ALL THE KING'S MEN

HEART OF THE WARRIOR

Heart of the Warrior

Published by Phoenix Press

Copyright © 2012 Donya Lynne

ISBN: 978-1-938991-23-3

This book is a work of fiction. References to historical events, real people, or real locales are used fictitiously. Other names, characters, places, and incidents are the product of the author's imagination, and any resemblance to actual events, locales, or persons, living or dead, is entirely coincidental.

Cover art by Reese Dante.

Licensed material is being used for illustrative purposes only and any person depicted in the licensed material is a model.

ACKNOWLEDGEMENTS

First and foremost, thank you to my readers. You are the reason why I write. You are why I strive to create an experience with my stories. I don't write for me. I write for you. If I'm not giving you an experience, I'm not doing my job. Please keep your feedback coming.

Thanks again to Reese Dante, cover artist extraordinaire, for another great cover. I hope we make many more beautiful covers together.

Once again, thank you to my editor, Laura, and to my wonderful beta readers. These stories wouldn't be what they are without your awesome, honest feedback. You make me better than I can be by myself.

To all you bloggers and book reviewers: Thank you for taking your valuable time to host me, promote me, and review my books. You all amaze me with your undying passion for all things books, as well as with your incredible blogs and websites.

A special thank you to Jowanna. What a wonderful addition to my life you have been. You're such a joy, and I love your drive for knowledge and blunt honesty.

To all of you I've met since my first book came out: I'm so pleased I've met you all and can't wait to learn more about you.

Books by Donya Lynne

All the King's Men Series

Rise of the Fallen
Heart of the Warrior
Micah's Calling
Rebel Obsession
Return of the Assassin
All the King's Men - The Beginning

Strong Karma Trilogy

Good Karma
Coming Back to You
Full Circle

Hope Falls Series

Finding Lacey Moon

Stand-Alone M/M Titles

Winter's Fire

Collections and Anthologies

All the King's Men Vol. 1 (books 1-3)
All the King's Men Vol. 2 (books 4-6)
Strong Karma Trilogy Boxed Set
Whispered Beginnings - A Romance Sampler

ALL THE KING'S MEN
HEART OF THE WARRIOR

DONYA LYNNE

DEDICATION

To the two of you. May you have no more
secrets and find happiness forever.
Your story touched me.

CHAPTER 1

CRACK!

The beam of wood splintered as it slammed into Severin's side and flung him against the dirty brick wall before he could catch himself. His shoulder protested and pain shot down his arm and across his upper back. Wincing, he pushed away from the wall and met the *dreck* head-on as the fucker came at him again.

But before the blue-toned shifter could repeat his Babe Ruth imitation and hit a home run on Sev's face, he leveled the dreck with a flying roundhouse worthy of the Ultimate Fight Club.

"Fucker!" With his fists up, Sev stalked after the dreck like he was Mr. T in *Rocky*, going in for the knockout punch as the guy stumbled backward and dropped his pansy-assed piece of useless wood.

A volley of fists flew back and forth between them, but the dreck was no match for Sev. With several lifetimes' worth of hand-to-hand combat training, few opponents could rival him in a fight, and he landed more hits than he took.

But Sev had one other benefit going for him, and when the dreck pulled out a gun and fired off two quick rounds, Sev sucked in his breath. The bullets pierced his jacket then bounced off his skin.

As in, pinball-off-the-bumper bounced.

Sev jolted backward from the impact and cursed as he poked his finger through the hole in his jacket. Fucker! This was his favorite jacket.

His angry glare shot to the dreck, and he almost laughed,

instantly forgetting about his wardrobe malfunction. The look on the dreck's face was priceless, all wide eyes and open-mouthed shock.

"Didn't know I could do that, did you?" Sev grabbed the asshole's long, blue-black hair and jerked back his head.

"But you…you're a…you're not—"

"A pregnant, female dreck? Yeah, I get that." Sev sneered, showing fang. "But my mom was."

The dreck's blue-toned fist flew at Severin and he caught it midair then flipped the dreck with a violent flick of his wrist.

"Ah, that looked painful. Did it hurt?" Sev looked down at the drug-dealing dreck lying on the damp pavement. "Here, let me help." He cocked back his arm, lunged down, and decked the guy into unconsciousness.

"As I was saying earlier, asshole, stop or I'll fuck you up."

He quickly glanced over his shoulder to make sure Malek hadn't been around to see his force field impersonation then dove into the dreck's thoughts and pulled out anything related to his Iron Man routine. Sev didn't need the asshole shifter blowing his iron skin secret to Malek or the others back at AKM. That would lead to complicated questions. And sure as shit, this dreck would have loved to spill Sev's secret to his teammates about exactly what kind of mixed blood coursed through his veins.

Yeah, I ain't no human mix. Sev clapped his hands together in dust-off fashion and stood up.

Good ol' Dad had been a full-on, full-blood, virile vampire. Extremely powerful. And a jackass. Sev had only met his father once, but the meeting had left an impression when the two had nearly beaten each other to death.

Centuries ago, Daddy-o had raped Sev's mother, a full-blood dreck named Felice, creating Severin in a harsh moment of suffering. Given how much love wasn't shared between the two races, female drecks usually killed themselves after a vampire raped them and conception resulted, but Sev's mother had refused. She had tried for centuries to have a baby, and all attempts with one of her own kind had resulted in failure. So, even though Sev's conception had been violent and at the hands of a vampire, Felice protected Severin and loved him as her cherished young right from the start.

As for what was referred to as *iron skin,* nature had granted female drecks, who struggled to conceive in the first place, a protective mechanism for when they did: impenetrable skin. After birth, the mother maintained her iron skin for a few years, as did the offspring. This ensured the young could develop until it was able to take care of itself.

In full-blood drecks, this trait eventually faded away, but Sev's mixed blood had misfired as he'd matured past the usual age when iron skin began to diminish. Instead, his mixed genes had mutated as all half-breeds' genes did, and rather than fade away, his iron skin became a trait he could turn on and off at will. It was the gift of his mixed blood.

But it was also a curse. If anyone found out he was half dreck, it could destroy his life, so he kept his special ability a tightly guarded secret. The war between the drecks and vampires had been over for a long time, but that didn't mean the two races got along. Huh-uh, no way. It just meant they barely tolerated each other on a good day.

But lucky vampires, they got the task of enforcing the peace between the two races, both because they were genetically superior and because of King Bain's contribution to the truce: All the King's Men Security. AKM was an enforcement agency that had evolved from policing drecks to working alongside humans in military ops, security details, and everything in between.

Where did that leave Sev? Was he supposed to police his own self? Was his vampire side supposed to kick his dreck side's ass every once in a while for good measure? And if his dreck lineage was discovered, would that be considered a conflict of interest that would require his removal as an enforcer from AKM? The dilemma was enough of a reason to keep his shit hush-hush.

Sev sighed and stepped back from the dreck at his feet and leaned against the alley wall. This was what he both loved and hated about patrolling Chicago's South Side. Drecks congregated here like flies on shit. Sev hated it because

South Side patrols weren't usually so exciting and mostly ended with a lot of tense staring and posturing that felt like foreplay with no score. But when he scored on the South Side, he scored big, and that's what he loved. In two months at AKM, this was Sev's third South Side brawl, and his first cobalt bust. You hardly got shit like this on the North Side, where even the drecks acted more civilized.

He looked at the unconscious dreck who had shifted back to his human form: brown hair, pale skin, and pink lips. Just like any number of humans Sev came in contact with every day. In their real form, drecks were blue. Blue skin, blue lips, blue-black hair, blue blood. Damn, they even smelled blue.

Funny, you would think they would remain in their natural state when unconscious, but since a dreck's natural tendency was to remain hidden within a disguise, falling unconscious rendered them back to that disguised form rather than their natural form. Remaining in their blue state, as some called it, required a conscious effort.

When was the last time his mother had shifted to blue? He couldn't remember, but then she didn't like to advertise what she was. She was different from the majority of drecks and kept her identity on the down-low.

The fact that his mother was a dreck made his line of work all the more ironic. Policing that which he was in his blood had the trappings of a moral dilemma, but Sev didn't think of it like that. Like a human policeman, Sev thought of his job as putting the bad guys away to save the innocent. It didn't matter what race they were. Being dreck had nothing to do with it. If you broke the law, you got punished. Dreck, human, vampire, or otherwise.

Exhilaration flowed through his muscles from the unexpected fight he and Malek had lucked into tonight. Sev lived for action like this. It made his insides all sizzly and warm, even if his exterior was a disheveled mess.

Case in point, strands of his long, blond hair fell over his eyes, loose from his ponytail, so he took a second to pull the elastic tie off then re-tie it.

"Nice work, Sev."

Severin turned to see Malek leading a cuffed dreck back into the alley.

"Thanks." He finished pulling back his hair.

"I thought I heard gunshots. You okay?"

Sev hid the hole in his jacket. "Yep. Fucker's aim was worse than his judgment."

He and Malek had stumbled on these two selling *cobalt* to a couple of vampires. The vamps—two females—got away, but not the drecks.

Sev leaned over and grabbed the unconscious dreck by the collar and yanked him up then slapped him back to the land of the lucid.

"Who were you selling to?" he said.

The dreck sneered, but in his human form, the gesture didn't look as sinister as it would have in his blue-toned shifted form. "Fuck you, vampire."

"Wrong answer." Sev punched him in the gut and the dreck doubled over.

"Sev!" Malek grabbed his arm. "Forget it. Let's just take them in."

With a scowl, Sev looked between the two drecks then back at Malek, whose long, jet-black hair hung loose to his shoulders and blew over his face. He had a bit of a shiner around his left eye. Looked like Malek had scuffled with his catch, too.

"I'm going after those two vampires," he said.

"They're long gone. Don't bother."

"No, I want to know who they are."

Cobalt consumption was growing out of hand in the vampire community, jeopardizing the truce between the drecks and vampires even further. Drecks had originally manufactured cobalt in the mid-80s as a designer drug for humans, which was bad enough, but unlike most human recreational drugs, cobalt actually affected vampires. It was a powerful drug and highly addictive. It hadn't taken long for vampires searching for recreational intoxication to figure out cobalt would succeed in giving them a higher high where cocaine, heroin, and meth had failed, and now it was becoming an epidemic.

After slapping cuffs on the dreck, he shoved him toward Malek.

"You can wait here or go back. It's up to you, but I won't be gone long. I just want to see if I can track them and find out who they are."

"Sev—"

But Sev was already dematerializing into ether. Some mixed-blood day walkers couldn't make like a mist, but he could. He was thankful for that. Going ethereal had its advantages. At least his asshole father had given him something useful.

He tracked the trail of the two vampires through the back alleys and out to the street. A few blocks later, the trail weakened where they had gotten into a car and driven off. In a flash, he zipped after the faint, lingering trail until it led him to a flying-by-the-seat-of-its-pants Jaguar XKR-S convertible with the top down.

Yes, those girls were flying high. One of the effects of cobalt was heat, and on a cold mid-March night in Chicago, no one put the top down and went for a spin unless they were seriously tripping.

As he landed in the car behind the two girls and rested his hands on the headrests of their seats, he got the sense these weren't regular females. These were the daughters of vampires with privilege.

"Nice car," he said.

The one who was driving screamed and swerved, and Sev nearly careened over the side.

"Whoa! Eyes on the road, sweets. Better yet, pull over."

She was already slamming on the brakes, and Sev flew forward between them, throwing out his right hand just in time to stop himself from smashing headfirst into the dash and windshield.

"Fuck!" He pushed back and sat up as the car finally stopped on the side of the road. "Damn it, female! Where did you learn how to drive?"

The two girls were drenched in sweat, hands trembling,

eyes wide like they were seeing rainbows and unicorns prancing in the street in front of them. Then the driver turned and looked at him.

"Who the fuck are you? What do you want? My father will have you killed if you hurt me." Her threat rattled and slurred out of her, but she held her head high. Sev got the sense she was a strong vampire, highly intelligent and feisty, as well as rich as sin.

Gold hoops hung from her ears—the real shit, too. Not the gold-plated stuff—and a diamond and ruby brooch adorned the left breast of her short-sleeved, pink angora sweater, which she filled out nicely with ample breasts. If Sev had been a straight male, he would have been impressed to distraction. Luckily for him, he didn't have to worry about that. He was one hundred percent into guys. Well, one guy in particular, but this wasn't the time to think about Arion.

A mink coat lay strewn over the back seat. The driver's blonde friend wore even more high-dollar bling, and the suede coat at her feet looked like it had set her back a good three thousand dollars. Good thing money didn't intimidate Sev. At least, not usually. These females were pushing the limits of his *intimidometer*, though.

"And just who might your father be?" Sev tapped the driver's seat headrest as he eyed her. "And I wonder how he would feel if he knew you were buying cobalt from a dreck on the South Side. Because it's obvious you're a North Sider with this swank-ass car and all the fancy rocks."

The female's lip quivered and Sev wasn't sure if she was angry or just tripping off the cobalt, but he got the feeling it was a little of both and that she didn't want to reveal who her father was. He could see her mental processes sorting through the drugged haze in her brain as if she were trying to assimilate what was real and what was drug-enhanced so she didn't say anything incriminating.

"Forget it," she said. "Just tell me what you want. You want money? I can pay you. Or...I can...I can give you a blow job." Her voice wavered nervously. "Will that make you forget you saw us? I can do that."

Sev got the distinct impression that she had never given a blow job in her life, so offering one to him showed just how desperate she was. Her friend nodded in agreement, and Sev got the same impression about her. These girls were young and sexually untouched. Daughters of privilege—progeny of members of the king's council, no doubt. That would explain their apparently intact virtue. Members of the king's council tended to live by the old ways, which included keeping their daughters chaste and marrying them off to approved suitors, whether those suitors had biologically mated their daughters or not.

Both females reached for his belt.

Sev grabbed their wrists and batted them away. "Stop! Hell no. I'm not into bribes, Barbie. You're not my type, anyway." Hell, they weren't even his gender.

Sev's mind shot unwittingly to Arion again. Ari was another member of Sev's enforcement team. Just the thought of him made Sev's heart skip a beat.

No, better not go there, Sev ol' boy. Not now. Head in the game, head on your job. You can think about Ari and that heartache later.

The busty brunette behind the wheel huffed and sat back in her seat, dejected. Her blonde friend did likewise, avoiding his gaze.

"So, what? You gonna bust us? You're an enforcer, right?" The short high seemed to be dissipating as the two girls turned and looked out the windshield.

"Maybe. Maybe not. What are your names?"

The two exchanged glances, their long hair hanging in sweaty ribbons over their faces and down their backs.

"I'm...Candy, and this is...Sue."

"And I'm the Tooth Fairy," Sev said. "Now, what are your real names?"

The brunette behind the wheel shot a glance at him as if she couldn't believe he had caught on to her lie, but really? Candy and Sue? How obvious could she be? Of course those weren't their real names. No sane vampire within the king's inner circle named their progeny such ordinary names, and Sev would bet everything he owned that's what he had on his hands here.

He cocked his head at the driver, waiting, but she only stared back, her lips pursed tightly.

With a sigh, he looked away. He wanted to bust these girls, but something told him to let this one go with only a warning. Otherwise, their high-powered parents might drag this into a major issue that wouldn't be worth the energy. Maybe this was enough of a scare to sober them up and keep them from making any more late-night buys or equally bad choices. Probably not, but he would give them the benefit of the doubt.

"Look, girls. I won't take you in this time, but if I catch your asses buying or using again, I'm hauling you in, and then you'll *have* to give me your names. Your *real* names. *And* your daddy's*." The last he said to the brunette. That seemed to get *Candy's* attention. "Understood?"

The two nodded.

"So, you're not going to arrest us?" The blonde gaped at him as if she had just fallen under a lucky star.

"Not this time, but consider yourselves marked. I've got your scent right here." He tapped the side of his nose. "I *will* be looking for you. Rest assured. Now, do yourselves a favor and get off the cobalt."

Sev met the brunette's eyes and held her gaze for a long moment before hopping over the side of the car. "Now get out of here before I change my mind."

The two girls glanced at each other as if they couldn't believe their good fortune, and without another word, *Candy* threw the car in gear and took off, leaving him standing on the sidewalk.

Shit. He needed to be less of a softy, but he liked giving people a break. One get-out-of-jail free card was all they got, though. He sure hoped he didn't see Candy and Sue, or whatever their real names were, again, but he probably would. Oh well, they had been warned. Next time, he wouldn't be Mr. Nice Guy.

Dematerializing, he misted back to the alley and found Malek waiting in the Suburban.

"Hey." He hopped in the passenger seat and yanked the door closed. "Thanks for waiting."

"Well?" Malek put the Suburban in gear and they started out of the alley.

"Two females in a Jag. Money falling out their asses. If I had to guess, I'd say they were recently-transitioned."

Recently-transitioned could mean they were anywhere from twenty-eight to sixty years old. By vampire standards, anything less than sixty was young.

"Damn. Makes sense, though. It's the young ones who seem to get tangled up in the shit these guys were peddling." Malek jerked his thumb toward the back seat.

Sev turned around and inspected the shackled drecks behind the iron grate separating the cab from the passenger seats. "How you boys doing? Comfy?"

The one with the home run swing sneered. "Fuck you."

Sev grinned and rubbed his shoulder. The bitch hurt like a motherfucker. "Maybe later." He turned back to Malek as they hit the main road and headed toward AKM. "Did you get names off them?" He bobbed his head toward their catch.

"Nah, just call them Tweedle-dee and Tweedle-dum. Or Dumb and Dumber. Although I don't know which is which."

Sev chuckled and looked out the window.

"So you didn't bust the girls?" Malek glanced sideways at him.

Sev snorted. "Hell no. With all the money in that car, I had a feeling busting them would end up a nightmare of monolithic proportions. Nah, I gave them a warning this time."

"This time?"

"Yeah. I marked their scents. I'll be looking for them, and if I catch them pulling this shit again, I don't care who their daddies are, I'm hauling their asses in."

"Is that the real reason why you let them go, bro?" Malek arched an eyebrow at him.

Sev shook his head. "I know what you're thinking, Malek, but I wasn't even remotely interested in tapping either one of them. Not my type." He thought about Arion again and wondered if he would ever get the male off his mind. He had been thinking a lot about Arion. Too much, actually.

Honestly, Sev was surprised at Malek's suggestion that he would be interested in the girls. Malek didn't normally talk about females. It was common knowledge that he had lost his mate centuries ago and had never fully recovered. Consequently, females weren't a big topic of discussion with him. He never dated, and he never even looked at a woman in that way, except for on the one night each month he went to the Black Garter. Even then, he only looked, didn't touch.

Maybe Malek was just growing more comfortable with him and opening up more. Sev was still considered the new guy, after all, and now that he and Malek were patrolling together on a regular basis, conversation flowed more easily. But Sev wasn't used to hearing him talk like that.

Malek let the subject of the two girls drop, and they rode in silence for a couple of minutes.

"So, what are you doing after your shift?" Malek said.

Sev inspected his fingernails. "I don't know. Maybe hit the training center then go home."

"You should come with us to Four Alarm."

Us—Malek, Io, Micah, Trace...and Arion.

Sev knew Arion would be at Four Alarm and he wasn't sure he could handle that. Ari was easily the finest-looking guy on the team, and he attracted enough females to prove it. Women, both human and vampire, gravitated toward him like bees to honey. And wasn't that just swell? Ari and his best friend, Io, another member of the team who was equally popular with the ladies, were quite the crowd pleasers at the team's regular hang-out. Going and watching that dagger-through-the-heart shit would prove just how much of a masochist Sev was, and masochism wasn't something he normally ascribed to. That shit worked well and good for the likes of Micah's old friends, from what he'd heard, but Sev didn't float that way.

"I'm not sure, Malek. I should really just go home."

"Come on. It'll be fun and you deserve a night to celebrate. You haven't taken any time to hang and have fun since Tristan promoted you to full status."

As the newest member of the team, Sev had only recently come off probation.

He glanced back out the window. Part of him wanted to go, but seeing Arion would kill him. Had it really been over a month since the night Micah brought his mate, Samantha, into AKM after giving her his venom to save her life? Arion and Micah had argued that night, and in his emotionally charged state, Micah had beaten the crap out of Arion. Then Sev had taken Ari home and...Sev's heart hiccupped as he remembered what had happened in Ari's kitchen. Oh, the things they had done to each other in that brief, heated interlude.

Damn, it *had* been over a month. Closer to six weeks. And Ari barely spoke to him now. The awkwardness between them felt like sludge, and Sev didn't know what to do or how to feel about the incidents of their first and only night together and all the uncomfortable moments between them since.

He shifted uneasily as he remembered the way their bodies had fit together so perfectly. Ari's mouth had brushed over his and hovered there as their bodies had slapped together. Sev had never experienced anything quite like what he and Ari had shared. Hell, there hadn't been any penetration, and yet, the experience had been the most erotic one of Sev's life.

And Ari had wanted him, too. He'd been too into him, too excited, too eager to touch Sev. Surely, Sev hadn't misread Ari's interest, but afterward, Ari reacted as if dismayed. As if he couldn't believe what had happened.

No, that wasn't exactly right. But there had been something in Ari's expression and body language that Sev couldn't quite put a finger on. Almost as if Ari had been in the midst of a revelation. He'd looked like someone who had always sworn he hated being near water, and then went to the beach one day and couldn't stop staring at the ocean. Before long, he's taken off his shoes and is walking in the surf, curling his toes in the wet sand, smiling in awe that he had missed this beautiful, wet world his whole life, asking himself what in the hell he'd been thinking.

That's how Ari had looked that night—like a man who

had been missing something his entire life and had only just found it.

But now, six weeks later, it was as if that night never happened. Ari never mentioned it, and Sev never brought it up.

Unfortunately for Sev, his world had shifted that night. Something had changed inside him. His heart had opened in a way it never had, and it scared him. Not even Gabe, who he'd lost a year ago, had made him feel this way. And if Sev was being honest with himself, the way he was feeling was the way a male felt in the early stages of taking a mate.

Hence his reason for being scared.

Male vampires lived in both excited anticipation and fear of the call to mate. Nothing possessed the power to lift a male vampire into the heavens emotionally the way the mating call did, while at the same time filling him with dread that reached the depths of Hell. Losing a mate could be fatal, and mated males never fully let go of that fear. It always hovered just at the back of their minds. And if a chosen mate didn't reciprocate? Well, that was like living death from the stories he'd heard.

On one side was the beautiful, erotic phase known as the *calling*, which all males lived for, while on the flipside he faced the painful *suffering*, which caused males to cower in fear. The *calling* lifted a male up, and the *suffering* made his life a living hell if his mate rejected him.

And right now, it looked like Ari was definitely rejecting him.

Lucky me.

The early stages of mating were a precarious time for a male, and Sev displayed all the signs of early *suffering*. His chest ached, he was moody as fuck, any little thing set him off, his mind obsessed over Ari to the point of distraction, and he was a nervous wreck.

How had this happened? How had he started to attach to Ari when it was apparent Ari wasn't feeling the same for him? All he wanted was to see Ari, but he fought to avoid him so he wouldn't feel the pain of rejection.

"So, what do you say?" Malek pulled him from his thoughts. "Huh?"

"About Four Alarm. You coming or what?"

"Okay, sure. I'll join you guys for a while." Had he really just agreed to go? His voice had simply come out of nowhere and betrayed him, and as soon as the words were out, he wished he could take them back.

Truth was, if he was mating to Ari as he suspected, he would slowly lose control of his conscious behavior as his subconscious pushed him to reconnect with Ari. The mating tether was a bitch to resist, pushing a newly mated male toward the *calling* so he could propagate the species with his fertile seeds. Too bad his mating side hadn't received the memo that he was gay and wouldn't be getting anyone preggers with his army of fertile soldiers unless a miracle occurred.

"Great. Drinks on me tonight, bro." Malek clapped him on the shoulder.

Sev watched the city pass by for the rest of the trip to the compound, and he made a conscious effort to keep a lock on his vocal cords before he made another colossal blunder, because Lord knew, he kept a lot of secrets hidden inside and needed to keep his yap shut.

CHAPTER 2

ARION SAT AT THE BAR WITH IO. A woman wearing barely-there clothes who'd introduced herself as Chloe was tucked between his knees and laughing at something Io had just said. She was built like a fitness model and had pretty eyes. She had a nice laugh, too. The way she pressed her perky breasts against him and snaked one arm around his back to dip her fingertips into the waist of his pants would have sent any man into fits of hard-on heaven. Any man except him, anyway. Because, honestly, he just wasn't into this scene, anymore. If he ever had been. And he was seriously beginning to doubt that.

For the past six weeks, he had begun to realize he'd merely play-acted being into females all his life. Every day it became clearer that his motor ran for men and men alone. It still shocked him how quickly the truth had awakened in him after his brief interlude with Sev, and he was still getting used to the idea, but there was no doubt. Ari was attracted to men. He realized that now, but he kept that newsflash under lock and key more securely than the government guarded Area 51.

Homophobia was just as rampant in the vampire community as it was in the human one, and he didn't need to deal with that shit. But lucky Arion, his best friend, Io, was a certifiable, card-carrying member of the anti-gay faction. So were his parents. They would disown him if they even thought he had switched teams and floated a hard-on for males.

Well, actually, one male.

Ever since that night with Sev six weeks ago, it had become clear who he wanted. With Sev, his libido had spiked, and, for the first time, responded to someone. None of the women he'd dated ever excited him the way Sev did. But then Ari had only been with women before he and Sev ventured down Gay Lane and turned onto Orgasm Boulevard with each other. The conclusion seemed obvious, didn't it? Women equaled ho-hum. Sev equaled oh my God yes!

The experience with Sev had given Ari a lot of food for thought, and after much soul searching, he realized he had gotten good at faking it with females. That alone should have tipped him off that he was gay. Looking back at all his short-lived relationships with females—none had lasted more than a few weeks—it was obvious he had never been heterosexual, only a poser. A gay male pretending he was straight.

One clue should have been that he'd never been able to keep his eyes open during sex. He kept them closed. And the female couldn't talk too much. That way, he could fantasize about men and get excited enough to get off. But it took major fantasizing—as in super focused this-is-really-a-man-and-not-a-woman-and-he-only-feels-like-a-woman fantasizing. Going with the ever-faithful doggie style made it easier, because then he could really get into the fantasy that he had a man bent over in front of him. But even with all that fantasizing, he had gotten so good at faking orgasms he deserved an Academy Award. More often than not, though, he forewent the agonizing roll in the hay and took his fantasies home with him and let his hand do the honors.

And his hand had been getting a lot of honors in the six weeks since he and Sev had dry-fucked against the kitchen counter. Well, not exactly dry, but hell, what did you call it when there was no penetration but you came all over each other, anyway? And what they did hadn't been masturbation, either. But, fuck, it had left Ari's blood boiling for more even though he was terrified of going down that road again. What if someone found out?

Ari's world was going to Hell with a first-class ticket, because while he was terrified of someone finding out about his "new leaf," he couldn't stop thinking about Sev. And it was driving him mad.

He had felt a connection with Sev almost from the first day Sev joined the team two-and-a-half months ago, but he figured they would just be good friends. Now he knew better. He was attracted to Sev. Really attracted to him. As in, he could hardly think of anything else and was in a state of arousal half the time as he replayed that night over and over in his thoughts. Even now he was aroused thinking about it.

Blind luck had pushed them together that night and he hadn't been able to resist. Sev's mouth had felt perfect on his, and so had his body, and he often wondered what would have happened if he hadn't gotten spooked. Would he have invited Sev to spend the day? Would Sev have agreed? If so, just how far would they have gone with each other? Ari knew the answer. He and Sev would have gone all the way. More than once. That's how aroused Sev made him. But things had gotten awkward that night, Sev had left, and now he and Sev hardly even looked at each other, anymore.

The evasive action was Arion's fault. He was afraid. No. Afraid wasn't the word for it. He was fucking terrified. What if his parents had seen them together? The thought was irrational, but he couldn't stop himself from imagining his parents standing at his window, watching him kiss and hump his cock against another male. And it wasn't just his parents that put the fear of God in him. What if Io found out? Io would rag his ass and he would never hear the end of it. Their friendship probably wouldn't survive it, and Ari didn't want to lose his best friend.

So, he continued living a lie. No matter how attracted he was to Severin, he couldn't be with him. It would cause too much trouble.

"Are you listening to me?" The woman between his knees pulled back and Ari realized she had asked him a question.

"I'm sorry. What did you say?"

She tsked and tilted her head. Her flimsy blouse sparkled in the dim lights blinking over the dance floor. The music was pumping loud and hard.

"I asked if you wanted to dance."

Ari glanced at Io, who had a girl tucked inside each arm and two sets of lips sucking on his neck. From the looks of it, shit was getting intense and Ari figured Io would disappear with them soon to do whatever it was he did with them in the back. Yeah, no mystery there. Io was going to drink well tonight while getting good and fucked. The thought that he and Io used to participate in these little banquets together made his stomach lurch.

"Sure." He scooted off the bar stool, and Io looked up long enough to give him an approving nod before turning his attention back to his fan club of two.

If Io only knew how miserable he was inside and why, he wouldn't show such encouragement. Arion almost didn't know who he was, anymore. He had lived the lie too long. Shit, he had gotten so good at acting hetero he had believed he was.

Until six weeks ago.

Chloe took his hand and led him to the dance floor just as the music changed to something slower. Grrreeeaaaat. Just what he needed, because sure as shit, Chloe would take the opportunity to cling to him like static. Her arms wrapped around him and he cringed inside as he slipped his arms around her waist.

"I've seen you in here before, you know." Her lips played against his ear as she spoke.

"You have, huh?" He tried not to roll his eyes at her come-on.

"Yes. You're a real ladies man."

"Looks can be deceiving."

Chloe snuggled closer. "Mmm, I don't know. I'm a lady, and you're definitely all man."

Ari's cock stood at half-mast from his recent Sev-dominated musings, and obviously Chloe had felt it against her hip as she rubbed him.

"You like me, don't you?"

No. "Sure."

"How about this?" She rocked the top of her thigh against his crotch more persistently.

Ari closed his eyes and imagined Severin holding him. It was the only way he could stomach Chloe touching him like she was. His arms tightened around Chloe as he wondered how Sev's hard body would feel pressed against him, dancing here and now for God and everyone to see. The thought alone was enough to scare the shit out of him, and he tensed and shivered.

"Mm, you do like me, don't you?" Chloe misinterpreted his body language.

"No, I—"

Chloe cut him off as she brought her face around and sealed her lips over his.

He almost jerked away before reminding himself he needed to keep the façade in place. The world was watching. And like his parents, Ari excelled at keeping up appearances. But kissing Chloe was near-revolting. She wasn't what he wanted.

Still, he forced himself to return the kiss. *Ugh. Please stop, please stop.* But she didn't, so Ari automatically fell into his mind as he always had in situations like this. Only this time it wasn't some random man he pulled into his thoughts. It was Sev, glorious Severin. Sev's image, front and center.

Ari was an expert at fantasizing himself into submission, and dreams of Severin made that easy. So, when Chloe opened her lips against his, he did likewise, chasing his memories, reaching for Sev through his mind. Once more, he was back in his kitchen and Sev stood in front of him, holding him, pressed against him, their lips drinking each other in like hot, weary travelers gulping from an oasis of cool, fresh water.

The fantasy kept him from pulling away. The fantasy of Sev kissing him made him drunk. As long as he kept his eyes closed, it was Sev he was kissing, not Chloe.

SEV FOLLOWED MALEK INTO FOUR ALARM and immediately saw Io in the clutches of two vixens at the bar. The bulge in his jeans left nothing to the imagination.

"Hey, Malek. Sev." Io's lust-glazed eyes looked up as he and Malek pushed through the crowd and compelled the people near Io to vacate their bar stools.

Malek tapped his knuckles on the bar and caught the bartender's eye then glanced at Io.

"Busy I see," Malek said.

Io grinned, his fangs already halfway descended.

"Um, bro..." Malek pointed to his own canines and gave Io a look that the other male instantly understood. He snapped his mouth closed before anyone else could see his fancy dental work. They didn't exactly announce to the general public they were vampires.

"How about you two save my spot while I go take care of this." Io shifted the girls as he stood and adjusted his erection inside his jeans.

"Sure," Malek said. "By the way, where's Ari?" He quickly ordered two Lags.

Io grinned as he pulled the girls away then dipped his head toward the dance floor. "Ari's getting his itch rubbed."

Sev turned his gaze in the direction Io was looking, and his heart stopped. As in, dead. No beating. And the resulting ache felt like a bomb blowing up behind his sternum, knocking the air out of him. Arion was lip-fucking a blonde with tits the size of melons, and through the shifting crowd, he caught sight of her hand giving his swollen crotch a slow, persistent rub-down.

Ari was certainly enjoying himself.

Sev turned away and grabbed the Lag as soon as it was placed in front of him and downed it in one gulp. He slammed the glass on the bar and gestured toward the empty. "Another. And leave the bottle."

Coming here had been a mistake. A big one. He could see getting shit-faced was in his very near future.

"Whoa, guy. Slow down. Micah and Trace aren't even here, yet." Malek turned and looked around the club.

Fuck. Micah. Six weeks ago, he had hated Micah for a whole other reason than why he hated him now. Back then,

Micah had used Arion for a punching bag every chance he got, and Sev had wanted to kick Micah's ass for messing with the object of his affection like that. Now, Micah was a fully and happily mated male. And that made Sev feel about as thrilled as a dying fish.

He glanced in Ari's direction again, but a mass of bodies prevented Sev from seeing him, which was probably for the best, being that Ari was lost in that blonde he had been lip-locked to a minute ago. Still, being unable to land eyes on Ari didn't stop Sev from being consumed by despair, and he kicked back another drink.

"Ah, there they are." Malek looked toward the entrance.

Sev turned and saw Micah walk in with a smile on his face, his arm pulling Sam close as they looked at each other with what Sev could only describe as complete love and devotion. He glanced back to the dance floor, and the sea of bodies parted just enough that he saw Arion still kissing the blonde. Sev swiveled his gaze back to Micah as Trace shouldered through the door behind him. Sev would never have what Micah had, would he? A mate of his own and the happiness that seemed to ooze out of every pore because of it.

Micah was a changed person from when Sev first met him. He'd been a dick, a real sonofabitch who had done what he wanted when he wanted, without a care for his own safety or the safety of others. When Sam happened along, all that had changed. Micah was still a lethal fucker in the field, but what made him so dangerous now seemed to be his undying love for Sam, whereas before it had been a total disregard for his life.

Sam leaned up and whispered something in Micah's ear and he grinned and turned in to nuzzle her neck as she threw her head back, laughing. Micah pulled away and laughed with her. From what Sev had overheard and witnessed firsthand, Micah never used to smile. Now he smiled all the time.

That was what love and being mated did for you. Or at least it was supposed to. Sev thought about his unrequited feelings for Arion then kicked back another glass of Lag and poured himself another as Malek held his hand out to greet the three newcomers.

"You two look good." Malek looked between Micah and Sam.

They did look good, which made Sev hate Micah even more. Lucky fucker finding true love and all that shit. And he worked the color black like a fucking supermodel, too. Sam wore tight faux leather pants and a modest top that showed just how a woman's body was supposed to look. She had smaller breasts and wore more clothes than any other woman there, but she was by far the sexiest. And that was something for Sev to think, being that he wasn't even into women.

He looked up and noticed Micah scowling at him as if he was reading his thoughts. And, hell, maybe he was. Even if Micah knew he was gay, he still wouldn't like Sev thinking about his female like that. Mated male dominion shit. You never coveted or admired a mated male's mate.

Trace reached past Sev and flagged down the bartender for a glass. As the bartender handed him one, he picked up the bottle of Lag and paid Sev a cursory glance. "You don't mind, do you?" Without waiting for an answer, Trace poured himself a triple and set the bottle back down.

"Apparently not." Sev regretted his decision to come here. He should have gone home, because this scene was rubbing him fifty ways wrong.

"What did you meatheads do tonight?" Trace said to Malek, ignoring Sev's retort. Trace sipped his drink then handed the glass to Micah, who took a healthy swig and handed it back.

Malek glanced at Sev then said, "Popped Sev's cherry and broke up a cobalt deal and bagged a couple of drecks."

"Nice. Did you bag the buyers, too?" Micah looked at him, his arm tightening around Sam as if he were trying to prove a point about who she belonged to and who had a right to look at and think about her.

"Nope." Sev downed another glass before pouring more.

Malek reached for the bottle to pull it away, but Sev snatched it from him and gave him a warning look. Tonight, Sev's mate was the bottle, and nobody would take Mr.

Lagavulin away from him, so help him God.

"Well, did you at least mark them?" Micah took the glass from Trace again and drank.

"Of course I did, asshole. Do I look like an idiot?" Sev squared Micah up. He really hated this guy. Mr. Perfect. Mr. Happy. Mr. I've-Got-It-All-And-You-Have-Nothing.

"Do you really want me to answer that, newbie?"

Malek held his hands up between them. "Hey, Micah, Severin's been promoted to full status. You know that."

Micah chuffed. "Yeah? Well, his attitude is for shit. I think he needs to get laid." The last he said softly, almost lethally soft, and with an edge as if he were laying down a dare or a challenge or something.

Sev's eyes narrowed, and he wondered what game Micah was playing. "You're one to talk about attitude." The alcohol was making Sev bold. Or maybe just stupid. He would decide the answer to that in the morning.

"Fuck off, *newbie.*" Micah handed the Lag back to Trace, and Sev could feel waves of aggression coming off the male as if he were ready to throw down. Micah was one of only a few males who could hold his own against Severin, and they both knew it.

Trace chuckled low and deep, but otherwise didn't get involved, sipping his drink instead, watching the two of them with a secret smile on his face.

The air bristled between Sev and Micah, and it looked like fists were going to fly for sure until Sam pressed into Micah's side and stroked her fingers down the slope of his neck as if trying to calm him.

"Sshh, baby," she said. "Don't I feel good against you? Huh? Look at me. Micah? Come on, look at me."

She must have been through this with him before, because he did seem to cool off. Within seconds, he turned toward her then pulled her close until she nuzzled the stretch of skin her fingers had just caressed. And just like that, Micah was a kitten again, grinning and purring into her ear as the two of them sank into their own secret universe. Severin was suddenly forgotten in their world. A nobody.

Again, that was what a mate did for a male. His mate kept him in check, cooled him off and heated him up when necessary.

Sev's eyes lingered enviously on Sam and Micah then drifted back to the dance floor. Ari was just breaking away from his blonde hussy and turned directly toward him as if he had known he was being watched. Their eyes suddenly met. Sev held his breath as Ari's gaze locked to his, and the other male flushed as if caught with his hand in the cookie jar.

But for a moment, with their eyes locked together, everything was perfect. Then the reality slammed into him with a nauseating punch to the gut. Yeah, he was a nobody all right, and not just to Micah.

Sev grabbed the bottle of Lag, his glass, and shoved his way between Trace and Micah as he departed for a table in the back, hopefully where no one would bug him so he could get good and drunk.

How could he even think he had a chance with Arion? He had no chance. The brief interlude they had shared six weeks ago was an anomaly, a joke, just a heterosexual male satisfying his homo curiosity. For Ari, the incident had meant nothing. Sev had received that message loud and clear. Hell, maybe their wild, sexy night hadn't even happened and Sev had daydreamed the whole thing. Whether real or not, Sev knew in his heart he was utterly lost to a male he apparently couldn't have.

"Hey."

Sev flinched back to the present and looked up to find Arion standing next to him.

"Hey." He looked back down at his glass.

"I haven't seen you here in a while."

Severin chuckled darkly at what came off sounding like a cheesy line. "Oh, yeah? What? Is that some kind of pick-up line or something?" Sev threw back more Lag and scowled up at Ari. "You use that on a lot of guys? Or just girls?"

"What's that supposed to mean?" Ari frowned at him.

"Nothing. Forget it."

Sev really couldn't explain where his animosity toward

Ari came from. Must be one of those fun-filled mated male things he would have to get used to. After all, violent mood swings were a side effect of the call to mate. But honestly, he was really more angry at himself than Ari. Ari just got the privilege of being his whipping post.

"I'm just saying I haven't seen you here in a while. I didn't think you hung out here, anymore."

"So, I can't come here and have a drink?" Sev poured more Lag in his glass.

"That's not what I said." Ari huffed. "What's wrong with you?"

Other than I want you so badly I can hardly stand it? "Nothing. What's wrong with you? Can't you tell I just want to drink in peace?"

Ari stood there for what felt like a lifetime then said, "I just wanted to...I just thought I'd say hi." Ari shifted his weight.

Heavy emptiness hung between them, the air swelling with a lot of unspoken words.

For just a heartbeat, Sev thought maybe—just maybe—Ari wanted to say more than just hi. But he only stood there, silent, staring at Sev with his trademark serious mask on. After several seconds passed, Sev looked away.

"Fine. Hi. There. Now you can get back to your bimbo. Or better yet, go join Io with his."

Sev didn't have to look at Ari to feel the stunned hurt and anger rolling off the guy.

"Fuck you, Sev." Ari turned and walked back to the bar, grabbed his jacket, and marched to the exit.

Sev's heart went with him, all *Wait for me!*

Yep, fuck you about summed it up as he watched Ari disappear through the door.

The girl Ari had been dancing with appeared a minute later, having just freshened up in the bathroom. She looked around, approached the bar, and said something to Malek and the others. She must have been asking where Ari was, and they must have explained he had just left, because the next thing Sev knew, she flushed red and snatched her own coat and stormed out.

Huh. Whatever. She was probably pissed because Ari hadn't helped her with her coat and walked her out. *Take a number, toots. Ari's a real gentleman like that.* Sev raised his glass in mock salute and downed its contents just as Io appeared with his two women. All three were disheveled and Sev could smell the sex coming off them from across the room.

Jesus. He needed to get out of here. *Note to self, don't ever come to Four Alarm again when you know Ari will be here.* Grabbing the bottle, he made his way toward the back exit and slipped out before anyone could stop him.

CHAPTER 3

GINA CARANO PULLED IN FRONT OF THE TRUMP HOTEL in Chicago. If she was going to kill someone, she might as well do it in style, right?

After parking, a bell boy greeted her at the curb and helped unload her luggage from the back of the SUV. While he took her bags inside, she pulled into the parking garage, freshened her lipstick, and then made her way to the lobby. She was the picture of elegance.

Gina didn't look like a killer, but that was the idea. With smooth, shiny, black hair cut blunt above her shoulders, and with perfect skin and a lithe body wrapped in a silk pantsuit and fur coat, she looked more like a model—albeit a short one—than a woman with vengeance and death on her mind. Indeed, several patrons in the lobby stopped and stared as she strode past, her Coach clutch firmly gripped in her gloved hand.

"Good evening. Welcome to the Trump International Hotel and Tower. Your name?"

"Gina Carano."

The attendant looked up her reservation.

"You'll be with us two weeks?"

"Yes, that's correct."

Two weeks should be more than enough time for her to finish the job she had come here to do. Maybe she would even do some sightseeing afterward. It would be nice to visit Millennium Park and shop on the Magnificent Mile, something every girl needed to do at least once. And she was craving a taste of Chicago's famous deep dish pizza.

Yes, as soon as she finished her job, a little food, fun, and shopping was in order to celebrate.

The desk attendant handed her the key card for her room and she gave him a warm smile, her eyes hidden behind fashionable sunglasses despite it being nighttime.

"Thank you." She followed the bell boy into the elevator and up to her suite. After he deposited her luggage and she was finally alone, she took out her cell and punched in a number.

"Hello? Gigi?" Gina's mom's voice. Her given name was Virginia, but her family always called her Gigi or Gina.

"Hi, Mom. I just wanted you to know I'm here."

"Oh honey, please. You don't have to do this. Your dad and I—"

"Mom. Yes, I do. I do need to do this, and you know why."

"Gina, you need to let this go. Do you really think your brother would have wanted this?"

"Well, Gabe isn't alive anymore to speak for himself, now is he? That asshole and his friends made sure of that. And now he has to pay like all the rest." She had been hunting down her brother's killers for the last year, and only one remained. She saved the best—and hardest—for last.

"Honey—?"

"No, Mom! I'm doing this. I just wanted you to know I'm here. I'll call you after it's done." She hung up and tossed her phone on the bed.

Gina took off her sunglasses and walked to the window that overlooked The Chicago River. Severin Bannon had betrayed her brother. He had betrayed Gabriel and killed him. Now she was in Chicago to ensure Severin paid for what he had done.

CHAPTER 4

SEVERIN COULDN'T SLEEP. Well, not really. After drinking Lag straight from the bottle and getting to where he couldn't feel anything but the misery, he somehow managed his way home, even if he couldn't remember how. He blinked and tried to focus on his surroundings in his basement studio. Mr. Lagavulin had performed admirably and now the bottle lay empty on its side on the floor next to his hand, which hung over the edge of the couch. Wait. Was that his hand? He slowly wiggled his fingers. Yep.

With a groan, he peeled his face off the leather cushion. It stuck where it made contact with the cowhide, and his mouth felt as if it had been swabbed with cotton then dried with a hair dryer.

Moan.

And what bunch of house trolls decided to take up residence inside his head to pound from the inside-out with pick-axes?

Blinking repeatedly, he looked around the dimly lit basement. His bed on the other side of the large room remained made since he had slept on the couch, and only one lamp was on in the corner where he painted.

Why was the lamp on? Had he painted last night? He painted when he was upset, stressed, or just needed a break, but he couldn't remember painting last night, although he had certainly been in the right frame of mind.

He glanced at the canvas on his easel and his stomach rolled. Ari's face stared back at him. Okay, so he *had* painted last night. Funny how he couldn't remember. He looked at the empty bottle on the floor. Well, maybe not so funny.

His gaze lifted back to the small canvas of Ari's perfect face. Even when he was drunk off his gourd, he could paint better than most sober people, but shit, that thing had to get out of his house. Like the ten other portraits of Arion he had painted in the last six weeks, he needed to get rid of it so he didn't have to look at it day in and day out and be reminded of what he couldn't have.

And after last night, it was clear he couldn't have Ari. Ari had been into that female. Maybe he was plundering her right now. The thought made his stomach turn again, and Sev stumbled his way to the bathroom before he messed up his floor. Not that his stomach contained a lot to upchuck, but still.

After the coughing and retching stopped, he turned on the faucet and splashed cold water on his face and neck. Over and over. *Splash-splash.* The cool moisture felt good. He cupped his hands and caught the running water then lifted it to his mouth. Sucking it in, he swished and swallowed. *Aaahh.*

Luckily, as with a cobalt high, hangovers didn't last long in vampires. By the time Sev downed a pain reliever with a mug of black coffee, showered, and dressed, he was feeling much better. So he whipped up some eggs and toast for breakfast and snarfed it down before calling his mother and inviting her over for a visit, as well as to take Ari's portrait.

"Hey, Mom."

"Hi, Sev. How are you?" His mom's voice sounded concerned. It was amazing how she was able to read his mood so easily.

"I'm okay. Hung over." He sipped his coffee. "Can you come over for lunch today?"

He could almost hear her compassionate smile through the phone. "You have more paintings for me, don't you?"

Sev sighed. "Just a couple." He looked down at his mug of coffee. "But I also thought it'd be nice to get together." Sev needed to talk to his mom. She always kept him grounded, and right now, he needed to be grounded in the worst way.

Otherwise, he was going to float away in a hot air balloon of despair.

"I'll bring a pot of chili."

Yeah, Mom knew he was hurting. She only brought him chili when he needed comforting. The last time she'd made him homemade chili was when Gabe died.

"That sounds perfect, Mom. I'll see you in a couple hours."

"I'll be there. I love you."

"Love you, too, Mom."

His mom was the reason he had moved to Chicago. She had come here years ago to open an art gallery. Sev hated being away from her, so when his undercover spec ops gig in Atlanta had come to an abrupt end a year ago, he'd packed up and moved here. Before that, he had fought in the human military Special Forces.

Sev had been born to be a warrior in one way or another, but under his hard exterior, he possessed an uncanny eye for art, hence his talents with paint and brush. Being that his mom was an artist, he often wondered if his artistic ability had been as much a gift from her as his iron skin had been.

Of course, then there was the matter of his talents with hand-to-hand combat and weapons. That would have been his dad's gift to him, right? Yay for Dad. The prick. Sev rolled his eyes.

After hanging up the phone, he cleaned the kitchen, which he hadn't done in a few days, then started the laundry. Sev had just thrown in his second load when the doorbell rang. He rushed to open it and his mom's smiling face stared back. She was holding a large pot, and the heavenly smell of chili instantly calmed him.

"Feelee." It was what he called his mom in public, because calling her mom would have raised eyebrows since she looked younger than he did. With his neighbor out working in the yard next door, Sev wouldn't take the chance. And being that her name was Felice, Feelee just came naturally.

"Hi, sweetie." She stepped past him, and he shut the door then followed her into the kitchen.

"Thanks for coming over."

She smiled at him then opened the fridge and made room for the pot. "I can't turn down my only son's invitation, can I?"

Sev smiled. "No, I guess not."

His mom had never had more children, so he knew she loved her time with him as much as he did.

She shut the fridge, poured a cup of coffee, then turned and leaned back against the counter as she blew over the surface of the hot liquid. Her eyes scrutinized him.

"How are you, honey? You look tired."

He smiled weakly. "I am tired."

"Why?"

Sev's mind flew instantly to Ari and last night at Four Alarm. "It's nothing, Mom. I'll be fine."

His mom clucked her tongue. "I know that look." She took a deep breath and sighed. "Boy trouble, huh?"

How did she do that? How did she know what was wrong with him from just a look? There was no hiding his sorrow from her. But wasn't that why he had invited her over in the first place? So he could talk to someone about what he was feeling? Well, that and to get rid of the two portraits of Arion, because not only did he have last night's water color, he also had an oil painting of Arion from last week he needed to get rid of.

"How do I have such bad luck with men, Mom? First Gabriel, and now I've fallen for a guy who is clearly into women, not men."

There had been other males, but Gabriel was the only one besides Ari Sev had considered special. He and Gabe hadn't been biological mates, but Sev had loved him. He had wanted to build a home with Gabe, but shit had fallen apart before they could.

Gabriel's death still haunted him because he could have stopped it. It would have destroyed years of undercover work, but he could have saved Gabe's life. Everything happened so fast that night, but having a year to think about all the could haves, would haves, and should haves made Sev see about twenty other ways that night could have gone down to keep Gabe alive.

Sev's fixated commander, Jonas, who had been Gabe's former lover, had let his jealousy and sorrow over Gabe's death throw Sev under the bus. When questions got asked about Sev's employment with Vampire Dreck Affairs, or VDA for short, Jonas had disavowed him, claiming Sev had never been a VDA agent, which made it look like Sev was a traitor working with the drecks to build the cobalt distribution network for the entire United States.

At least now Sev knew why he had been the only agent sent in to the factory that night. Jonas had known a raid was planned, and from what Sev had pieced together, Jonas had hoped to get rid of Severin. Only he hadn't expected such a large presence of military-grade drecks to show up to guard an outbound shipment. Big mistake. Instead of killing Severin, Jonas had ended up killing the very person he wanted to protect: Gabe.

"Gabriel wasn't your fault, honey," his mom said. "You need to stop blaming yourself for that."

"I know, but I can't help it. I could have done things differently." Sev traced a pattern in the granite countertop with his finger. Gabe had never known that he worked for VDA. Sev hadn't told anyone other than his mom, because his cover had been that deep. Maybe he should have told Gabe. At least then Gabe wouldn't have died thinking Sev had betrayed him, and Gabe's sister wouldn't be after his ass right now. It was obvious she had stripped Gabe's memories before he passed.

His mom tsked. "Sure, and jeopardized your own life and the lives of so many others in the process. You did what you could, Sev. Stop beating yourself up."

"Yeah, but my commander didn't disavow the others. He disavowed me. So, my life *is* in jeopardy if someone tracks me down."

"I'm sure if anyone was going to track you down, they would have come for you by now. Let it go."

His mom was right. He needed to let it go, but he just couldn't, especially with Gabe's sister out there God-knew-where, because he knew she was and that she was pissed off.

"So, are you going to show me those paintings or not?" His mom tapped a long, elegant finger against her coffee mug, changing the subject as deftly as she always did when Gabe came up in conversation.

"Sure, yeah. They're downstairs."

She followed him to the basement, and he clicked on the overhead lights.

"Oh, that's lovely." Her eyes fixed on the canvas resting on the easel.

Sev's heart broke as he looked at the painting and remembered the night before and Arion kissing that woman. Lucky girl.

"So, this is who you were talking about, right? This is the one who likes women that you're in love with?"

"I'm not in love with him." Sev skulked to the opposite side of the room and crossed his arms as he tried to look casual.

"Uh-huh." His mom didn't sound like she believed him. "But this is him?"

He nodded and looked at the floor, letting his long, blond hair cover his face so she wouldn't see his anguish.

"Thought so. Not that it was hard to figure out with all the portraits you've been painting of him and handing off to me."

Sev had a feeling she'd already figured out the four-one-one on the sitch by now. After all, Arion was all he had been painting for weeks. And each painting was as tragic to his heart as the last one. No doubt his mom had figured out a while ago he was fixated on the male.

He cleared his throat and stepped forward to pull the oil painting away from the wall and set it on an empty easel. "This one, too."

He averted his gaze uncomfortably from the painting of two men standing together, arms around each other, their foreheads touching. It hurt Sev to look at it. It was a pose he now knew would never become reality.

"You've captured the moment perfectly," she said.

His mom paced to one side then back, one arm across her torso, the elbow of the other pressed against it as she rested her chin against her thumb and forefinger as if in contemplation. Her eye was all professional, while his only saw the personal component of his work.

"I can tell you were personally inspired. I can feel the emotion." She leaned toward the oil painting then stood back again. "I feel the love between them, but the dark colors show the pain."

His mom turned compassionate eyes on him, and she smiled warmly.

"Don't look at me like that, Mom."

"And how am I looking at you?"

"Like you want to give me a bowl of ice cream as if that will make it all better. But it won't. It won't make it all better." He turned away so she wouldn't see the tears of frustration well in his eyes. "Damn it, Mom! I hate this. I fucking hate this!"

His mom's hand touched his shoulder. "I knew it. You love him."

If only she knew. What was happening between him and Ari—at least on his end—went way beyond mere love. But he wasn't ready to reveal to his mom that he was forming a mating connection to the other male. He didn't want his mom to worry.

With a quick swipe of his hand, he wiped away a tear and chuffed sarcastically. "Yeah, well, it doesn't matter if I love him or not, because he doesn't love me back. So, I just need you to take those paintings out of here so I don't have to look at him every day."

"You know I will, Severin."

They stood silently for a moment then his mom said, "Have you told him how you feel?"

He frowned with contempt. "No, but he should know."

"Why is that?"

"Because I kissed him, and, well…" Sev chuffed again, not wanting to go into all the details about the other stuff they had done. "And he kissed me back, but it was obviously just homo-curiosity, because it's clear he isn't interested in me like that."

His mom pulled back and stepped around to look at him.

"When did this happen?"

"Over a month ago."

"Okay, and then what?"

"Nothing. Absolutely nothing. He hasn't brought it up again, and we've hardly said two words to each other."

"You work with him?"

"Yes."

"Well, maybe he's afraid this will affect your work. You say he hasn't brought it up since you two kissed. Well, have *you?*"

Sev shook his head. "No."

His mom tsked. "Well, for Pete's sake, Sev, why not? Maybe he's just waiting for you to make a move?"

"Doubt it."

"Oh, and it's better to just be miserable than to actually take a chance at happiness? I see."

"Huh?" Sev frowned at her, a bit jostled by her frankness.

"Well, it sounds to me like both of you are waiting for the other to make a move, and neither one of you has the damn balls to do it. How about you try actually talking to him about how you feel, knucklehead?"

His mom had a way of making him feel like such an idiot sometimes, but he couldn't fault her for it. She was usually right, even when he didn't want to admit it.

"What's the point? I already know how he feels. He was lip-locked to a woman last night at some club we all went to after our shift."

"Oh, and that automatically means your time together didn't mean anything to him?"

Sev scowled. "Well, what else would it mean?"

She shook her head, turned back toward the portraits, and grabbed one in each hand. "Children. No matter how old they are, or what generation, they all act the same when it comes to love."

"Oh? And how do they act?" Sev huffed at her as he crossed his arms.

"Like idiots without brains," she said, squaring him up.

With a guilty frown, he took one of the paintings from her, followed her back upstairs, and set the painting in the hall by the front door. Was she right? Was he acting like an idiot? Could Ari just be waiting for him to make a move? The thought of talking to Ari right now made his stomach squirm like a squeamish medical student watching his first surgery, but maybe that's exactly what he needed to do. Talk to Ari.

As long as he didn't do most of the talking with his fists. Uh-huh.

After setting the paintings in the front hall, his mom turned and walked to the kitchen. "Come on, let's have lunch."

Seemed the conversation about Arion was over, at least for now.

They returned to the kitchen and he pulled the pot of chili from the fridge and set it on the stove to heat while he worked on a salad. His mom sat down at the table.

"Have you ever thought of doing a showing, Sev? I'd love to feature your work in the gallery. It's so unique and full of emotion. Better than the work I get from humans."

"That's not how I paint. You know that," Sev said.

"Maybe you should. You know, give the wars and fighting a rest and take some time off. Maybe you could use it to take your mind off this guy you're swooning over."

Sev looked back at the paintings in the hall and felt his heart wrench like two fists gripped and twisted it in opposite directions, wringing it like a wet towel. Time wouldn't help him deal with Arion. It would only make things worse by giving him too much freedom to dwell.

"You know I can't. I just started at AKM." His gaze drew away and he habitually scanned the room, noting that the door and windows were locked before he scanned the back yard.

If a team of drecks showed up, what would I do? Would I see the danger in time to protect myself? Could I protect my mom?

This was how his mind worked. It didn't matter if he was home, at AKM, shopping for groceries, or on patrol. He planned for the worst, always preparing, always ensuring he had an escape plan in case of attack.

And it wasn't just drecks he watched out for. About half-a-dozen military organizations around the world would have loved his head on a stake. And he was sure Gabe's sister would love his skull in her trophy case. She had been out for his blood the last time he saw her.

"Yes, you can. You just have to choose." His mom pulled him from his thoughts and sighed. "You've been fighting wars for so long do you even know how to live freely, anymore?"

"I live freely."

"No you don't. You live waiting for the next attack, always looking over your shoulder. Even now you glance around your own home like it's booby-trapped and someone will jump out from behind the bushes in the backyard. You. Can't. Relax. Severin."

Sev felt himself blush, realizing she had caught him casing his own home like a battle planner. "This is just how I'm wired, Mom."

"Maybe it's time you hired an electrician and got yourself re-wired." She stood and helped herself to a glass of water. "Maybe *he* can rewire you."

"Who?"

She nodded toward the paintings.

Sev shook his head. "He's a figment of my imagination, Mom."

"Bullshit. You make him a figment by not talking to him about how you feel."

"It's not that easy. Besides, it's Dad's fault I'm the way I am. Thank him for giving me his warrior blood." At least he knew he and his mom agreed on just how big of an asshole his dad was.

His mom walked uneasily back to the table and sat down.

"About your dad," she said.

Sev's skin prickled and he looked at her. Her gaze flicked warily to his.

"What about him?" he said.

"He contacted me again."

"When?" Sev didn't like this. His father had been trying to

get in touch with his mom for over ten years now.

"Last Tuesday."

"And?"

His mom hesitated and took a deep breath, held it, then blew it out. "Sev, I agreed to see him."

Sev's hands clenched into fists. "Why?"

"He's changed, Severin. Somewhere along the way, your father developed a conscience and he wants to see me to set things right. And he wants to see you, too."

"Not. Interested." Severin rinsed the lettuce in the sink.

"He asked about you."

"Oh yeah? Well, fuck him."

His mom sighed. "Just shows you can't run forever, son."

"Well, I have no interest in seeing him or talking to him." He paused. "What did you tell him about me?"

"That you're here in Chicago. That's all. I figured I would let you decide what else to tell him when you joined us for dinner."

Sev spun around. "Mom! Dinner? I don't even want to pretend he's my father, let alone have dinner with him, for Chrissake."

She stood and went to the stove and stirred the chili. "He'll be here in a couple of days. I'd like it if you stopped by."

"Don't hold your breath."

"For me. Could you do this for me, Sev?"

"Don't ask me to do that, Mom. Please, don't ask me." Severin's hands temporarily balled into fists.

"Severin, if I can forgive him for what he did to me, why can't you?"

"Because he's an asshole." He set the colander of lettuce on the counter to drain onto a towel.

"Well, he gave me you, and that's something, isn't it?" His mom placed her palm on his cheek and smiled.

Sometimes Sev felt guilty for what happened to her, as if he were to blame. They had to keep their relationship a secret because it would cause them both too much pain if people knew they came from two separate sides of the old war. She would be ostracized by the drecks if they knew she had kept a vampire's offspring and carried it to term rather than kill herself. He would be seen as a threat or, at the least, a dreck sympathizer if his teammates or other vampires learned of his dreck bloodlines.

This was what they called being between a rock and a hard place.

"Do you ever regret keeping me, Mom?"

"*What?* Of course not. Why would you even think that?"

"Sometimes I just hate that I can't call you Mom in public, or that I can't introduce you to people as my mom. And maybe I feel like I hold you back."

His mom hugged him. "Severin. You don't hold me back. And you and I can do what we have to do to make sure it doesn't get complicated for either one of us. Don't worry about any of that. I love you and wouldn't trade you for anything. I'm proud of you, even if I feel that you're a little misguided at times."

"I love you, too, Mom."

"Come on, let's eat."

As his mom grabbed bowls and silverware, Sev glanced back at the portraits leaning against the wall in the front hall. He wondered what Arion was doing right now then realized he probably didn't want to know.

CHAPTER 5

Arion awoke in his dorm at the compound around three o'clock. He had slept like shit, waking up every forty-five minutes or so to toss and turn and nod back off. Dreams of Severin had haunted him all day. Sev dancing with him, kissing him, rubbing his aching erection…and more.

Fuck, he had morning wood. Nice and firm and all *Good morning, Ari.*

Well, too bad. He was tense and wasn't in the mood to give his fifth appendage a handshake.

What the hell had been up Sev's ass last night? Sev had treated him like a second-rate citizen.

Arion shook his head and looked down in reluctant surrender. Okay, so he wasn't that dense. He knew what the problem was. He just didn't know how to fix it. He couldn't give Sev what he wanted—or at least what he figured Sev wanted, which was more of what they had shared in his kitchen six weeks ago.

Then again, maybe Sev felt as uncomfortable about what had happened between them as Ari did, and this was his way of dealing with it.

Ari should have never let them get so carried away last month. He should have stopped their tryst before it began. But he had been woefully weak, and Sev had been enticingly close, and for the first time ever, Ari had succumbed to the urges of his body, as well as to his attraction for his teammate.

Ari dropped his face into his hands and groaned. He had royally fucked up. Not only was he more confused and upside-down about his own sexuality than ever, but he had alienated the one male he was attracted to by screwing around with him out of turn.

What was wrong with him? Until that night six weeks ago, he had known deep down he liked males but had kept that part of him hidden away, accepting superficially that being with a male was out of the question. In fact, his self-deception had been so convincing, he had assured himself he was heterosexual. As if having sex with his eyes closed and fantasizing about men was normal heterosexual behavior for a dude.

It was what it was, and living the life of a heterosexual male was sacrosanct in his parents' eyes. Not to mention, his best friend, Io, would string him up by the balls if he thought Ari was batting for the other team. Ari couldn't stop reminding himself of the reactions of his family and best friend, as well as the consequences, if his newfound sexuality came out. The constant reminders were the only things keeping him from acting on the strengthening impulses to get Sev alone again and do unspeakable things to him. Sev's soul seemed to call to his, and every day Ari felt himself lose a bit more resolve to keep his distance.

Unbidden thoughts of how good Sev had looked last night danced in his mind like marionettes controlled by the Devil. Sev had been a major asshole, but the male rocked blue cashmere sweaters and black slacks better than anyone. And with his hair pulled back in that mussed ponytail secured at the nape of his neck, Sev's sexy mug had been positively lickable.

Maybe Sev had been an ass last night because seeing him kissing Chloe made him jealous, and if Sev was jealous, didn't that mean there was a chance Sev liked him in *that* way? The thought filled Ari's heart with a healthy dose of hope he had no right to feel so good about. His pulse raced with excitement, and he rubbed his hands over his bare thighs. If Sev was attracted to him and he was attracted to Sev...? He took a nervous breath and blew it out. If Sev *did* like him, could he somehow find a way to make a relationship with Sev work despite his need to keep up the image he was heterosexual?

He couldn't believe he was even thinking it, but for the first time in his life, he wanted someone. A very specific someone. He wanted Severin.

With a surge of determination, Ari stood and paced as he raked his fingers through his thick, dark brown hair. How could he make this work? Should he even try? What if his parents or Io found out?

Get Real, Ari. Who are you kidding? He stopped and hung his head in despair. Trying to have a relationship with Sev was a foolhardy idea. They would both get hurt in the end, and it would tear up the comfortable order in Ari's life.

He looked down at the tent in his boxers. "Sorry, buddy. Get used to disappointment." Disappointment had been the story of Ari's life, so why shouldn't his pecker share the pain?

With a sad, reluctant sigh, he turned toward his twin-sized bed then meticulously pulled the sheets and blankets into crisp lines. He tucked in the sheets, then patted the covers under the single pillow and smoothed out the wrinkles in the bed spread. Perfect. Like everything else in his life. Except that the perfection was just a mirage, an illusion to trick everyone into thinking he was someone he wasn't.

His phone rang and vibrated on top of the simple desk against the wall. He frowned and rolled his eyes as he picked it up and saw who was calling.

"Dad? This is a surprise. I was just thinking about you." *Yeah, thinking about how I live a miserable life so you and Mom can be happy.*

"Oh? All good, I'm sure."

"Of course." He had gotten so good at lying to his parents he didn't even have to try, anymore.

"You're well, I hope?"

"Yes. Everything's great." Lie, lie, lie. "So, what's up?"

"Your mother wanted me to call and tell you we're inviting your whole team to our party next weekend."

"You are?" He hated this. He didn't even want to go, let alone have his whole team along to see the debacle of embarrassment he contended with on a regular basis. "Um, but I think we're working that night."

"I took care of all that. I already spoke to Tristan and worked it all out."

Ari closed his eyes in frustration and pinched the bridge of his nose between his thumb and forefinger. His dad loved throwing around his money and his power as the king's liaison like they were nothing. Dad had been part of the King's Guard for centuries and now lived in exceptional comfort as a close personal advisor to the king, who preferred to stay out of the public eye. No one ever spoke directly to the king. That was what his liaisons and consultants were for.

"Well, sounds like you've got it all taken care of. Why did you call me?"

"I wanted to remind you to make sure you get here early to help us greet all the guests."

His dad hoped to groom him for a more political position someday. Ari wasn't remotely interested but he played along, anyway.

"Fine. What time should I get there?"

"Better make it nine o'clock. With the time change, I think that's the earliest you can get here, anyway."

Ari hated Daylight Savings Time. It meant the full-bloods would have to use their dorms at AKM more often rather than be free to go home during the day. Severin would likely be assigned day patrols to compensate for the shorter nights, too. The thought of not seeing Severin every night made his heart ache. And wasn't that an odd feeling? Ari had never felt such a dull, throbbing ache in his chest before.

"Okay, Dad. I'll be there. Tell Mom I said hi." He rubbed his thumb absently over his sternum, trying to soothe the ache.

"I will. Take care, Arion."

They hung up and Ari wondered if he would be able to get out of the party. Probably not. Damn it. He needed to toughen up and just plan to make the most of it. Maybe he would be allowed to play the piano. That would be worth it. He loved playing and didn't have nearly enough opportunities to do so.

Okay, enough pussy-footing around. Time for a quick shower and a workout. He grabbed the folded towel and stack of clothes he had set out last night, along with his shaving kit, and stepped into the deserted hall.

AKM was a veritable ghost town during the day. Except for the medical wing, the building was windowless to protect the few full-bloods who rotated day shifts to monitor dispatch and the data center, but it wasn't until nightfall that things started hopping inside the facility.

The community bathroom was empty and he cranked on one of the showers to get the water heated up, which usually took a couple minutes. While he waited, he brushed his teeth, shaved, and used the facilities.

Showering made him feel a little better about the shit in his life. Then he got dressed in nylon gym shorts and a T-shirt after combing his hair and slicking it down with gel.

Okay, so what if he showered before working out? He got made fun of for showering before and after going to the gym, but he didn't care. Showering was to him like coffee was to other people. It woke him up, invigorated him, and got him ready for his day. Fuck what everyone else thought.

Hmm, maybe he should take up that attitude with everyone who wanted to control who he did and didn't go out with. Wouldn't that be interesting?

Yeah, right. Like that would happen.

After depositing his things back in his room and tossing his boxers into his dirty clothes hamper, he grabbed his gym bag then stopped by the kitchen for an apple and a bottle of water on his way to the training center. His footsteps echoed in the empty hall. He liked it here when it was like this. Quiet, calm, peaceful. The evening bustle always made him tense.

He was good at his job and all, but it wasn't what he loved. It wasn't that he hated being an enforcer. He just would have preferred being at home writing music or playing in one of Chicago's jazz clubs every night instead of chasing drecks and other criminals.

He was just sinking his teeth into the last bite of apple when he pulled open the door to the training center and came to a dead stop. Sev stood in front of the mirrors grinding out a set of bicep curls. His gaze jumped to Ari's in the mirror and his arms hesitated for a split-second in their upward swing.

Fuck. Ari hadn't expected to see Severin here today. This was going to be uncomfortable.

SEV'S STOMACH PIROUETTED INSIDE HIS BELLY when he saw Arion.

"What are you doing here?" He set the dumbbells back in the rack but didn't turn around. Arion was the last person he had expected to run into when he'd decided to come in for a workout after his lunch with his mom.

"I could ask you the same thing," Ari said.

"Yeah? Well, I asked you first." He was being intentionally antagonistic and he knew it, but damn it, he didn't need the reminder of last night. He had come here to forget about Arion, not see him. And now the male was in the same room with him, looking and smelling fucking fantastic to boot.

"I spent the night here." Ari discarded what looked like an apple core and walked into the large room.

"With the woman you were with last night?" Sev's voice held an edge to it. He knew Ari hadn't brought that woman back here, though. Ari didn't break the rules, one of which was no outsiders inside AKM. Family was okay, but no one-night stands, as it were. Micah could get away with that shit, and he had with Sam—partly because she ended up being his mate and required special medical attention—but Ari would never do something like that. He flew too close to the arrow to break rules.

"I wasn't *with* her." Ari bit the words out and shot him a you're-being-an-asshole look before hopping on a bike to warm up. "And no, she didn't come back here with me. I was alone."

Well, good then. Sev harrumphed and turned back to the dumbbell rack. He felt like punching something. Maybe he could go out on a day patrol and find some drecks and kick their asses for the fun of it. Yeah, and then he would find himself out of a job for starting another war between the two races. No thanks.

He picked up the next heaviest weight of dumbbells and pounded out another set of curls. Without another word to Ari, he worked through his biceps routine before moving to chest. After loading a bar, he glanced at Ari's reflection in the mirror and saw him looking back at him. He quickly glanced away then laid down on the bench and un-racked the bar.

"Need a spot?" Ari appeared beside him, out of nowhere.

"No." The word shot out of Sev like an angry dart.

"Suit yourself." Ari shook his head and grabbed a forty-pound dumbbell and pushed out a warm-up set of triceps extensions as Sev grunted through his set of presses.

Tense silence stretched between them as they peered at each other out of the corners of their eyes, scowls firmly in place and brows bunched in irritation.

Sev looked away and finished his set of presses and sat up to catch his breath while he rested. His gaze drifted to Ari once more. The male was built. His sculpted triceps popped on the flexion then stretched through the negative motion. Sev wanted to trace the outline with this fingers. Or better yet, his tongue.

Ari wasn't as large as some of the other members on the team, but his body looked like it had been chiseled from stone. By the gods, no less. He was hard in all the right places with about five percent body fat, but then that could have been his vampire genetics. He was rumored to have strong bloodlines.

Ari's gaze caught his in the mirror again, and Sev quickly looked away and eyed the sparring mat in the center of the room. He could sure go for a match right now.

"Hey, Ari, didn't you say you wanted to spar with me sometime?" Maybe working out his aggression against the very person keying him up would set things right. Or maybe it wouldn't. All Sev knew right now was that he needed to work off his pain and this was as good a way to do that as any. And why not hurt the one who had hurt him? Sounded good to Sev.

"Yes, I did." Ari's tone held an edge of its own, as if he were thinking the same thing or at least something similar.

Sev stood and walked toward the mat.

"This is as good a time as any then, don't you think?" He turned to see Ari following him.

Ari's brow furrowed and his jaw clenched. The muscles by his ears on either side of his face bunched and flexed as if he were holding back a verbal lashing by clenching his jaw.

"Sure." Ari's eyes narrowed on him as if he were ready to exorcise a few demons of his own.

They squared off at each other on opposite sides of the mat, arms raised, feet wide in solid stances, gazes locked.

"You think you can hang with me?" Sev said.

"We'll see."

Sev swung and Ari dodged, blocked, and retaliated with a side-arm that connected with Sev's cheek as they whipped past each other.

Sev's head ricocheted to the side from the impact, and he jerked back around to the front. "Lucky shot." He flexed his jaw and touched his cheek, actually surprised at Ari's fast reflexes.

"It's not luck." Ari surged forward and swung again.

Sev caught his arm and shot sideways to let Ari's momentum carry him over as Sev flipped him.

Ari's body crashed to the mat, and for an instant Sev wanted to end the fight before he hurt him, but then Ari spun on his back and caught Sev's legs between his ankles and knocked him down.

He suddenly found himself pinned as Ari jumped on him, gripped him with both his arms and legs, then heave-hoed Sev across the mat. Shit! Ari was a strong fucker. Sev's long hair flopped over his face, disorienting him as he crashed against the mat again.

Okay, no more playing games. He hopped up and threw back his hair as he glared at Ari, who was already up and dancing around on the balls of his feet like a boxer.

"So, you've got some moves of your own, huh?" Sev said.

"I'm just full of surprises." Arion stopped hopping from foot-to-foot and walked it off, glowering right back at Sev.

Damn, but Ari looked sexy all pissed off, his brow knitted tightly, his eyes narrowed and resolute.

Okay, so Sev didn't need to be thinking that way right now, because it was causing him to get his ass beat. He normally didn't struggle with hand-to-hand. Maybe he was simply too emotionally vested in this sparring match to perform. Or maybe it really was that Arion's physical beauty distracted him. Whatever the reason, he needed to gather himself.

He tied back his hair with an elastic band and cracked his neck with a couple of side-to-side flexes.

"I bet you are, and not just on the mat." The words spat out with more venom than Sev intended.

"What's that supposed to mean?" Ari's frown deepened, making him look even sexier.

Sev chuffed. "As if you don't know."

"Enlighten me, asshole, because yeah, I *don't* know." Ari's glare was positively electric by now, all kinds of daggers and knives shooting from his topaz-colored eyes.

Sev sneered and looked away, not about to answer. Big mistake, because Ari came at him again. Turning back just in time, Sev avoided being served a dish of knuckle sandwich and dodged out of the way, shooting his knee up to gut-check Ari. The air burst from the male's lungs and he doubled over, coughing as if his diaphragm was in his throat while Sev danced away from him.

A part of Sev ached watching Arion suffer. It didn't feel natural beating the guy up like this, and he almost wanted to apologize. Almost.

"Did your girlfriend teach you how to fight, Arion?" He walked a semi-circle around Ari, glaring, seething, needing to let go of all his anguish.

"What? Who...?" Ari was still bent over and looked up, his face a mix of pain and anger as he coughed again.

Sev reversed direction and paced back the other way. "You heard me. Did she teach you how to fight while you were fucking her?" His face screwed up with annoyance.

Arion frowned as he finally righted himself and pulled back. "What's your problem, Sev? Huh?"

Sev glowered and sneered. "She was a real class act, buddy. I love how her hand was surgically attached to your crotch. Did you enjoy it? Did you like getting your rocks off in the middle of the dance floor?"

"What the fuck, asshole!" Ari stepped back and his frown deepened further, casting alluring shadows over his eyes. "You sound like a jealous boyfriend. I didn't know my sex life was so important to you."

"It isn't! Who said it is?" Sev surged forward and shoved Ari hard, but the male pushed back, knocking Sev's arms to the side.

"Like hell it isn't! Listen to you. We had one heavy scene in my kitchen and now my sex life is your business? When you haven't said two words to me since? What the hell? You fucking hypocrite!"

The two were practically chest-to-chest and nose-to-nose, tempers flaring, vampire testosterone flowing like rolling lava. Ari's toss-out about what had happened between them last month caught Sev off guard. So, Ari hadn't forgotten. He had just chosen to avoid the topic of their brief love fest on purpose all this time. That shit hurt like a razor gashing his heart.

"I don't give a fuck what you do or who you do it to!" Sev pushed against Ari's shoulder and knocked him backward.

"You sure about that? Because you sure seem suddenly interested in my dick and where I put it."

"Fuck you, Ari!"

Ari chuffed sarcastically. "Fuck *you*, Sev!" The two stood a few feet apart, all heavy breathing and torqued aggression, glaring at one another as if nothing but hatred stood between them.

Finally, Ari's face twisted with rage and the dam burst. "Damn you, Severin!" Ari rushed him and tackled him to the mat. Their bodies tangled as they scrapped and fought to get the upper hand. Just as Sev thought he had Ari pinned, Ari scissored his legs around Sev's waist and sling-shot him to his back.

Sev growled. He was angry, out of breath, and hurt. Why

hadn't Ari said anything about their time together before now? Had it been that bad? Was Ari that ashamed of what they'd done?

"Fucker!" Sev tried to wrench free, feeling shattered and used. "Was our night together nothing to you?" The words blurted out of nowhere as he struggled against Ari's hold. "Did you just *use me* to satisfy your gay curiosity? Is that it? Was I just some random, homo-curious fuck-for-the-night, and then it was back to your safe, hetero life like what we did meant nothing to you? Like *I* meant nothing? Am I *nothing* to you, Arion?"

"**WHAT?**" ARION'S FACE SCREWED UP in stunned surprise as Sev's words sliced into his heart.

Nothing? Sev wasn't nothing. He was everything. Okay, sure, maybe there had been some curiosity surrounding what they'd done, but not because he wanted to give gay sex a try. The curiosity had been about his own self-discovery. Arion had been learning about himself in that short twenty minutes that Sev had been in his home, so of course he'd been curious. But he hadn't used Severin, had he? That hadn't been his intent, but now that he thought about it, that's exactly how it looked. Like he'd simply had his fun then tossed Sev aside like refuse after he was finished with him.

Arion scowled, but his aggression was directed at himself. He'd never meant to hurt Sev, and yet he had. He'd inadvertently allowed Sev to think he'd used him.

And now he was too disgusted with himself even to apologize. Sorry just didn't seem a grand enough word to atone for his abhorrent behavior of the last six weeks.

He released Sev and jerked back and away, not wanting to cast his negative shadow over the male he adored more than anyone he'd ever met.

Sev rolled to his side and stilled as if the life had abruptly drained out of him. "Fuck you, Ari. Fuck you for playing with my emotions like that." He paused. "Just leave me alone."

Ari couldn't see Sev's face, but he imagined if he could, he would find nothing but pain and heartache there. Sev's voice sounded so far away and wretched. And sad. No, not sad. Miserable. Dejected. In utter despair.

"Sev..."

"I said fuck off." Sev stood, keeping his back turned on Ari. "I'm such an idiot." He shook his head, his voice willowy thin. "You just used me. You never had any intention of being with me."

Severin turned and marched to the locker room in silence. Discussion over.

Arion could only watch him leave. What the hell had just happened here? He looked down at the mat, at a smear of moisture—Sev's sweat. He reached out and dabbed it with his fingertips and lifted it to his nose.

Aaaahhhh. Severin. Pure and strong.

His gaze swept back to the locker room door and that dull, throbbing ache awakened in his chest again. He had hurt Sev. Sev thought he had simply been using him, but that wasn't the intention at all. Arion had wanted what happened six weeks ago. He had never meant to hurt Sev.

But he had. Sev was most definitely in pain.

Shit.

Arion felt about an inch tall, and he needed to get out of there.

Rubbing his thumb up and down his sternum, trying to ease the ache, he gathered himself and stood. With one last look toward the locker room, he took a deep breath, blew it out, and hurried for the exit.

After rushing down the deserted hall in a fit of emotional upheaval, he reached the elevators and smacked the up button then looked back in the direction of the training center. Sev was in there, likely in as big an emotional mess as he was. Probably wondering where it had all fallen apart.

He needed to explain. He needed to apologize. He needed to somehow let Sev know that none of this was his fault. It was Ari's fault. All of it.

His thumb continued rubbing rhythmically up and down

the center of his chest as the ache deepened. When the elevator door opened, he stood there for a second. Then he took a step forward. Then stopped. Then closed his eyes and leaned forward on one outstretched arm pressed against the wall.

He couldn't leave Sev.

Turning, he let the elevator door close behind him as he began the hesitant walk back to the training center.

This was crazy. Ari stopped in the middle of the hall. If he returned to the gym, he knew how things would end up. He wouldn't be able to hold himself back from Sev. He wanted him. The scent of his sweat still invaded his senses, and it was a better high than a snort of cobalt could provide.

No, no. He could hold back. He would be able to control himself. He owed Sev that much.

With purpose, Ari started walking again, holding his head high and pushing his shoulders back. The ache in his chest diminished as he neared the gym and opened the door. After stepping inside, he halted abruptly, his lungs pumping hard. Was he nervous or just keyed up? Was he afraid someone would see them and figure out what happened? Or was his sudden, erratic breathing caused by something else? Desire perhaps? Or his struggle not to give in to temptation and claim Sev's body as he had six weeks ago.

Fucking hells, maybe he should just bolt and do this shit later.

A sudden jolt of pain hit his chest. *No. you need to do it now. You need to take away Sev's pain, you chicken shit. Suck it up, grow some balls, go in there, and apologize. Set things right.*

Nodding to himself, he took a deep breath and stalked the length of the gym to the locker room, pushed the door open, and proceeded directly to the bay of lockers reserved for Tristan's team.

As he rounded the corner, he sucked in his breath at the magnificent, beautiful male who greeted him. Sev sat on the bench, his face already turned toward him, his guarded eyes red and full of tears, his thumb poised against his sternum as if he had been rubbing it.

Sev slowly stood up. "Why are you here?"

Suddenly, everything Ari had wanted to say escaped him. Like a fleeing antelope, his words bounded away, leaving him only with his breath, his body, and the vision of Severin in front of him. And the scent of Sev's sweat. And the memory of Sev's mouth on his, their bodies perfectly matched and pressed together. All he could do was stare and remember how incredible Sev had felt against him and in his arms.

"Ari?"

Without a word, Ari charged forward, grabbed Sev, and thrust him back against the metal lockers with a loud clank as he came nose-to-nose with him, his senses spiking to DEFCON 1 as he panted with arousal.

"I didn't want her." His voice growled low in his throat.

It took a moment for Sev to react, but he didn't fight him or try to pull away. On the contrary, his body seemed to light up with as much heat as Ari felt lighting up his blood.

"What? What do you mean?" Sev blinked in confusion. Or maybe he was just dazed.

Arion's grip on Sev's shoulders stayed firm as his gaze danced over Sev's face. He was hungry for this male. Physically and emotionally hungry for him. "I didn't want her." He spoke more softly this time. More reverently.

Sev licked his lips, and it was all Ari could do not to lean in and quickly snag that alluring tongue with his teeth.

"Who?" Sev said quietly.

Ari could tell Sev knew he was talking about Chloe, but he seemed wary, as if he couldn't believe he was hearing him right.

"Any of them. I didn't want any of them." Ari hadn't wanted Chloe or any woman he'd ever dated. In a moment of pure clarity, he knew that what he wanted was right here in front of him.

Their noses touched as their gazes held and locked on to each other. Ari could feel the warmth of Sev's breath on his own mouth, and it made his stomach muscles quiver, taking him back to his kitchen and how they had devoured each other that night.

Sev's eyes searched his as he remained pressed against

the lockers. "Who *do* you want, Ari?" He kept his voice soft then held his breath, as if not daring to hope for the answer he wanted.

"I think you already know." Ari could see the realization dawning in Sev's blue eyes. The connections being made. The knowledge that what had happened six weeks ago hadn't been a fluke, an accident, or just some curious adventure.

Sev's eyes tightened and his breath hitched. "Please tell me. Who do you want?"

Ari glanced down at Sev's perfect lips then prowled his gaze back up to his eyes, seeing his future in their blue depths.

"You." Ari closed the last inch between them in an instant, locking his lips to Sev's.

Air pushed out their noses as they both moaned in what sounded like relief.

Sev's body instantly uncoiled and softened within Ari's grasp.

Their lips fused and separated, re-fused, twisted together, opened and devoured. Their tongues danced against each other, lapping and licking and drinking in the other's taste. Sev's teeth banged against Ari's, but neither of them seemed to care as long as the connection between them remained intact.

"Ari...when? How?" Sev's hands explored down Ari's stomach as he spoke against his mouth.

"Ssshhh." Ari brushed his lips over Sev's again, lingering, their tender skin clinging together.

Sev moaned and his eyes closed dreamily as he gently squirmed, feeling and touching Ari.

Damn, but his hands felt good creeping lower like that. Ari thought he would hyperventilate as he began panting, drawing his mouth away from Sev's so he could look down at that big hand inching toward his erection.

Sev shifted and leaned into Ari, resting his forehead on his shoulder and wrapping his other arm softly around the small of Ari's back, holding him, caressing, keeping him close.

Not a word was said as they both watched Sev's hand slide the rest of the way down and over the mound of hard flesh in Ari's shorts.

"Oh, God." Ari swayed forward, shuddering, growing weak in the knees. Sev's arm tightened around him and Ari's fingers curled and gripped the tops of Sev's shoulders like hooks to hold himself up.

They both watched Sev's palm rub slowly up and down his hard column. The satin material slipped erotically over his cock, tantalizing him and licking lust into an inferno inside his belly. Then Sev curled his fingers around him, holding him through his shorts, applying delicious pressure that seared his senses and made him shiver.

He just wanted to take Sev. Here. Now. Just throw him over the bench and fuck the ever-living rocks off him.

Sev groaned and rubbed him harder. "Is this for me?" Sev's deep voice and the warmth of his breath against his shoulder awakened another unnerving shiver down his spine.

He nodded, trying to swallow a gasp that choked through his throat. Ari closed his eyes. This felt too good to believe. "Y-yes." He stammered over the words, lust turning his voice to gravel.

Something was building inside him. Need. A craving. Desire. His whole body rose and fell with each breath, and he whimpered as Sev pulled away the waist of his shorts and dipped his hand inside.

Fuck! That nearly undid Ari. His legs buckled and his abdomen spasmed uncontrollably.

Getting a hard grip on Sev's shoulders again, he slammed him back against the lockers once more and bit down on Sev's bottom lip, purring so hard it sounded like a growl.

The purr. The sound of an aroused male. And Ari was way beyond aroused.

Sev pushed him back and spun him around, nearly crawling inside his body as he shoved him toward the shower room while keeping one arm secured around his waist and his other hand down the front of Ari's shorts.

"Where...?" Ari nearly fell over from the pleasure of Sev's

hand stroking him.

"Showers. Now." Sev clumsily directed him forward.

They barely avoided tripping over each other in their haste to get into the farthest stall to the right.

The showers were typical gym showers, with a curtained outer area for towels, robes, or other clothes, and a second curtained area for the shower itself.

Sev yanked open the outer curtain and pushed Ari in before pulling the curtain shut behind them. In a tangle of arms and fervent kisses, they started pulling off each other's clothes as Sev reached in and cranked on the water.

Sev tugged off his shirt as Ari discarded his to the marble bench behind him. Hands found waistbands and pushed. Feet toed off gym shoes. Shorts fell down their legs. Two powerful, masculine bodies pressed together and spun into the spraying water. Their hands combined to throw the inner curtain closed with the satisfying sound of metal shower rings swooshing over the bar.

"I've had fantasies about this since—" Ari was cut off by Sev's mouth clamping down on his in a heated kiss.

"So have I." Sev pushed him back against the cold tile wall and skimmed his hands over the curves of his back to his ass, sliding the fingers of his left hand softly between his cheeks.

No man had ever touched him there and Ari's knees nearly buckled again from the pleasure of having Sev's fingers dip into the place he had only ever dreamed of being explored.

"Sensitive?" Sev chuckled lightly as he pushed closer and deepened the caress.

"You have—Oh my God!—no idea."

The earlier tension was gone. The aggression between them had dissipated, replaced now by something primal that seemed to originate from somewhere far back in their vampire genetics. It felt almost like instinct, as if an innate drive propelled them toward one another.

"I never meant to hurt you." Ari skimmed his hands with fascination over Sev's bare chest. He was massive. Broad and wide of shoulder and pure muscle. Fucking sexy as hell.

"That's past now." Sev purred and found Ari's mouth, locking them together.

He tasted perfect. Magnificent. Ari opened for him and licked the seam of Sev's mouth, urging his lips apart as Sev pressed him more intently into the cold, tile wall.

They both moaned and sighed against each other.

It was suddenly clear Ari couldn't be without Severin. He would have to find a way for them to be together so that no one found out, because he had to have Sev in his life as more than somebody he worked with. He wanted him too badly. Trying to deny his attraction felt akin to asking water not to be wet. It just didn't make sense and wasn't possible. Doing so would be living a lie. An even greater lie than the one he had been living already.

Sev's fingers dove deeper, spreading the cheeks of his ass to graze the tight opening that no one but he had ever played with. He shuddered violently and sucked in his breath as his knees almost gave.

"Okay, I've got you." Sev gripped him securely around the waist with his other arm, holding him up as Ari latched onto his shoulders.

"Don't stop. Please." Ari couldn't believe this was happening. He had only ever wanted to feel normal and to have a sexual experience where he didn't have to force fantasies of men touching him like this so he could get off. Now that it was actually happening, he had a feeling he would go into major meltdown if Sev stopped.

Sev abruptly lifted him and his back slapped against the wall. "Wrap your legs around me."

Ari did as he was told and locked his ankles above the curve of Sev's bottom.

Sev's hand gripped his ass cheek and his fingers crept into the previously unexplored crevice once more. Arion arched away from the wall, grinding their cocks together as Sev leaned forward and closed his mouth over his nipple.

"Oh, God," he said softly.

This was better than he had ever imagined. He reached down and started stroking himself as he watched Sev's tongue flick up and down over his nipple before his lips closed over it again and sucked. For the first time, he didn't have to close his eyes to find something to sexually excite him. Sev's masculine face and his hard cock gave him an arousing visual feast that kicked his libido into a dimension it had never known, and no way was he about to close his eyes. Nothing his mind could conjure would turn him on more than the very real, very sensual male holding him against the wall.

Sev's fingers dug into the fleshy cheek of his ass, so close to his tenderfoot trail, and the anticipation was almost enough to send him over. God! When had he ever been this turned on? Sure, he had toys and dildos he used on himself when he masturbated, but this was different. This was Sev, whose fingers were so close to going where no man had gone before. It was enough to make his cock weep with anticipation.

Suddenly, the sound of another shower cranked on and Sev pulled his mouth off his chest and looked up at him.

Ari's lungs pumped as hard as his hand and he must have looked desperate because Sev nodded once and pressed forward to claim his mouth. He whimpered softly against Sev's lips, cranking his shaft harder. His orgasm was close and he couldn't stop, not when he had waited for this moment forever.

"I need this. Please." He said the words so softly against Sev's mouth that he worried Sev didn't hear him.

"Then take it." Sev spoke just as softly, but his words held an edge of desire that nearly blew Ari's toes off.

It was then that Ari realized Sev was pounding his own cock, their hands in perfect unison with each other. He looked down at their pair of ruddy heads glistening with water and pre-cum just as Severin poked his finger inside his ass. He nearly blacked out from the pleasure, jerking and stiffening. Shit, he didn't even have time to think. He came instantly, biting back a grunt as his entire body spasmed and his legs stiffened and clamped around Sev's waist as his release flew out of his cock.

Ari undulated against the wall, levering himself up with

his legs, which were locked hard around Sev's waist. And still he continued to come as Sev's finger probed deeper, staying with him as he slid up the tiles and tried like hell not to cry out as wave after wave pounded through him and out his cock. Finally, his body relaxed in post-orgasmic reverie, and he slipped back down and into Sev's waiting hold.

Shocked, he lifted his dumbfounded gaze to Sev's as beads of semen continued to flow out of him and over his hand.

When their eyes met again, Sev stiffened and sucked in his breath.

"I'm coming, Ari. Look. Watch me." Quiet, Sev was so quiet.

How could he not watch? They both dropped their gazes and Ari held his breath in a dazed stupor as Sev's cock erupted and shot his release over Ari's stomach to mix with his own. Air rushed out of him as the creamy fluid splattered his skin, and he raised his hand to smear it over his torso with a sense of wonder, as if he needed to touch it to know it was real.

Sev shook and convulsed. "Fuck, but that's sexy. Watching you rub my cum over you."

It felt sexy, too. Ari couldn't stop rubbing the viscous fluid over his body. He wanted to wear Sev's scent like a badge of honor. He couldn't explain it. It just felt right to want Sev's smell on him, and to want everyone to know Sev was his.

But he couldn't let that happen, could he? If everyone knew, then it was only a matter of time before his parents and Io found out. And then all hell would unleash. So, he was at odds with himself. His heart and every instinctive urge inside him wanted to layer Sev's scent over him, but his conscious mind protested and shot his subconscious down, telling him he was being irrational.

The other shower shut off and whoever was there flung their curtain open, probably to grab their towel. Ari wondered if whoever it was could smell them and what they had just done. It wouldn't be the first time the showers had been used for sexual recreation. More than one gay couple worked at AKM and sometimes a guy had to do what a guy had to do. Or a couple of guys, as the case may be.

Still, Ari didn't want anyone to know it was him doing the rainbow dance in the shower this time.

They waited, holding each other with Sev's finger still probed up his ass and their hands still ringed around their cocks, almost as if they both feared moving would make their time together disappear. Ari didn't want it to disappear. He slammed his eyes closed against the sting of tears and swallowed his emotions as Sev kissed the side of his neck.

This had been the most wonderful sexual experience of his entire life and he wanted to hold onto Sev forever. Forever! He liked Sev. A lot. As in, he wanted to see him again, date him, and spend time with him that went beyond just hanging out and catching a beer. He wanted to *know* Sev and learn about his life.

Why? Because he wanted to have a relationship with him. There. He admitted it. Maybe he hadn't declared his intentions out loud to the world, but confessing them to himself was a start. He was happy—happier than he could recall in a long time. And the day had started out so bleak, too. Who could have known this would happen?

When the water started to cool, Sev finally stood back and quickly splashed them both to rinse away the residue of their orgasms. Ari unlocked his legs from around Sev's waist and stepped down. The moment was over too soon.

"I'll go first," he said, sounding sad.

Sev quickly grabbed him and yanked him back, kissing him hard.

They looked at each other, and Ari knew he probably appeared like a deer in the headlights. A happy deer, but in the headlights nonetheless.

He grinned secretly at Sev then stepped into the outer curtained area to retrieve his clothes before darting to his locker. He quickly unlocked it, grabbed his towel, and dried off before pulling his clothes over his still-damp skin.

Severin joined him a couple minutes later and did likewise.

They were silent for a minute.

"So..." Ari said, the magical tension blossoming between them again like a blooming rose.

Everything had just changed between them. Their shower encounter hadn't been a repeat of six weeks ago—a clumsy, spontaneous outburst of sexual discovery in Ari's kitchen. What had just happened had been something else, premeditated. Not spontaneous. They both knew what they were doing this time around. They had both wanted it just now, and it was clear they both wanted it again. For Ari, the time of holding back and restraining himself from following through on his feelings was gone. There would be no going back from where he and Sev were with each other now.

Sev turned and sat down beside him, straddling the bench. "So..."

They stared at each other. Ari felt himself losing control of his emotions again, his heart splitting wide and yearning to be back in Sev's arms. He took several shorts breaths then swung toward Sev as if he'd been pushed. In one fluid motion, their lips locked together again and Sev's hand cupped the back of his head.

He needed him. Oh God, but he needed him. Not just sexually, but as in Sev was the other half of his life and he didn't think he would survive if Sev wasn't there. He didn't know how he knew this. He just did.

The door to the locker room clanked on the other side of the locker bay and the two jerked apart. Ari leaned into his locker as if he were looking for something.

"Hey." Bauer, one of the day walkers from Stryker's team, shuffled into view. "I thought you guys were off tonight."

"Yeah. We are," Sev said. "But you know how it is. Can't get away from the place even on a day off, know what I mean?"

Bauer nodded. "Fuck, yeah. I know what you mean." He rolled his eyes. "Well, have a good one. I've got to get ready for my shift."

Bauer disappeared into the showers, and Ari quietly shut his locker before glancing at Sev. "What are you doing tonight?"

"Nothing. Why?" Sev playfully bumped his knee against Ari's.

Because I need you. "Want to come over and watch the game?"

He nudged his foot against Sev's.

"Who's playing?"

Who cares? "The Bulls."

"Want me to bring anything?"

Just you. "Only if you want."

"I can bring beer."

Can I pour it over you and lick it off? "That's fine. I was going to order a pizza."

"What time you want me there?" Sev scooted closer on the bench and surreptitiously stroked his fingers against the side of Ari's leg.

How quickly things had changed between them. Not even an hour ago, they were at each other's throats, and now they acted like two men who were in love and never said a harsh word between them. Clearly, both of them had been holding in a lot of repressed emotion from their first encounter. Ari knew that was true for him.

He suddenly realized the ache he had suffered in his chest off and on for weeks was gone, and he knew it was because he had finally acknowledged his feelings for the male next to him.

Ari glanced down at Sev's hand. The back of one strong, masculine finger stroked the nylon fabric that covered his thigh, creeping lower until it dipped under the seam and grazed bare skin. He swallowed and took a shivering breath as he lifted his gaze to Sev's.

"Right after sundown would be good. I can't go home until then."

Sev leaned toward him. "I could stay here with you." The timbre of his voice was suggestive, seductive in a way that nearly broke Ari's will. Sev's fingers crept higher on his thigh and his body heated.

"Too many eyes here. It's too risky. Let's wait until tonight."

Their eyes met again and Ari's heart backflipped.

"Tonight then." Sev nodded but his hand stayed under Ari's shorts.

They were only inches apart, drifting closer to one another until their lips drew together again like magnets.

Ari couldn't get enough of Severin. It was like the proverbial dam had burst and he was overflowing with his need to be in constant contact with the guy, especially mouth-to-mouth.

Sev held him like a cherished treasure, their lips sliding easily against one another in long, languid caresses as his hand slipped to the inside of his thigh and squeezed. Ari's fingers wove into the long, damp tresses that hung around Sev's face and his mind carried him back to the shower and Sev's gift. His first real experience with a male. The rushed encounter in his kitchen didn't count, because Ari hadn't known what he was doing then. Now, he did. Now, he knew exactly what he was doing and what he wanted.

Warmth filled him, and the feeling was pure joy. Always until now, sexual experiences had been cold and unfulfilling, even miserable, because he had been forcing himself to be something he wasn't. Not anymore. Severin had shown him who he was and what he wanted to be, and right here in Sev's arms was where he belonged.

The shower shut off and Ari jerked back, remembering where they were.

Sev gently pulled his hand out of Ari's shorts and smiled at him as if he thought Ari was the most adorable creature he had ever seen.

"Okay, so, yeah." Ari cleared his throat and took a deep breath before adjusting the semi in his shorts and standing up. "I'll see you tonight then?"

"Count on it."

Ari nodded and looked over his shoulder then at the floor then back at Sev. "Good." As he started to walk away, he held his hand ever-so-slightly away from his body, his palm facing Sev, who glanced at it before looking away and lifting his own hand just enough so their palms slid one over the other. Their fingers lingered together for just a moment and curled around each other before Ari broke the connection and headed toward the exit.

Don't turn around, don't turn around. He knew if he did, he would never be able to walk away.

CHAPTER 6

SEVERIN WATCHED ARION until he disappeared behind the bay of lockers then grinned. When he had decided to come to AKM for a workout today, he hadn't counted on the heavens breaking open and raining down a whole lot of good fortune. Hell, he hadn't even known Ari was here. If he had, he wouldn't have come, and what a mistake that would have been in light of what had occurred in the past hour.

He and Ari were on new ground with each other, and Sev knew the field of play was a brighter, happier place all of a sudden.

The door to the locker room opened and closed and Ari was gone, leaving him with his big-ass cheesy smile and the most incredible sense of contentment he'd ever felt.

Sev couldn't have been imagining the powerful feelings spilling out of Ari, but this had all happened so suddenly. He looked back in the direction Ari had gone, wanting to go after him. He didn't care who knew how he felt about Ari, and he didn't care who found them together. He was in love, and he had been for a while. He knew that now. But it seemed Ari wanted to keep things low-key.

Was that why he hadn't said anything about what had happened six weeks ago? Had Ari simply wanted to stay under the radar? Who knew? It didn't matter anymore. He and Ari had just taken a huge step in the right direction. And yay him! He had a date with the guy tonight.

Bauer appeared from the showers wearing a towel around his waist, and Sev stood up like he had just been getting ready to head out instead of sitting there like a love-struck dummy.

"See you later, man. Don't work too hard," he said.

Bauer smirked and rolled his eyes. "Yeah, yeah. Stop rubbing it in that you've got the night off and get outta here."

Bauer disappeared and Sev shut his locker, grabbed his duffel, and made for the exit. As he passed through the gym, he stopped and stared at the sparring mat where everything had started. He grinned. Ari was a scrappy fighter, full of surprises, and had tossed Sev around a couple of times, which was saying something with his skilled hand-to-hand background.

He wondered if Ari would toss him around tonight, and the thought turned him on. What was Ari like in bed? Did he take control or enjoy being more passive? Would he make the first move, or would Sev have to? Shit, what was he thinking? It was just a date. There were no guarantees they would even have sex, and it was probably better if they didn't. They really needed to talk, like his mom had suggested.

He was still lost in thought when he pushed through the door of the training center into the hall and almost ran into another member of Stryker's team, Devon.

"Oh, excuse me."

Devon gave him an odd look then stepped back as if he had a contagious disease. "No, that's okay." Devon quickly looked away and hurried off.

What the hell was that all about? Sev stared after him for a second, paranoid. He always worried someone would find out about his mom and then he would be up shit creek. Surely, Devon hadn't learned he was half dreck. He kept that secret too tightly guarded.

Well, whatever was up Devon's ass would have to keep. He needed to scoot.

It took everything he had to keep walking past the elevator instead of taking it up to the third floor to Ari's room, but he forced himself to continue toward the exit. Tonight. He would wait until tonight. He checked his watch. Just a few more hours until sunset. Would he survive that long?

CHAPTER 7

GINA AWOKE FROM HER NAP and rolled toward the windows. She had drawn the vertical blinds then closed the opaque drapes over them to shut out the sunlight, so the room was pleasantly dark. A check of the time showed it was almost nightfall.

Her stomach growled and she recognized the familiar ache for blood riding just underneath her need for food.

Time for room service.

She called down and ordered a full dinner then hopped in the shower while she waited. The knock came on her door just as she finished drying her hair. She answered wearing only a silk robe and matching satin bra and panties.

"Room, uh, service." The uniformed man tried not to gawk, but his gaze performed a cursory sweep of her revealed skin, and his feet refused to move.

"Good, come in." Gina gripped his mind into compulsion.

The glands in her mouth were already secreting the tiny dose of venom that would both numb the pain of her bite as well as heal it. He was a handsome fellow. If she had more time, she would keep him there for a while. He could please her body's more physical needs in addition to her hunger for blood.

He did as he was told and closed the door behind him as she directed him to push the cart of food to the foot of the bed. Then she pulled him to her, licked his neck twice, and sank her fangs in to his flesh.

Aaaahhhh, that's what she needed to get her night off to a good start.

He didn't know it, yet, but he was catching a cold. Her body would process out the virus so she didn't have to worry about getting sick, but still, it made his blood weaker than she preferred. Even so, it was delicious and would get her by.

After taking her fill, she released him, and the bite instantly sealed. He grinned like a lovesick puppy from the euphoric side effect of the small dose of venom she'd injected. Not enough to kill him, but enough to make him feel really good for a few minutes and heal her bite. She imagined he was sporting half a hard-on in those black uniform pants, and she casually glanced down. Sure enough, he was a happy fellow.

If only she had time to play. He looked like a hung specimen, and it had been a long time since she had felt a male body against hers. But alas, there wasn't enough time.

She handed the young man twenty dollars and released him from compulsion. "Thank you."

He blushed, probably because he realized he was staring at her satin-covered breasts and displayed a decent woody begging for attention. Gina pretended she didn't notice as she opened the door for him.

"Please do come back," she said.

"Uh...um...sure. Enjoy your dinner, Miss Carano."

She smiled and watched him walk out then shut the door.

"Well, I already had my appetizer," she said under her breath, and then licked his taste off her mouth.

With a satisfied smack of her lips, she plopped down on the foot of the bed and flipped on the TV before addressing her dinner, which was a salad, gourmet cheeseburger, and French fries. For dessert, a wedge of chocolate cake that looked like Heaven on a plate beckoned her to eat her dinner in reverse order. But no, she would be good.

As she ate her salad, she clicked the channel changer until she came to the pregame show for tonight's basketball game. She might be able to catch the first few minutes, but not the whole thing. She had work to do and a vampire to kill. She would have plenty of time to goof off and catch up on her sports after Severin was dead.

CHAPTER 8

ARION'S FOOT BOUNCED IMPATIENTLY as he sat in his living room with the TV turned on to the pregame. The sun had set twenty minutes ago and he was starting to think Sev had changed his mind when the doorbell rang.

In a flash, he was up and hurrying to the foyer.

He swung the door open and smiled when he saw Severin. "Hi."

Sev looked good. His long hair fell in wavy blond cascades over his shoulders and looked feather soft. He had on jeans, a pale-blue, knit sweater that brought out his eyes, and what looked like broken-in combat boots.

"Hey." Sev stepped in and snaked an arm around his waist before kicking the door closed behind him. "I missed you."

Ari closed his eyes and inhaled the soft fragrance of aftershave and soap. When he opened them again, Sev was watching him with a hunger that stirred Ari to the soles of his feet.

"I can tell."

"I thought about you all afternoon." Sev burrowed his nose into Ari's hair.

He thought he might implode from the heat that fired through his loins.

"Me, too."

It was clear what tonight was about. He had obviously used the game as a ruse to get Sev there, and they both knew it. Ari's hunger for Sev wasn't quenched, yet. In fact, what had occurred in the gym had only whetted his appetite. He felt like a kid after eating his first homemade chocolate chip cookie and couldn't wait to get his hands on another one. Or a whole batch of them.

"You want a beer?" Sev said.

No, I just want you. "Sure."

Sev pulled away, took his hand, and they walked to the kitchen, where Sev set the six-pack on the counter and pulled out two bottles before twisting off the caps and handing one to Ari. They both drank, staring at each other. The air between them was electric. It felt like a hundred invisible threads of desire reached from Sev's body to his. They stroked him, caressed him, and burrowed into his skin.

Then the dam broke. In a blink, the distance between them vaporized, and Ari was in Sev's arms again, just as he had been in this very spot six weeks ago. Sev spun him around and slammed his back against the refrigerator before clamping his mouth over his.

Flames burst through his groin and up his spine before shooting through his limbs. The chemistry between them was unreal. Off the charts. Almost supernatural. They were like two land masses crashing together, causing an earthquake that shattered them to their core.

When had a kiss ever assaulted his senses like this? Was this what a kiss was supposed to feel like? As if a waterfall of heat was pouring through his body like a tidal wave from the pit of his stomach? His knees wobbled, his hands trembled, butterflies danced in his abdomen, and his cock hardened in an instant. Was that normal? His body never reacted this way from kissing a woman. With a woman, he never got hard without having to fantasize, and even then it had never felt like this—like he had a steel rod in his pants. And what was that noise? Ah, hell. That was him, moaning deep in his throat with every breath he took. God, he was completely lost in Severin's kisses.

"Sev..."

"Mmm?"

"Spend the night with me."

Sev made a noise that sounded like yes and assaulted his lips with increased fervor as his hands started to lift up his shirt.

Suddenly, a loud pounding at the front door jolted Ari back to reality. He jumped and pushed Sev away. Breathlessly, he glanced over his shoulder in the direction of the front hall.

"Fuck." He tried not to laugh at how jumpy he was, but ended up chuckling and shaking his head at himself. "That must be the pizza, but shit, they could have used the doorbell, for God's sake."

Sev chuckled at him and grabbed his beer off the counter then took a drink.

Pound-pound-pound!

"Okay, okay, I'm coming!" Ari called.

"Not yet, but you will." Sev's voice and the heated sideways glance he threw Ari hinted of promise, and he grinned mischievously as he stepped aside to let Ari leave the kitchen.

Ari's breath quickened, and he smiled. "I hope so."

"Hey-hey! Anyone home?" Io called from the front porch, knocking again.

Fear gripped Ari's throat as panic rose in his heart. He froze in his footsteps.

"Fuck, what's Io doing here?" He glanced back at Sev with wide eyes. He hadn't been expecting Io tonight.

"Just tell him to get lost. You're on a date."

Oh, yeah, that would go over great with Io. He couldn't even let Io get an inkling of an idea as to why Sev was here.

He gave Sev a get-real look. "He's my best friend. I can't tell him to get lost. And I can't tell him I'm on a date, either."

"Why the fuck not?" Sev frowned at him.

Ari shook his head. He didn't want to have this discussion right now. "Just hold on. I'll deal with him."

Sev sighed and meandered out of the kitchen to the living room as Ari checked himself to make sure the bulge in his jeans was covered by his untucked shirt, and then he took a deep, steadying breath before hustling down the hall to the front door.

"Hey, bro! What's shaking?" Io barged past him and into the kitchen.

"Just getting ready to watch the game with Sev." Ari

closed the door and tried to act normal, even though he was nervous as hell. He hoped his attraction to Severin wasn't as obvious as he thought it was.

He followed Io into the kitchen. "Why are you here? I thought you had a date tonight." Well, dates. The two girls from last night at Four Alarm had apparently been good enough for a second go-round. Io didn't usually dip into his women twice, but he supposed there was an exception for every rule.

"I do, I do. On my way there now, bro." He stopped when he saw Sev on the couch in the living room. "Oh. Hey, Sev." Io glanced over his shoulder at Ari as if he needed to talk to him in the worst possible way.

Sev nodded and held up his beer in greeting. "Io." He sounded irritated.

Tonight was turning into a major bust. This wasn't what he had wanted to have happen on his first date with Sev. And it *was* a date. Just as Sev had said.

Ari drew up next to Io as he pulled one of the beers out of the six-pack. *Fzt.* He twisted off the cap and guzzled a healthy gulp.

"Io, come on, why are you here?"

"What's up your ass? In a hurry or something?"

Actually, yes. "Of course not. It's just...well, the game's getting ready to start."

"Come here a sec." Io kept his voice low and motioned him into the other room. When they were alone, Io snickered. "Hey, I think Sev might be a faggot."

Ari felt the color drain from his face, and he stammered. "Uh-wh-huh-what?"

Io huddled in close and chuckled quietly. "Yeah, man. I stopped by AKM to grab my laundry and bumped into Devon. Devon was in the showers today and heard two guys fucking each other or some shit. A little while later, he was walking past the gym and Severin was coming out. His hair was wet." Io looked at him as if he was waiting for Ari to connect the dots. "You understand? Sev was one of the guys."

Ari was numb. What if Devon had seen him, too? What if

he knew? What if...? Fuck, it was just a matter of time before everyone knew and it got back to his parents. This was bad. So, so bad.

Okay, he needed to slow down and chill. If Devon hadn't told Io about him, then maybe he'd gotten out of the gym before Devon saw him. "Did Devon say who he was with?"

"He thinks it was Bauer. Bauer came out of the gym freshly showered right after Sev did." Io kicked back another swig of beer, waggling his eyebrows at Ari. "Can you believe it? Sev and Bauer? Faggots? Shit, bro, we've got a fag on our team. And Bauer? Shit, I never would have thought. I've seen him with chicks. Hmph, maybe he's bi. But Sev? A faggot? I mean, he's pretty enough, but..."

This was Ari's worst nightmare. "Stop calling him that, Io. You don't know."

Io rolled his eyes. "Think about it, Ari. When do you ever see him with a girl? With anyone? Sev's a fairy, admit it."

Ari shook his head and tried to think of something to say, but couldn't.

Io pointed at him as he drank then said, "You better be careful having him here. He might try to rape your ass." Io broke into fits of hushed laughter.

"Ssshh. Keep your voice down, jackass. He's just in the other room. And you don't know what happened. Devon could have been mistaken."

"Not likely."

The doorbell rang, saving Ari from further humiliation.

"That's pizza." He led Io back through the kitchen to the front door. He could smell the pizza before he opened up, and it almost made his stomach turn with the shit Io had just unloaded on him.

"Hi, that's twenty-four fifty-nine," said the delivery boy.

Ari pulled thirty bucks out of his pocket and handed it over. "Keep the change."

The boy nodded and tucked the money into his cash bag and trotted off.

Ari closed the door and turned back to Io. "Io? Is that why you stopped by tonight? To tell me you think Sev is gay?

Please tell me that's not the reason." Ari was ready to boot Io out. It made him angry to hear him talk about Sev like that, and not just because it was Sev, but also because he knew that's how Io would talk about him if he ever found out that he was gay, too.

"No, man." Io seemed taken aback. "I wanted to know if you had changed your mind about going out tonight. I mean, hell, I've got two girls. We can share."

"No, thanks. I'm not in the mood." In fact, Ari was feeling a little sick.

"Hey, that's cool. More for me." He snuck his hand inside the pizza box and swiped a slice. "See you tomorrow." Io winked over his shoulder toward the living room. "Remember, bro. Watch your back door."

Yeah, my back door was gonna get good and unlocked before you stopped by, fuck you very much. This had been a disaster.

Io saluted him and headed down the hall. And just like that, Hurricane Io swept out the door. He had spun in, done his damage, destroyed the wonderful mood Ari had been in, then blew out to leave mass destruction in his wake.

Ari leaned back against the counter, the pizza box still in his hand. What was he doing? How was this going to work? Shit, he couldn't even have Sev over without Io busting in like a wrecking ball.

"Hey, is that pizza I smell?"

Ari looked up and saw Severin leaning against the doorway into the kitchen, concern in his eyes.

He lifted the pizza box and tried to smile, but he was sure it came out looking as pathetic as he felt. "Yeah, sorry."

Sev stepped toward him. "Do you want me to leave?"

"No." That much Ari was sure of. "Please stay. I want you to stay."

"You sure?"

Ari nodded. "Yes."

"You're not afraid I'm going to rape your ass?"

If any color had remained in Ari's face, it drained out.

"You heard us." Ari dropped his gaze to the floor, ashamed of how Io had talked about him.

Sev chuffed. "Hello. Vampire here. Yes, I could hear you. It wasn't like Io was really trying to keep his voice down."

"Look, I'm sorry about that." Ari felt guilty.

"Fuck, I've heard worse shit than that, Ari. I'm used to it. Although I'm surprised your best friend would talk like that."

"He doesn't know."

Severin took the pizza box and placed it on the counter before digging out a slice. "Doesn't know what?"

"That I'm gay."

Sev froze. "Say again."

Ari sighed heavily. "Io doesn't know I'm gay."

"Why not?"

Ari dropped his head back. "It's complicated, all right?"

"Well, uncomplicate it. How the hell does your best friend not know you're gay?"

How did he explain this to Sev when he was only really beginning to understand it himself?

"Because until last month...when you and I...well, when we were together...I wasn't even fully aware that I *was* gay, okay?"

Severin stopped with his slice of pizza halfway to his mouth, and the two stood and stared at each other in stunned silence.

"Come again?" Sev lowered the pizza back to the box. "Is this some kind of joke? Are you fucking around with me, Ari? If you are, tell me now. I mean, if I'm just some homo-erotic experimentation for you, let me know, because I don't think my heart could survive if you—"

"I'm not playing with you." Ari stepped forward and placing his hand over Sev's mouth to quiet him. He stared at his fingers and felt Sev's full lips press against them. Then he locked his gaze to Sev's and repeated with conviction, "I'm not playing with you. This isn't a game, a joke, or some homosexual fantasy I want to act out. I don't know why it took me so long to figure things out, but Sev, when you came here and we did what we did right in this very spot...I can't explain it, but suddenly I knew. I knew I had been living a lie. I knew I was gay." He paused and lowered his hand. "I knew I wanted you and no one else."

Sev watched without saying a word, and the silence stretched for what felt like forever.

"God, Sev, please say something. I'm dying here. I don't know what to do. I've never been with a male before, but I can't stop thinking about you. I can't get you out of my mind." He stepped closer, ran his hands up Sev's chest, and inhaled a shaky breath as he felt himself drift further into Sev's personal space.

Sev remained stoically still while following Ari with his gaze.

Ari closed his eyes as if fighting himself then opened them and looked back into Sev's.

"I've never reacted to women the way I react to you. I just figured something was wrong with me, or that it was normal—as dysfunctional as it sounds—that I had to fantasize about men to even tolerate being with females. But then you..." Ari's voice trailed off, and before he could stop himself, he leaned in and ran his nose up the column of Sev's neck so that his lips brushed over his skin.

He wasn't sure, but he thought he heard Sev purr softly as his body rippled ever so slightly.

"You came along, Sev. You changed everything. I know who I am now because of you." Their bodies had slowly come together, and they stood chest to chest. "I was meant to be with you."

Sev's head turned into his. Ari felt him exhale more than heard it as Sev slid his cheek over Ari's hair then dipped his nose against his scalp. Ari felt like he was being claimed by a giant feline, which was fine by him. He wanted to be claimed. And Sev made the perfect lion with his mane of blond hair.

He stepped back and lifted Sev's hand to his mouth. Slowly, he drew his tongue around the tip of Sev's index finger then sucked it between his lips, tasting a hint of pepperoni from the pizza Sev had been holding a moment ago. He moved to his middle finger, then his ring finger, his pinky, and finally his thumb.

Sev stared at him, his mouth opened slightly, his gazed fixed on Ari's mouth like he was hypnotized.

Ari had never seduced anyone, man or woman, but with Sev it felt completely natural. In fact, his body was almost commanding him to seduce Severin. He had never felt such a powerful pull to be with someone, but Sev had him enthralled.

He released Sev's thumb with a pop and leaned in close.

"So, see, Io had it all wrong." He tugged on Sev's sweater and slid one hand underneath it to play his fingers over the waist of Sev's jeans. "It isn't me who needs to worry about you. It's you who needs to worry about me, because I want to invade you in the most unbelievable way right now." Ari had no idea where his words came from. He just knew that he was ready for more. "I haven't been able to stop thinking about you for weeks. I've waited all my life for you, Sev. Now that I've found you, don't make me wait, anymore."

In a rush of movement, Sev growled, gripped Ari's hips harshly, and shoved him back. "Bedroom?"

"Downstairs."

"Show me."

Pent-up energy exploded between them, and Ari batted Sev's hands away and spun him around before driving him out of the kitchen and directing him toward the stairs that led to the dimly lit basement. After nearly tripping over each other to get to the bottom, Ari gripped Sev's long hair like it was a horse's mane and jerked his head back as Sev groaned and cried out.

"I love your hair," Ari said, giving it another sharp tug. "I love pulling it."

Where was this side of him coming from? It seemed more than just his homosexuality had been in the closet his whole life. Finding the one he was meant to be with was waking up all sorts of new feelings and emotions, as well as a darker side to his libido.

"Please, more. Harder." Sev seemed to enjoy the rough action as much as Ari did.

Ari thrust his hand into all that glorious hair and

maneuvered Sev to the bed and shoved him down face-first. Sev bounced then rolled over and they both hastily pulled off their shirts and unfastened their jeans, stripping off their clothes in seconds.

Sev crawled backward into the middle of the bed as Ari rode up with him, hovering and stalking him. He had never wanted to have sex with anyone so badly he lost all inhibition, but it was as if he were suddenly someone else. And based on Sev's reaction, he loved who Ari had become.

Sev's arms wrapped him up, and their mouths connected once more, hungry and greedy for each other as their cocks rubbed together to send tingles down his legs and around the insides of his balls like tiny lightning strikes.

Ari loved how Sev touched him and how he felt. Sev's touch was unlike a woman's. His hands were bigger, and the way he handled him was strong and gruff, full of lusty intent. No woman had ever touched him this way, and it was clear that this was how he had always wanted to be touched. It turned him on.

What was even clearer was that Sev's was the kind of body he had always wanted beneath him. Powerful and masculine, with hard, rounded pecs topped with large, dark nipples. And God, the male had the widest shoulders he'd ever seen. He was built for brawn.

"Fuck, you feel good." Ari trailed his lips over razor stubble—actual fucking razor stubble—and shivered with excitement. The faint beard growth was just one more physical sign that this wasn't one of his fantasies and that he was finally living his true self.

"Mmm, so do you."

And that was another sign. Women didn't have such sexy, deep voices that rumbled with masculine intensity in a way that shot a whole lot of sexual excitement up the backs of Ari's thighs to whip around the base of his spine before shooting down to his dick.

Ari moaned and drew his mouth down to Sev's chest. His skin was smooth and hairless—not uncommon for a male vampire—and he tasted incredible. He had a distinct manly flavor that turned him on.

Sev arched into him and groaned as Ari found one dark nipple and drew it into his mouth. A man's nipple—Sev's. Rarely had Ari suckled a woman's breast, but taking Sev's between his lips felt perfect in all the right ways. Flat and hard, not soft and buoyant. Sev's nipple still puckered and hardened against his tongue, but in a completely different way than a woman's.

His palms caressed over hard muscles which bunched and flexed unlike a woman's, straining and tensing in such a masculine way. Oh God, this was what he had been missing all his life. This had been what he had always wanted. The reality was so much better than the fantasy, and Ari found himself being swept away with his need to feel all of Sev.

His mouth worked its way to the other side of Sev's chest, closing around his other nipple, sucking it harshly and flicking it with his tongue. He wanted to please Sev. He *needed* to please him.

"Babe, you're driving me wild." A purr released inside Sev's chest.

A fucking purr! Ari felt like he was in the middle of a smorgasbord of revelations and new discoveries.

Female vampires rarely, if ever, purred. Ari had never been with one who did. Hearing the telltale sign of arousal from Severin was mind blowing, and he surged up Sev's body to close his mouth over his throat, sucking hard, wanting like hell to bite him and sink his cock in deep to claim him.

Sev shuddered violently as he purred again, more loudly this time, and with a flip, Ari was on his back and Sev rose up over him, grinding his hips forward and back in a fucking motion. Ari looked down to watch their dicks slide against each other, and his body visibly shivered. The visual heated him instantly, pushing him closer to the edge as he panted and a purr emanated from his own chest, surprising him. When had he ever purred before except when he was masturbating?

His eyes shot to Sev's, wide and shocked.

Sev smiled down at him. "Let me guess. You've never

purred during sex."

He shook his head. "That was a first. God, this is a lot of firsts for me."

Sev moaned and seemed to melt a little against him. "Babe, you can't say shit like that to me."

Ari frowned in confusion. "What do you mean? Why not?"

"Because…" Sev rolled his body along his again, lowering himself so his lips hovered over Ari's. "It drives me crazy." He kissed and rocked against him. "It makes me want to do…*things* to you." Another kiss and body roll. "Fuck, you're sexy as hell."

Ari thought he might just die right there. The man of his dreams was undulating over his body like a lava flow, and their cocks glided up and down against each other, sending increasing signals that he was going to come any minute if this didn't stop.

Somehow his arms wound around Sev's back and his hands threaded up under his armpits to grip his shoulders underhanded. His legs shot around Sev's and he pulled him down, forcing their mouths to crash together. A chorus of low purrs echoed back and forth between them as their bodies cavorted against one another and their tongues wrestled, licking long and deep with each oral embrace.

"I want inside you. I need to fuck you, Sev." Damn. Either he was growing bolder or the brain-to-mouth filter wasn't working. Had he really just spoken those words aloud? He cleared his throat and felt his face heat up. "Uuhh…yeah. I didn't mean…um…"

Sev grinned down at him, obviously humored. "Where's the lube?"

Ari flushed and grinned back, realizing that while this was all new to him, Sev wasn't as inexperienced and could handle the man-to-man dirty talk. "In the drawer." He began to reach over, but Sev stopped him.

"I'll get it."

"No. That's okay." Ari pushed up on his elbows and tried to beat Sev to the drawer. Too late.

Sev stilled on top of him, his arm outstretched, his gaze

locked on the contents of the nightstand. One brow lifted and a crooked smile curved Sev's mouth as Ari collapsed back to the mattress, mortified.

"Mmmm, what do we have here? Toys?"

Oh God, kill me now. Ari cringed and tried to look away but ended up rolling his head back to look at one of the dildos Sev had pulled from the drawer. Yeah, *now* he looked away, grimacing with embarrassment.

Sev dug around inside the drawer. "There are so many."

Uh-huh. Ari had a lot of toys. Dildos, vibrators, some big, some small. He even had a cock sleeve. He liked his toys, but until now, he had been the only person who knew about them.

"I wonder, Ari," Sev said, "what do you do with these?" He held up one of the vibrators. It was cylindrical with a T-shaped handle.

God, why haven't you killed me, yet? Ari pushed out from under Sev and rolled to his side, horrified Sev had found his stash.

"Hey, Ari. Come on. I'm only kidding." Sev scooted up behind him and kissed his shoulder.

Ari groaned and rolled to his stomach, burying his face in his pillow. He managed a pathetic chuckle of embarrassment, but didn't look up.

"Come on, babe. Look at me."

With a sigh, Ari shook his head and turned to look back at Sev. He knew he had to be thirty shades of crimson.

Sev smiled warmly at him. "I didn't mean anything by it," he said. He snuggled closer. "I like toys, too."

Ari groaned and buried his face in the pillow again. "I'm so embarrassed."

"Why?" Sev stroked his fingers up and down Ari's back. "There's nothing to be embarrassed about, babe."

He turned back and looked into Sev's gentle, blue eyes. Sev was propped on one elbow, and his hand on his back felt soothing. Nice. Sensual.

"I masturbate with them," he said quietly, closing his eyes and turning away again.

Sev laughed. "What's wrong with that?" He pressed closer

and Ari felt Sev's erection press against the side of his hip. "I masturbate with toys, too."

Ari glanced back at him. "Really?"

"Fuck, yeah. It makes me hot." Sev's hand dipped lower and brushed over the upper swell of Ari's ass, setting off a storm of tingles deep in his groin.

Ari closed his eyes and breathed deeply, enjoying the sensations.

Sev's hand swooped lower still and pressed more firmly against Ari's bottom, gently squeezing one cheek. "Do they make you hot, too?"

Ari's breath quickened. He kept his eyes closed and nodded. "Yes," he said softly.

"Mmm."

Sev knew just what to say to put Ari at ease. He knew just what to do. His hand worked even lower and his fingers skimmed up the part in his bottom, making Ari tremble and tense.

The mattress shifted and Ari felt Sev sit up and move behind him, and still he kept his eyes closed. What was Sev going to do? Fuck him?

He heard the click of the cap on the lube pop open, then Sev's slickened fingers dipped between his cheeks once more, causing him to moan. The anticipation was killing him.

The sudden, soft whirring of the vibrator told Ari he was about to get a touch of the familiar. And sure enough, as Sev's weight shifted over him again, he felt the tip of the vibrator brush lightly down the center line of his ass.

A jolt of fire shot straight to his cock and his hands fisted the blanket as his toes curled.

"See. Toys are fun, aren't they?" Sev rubbed the vibrator more forcefully against him, pushing it deeper until it nestled against him in just the right place. If Sev gave a gentle nudge, the vibrator would breach him.

Ari trembled. "Y-yes."

Sev chuckled and bent down to kiss the back of Ari's neck. "Come on. Get up for me, babe."

Get up? Ari wasn't even sure he could breathe right now.

And Sev wanted him to push himself up off the mattress? Okay, he would give it his best shot.

On shaky arms and legs, as his chest began pumping hard for air from the sheer arousal coursing through his veins, he pushed away from the mattress. Severin's arm slipped around his waist and pulled him up to his knees as his other hand pushed the vibrator in.

"Oh! Fuck!" Ari's eyes popped open and his head fell back against Sev's shoulder.

Sure, he had used his toys on himself before, but this was the first time a male had done the honors for him. The heat level was significantly higher under the circumstances.

The two of them struggled to find a balance, and Sev had to do his best to hold Ari up as he gasped for air and squirmed.

"You're so damned sexy. So responsive," Sev said, nipping his neck. "Is this better now?" His voice held an edge of humor alongside his growl of arousal.

Ari nodded, but was too blissed out to speak. He was in Sev's arms. Sev—the man of his dreams. And he had a vibrator tantalizing him up his back side. And now that the vibrator was secured, Sev let go of it and reached for his—

"Oh God!" Ari cried out and reached around with both hands to grab Sev and hold on as Sev stroked his cock.

Damn, Sev felt good, large and strong, holding him. Ari looked down at the thick arm secured around his torso. Then he glanced lower at Sev's large hand wrapped around his cock, stroking his shaft, palming the head every sixth or seventh pull. The moment was surreal. It was as if he were watching as an observer, and this couldn't possibly be happening to him. But it was.

To prove it, he began to thrust his hips forward and back in time with the tempo of Sev's hand, fucking his fist, intensifying the contact between them as he continued to watch. Sev's chin brushed over his shoulder as he pushed forward and joined Ari in watching the action down below.

"Fuck, Ari." It sounded like Sev was about to lose control of himself.

Ari turned and their eyes met briefly before he pulled on the back of Sev's head to urge their mouths to join. So good. So goddamn good. Feeling Sev's mouth on his, Sev's hand fisting his cock, and the vibrator whirring away and stimulating him from the inside was about the closest thing to sexual heaven he had ever experienced. And he didn't want it to stop.

"Didn't you say you wanted to be inside me?" Sev spoke against his mouth then licked his lips. "Didn't you say you wanted to fuck me?" His breath washed over Ari's mouth. Only now did Ari realize Sev's hips were thrusting gently against Ari's lower back in rhythm with his hand.

"Yes." Ari had said that. He had wanted it. Still wanted it.

"Then do it. Fuck me." Sev turned him around and laid him back on the bed, climbing up and straddling him.

"What are you doing?" Did men fuck like this? Ari slid his hands up Sev's thighs.

Sev reached for the lube and poured it over Ari's cock then capped it and tossed it aside as he positioned himself while working the lube up and down with his palm.

"I like being on top." Sev's hand stilled and he lifted up on his knees.

"How—?"

Ari's eyes shot wide as Sev lowered himself, slowly taking Ari's cock inside him.

Oh, fuck!

"Oh God, oh God." Ari had never felt anything like this. Sev was so tight around him. So damn tight.

"Good?"

Ari nodded like a damn fool bobble-head doll. "Hell yes."

He must have looked like a gaping idiot, too, his head lifted and his eyes wide as he gasped repeatedly, watching every inch of his hard-on disappear inside Sev. He didn't even know sex was possible this way between two men, but he wasn't complaining.

"You like that?" Sev pushed his palms against Ari's chest as he took the last of his cock and moaned approvingly.

"Fuck." Ari could barely keep himself still. He bent his

legs and grabbed Sev's thighs in a death grip. "Oh, fuck." He wasn't going to last long. He was too torqued—too turned on. And Sev felt incredible.

"Mmm, you like it?" Sev lifted and lowered again, then again.

All Ari could do was give a hurried nod and labor for breath. This was his fantasy come to life. Looking up to see Sev's chiseled, muscular body poised over his was better than amazing. Just the visual feast alone was enough to bring him off, but to have Sev stimulating his cock, too? No, he definitely wouldn't last more than another few seconds.

"So do I," Sev said.

Sev did all the work, bobbing up and down, their gazes locked together and Sev's erection sticking straight out from his body.

"Sev! Oh God, Sev! I can't—"

Between the vibrator, the view, and the tightness of Sev's ass around his cock, along with the fact that this was the most turned on he had ever been, Ari couldn't stop himself. They had been at it less than a minute when he shot his load. His body shuddered and jerked as he cried out in stunned climax, his eyes open wide as he jacked up off the bed. His fingers squeezed Sev's hips like he had him in a vise. The force of his orgasm was so strong, the vibrator popped out of his ass.

"Fuck, but you're sexy when you come, Ari. I can feel everything."

Sev had stopped working up and down on him, but Ari's cock continued to pulse and twitch while Sev pumped his own erection in his fist. Ari's chest worked for air as he watched the swollen head of Sev's cock disappear and reappear in his hand. Shit, but he felt like the room was spinning. He was still coming. He had never come so hard. His unfocused gaze swam down again to watch Sev pump himself, his mouth hanging open as he gasped for air, his eyes hungry to see Sev come if he could just get them to focus.

"Yes, yes." Sev's hand momentarily stilled then resumed

with light, rapid strokes as streams of semen spilled over Ari's stomach. His ass clenched on Ari's cock. "Aaughh."

So, this is what real sex felt and looked like.

Ari stared in awe at the magnificent male tensing and relaxing through each orgasmic wave. Everything about this scene was right. Severin, him, the two of them together, coming on and inside each other.

Having sex with Sev hadn't been work like it always was with women. It didn't leave him unsatisfied, angry, miserable, or any of the other morbid or frustrated emotions having sex with women always left him feeling. It didn't leave him wanting to get dressed immediately so he could bolt. For the first time, he wanted to hold someone after sex. And not just hold him, but sleep beside him, wake up next to him, and make him breakfast.

Sev reached down, picked up the vibrator, and turned it off. "What are you thinking about, babe?"

Ari glanced up to see Sev grinning down at him, his face and neck flushed and radiant as his large, sweat-covered chest pumped hard for air.

"Huh?" Ari said, still stunned stupid, but in a good way.

"You've got this look on your face. Kind of a goofy, happy look." Sev rubbed his palms up Ari's stomach and over his chest, smearing his release over his skin.

Ari ran his hands up Sev's legs as he sighed contentedly. His body still tingled, and he could still feel the effects of his orgasm. "Maybe it's because I *am* happy."

Sev lifted off his spent cock and laid down next to him, facing him. Ari got the feeling that Sev's smile matched his own as he rolled onto his side to face him. He didn't even care that Sev's release still coated his stomach as he pushed in close so they could hold each other.

"That was your first, huh?" Sev said, stroking his fingers down his back.

He nodded, and his hold tightened.

Sev kissed his cheek. "How was it?"

Ari didn't think he could put into words how incredible the entire experience had been.

"Perfect. It was perfect, Sev." Ari rested his forehead against Sev's and gazed into his crystal blue eyes. "Sex with women was never this satisfying."

"Well, when you're gay, it shouldn't be."

Was Ari gay? Really? And was he even still asking himself that question? Because it was pretty clear he was, in fact, gay. Women were never meant to be on his menu.

"I love your body. I love watching you." Ari tried to burrow in closer and rubbed his hand over Sev's chest. "You feel amazing against me."

Sev chuckled then kissed him. "Look at you. All full of man-love. It sure took us long enough to get our heads out of our asses, didn't it?"

"You mean all that stupidity after what happened last month?"

Sev nodded and their lips met briefly. "Yeah. I thought you regretted it."

Ari kissed him again. "No, I just didn't know what to think about what happened. I didn't know what to say or do. And I thought you were having second thoughts since you didn't mention it."

Sev's hand ran over the cheek of Ari's ass before gripping the back of his thigh and pulling him on top of him as he rolled to his back. "No. I wanted you. The only second thoughts I had were whether you had really wanted me." Strong arms encircled Ari and held him close.

"I wanted you. I still want you. So help me, but it feels like I'll never stop wanting you." He pushed his arms under Sev and held him close as he pressed his face into the side of his neck and breathed more easily than he could remember. He felt good here against Sev, as if he belonged and the curves of his own body were made exactly to fit those of Sev's. Now he knew what people meant when they referred to someone as the puzzle piece that had been missing from their life. Because that's how he felt about Sev. Perfect puzzle pieces finally locked into place against one another.

Now if he could only figure out how to mesh this new, real life with the fake one he had lived since birth. Because even though he had finally found his other half, it was critical their relationship remain a secret. No one could know the truth about who he was. No one but Sev.

CHAPTER 9

ONE YEAR AGO

"Multiple enforcers down!" Gina's heart skipped a beat as the call came through her radio. Even before the report confirmed that it was the raid Gabe was involved in, Gina knew.

She slammed on the brakes of her SUV, turned around, and high-tailed it to the factory. Ten minutes later, she rushed into the stench of death and found Gabe bleeding out. He had been shot several times with artillery powerful enough to pierce his vest. That was some fancy-assed ammo in those drecks' arsenal.

"Gabe, oh God. Stay with me, Gabe!" She ripped off his shirt and vest and tried to stop the bleeding by releasing her venom into the wounds, but there was too much damage.

"Sev was with them," Gabe said, his voice weak. "I can't believe it. Sev." He kept repeating the words over and over.

"What? Sshh, Gabe, don't talk. The medics will be here soon. They're on the way."

"No, Sev's one of them. I can't believe it. He has iron skin. He's half dreck. Gigi, he's half dreck."

Sev? Gabe's boyfriend? What did he mean, Sev was half dreck and that he was with them? Gina knew she didn't have much time with Gabe. He was dying in her arms. Whoever had done this would pay. She dove into his mind to capture what she could of the incident and to figure out what he meant about Sev, who she'd only met once.

Quickly, she pulled Gabe's memories from him, marking each face and identifying the scents in the room that went with each one, and then she saw what Gabe meant. Severin was there. Dressed in the same uniform as the drecks. He certainly looked like he was with the drecks. Maybe he was an agent? She considered the possibility then remembered that VDA reported that no agents would be there tonight. And there were no other agencies besides Atlanta AKM assigned to the operation, which meant Sev was a traitor of the vampire race. He had betrayed Gabe.

Anger boiled in her veins as she felt the shots hit Gabe through his mind, and then Sev was running toward him, knocking him to the ground. It felt like the memories were flowing in slow-motion even though she was flying through them. Why had Sev knocked Gabe down? He had already been hit.

Shots rang out from somewhere and hit Sev as he stood over Gabe. Sev winced and jerked from the impact, but— holy shit! The bullets bounced off his body. Suddenly, Gina understood. Gabe had told her Sev was a day walker, which meant he was a mixed-blood. She had just assumed his mix was human, but his mix was dreck, wasn't it? And he had inherited dreck iron skin.

How did you kill someone who boasted iron skin? She had to find a way, because she wouldn't let Severin get away with this. She would make him pay for his duplicity.

"Does he always have iron skin, Gabe? Gabe?"

He was unconscious. She was losing him. Racing through his memories, she tried to find an opening. Any way she could kill Sev. The rest would be easy enough to assassinate, but Sev with that iron skin of his would be tricky. But he would pay for what he had done to Gabe and the others. Everyone possessed a weakness, and despite Sev's iron skin, she would find his.

She saw Gabe's memories with Sev: kissing, holding, making love, Sev asking Gabe just a few days ago to move in with him, but nothing—no, wait! There it was. Sev had cut himself with a knife while preparing dinner with Gabe. And she suddenly realized that Gabe would have noticed if Sev wore iron skin all the time. As much as he touched him, he would have noticed something as obvious as that, which meant Sev seemed to be able to control his natural force field.

Abruptly, the memories ceased and Gina gasped as her mind was thrown out of Gabe's.

"Gabe? Gabe?" She shook him, but he didn't answer. "GABE!" She felt for his pulse, but found none. He wasn't breathing. Oh God, he was dead. He had died in her arms.

"Is he dead?"

Gina spun around to see Severin climbing through a window.

"Traitor!" She stood up and pulled her gun.

"No, wait! I'm an agent." Sev froze.

"Liar. There weren't supposed to be any agents here tonight." She fired her gun, hitting him, but the bullet bounced off.

Sev's eyes shot wide with shock, but he froze as if he knew not to push his luck. "I'm an agent. Call it in. Why would I lie?"

She didn't trust him. "You're not going to sucker me in like you did my brother, Severin."

"Just call it in!" His gaze dropped to Gabe.

Checking to make sure he was dead, no doubt.

Sev remained poised half inside the window and half out while she radioed her boss, who got on the horn with the VDA commander.

A minute later, her radio crackled to life. "That's a negative, Gina. VDA command has no knowledge of an agent named Severin Bannon."

"No!" Sev held up his hands as Gina unloaded her clip on him.

By the time she clicked her trigger to empty air, Sev was gone. Mother fucker, she would get him. She would find a way.

GINA WIPED AWAY A TEAR at the memory. She had been monitoring the AKM building for four useless hours. Sev had never shown up, and, in her boredom, she had found herself recalling yet again the night Gabe died like she had so many times before. Her memories served as a reminder as to why she needed to kill Sev. She had killed the others, and now it was Sev's turn.

She sat back and looked up at the stars. Where was Gabe now? Was he in Heaven? Was there a place in Heaven for vampires, or did they go someplace else when they died? She liked to think that Gabe was in a better place and that he could hear her when she spoke to him, as she often did.

"I miss you, Gabe. Every day, I miss you." Another tear trailed down her cheek. She had been close to her brother. "But I promise you, I will avenge you. I won't let them get away with this. I'll make Sev pay for what he did to you."

Sev's behavior still baffled her. How could Sev have asked Gabe to move in with him when he'd been betraying him all along? Well, she supposed that if they lived together, it would have been easier for Sev to fuck him over. But damn, that would have also made it harder for Sev to keep his own truth a secret.

Whatever. She didn't know how Sev's demented mind worked or what his motives were. What she did know was that he had lied and had been involved in Gabe's death. That was all she needed to know. Oh, and that he was half dreck, which made the connection clear as to why he was working with them.

How would the other enforcers in Chicago react if they learned Severin was a half-dreck? Hmm, maybe she could use that to her advantage if an opportunity presented itself. One way or another, she was taking Sev down.

SEVERIN WALKED OUT OF THE BATHROOM and smiled. Ari was sprawled on his stomach where Sev had left him, one arm hanging over the side of the bed. The guy was spent and passed out.

For the past two-and-a-half hours, they had done nothing but explore each other, make love, rest, and start over again. Ari had finally been able to reach fifteen minutes before shooting his juice, but from the looks of it, that had only been because Sev had worn the poor guy out.

With a chuckle, he slid back onto the bed and propped himself up on one elbow so he could watch Ari sleep. The male was unbelievably responsive, and he had been eager to try anything Sev suggested, and like the owner of a new Camaro on the open road, Ari had taken his newfound sexuality out for one hell of a test drive.

Ari's eyes blinked open and Sev grinned at him as he brushed back a tuft of his thick, dark-brown hair. "Hey."

"Hey," Ari said sleepily, turning into Sev's touch as he shifted and pulled himself into Sev's body.

"You're a sexy mess." Sev combed his fingers through Ari's short, tousled hair, trying to smooth it out. "You hungry, sleepyhead?"

"Mmm, yeah actually, I am. What time is it?"

"Going on two in the morning."

Ari slowly sat up. "That's all? It's still so early. I can't believe I dozed off."

"Well, I tired you out." Sev sat up next to him. "Sex can be very tiring."

"Mmm, it can, huh?" Ari's bedroom eyes did an enticing unspeakable to Sev's cock.

"Yeah, especially when you do it right." He grinned and took Ari's hand, outlining each finger with the tips of his.

"Oh? I see. I've just been doing it wrong all these years." Ari chuckled softly, the air blowing out his nose in sharp, just-awakened bursts.

"Yes, you have, because you've been doing it with women when all along you were supposed to be doing it with me."

Sev already knew he wanted to spend the rest of his life with Ari. He could already feel his body's vampire biomechanics latching on to him as his mate, completing the bond that had started to form over a month ago. He had a feeling the same was happening to Ari, and that what they'd just spent two-and-a-half hours doing was the start of their *calling* phase with each other.

What a surprise this evening was turning into. Ari was his mate. He wanted to ask Ari if he could feel it, too, but was too afraid it would scare him, so he bit his tongue. That conversation would happen soon enough. If Ari's biology had chosen him as his mate, too, there wasn't much he would be able to do to sever the link between them, anyway.

Fuck that. There was nothing he could do. Once a male's soul chose a mate, that was it. End of story.

Ari turned his face toward his, and he tenderly kissed him. "Well, I'm glad we remedied that, then," Ari said. "I would have hated spending the rest of my life fucking when I could have been making love to you."

"Such a romantic." Sev pecked him on the lips again.

"It's your fault."

"Guilty, as charged."

Ari laughed at him. "Come on. I need a shower and then we can go up and eat."

"I just took one. I hope you don't mind."

"No, that's cool." Ari stood and stretched. "God, my body feels…I can't describe it."

Sev stood up next to him. "Sore? Well-used? Tight?"

Ari smiled then laid his forehead on Sev's shoulder as his hands skimmed up his sides and around his back. Then Ari looked up and met his gaze. "That wasn't exactly what I was thinking, but yeah, okay. I'm all those things, but in a good way. You know what I mean?"

"Yes, I do. I feel the same way." They gazed into each other's eyes for a moment. "Damn, Ari, but for a guy who's never been with another guy, you sure know what you're doing." Ari had manhandled him like a rodeo cowboy roping a calf. The sex had been hard, rough, active, and fast. And fucking hot as hell. Sev couldn't remember the last time he had been with someone who pleasured him so thoroughly.

"I think it's my partner, not me. And just because I've never been with a man doesn't mean I haven't had sex or that I haven't fantasized about what it would be like with a guy. Shit, Sev, but that's the only way I've been able to have sex all these years, by fantasizing I had a man under me. It's kind of nice bringing the fantasy to life."

"I like your fantasies, then," Sev said. "Especially the ones where you pull my hair." He leaned in and nuzzled Ari's throat, purring against him.

"You like that?" Ari tipped his head back and purred in reply.

Sev growled against his throat. "I fucking love it."

Ari's stomach rumbled and they both froze then laughed at the rude intrusion to their play.

"Maybe I had better...." Ari pulled away and pointed toward the bathroom.

"Get going. Point me toward clean sheets and I'll re-make your bed while you take a shower." He looked down at the bed. "These sheets are done." Done wasn't the word for the state of Ari's well-soiled sheets.

Ari gestured toward a closet. "In there. But you don't have to make my bed, Sev."

"I want to. Now go."

Ari held up his hands in submission and chuckled. "Fine, I'm going."

The bathroom door closed and Sev shut his eyes and took a deep breath. *Thank you, God. Thank you, thank you.* His heart skipped in his chest. He had a mate. He had never taken a mate before, but all the early signs were there that he and Ari were mating.

Most of the time, when a vampire mated to another, the other vampire mated back. Sure, Micah had been an anomaly when he had mated Jackson last year and Jackson hadn't returned the favor, but that was rare. Leave it to Micah to be the oddball and take a mate that didn't requite.

But now Micah had Sam, and to hear him talk, Sam had been his rightful mate all along and Jackson had been an accident, so it had all worked out for the guy in the end. Sev just hoped it worked out between himself and Ari, too.

Sev slipped on his boxer briefs and stripped the bed then grabbed fresh sheets out of the linen closet. His mind drifted back to Micah and Sam in Four Alarm and the way she had been able to calm him and direct his attention. He and Ari would be able to do that for each other now, wouldn't they? As mates, they would be able to bring balance to each other's emotions and keep each other focused. Sev secured the fitted sheet to the mattress and looked at the bathroom door. His mate was in there. Shit! Wow! He listened to the shower water splash against the tiled floor as if Ari was sweeping it off his body as he rinsed.

He hated even this meager separation. He hated that he couldn't see Ari and make sure he was safe and protected. He had to physically resist the pull to go into the bathroom and get into the shower with him simply so there was no distance between them. Thank the *calling* for that.

The *calling* was what he had in store for him as their link to one another deepened. In reality, it had already started. The drive for constant sex was already tugging at Sev to go in there and make love to Ari again. He couldn't really call it fucking, though, because there was too much emotion behind it.

And those were all signs of the bond that was forming to connect him to Ari on a deeper level than just friends or lovers. The *calling:* The ache in his chest when Arion wasn't near; the moodiness; the carnal need to be on and in his lover twenty-four-seven. These were all signs of the mating link strengthening to bind them to one another forever.

Mates.

Sev blinked back shocked, happy tears. This was what he'd always wanted but never thought he would find. For some reason, he thought that since he was gay, the mating call would pass him over. Which was ridiculous since plenty of gay couples mated one another, but he thought his dreck blood would prohibit it.

Oh God. That posed another problem, though. He would have to eventually tell Ari who and what he was. After what had happened with Gabe and his sister, he had decided that if he ever took another boyfriend, he would be honest with him. And being that Ari was his mate and not just a boyfriend, there was no question. He had to tell him everything. Even if it meant Ari might reject him. Then again, Ari couldn't reject him if he was mating to him, too.

Still, Sev wouldn't put another person in danger without letting them know up front what they could be in for, and with the imminence of Gabe's sis hunting him down, Ari needed to know.

The shower shut off, and Sev quickly tucked in the sheet and unfolded a fresh bedspread. He was smoothing it over the mattress when Ari opened the bathroom door and stepped out with a towel wrapped around his waist. He was combing his fingers through his short, wet hair, and looked magnificent. Ari's body was amazing. Tall, ripped, with the sexiest tattoo sleeve running the length of his left arm. Sev just wanted to kneel in front of him and outline his six-pack abs with his tongue.

"You okay, Sev?"

He lifted his gaze to Ari's topaz eyes to find the male smiling at him as if he was on the verge of laughter.

"Yeah, why?"

"Just the way you were looking at me. You looked... hypnotized or something."

Sev walked around the bed and slid his arms around Ari's waist. "I *was* hypnotized. You do that to me." He kissed him sweetly and patted his ass. "I'll meet you upstairs."

He knew if he didn't pull away now they would end up on the bed again. Not that that was a bad thing, but they did need to eat and a break in the action would be good to get their strength up.

Pulling away, Sev hustled up the stairs and returned to the kitchen. The pizza box still sat on the counter, and the TV was still on in the living room. He snagged a cold slice of pizza and took a bite. It tasted fine, just needed to be heated up.

He shoved a few slices in the toaster oven, and a couple minutes later Ari walked in wearing boxers. He looked somber.

"You okay?"

Ari nodded. "Yep, just got a lot on my mind."

"Such as?" Sev hoped he hadn't misread the sitch downstairs.

"Just stuff." Ari was being evasive and that made Sev nervous.

"Are you having second thoughts about all this?" Sev motioned back and forth between them.

Ari's head swung around. "No. No, that's not the problem."

Relief relaxed Sev's body and he breathed more easily. "Okay, so what is?"

Ari went to the fridge and grabbed two cold beers and handed one to Sev then leaned back against the counter and twisted the cap off his. After taking a drink, he shrugged. "Where do I start, Sev? Io. My parents. My life. My job."

Sev held up his hand. "Whoa, slow down." He joined Ari and leaned against the counter beside him. "Maybe you should start at the beginning."

"I don't want to dump all my problems on you, Sev."

But Sev wanted him to dump his problems on him. That's what mates did for each other. "You're not dumping anything on me, babe. You've obviously got something on your mind—something that's bothering you. You'll feel better if you get it out."

"Or not."

Sev gently nudged him, and the corner of his mouth turned up. "You won't know until you try."

The timer on the toaster oven dinged and Ari grabbed them a couple of plates and held them out while Sev placed two slices of pizza on each.

"Okay, I'll try," Ari said.

They went to the living room, turned off the TV, and sat down on the couch.

They ate in silence for a couple of minutes, and Sev could tell Ari was trying to figure out where to start.

Then suddenly, Ari said, "My parents. They're pretty old-world conservative." He kept his eyes down. "My dad, well, he used to be a member of the king's personal guard."

Sev's jaw dropped. "No shit."

So that's where the rumors of Ari's strong bloodlines came from.

Ari frowned as if he were uncomfortable or ashamed. "Yes.

So, he's a close friend of the king, right? And I was expected to follow in my father's footsteps and all that shit."

Sev wasn't sure where this was going, but he was intrigued.

Ari looked up and caught Sev's eye. "Sev, what I'm about to tell you stays between us, okay?"

Sev nodded. "Sure, babe. I can keep my mouth shut."

Wasn't that the truth? He had kept his own family secrets locked up for decades.

Ari took a deep breath and blew it out between pursed lips. He was obviously nervous and uncomfortable.

"Hey, Ari, are you sure you want to be telling me this?"

Ari gave a brisk nod. "Yes. I've just…well, I've just never told this to anyone before. I think it's harder to admit it to myself more than anything. I mean, the minute I say it out loud, it's real, you know?"

Sev wondered what was so important that Ari would keep it a secret from everyone to the point he struggled to finally reveal it to him. "Just take your time, babe. I'm not going anywhere." He shoved in his last bite of pizza and sat quietly, waiting for Ari to work up the courage to speak.

Minutes passed and Ari finished his own pizza, set down his plate next to Sev's on the coffee table, then turned to Sev. "I never wanted to be an enforcer."

Sev frowned. Was that it? Was that the big secret? "Okay."

Ari shook his head as if he could hear how lame his statement was. "I know it sounds like no big deal, but you have to understand my dad."

"You became an enforcer because of your father?"

Ari nodded. "My course was set before I was born. It didn't matter what I wanted to do with my life. My mind wasn't mine to make my own decisions. I've always done what my father expected of me. I've always put my own feelings and my own desires second."

"If you don't want to be an enforcer, then what do you want to be?" He took Ari's hand in both of his, turning toward him.

The hard lines on Ari's face softened. The tension around his eyes eased. He smiled softly. "A musician. That's what I want to be."

"Then do it."

The hard edges and tension returned. "I can't."

"Why not?"

"You don't understand the influence my dad has on me, Sev. I can't defy him like that."

"It's your life, Ari, not his."

"I know. Shit, I know, but it's hard."

"Nothing worth having in life is ever easy, Ari."

Ari looked up at him and Sev got the feeling there was more. A chill of dread wrangled his spine. He didn't have to wait long for the hammer to drop.

"My dad is also homophobic. So is my mom. As in, I-am-so-dead-if-they-find-out-I'm-gay homophobic." Ari paused. "They can't know I'm gay."

Thud. That was the sound of Sev's heart falling. If Ari couldn't go against his father when it came to his occupation, it stood to reason he couldn't oppose him about his sexuality, either. And where did that leave Sev? Hopefully not outside standing in the cold rain without an umbrella.

"What are you saying, Ari? That this has to end right now before it even begins?"

"God no!" Ari gripped his hand.

"Then what? How is this supposed to work if you can't even admit to your own parents you're gay and that we're," he almost said mates but quickly corrected himself, "... together?"

"I don't know. But it has to."

"Why?" Sev wondered again if Ari was feeling the truth of what was really happening between them.

"Because..." Ari's gaze dropped. "Because I can't lose you now that I just found you."

Well, that was something. Sev would have preferred to hear *because you're my mate,* or even *because I love you,* but under the circumstances, this was better than nothing.

"I don't want to lose you either, Ari, but sooner or later you'll have to tell your parents about me. Io, too."

Ari flopped his head against the back of the couch and stared up at the ceiling as he blew out a heavy breath. "You heard him tonight, Sev." Ari rolled his head and glanced at him. "You heard what he called you."

"Yeah, so? Like I said earlier, I've heard worse."

"Io would make our lives together a living hell."

"Only if we let him, and I know I won't." Sev gave Ari a hard look, challenging him.

"He's my best friend, Sev."

"And what am I?"

Ari gazed at him then looked down shamefully, clearly understanding what he meant by the question. In a way, Sev felt he was being unfair to Ari, because he had known Io a lot longer than him. But shit, Ari and Io had never engaged in sex, and Ari certainly hadn't been honest with the guy. Otherwise, Io would have known Ari was gay and Ari would have told him that he never wanted to be an enforcer. So, obviously Ari already trusted Sev a lot more than he trusted Io.

Does he realize we're mates?

"Look, Ari. If Io really is your best friend then he'll understand this. He'll support our relationship. That is, if you want a relationship with me. Do you?"

Ari lifted his hand and kissed it. "More than anything. I've never been this happy with someone, Sev. I've never wanted anyone the way I want you."

He caressed Ari's cheek. "Me neither, babe, but I don't want to be just another one of your secrets."

Ari turned his face into Sev's palm and kissed it before turning to look at him again. "I know. I don't want you to be, either, but I need to work through this. Just be patient with me, okay?"

How could he resist anything his mate asked of him? "Of course I will, babe. But please don't make me wait forever."

Ari paused. "I won't. I promise."

"Once everyone sees how happy you are, they'll understand. Everything will be fine."

"I hope you're right, because I want this. I want you."

Sev scooted closer and kissed his cheek, right by his ear. "I can't say I'm sorry that your dad made you be an enforcer, though. I wouldn't have met you otherwise."

"I know," Ari said. "At least one good thing came out of it."

"You're a good enforcer, if it's any consolation." He kissed him, just once, a slow and simple kiss.

"Sure, I'm good at it, but I don't love it. Not like you do." The mood in the room eased in one respect, but ramped up in another as Ari pressed nearer and licked Sev's neck.

Sev grinned and scooped Ari onto his lap with one arm. "I was born to fight. I was made to fight." He thought about the iron skin his mixed blood had given him. If he hadn't been built to fight, then he didn't know who was.

"Not me." Ari stole another taste of Sev's neck as he tugged him by the hair to grant better access.

He loved that. Ari gripping his hair and pulling was the most mind-bending turn-on.

"What were you made to do?" Sev settled under him.

"Besides music?" Ari nipped his neck.

"Mmm, yes. Besides music. What were you made to do, Ari?"

Ari purred and Sev's toes curled from the erotic sound. "Make love to you," Ari said. "I was made to make love to you."

Sweet Jesus. That was what he wanted to hear.

Their hands worked together to push Sev's boxers down to reveal his erection.

"Do you want to know what I was thinking about last night when I was kissing that woman at Four Alarm?" Ari said.

The way Ari asked with a secret smile on his face made Sev grin.

"Tell me."

"You. I was thinking about you."

"Oh yeah?" Sev felt like he was melting into the couch as Ari's hand wrapped around his cock and slowly stroked him.

"Uh-huh." Ari's lips closed on his neck and sucked.

"God, that feels good." Sev's head swiveled to the side. "What exactly did you think about?"

With a pop, Ari's mouth released his throat and his tongue lapped over the love bite he'd just given him.

"I thought about us six weeks ago, in the kitchen. I thought about kissing you." Ari licked him again and trailed his tongue to the other side of his neck. Sev sighed and rolled his head in the opposite direction. "I thought about what might have happened if I'd asked you to stay. I imagined your hand on my cock, stroking me."

He found Ari's erection. It had peeked out through the separation of fabric in his boxers. He swirled his palm lightly over the head, then closed his thumb and fingers around him for a few good strokes.

"Mmm, yes, I imagined you stroking me just like that, Sev."

"What else did you imagine?" Sev turned his head into Ari's neck and lightly bit him, making him purr again.

"That you *did* stay the night with me six weeks ago." Ari's lips brushed over his ear seductively as he whispered with erotic heat. "That I bent you over the kitchen counter and fucked you."

It was Sev's turn to purr, along with shiver, followed with a shot of growl.

"Fuuuuck."

"Can you see why I was so into kissing her?" Ari said, grinding into Sev's hand.

"I thought you wanted her."

Ari shook his head and scratched his fangs against Sev's skin. "No, I wanted you. I want you now. I want you tomorrow. Fuck, I want you forever, Sev."

Mates. Is Ari aware of what he's saying?

He could hardly contain himself and reached around with both hands and gripped Ari's ass. With a harsh yank, he pulled Ari further up his lap so their cocks pressed together. Ari quickly adjusted his grip and wrapped his hand around both of their hard-ons.

"What are you saying, Ari?"

Ari brought his mouth to Sev's but didn't kiss him. Nose-to-nose, mouth-to-mouth, he searched Sev's eyes as they breathed each other's air.

"I don't just want you to be my first, Sev. I want you to be my last. My only."

He feels it, but he doesn't realize it, does he? Give it time.

Sev stared back into Ari's topaz eyes and found sincerity,

honesty, and trust. Ari was serious. Perhaps he was oblivious to the developing bond between them, but it was clear Ari felt it even if he didn't recognize it for what it was.

Sev already knew he was head over heels in love with Ari, so nothing would please him more than for the two of them to be together. As in, *together.*

"I want that, too. I knew within a week of meeting you that I wanted this." He pumped his hips in time with Ari's hand as he masturbated them both.

Sev knew they had a lot to work out together. Ari was dealing with heavy shit. Io and his parents were huge influences on his life, and he was only just now growing the wings to take off on his own path. Sooner or later, Ari would have to come out to his family, Io, and everyone else if a relationship with him was to work. But he seemed to be on the right path to make that happen.

"It won't be easy, you know," Sev said.

"I know, but I want this. With you. I want you."

Ari's chest pumped hard against his.

"It feels good, doesn't it? Opening up like this? Knowing who you are?" Sev had never worried about hiding who he was. His mother had known early on, and he never purposely tried to keep his homosexuality a secret. He didn't simply volunteer the information, but if it came out, so what?

"*You* feel good." Ari's free hand ranged up Sev's chest.

He was fast-approaching the breaking point. His cock felt good nestled against Ari's, his hand massaging them both. Up. Down. Up. Down.

"Kiss me, Ari. God, kiss me."

Ari's mouth plastered over Sev's and his tongue plunged deep to wrestle with his. Fuck. So good. Ari felt so good. He was close. His scrotum tightened, his spine tingled, his chest heaved for breath as Ari claimed him. His imminent orgasm reared up.

With an assertive growl, Sev gripped the back of Ari's boxers and pulled. The back seam ripped open and Ari groaned against his mouth, knowing what Sev wanted, wanting the same thing.

Without breaking their deep lip-lock, Sev pulled Ari up and parted his ass cheeks as Ari rose on his knees and positioned the head of Sev's cock at his puckered entrance. As he sank down on him, Sev shoved his hips up. They met in the middle, each grunting against the other's mouth.

Thrust-thrust-thrust then shuddering bliss.

Just that quickly, Sev exploded inside Ari just as Ari's body stiffened and trembled. Hot spurts of semen shot out over Sev's stomach, and he pulled his mate down so he could share the offering with him, rubbing his stomach up against Ari until they were both coated with his erotic fragrance.

Only then did Ari finally release his mouth as the two gasped for breath. "Oh my God, wow."

"Mmm." Sev rolled Ari's nipples between his thumbs and forefingers, grinning with contentment as his receding orgasm continued thrumming through his muscles. "We're good together, aren't we?"

Ari's body shivered again and he squeezed his eyes shut through another grunt as one last spasm emptied his cock. Sev felt the tiny convulsion through the wall of Ari's rectum.

"I take that as a yes," Sev said.

"Yes, fuck, yes." Ari collapsed against him. "What have I been missing all these years? Is it always this good?"

Sev wrapped his arms around Ari. "Usually. As long as you're with the right partner, anyway."

"Don't ever leave me then. God, I think I'd die if you did."

Yes, you would, my mate.

"I know I would." For Sev, the connection forming through the mating link was already strong enough that if Ari walked away, it would kill him. He knew it would. A lot of males couldn't survive the loss of a mate, and Sev knew he would be one of those statistics if he lost Ari. God, he hoped Ari acknowledged his side of the mating bond before it was too late.

"Huh?" Ari said.

"Nothing, babe. Just let me hold you."

The two embraced on the couch, letting their bodies calm down from another set of intense orgasms. Eventually, they would get up and go back to bed, but right now, this was fine. This was perfect.

CHAPTER 10

THREE HOURS BEFORE SUNRISE, Lakota Bannon pulled into Chicago. He was a day early, but he had made unexpectedly good time during the night. After stopping at a gas station to fill up, stretch his long legs, and buy a bottle of water—he didn't drink alcohol, anymore, whether he was driving or not—Lakota got back in his Suburban and checked his GPS. He was only a few miles away from Felice's house.

He was nervous. In truth, he was shocked Felice had finally agreed to see him. It had been centuries since he'd—he didn't want to think about what he'd done. He dropped his head in shame, the guilt nearly overwhelming him. She was a better person than he was, dreck or not, because he didn't deserve a second chance. He didn't deserve her kindness. And yet she was willing to give him both.

With a fortifying, deep breath, Lakota brushed back his pale, shoulder-length hair and put the Suburban in gear. After pulling out onto the street, he checked his GPS again and followed the directions toward Grant Park until he slowed in front of a row of quaint, brick townhouses on East Benton. He ticked off the house numbers until he stopped in front of the one where Felice lived.

Sitting in his Suburban, staring at the cozy home, Lakota trembled with shame and fear. How ironic that a male as tough and strong as he was would be reduced to a quivering wuss over a decision as simple as whether or not he should ring her doorbell. He checked his watch and huffed. Shit. It was too late and he needed to get to his hotel. She was probably asleep, anyway.

Yeah, yeah, you're just making excuses, you big chicken.

He heard clucking, squawking chicken noises in his mind as he put the Suburban in gear. *That's right, bwaaaak, bwak, bwak, bwak. I'm a chicken. So what?*

After circling Lake Shore East Park, he pulled out on Wacker, drove down to Wabash, crossed the bridge, and arrived at the Trump Hotel.

Everything he owned was in the Suburban. He had sold or donated everything else so he could start over fresh here in Chicago, near his daughter. The fact that his firstborn son, Severin, also lived here was simply a bonus. One way or another, he would atone for his sins and make things right. He had already missed too much of Severin's life.

After parking in the Trump garage, Lakota grabbed his overnight bag and suitcase, locked up the Suburban, and headed inside to check in. Tomorrow night, he would have no excuses. He would meet Felice as planned, take any shots she hit him with, and begin forging his new life.

Gina entered the hotel after getting back from pulling recon on AKM and walked up to the desk.

"Good morning." The attendant smiled warmly at her.

Yes, it was morning, wasn't it? Gina was ready to settle down to sleep after a meal and a relaxing bath. "Good morning. Could I place an order for room service?"

"Certainly. Do you need a menu?"

"Yes, please."

The desk attendant handed her a menu, and while she considered her options, a tall man with shoulders as wide as the state of Illinois stepped up beside her and plopped his suitcase on the floor.

"May I help you?" The clerk stepped over to him.

"Reservation for Lakota Bannon."

Gina's ears pricked up. Bannon? That was Severin's last name. Without wanting to appear like she was being nosy, she casually glanced up at him and grinned as he looked over and caught her eye. The eyes were bluer, and the hair was a lighter shade of blond and shorter, but other than a few differences in their features, Lakota could have been Severin's brother. Or even his father. With vampires, it was hard to tell.

"Morning," he said to her.

"Morning." She looked back down at the menu while the clerk processed Lakota's reservation. Did she really have one of Severin's relatives standing next to her? Could she have fallen under a luckier star? The name was right, and he sure looked like Severin. This was just too much of a coincidence. Maybe getting close to Severin would be easier than she thought if she could find a way to use this to her advantage.

She realized he was looking over her shoulder at the menu in her hand, and she glanced up at him again. He really was a striking male. Perhaps she could mix a little business with pleasure, get close to him, and use him to get close enough to Severin to kill him. It was worth a shot.

"Oh, sorry. I was just taking a peek at the menu." His voice was deep and resonant, full of power. "My name is Lakota." He smiled at her.

"Gina." She tilted her head in greeting. "Are you hungry?" She flashed the menu at him.

"Yes. I've been driving all night. Us night owls, huh?" He gave her a look that made it clear he knew she was a vampire, too.

The attendant addressed Lakota, "Would you like to order room service as well, sir?"

He looked away from her and nodded once at the attendant. "Yes, I think I would."

The attendant handed him a menu.

"What brings you to Chicago at such an odd hour?" she said.

Lakota's gaze browsed over the selections. "Family. You?"

Oh, I'm just here for a little assassination. No biggie.

"I'm on vacation." The lie came easily, but it wasn't like she could just come right out and say that she was here to kill someone—most likely his son or brother.

They continued looking at their menus in silence, but she could tell Lakota was intrigued. She looked up at the desk clerk. "I think I'm ready to order."

He stood at his computer. "Certainly. Go ahead."

"Yes, I'd like the red eye—"

"With or without the egg?"

"With, please."

He tapped his fingers over the keyboard.

"And I'll also take the Wimbledon strawberry bowl, with cream, as well as the Mexican breakfast, no shot."

Lakota made a sound of approval. "You have a healthy appetite."

"I'm a growing girl." She tossed him a come hither look.

He cleared his throat. "If you don't mind my saying, you already look all grown up." His eyes darted away almost shyly, or maybe that was guilt in his expression. Either way, she found both responses odd for such a big male.

"That I am, Mr. Bannon." She handed her menu back to the attendant and confirmed her room number for room service then turned toward Lakota. "Well, you have a nice day. Enjoy your breakfast. Maybe we'll see each other again."

"That would be nice," he said.

She made sure he was watching her before she sashayed toward the elevators. As the doors opened, she glanced back to find his gaze still on her. She smiled then stepped into the elevator.

Gotcha.

CHAPTER 11

"OPEN YOUR EYES, ARI." Sev's strained voice caught Ari by the balls.

Shit, he had closed his eyes again. Habit. Damn. He snapped them open and caught Sev's gaze as he thrust into him, taking him hard. Again.

"That's better. Yes. I love your eyes." Sev wrapped his arms around Ari's back as they rocked the mattress and banged the headboard against the wall. "I love when you watch me."

And Ari loved watching Sev. He was beautiful during sex. A male worthy of the gods, as far as Ari was concerned.

"I'm close," he said, his voice filled with urgency. "Oh God, Sev!"

"That's it, babe. Don't stop." Sev's hold on him tightened. "Come for me."

"Sev! I'm coming! I'm coming!" Once more, his body released and his muscles ripped apart. He would be lucky if he was able to move tomorrow at the rate they were going.

When his latest release finally subsided, Arion collapsed against Severin's body, shuddering through the tail end of his orgasm as Sev held him close and brushed one hand down his spine.

How many times had they had sex in the past several hours? Ari had lost count. What he did know was that he had never demonstrated such stamina with any of the women in his past. In fact, with Sev he could hardly keep his cock deflated. Ari had never experienced anything like this. Ever. The floodgates were fully open now, and there would be no going back.

"Wow." He snuggled against Sev's chest, a gentle pulse

weeping the remnants of his release inside Sev. Face-to-face sex had never been this good before. Now if he could just learn to keep his eyes open, everything would be perfect. Old habits die hard, but he had a feeling it wouldn't take long to remedy that one. He loved watching Sev during sex. He loved looking at him and matching Sev's body's movements and his facial expressions to the sensual noises he made.

"Wow is right, babe." Sev kissed his sweat-dampened forehead. "I've never seen anyone with so much stamina."

Ari huffed out a weak laugh. "Honestly, I didn't know I had it in me. I guess I'm making up for lost time."

The sheets were soiled again, but he didn't care, and Sev didn't seem to mind, either. He loved how their combined scents filled the room and surrounded them.

"Can I stay with you today?" Sev's voice caressed his ears like a soft breeze.

Ari burrowed in close, shoving his arms around Sev to hold him tightly. "If you try to leave, I'll stop you."

Sev chuckled, and the vibration rumbled against Ari's chest. "Okay, I'll stay. Twist my arm."

They held each other like that for several minutes then Ari finally forced himself to pull himself off Sev's body. His spent cock pulled free and the cool air felt all wrong on him after being tucked inside Sev's warmth. He lay down next to Sev and they turned to face each other.

Sev touched his face, caressed his cheek, and smoothed back his hair. Ari closed his eyes, enjoying the affection.

"I—" Sev cut off abruptly then started over. "I want you to spend the day with me tomorrow. After our shift, spend the day at my house. Will you do that?"

Ari got the feeling that wasn't what he had originally planned on saying, but he let it go. "Mmm, yes. I'd like that." At least they wouldn't have to worry about Io or anyone else stopping by unexpectedly if they were at Sev's.

"So would I."

He opened his eyes again. Sev's long hair hung in sweaty, damp tendrils over his face and down his neck past his shoulders. Tonight, Ari had used that hair like a horse's mane, pulling, yanking, directing Sev's head where he wanted it. And true to his word, Sev had loved it. He'd cried out with pleasure, begged him to pull harder, and pleaded with him to be rough and not hold back.

Both of them were marked with love bites and bruises worthy of battle, and he smiled softly as he reached up and trailed the tip of his finger over one of the fading black and blue marks on Sev's chest where he had sucked on his skin.

"We're a mess," he said

"But in a good way." Sev brushed his hand over Ari's cheek then down to his arm.

He nodded. "A very good way."

Sev's fingers traced the lines of his tattoo sleeve. Up, down, around. Ari had already learned Sev's nuances enough to know he wanted to take him again. It was in the way his gaze followed his fingers down the pattern on his arm and the quiet purr deep in his chest. And Sev hadn't finished during their latest bout of orgasmic pyrotechnics, so he probably needed the release.

"Yes," Ari said.

Sev's gaze flicked to his. "Yes, what?"

"Yes, I want you to make love to me again." Hell, he was ready to go again himself. This was insane. Where was this incredible sex drive coming from?

The corners of Sev's mouth curled upward. "You're not too tired?"

Ari shook his head. "No."

"We've been at it all night, babe. I thought you'd need a break."

"That's okay. Like I said, I'm making up for lost time. Besides, you drive me wild."

Sev tenderly pushed him to his back as he rolled with him and settled on top. "You're driving me crazy, Ari."

"I can't get enough of you." He pushed his hands through Sev's hair as the other male pushed his legs open and pressed the head of his erection against him. Could they just stay in bed for the rest of the month? Ari really wanted to stay in bed with Sev for a few weeks. At a minimum.

"Me, neither." Sev drove forward and dove inside Ari in one fluid thrust.

"Oh, God, yes," he said, gripping Sev's shoulders.

Yes, just one more time and then they could sleep. Maybe.

CHAPTER 12

THE NEXT NIGHT, Lakota woke up just after sunset and opened the curtains then the blinds and looked south over the Chicago River. He already liked it here and couldn't wait to buy a place. His son's reaction, on the other hand…well that was another story.

The last time—the only time—he had seen Severin, they had almost killed each other. In a way, he was proud of how hard Sev had fought him. The boy was strong and lethal. Well, Sev wasn't a boy anymore. He was a mature male now. An adult.

Was Sev mated? Did he have a wife? Children of his own? Felice had only told him Sev was an enforcer, but she hadn't elaborated on personal details, so Lakota could only guess what Sev's life was like. Did Sev ever think about him? Probably not. But then, if he were in Sev's shoes, he wouldn't think about him, either. Who would entertain thoughts of a father who raped his mother, gave her a child, and took off?

He had been such a bastard back then. But the love of a human had changed him, and he would be forever grateful to Mary for opening his eyes. He still missed Mary, his beloved wife who he had cherished with all his heart. She had shown him so much love and had opened his heart to how awful he had once been and how good he could be as a person, husband, and father.

His cell phone rang and he smiled at the caller ID.

"Marie? You must have known I was thinking about you."

He had insisted their firstborn daughter be named after Marie, because he knew one day Mary would die and he wanted one of their offspring to remind him of her. That day had come six years ago, when Mary passed away at the age of sixty-two, just days after suffering a stroke.

"Dad? Are you here?"

Marie lived on Chicago's North Side, and her mixed blood had given her an uncanny extrasensory ability. Unfortunately, the price for her third eye was the loss of her physical sight by the time she had turned eighteen. Marie was blind. Funny how mixed blood worked. Marie could see the unseen with her special abilities of perception, but she could no longer see the physical. No doubt she had felt his arrival in the city last night.

"I knew I should have called," he said.

"Yes, you should have." Her chastising voice held the sound of a smile.

"I'm sorry, honey. Yes, I'm here in Chicago."

"I still don't understand why you insisted on staying downtown. You could have stayed with me, you know."

"I know, but I wanted neutral ground. You know how hard this is for me."

He could almost see Marie nodding her head in understanding. "I know it is, Dad. Have you seen her, yet?"

"No, but I'll see her tonight."

"She's ready to put the past behind her. I think she'll forgive you."

"What about Severin?"

She didn't say anything for a few seconds. "You'll have a tougher time with him."

Just what he thought. He sighed in frustration.

"Give it time, Dad. Severin's like you. He's stubborn and determined. He hurts easily and doesn't forgive quickly."

"And I hurt him." He said that more to himself than to Marie.

"Well, you hurt his mother, and to him, that's the same as hurting him."

Knowing that made him all the more proud of Severin. Unlike him, Sev was a male of honor and integrity. He was a worthy male—a male worth mating. Who would make a good father.

"Don't ask me that, Dad," Marie said out of nowhere.

"What?"

"I know you want to know if he's taken a mate and has children, but you know I won't answer you." She paused. "Although...I sense he's going through an interesting time right now. I see pain."

"Pain?" Lakota was suddenly concerned.

"That's all I can say, Dad. I've already released the vision so I'm not tempted to tell you more."

He had told Marie not tell him anything personal about Sev for a reason. It would make him work that much harder to get to know his son again. He didn't want to rely on Marie's special talents and ESP to learn details about Sev's life that he needed to earn the right to know directly from his son. But the idea his son could be in pain was troubling.

God, he hoped Sev forgave him. Marie wanted to meet her half-brother. She had made that clear. But she didn't want to do it until Lakota and Sev reconciled.

"You're a good daughter, Marie. Just like your mother. You're such a good person."

"She would be proud of what you're doing, Dad."

"And you know that because...?"

Marie laughed quietly. "Yes, Mom and I have communicated about what you're doing."

Meeting and marrying Mary had been the best thing that had ever happened to him—until their first child, Marie, was born. Becoming a father and actually sharing the responsibilities of raising children had affected him deeply and made him realize his failings with Severin.

It was still hard for him to believe after being a bastard for so long that he could change and feel so much love for another as he did for his deceased wife and their children. A rare second chance had been granted him, and now he wanted to make things right with his firstborn son, too.

"How is she?" He had reconciled the fact that Marie could still communicate with Mary, and it no longer filled him with pain when Marie mentioned it.

"You know how she is, Dad."

"You know what I mean." Lakota already knew Mary was in Heaven and that she was happy and no longer attached to her earthly emotions, but he liked asking how she was, anyway. It made him feel normal when talking about her. "Does she have any messages for me?"

"Just that you're doing the right thing and that it's time for you to move on. She wants you to find someone else. You're meant to find someone else."

Lakota's mind darted to the dark-haired female he had met in the lobby. She was attractive. Could she be the one? Was there a connection between Mary's message and him meeting Gina.

"Did she say who?"

"No. She says you have to figure that out for yourself."

As when she was alive, Mary's life lessons continued on even in the afterlife.

"I love you, Dad. I have to go. I have a client coming in a few minutes."

Marie was a massage therapist who worked with both humans and vampires. He could sure use one of her massages right now for all the tension in his shoulders. "I love you, too, honey."

"Come visit me tomorrow night. I'll make you dinner."

"I wouldn't miss it."

They said their goodbyes and Lakota hung up and took a deep breath as he checked the time. It was now or never. Time to get ready.

He went to the closet and pulled out the dark grey cashmere sweater and black slacks he had so meticulously steamed the wrinkles out of with the steam iron that came with the room.

After grabbing a quick shower, he blew dry his shoulder-length hair, shaved, splashed on just a dab of aftershave, and dressed. He tucked the long, silver chain he wore with its cross pendant—a gift from Mary—under his sweater and looked at himself in the mirror. For such a large male, he felt about a foot tall and an inch wide for all the shame he shouldered.

Time to go, big guy. You don't want to be late. You've already caused Felice enough pain. Don't add being late to dinner to the list of reasons she should hate you.

With another deep breath, he grabbed his keys and left the room.

AFTER AWAKENING TO ARI'S MOUTH suckling his nipple and his hands roaming his body, Severin had made love to Ari once more in the shower before forcing himself to leave. He needed to go home and get ready for work, but his body felt gloriously well-used and ready for more, which made for an annoying distraction.

He was sooooo in the throes of the *calling*. It didn't matter that he couldn't get Ari pregnant. His body didn't know the difference. All his body knew was that he was now a mated male, and all instincts within him resolved to one purpose: plant his seeds as often as possible.

He had almost told Ari last night that he loved him but stopped himself at the last second. It was too soon to be making such proclamations in light of the fact that Ari was still sorting through his own feelings.

Give him time. He already feels the mating call pulling him to you.

That much was obvious, at least to Sev. Ari had been unquenchable in his thirst to take Sev over and over again. And when Sev left his house late this afternoon, Ari's body had visibly tensed as if he couldn't stand the idea of being separated from him. Even now, Sev could still feel Ari's anguish at their parting as if it had been his own.

Absolutely, he's mating to you, Sev, just as you are to him. He won't be able to part from you for long.

How were they going to make it through their *calling* phase if they had to keep what was happening between them a secret? If Ari would just realize that they were mates, he would know that they needed to tell someone. Newly mated males usually dropped out of the public eye during their *calling*. They were too dangerous during that volatile time.

Any little thing could set them off, and the peaks and valleys of their moods resided at severe extremes.

Somehow they would have to make it work.

Sev itched to see Ari again, and he pushed down on the accelerator, weaving in and out of traffic to get to the compound. He could have just dematerialized to AKM, but that wouldn't have made Ari get there any sooner and would only have driven him nuts. At least in his Challenger, he could work off some of that extra adrenaline by hitting the gas.

Before he knew it, he was pulling into the underground parking at AKM then taking the elevator to the main floor.

On his way past Dispatch, Adam caught his eye and waved. "Hey, Sev."

By now, everyone at AKM knew Adam was gay. Most accepted it without incident, but some ribbed the kid behind his back. It pissed Sev off. Adam was a good kid. He was talented, too, and in only a short time had risen to the rank of dispatch supervisor, probably because he was the only one who had followed procedure two months ago when Micah had gone missing. Shit had certainly hit the fan over that. One supervisor had been demoted for ignoring Adam's concerns over Micah's lack of response to calls.

"Hey, Adam. How's it going?"

The kid's shaggy blond hair hung over his forehead. "It's actually kind of quiet tonight. So far, anyway."

"That'll change."

"How come?"

Sev made a face and bugged out his eyes. "Because I'm here now." Then he laughed.

Adam chuckled. "You're certainly in a good mood."

"What do you mean?"

"You're always so quiet, is all." Adam blew over his mug of coffee and sipped.

"I guess I'll have to do something about that, huh?"

Adam laughed again and shook his head. "Get out of here, Bozo."

"Ten-four. You'd better get to work, too, before the supervisor catches you loafing."

"Ha ha."

Severin mock-gasped. "Oh, that's right. You *are* the supervisor." He grinned at Adam and high-fived him then left him to his work. Sev realized Adam was right. He *was* in a good mood. He even had a skip to his step, as if he couldn't quite keep all his happy energy bundled up.

He hit the prep room and practically popped a button on his pants when he rounded the corner and saw Ari securing his shoulder holster. His face jerked up and he let out an audible sigh of relief when he saw Sev.

"Anyone else here?" Sev eyed him hungrily.

Ari shook his head. "Just us, but I expect—" He didn't have time to say anything more because Sev swooped down on him like a hawk catching a field mouse. Their mouths fused with enough heat to melt steel as he spun Ari around and slammed him against the lockers.

Ari gave in to the kiss for a couple of seconds then gripped his shirt and shoved him back. "No, Sev. Not here. Not at work." He glanced around as if making sure no one had seen them.

"Fuck, Ari. I don't care who sees us."

"Well, I do." Ari pressed his palms against Sev's chest, holding him off.

"Fine. I'll give that to you, but after our shift, when I've got you to myself, I'll make you pay for denying me." He grinned at the way Ari's breath hitched and the way he licked his lips as if reconsidering pushing Sev away.

"Tease."

Sev chuckled and backed toward his own locker. "You know it, but you? Your ass is mine in the morning."

"Sshh." Ari frowned and pushed his hands down through the air as if to tell Sev to put a lid on it.

He laughed at him, but in a way it bothered him that Ari was so concerned with what other people thought. Who cared? It wasn't as if he would be able to hide what was happening from the others forever. Because when you mated, it became pretty clear to everyone around who your mate was.

Hell, no one had even met Sam when it became vividly clear that Micah was mated to her. A mating wasn't something that a male could hide for long.

The door swung open, and speak of the devil, Micah walked in, followed closely by Trace. Those two couldn't be seen anywhere, anymore, without the other in tow. They were joined at the hip, as it were, and Micah refused to patrol with anyone other than the tall, dark male with the shaved head. But at least Micah was patrolling with a partner now. Until his meltdown last month, he had apparently bucked protocol on a regular basis, insisting on solo patrols. Tristan had let him get away with it, but now the problem seemed to have sorted itself out.

"Hey, homos," Micah said.

"Wh-what?" The color flew out of Ari's face.

Trace laughed.

"I'm just fucking with you, Ari." Micah opened his locker and shoved in his coat. "Wouldn't want to get you in trouble with your boy, Io, now would I?" Micah glanced at Sev knowingly. "We all know how much of a fucktard homophobe *he* is."

Severin narrowed his gaze on Micah. He knew. Somehow, Micah knew. He wondered if the rumors he had heard about Micah always seeing inside others' thoughts were true. From the looks of it, they were.

Ari laughed awkwardly and checked his clip before smacking it back into his gun. "Yeah, he is that, isn't he?" Ari turned away to fish his knife out of his locker.

Micah looked from Sev to Ari and back again. "He should mind his own business, if you ask me. Let people be with who they want to be with."

Sev wondered what Micah's game was and frowned at him. Micah just arched an eyebrow and threw him a challenging look. It was almost as if Micah was daring him to deny it.

"How's that?" Ari said, turning around.

Micah looked at Ari and shrugged. "What do I care where a guy dips his wick. If it makes him happy, who gives a fuck if he's doing a guy or a girl?" He paused. "You don't think I know about the shit he said about me while I was with Jackson? Little cocksucker knew not to say it to my face, though. I'd have beaten the stupid out of him."

Trace chimed in. "Io had better not bring that shit to my door. I'll shove my hand down his throat."

"Down whose throat?" Malek pushed through the door, followed by Io.

"Nobody," Micah said, turning back toward his locker.

"I'm always the last in on these scintillating conversations, aren't I?" Malek said, opening his locker.

"Don't take it personally." Micah slammed his locker closed. "We'll see you fuckheads in there."

He and Trace left, and Io regarded Sev casually as he passed him and held his tattooed right arm up to Ari. "Hey, bro! You survive your night off unscathed? No, uh, surprise attacks?"

Sev knew what Io meant. He was checking to make sure Ari's back door hadn't been violated by Sev's gay dick. Io's obvious poor humor and lack of tact made him want to punch the guy for making light of his sexuality, given how he felt about Ari and how Ari obviously felt about him.

Yeah, this is the calling *phase getting good and pissed off right here.*

"Nope. It's all good. How about you? How was your date?" Ari acted like nothing had even happened between them.

How the hell could Ari talk to that asshole like he was okay with how Io felt? How could Ari stomach knowing that Io had made fun of him, was making fun of him now, and would probably make fun of him again later? Sev looked into his locker, but he wasn't sure for what. He was done getting ready. What was he waiting for?

Ari, you're waiting for Ari, you mush head.

Io sniggered. "Ah, man, it was hot. Those two girls can party. I'm taking you with next time, bro. You would definitely like that scene."

"Okay, yeah, sure. Whatever. Let me know when," Ari said.

"I'll line it up for next weekend." Io holstered his pistol.

"Yeah. Great. Sounds good." Ari pulled the jacket from his locker and shut it.

Severin's heart felt like it was in a vise. What the fuck? Had Ari just agreed to go with Io the next time he got together with those women? For what? Tea and crumpets? To share pointers on how to fuck a man? It was as if they hadn't just shared twenty-four hours of unbelievable intimacy with each other. Had it all been a lie?

"Hey, Sev, how you doing?" Malek glanced over and chucked his shoulder.

He slammed his locker shut. "Fucking great. How are you?" He didn't wait for an answer and stormed out.

"Uh-oh, we've got another Micah on our hands," Io said with a laugh.

"Shut up, Io." Ari sounded testy as the door to the prep room closed.

Sev skulked down the hall to Tristan's office for their weekly meeting. He strode in and plopped down on the couch where he normally sat and crossed his arms. He was certain a grey cloud hung over his head to match the scowl on his face. So much for that good mood he'd been in earlier. But then, his mated side hadn't felt spurned fifteen minutes ago, either.

Hello, Sev? This is your calling calling. Ha ha, buddy. Get good and comfy, because I'm here to stay.

"What's eating you?" Micah's eyes narrowed knowingly.

"Nothing." Sev wasn't buying for a second that Micah didn't know what was going on. Somehow that fucker knew.

Micah chuffed. "Uh-huh, sure."

"Fuck you."

Tristan sighed from behind his desk. "Well, it looks like tonight is starting off as usual."

"Yeah, but it's usually Micah with the attitude," Traceon said. He pulled out a matchstick and stuck the handle between his teeth.

"Am I going to start having problems with you, Sev?" Tristan glanced over at him.

Ari and the others chose that moment to enter the room

and Sev could feel Ari's eyes on him. "No, sir."

"You sure?" Tristan tapped his pen on the desk. "Maybe you should stay after the meeting and we can talk about it."

"No. I'm fine."

"You don't look fine. You look like a loose cannon about to blow. What's up?"

"Fuck, Tristan. I'm fine, all right?"

"Leave him alone, Tristan," Micah said. "It's that time of the month is all."

"Yeah, fuck you, Micah!" Sev lanced Micah with his glare.

"Fuck you back, Sev!"

"Fuck the both of you!" Tristan stood up and threw his pen across the room. Trace grinned as he watched it ricochet off the wall.

"Enough of this shit! I have got to have the most dysfunctional team in this whole fucking compound. Now straighten up! Sev, get out of here. Take the night off and cool out. I'll call you later and you *will* talk to me." His massive arms flexed as he pushed against the top of his desk and glared a warning at Sev. "The rest of you, we need to talk about this cobalt issue." He paused, glancing back at Severin. "Sev, I said get out! Now! You're pissing me off for real."

"Fuck all of you." Sev shoved himself off the couch and wouldn't meet Ari's eyes as he barreled out of the room and charged down the hall to the parking garage elevator.

"Hey, you going so soon?" Adam said as he blew past Dispatch.

He didn't answer. Yeah, where was the good mood he had walked in with? Sev chuffed. It had left town with Ari's spine.

CHAPTER 13

LAKOTA PULLED UP TO THE TOWNHOUSE on East Benton and shut off the engine. His hands were shaking. Amazing what developing a conscience could do for a guy.

Even though he no longer drank, he wished he had a shot of Jack sitting in front of him to chill his nerves.

He got out and trudged the short distance to the front door. Since the first time he tracked Felice and Severin down right after marrying Mary (it had been her idea to find his firstborn son), he had kept tabs on them. Or tried to. Felice had been easier to stay in touch with. Sev, on the other hand, traveled all over the place. His son had fought in more wars than a Navy SEAL, Green Beret, and a career soldier combined. It was a wonder he was still alive.

Suddenly, the door opened.

"Are you ever going to ring the doorbell?"

He looked up to see Felice standing with one hand on her hip, head tilted, door propped against her other arm. It dawned on him he had been standing on her front porch for at least a couple of minutes.

"U-Um...I'm sorry, I guess I—"

She lifted her hand to shut him up. "Just come in, Kota."

He entered her home and she shut the door behind him.

"Wine?" she said, walking back toward the open kitchen. The townhouse was lovely. Well-lit with an open floor plan. And the place smelled wonderful, like she had spent the day cooking Italian food.

"Uh, sure." He followed her and stood back as she poured two glasses of red wine. "Actually, no. I'm sorry. I don't drink, anymore. I'll just have water." He was so caught off guard by her welcoming demeanor he had temporarily forgotten he had given up alcohol.

"Oh, okay." She sounded surprised but grabbed a clean glass and filled it with water.

"Thank you."

"I figure we can eat up on the terrace," she said, handing him the glass.

Okay, so he was thrown for a loop here. He hadn't expected Felice to be so inviting. After what he had done to her, even though it had been a lifetime ago, he assumed she'd only agreed to meet with him to get him off her back and would hustle him out as quickly as possible. Dinner and wine—well, water—were a surprise.

And that was only the half of it. She was a dreck. He was a vampire. The two races didn't exactly mix well.

"You didn't have to do all this, Felice," he said.

She flipped her short, red hair off her shoulder and glanced at him. "Don't be silly. Why wouldn't I?"

Lakota shrugged. "Because of what I did."

"Shush about that for now." She filled two plates with spaghetti, spooned homemade meat sauce that smelled like a gift from the gods over both, then placed two pieces of garlic bread next to each.

Just two plates.

"Severin's not coming?" he said.

She shook her head. "He's not ready to forgive you."

"But you are?"

She handed him a plate as she clucked her tongue. "It's time to move on, don't you think?"

Forgiveness and moving on were why he was here. He just wished Sev had come. He wanted to see him.

"Yes, I think so."

She led him up to the terrace, where outdoor heaters took the chill out of the air. They sat down in a pair of cushioned chairs at a small table.

"I like the new hair color, by the way," he said. "It's nice."

As shifters, drecks could change their human appearance

at will, but their dreck imprint remained the same. Luckily, Felice had never changed much about her shifted form other than her hair color. It had made finding her easier. He paused and nodded at her. "You look good, Felice." He swirled spaghetti on his fork and admired her fair skin. By human standards, she didn't look older than her late twenties.

"So do you. It's amazing how much Sev looks like you."

It was the vampire genes. They trumped dreck and human genes every time. It was why mixed babies always turned out vampires. Vampires with a twist, but still vampires.

"How is he?"

"He's good."

"Is he mated?" He stopped and held up his hand. "No. Wait. Don't answer that. I made a deal with my daughter—her gift is psychic in nature—not to tell me anything about him. That way I have to work harder to get to know him. So, you can't tell me anything about him, either. It would be like cheating. I need to earn it first."

Felice nodded approvingly. "You have changed, haven't you?"

"Yes, I have. As you've seen, I don't drink, anymore." He lifted his water glass to prove his point then hesitated as his mind fell back on the terrible things he had done to her and others so long ago. "And now I *protect* the innocent rather than hurt them." He set down his water and fork then reached for Felice's hand. "I am so sorry, Felice. I am so sorry for what I did to you. Our races don't get along, but what I did to you was inexcusable. Before we go any further, I need to beg for your forgiveness."

Her eyes misted over and she squeezed his hand. "No need to beg, Kota. I forgive you." She smiled warmly. "I'm just in awe that you've turned your life around the way you have."

"Mary helped me find my way again." He had told Felice about Mary on the phone.

Felice sipped her wine and smiled. "So she did. Do you have a picture of her?"

He pulled out his wallet and slipped a family photo from inside and handed it to her. "Don't get me wrong. I'm no saint. I still hunt. I still fight. But I do so now with a conscience."

"She was a lovely woman," Felice said. "And so are your children." She handed the picture back.

"Marie is the oldest. She lives north of here. I'm going to see her tomorrow."

"I bet she'll be glad to see you."

Lakota took her hand again and gave her a serious look. "You're a better person than I am, Felice. I don't think I could forgive someone who did what I did to you."

She waved her free hand at him and looked away almost shyly, as if she were struggling to hide her emotions. "Everything happens for a reason, Kota. You gave me Sev. That's how I prefer to look at it now." She patted his hand. "Now eat. No more dwelling on the past and what we can't change. All we can do is look forward and live for now."

Lakota realized he had been nervous for no reason. The evening was actually turning out enjoyable.

GINA SAT BACK ON HER HAUNCHES. This was turning out to be a major bust. She had followed Lakota tonight with the hope that he would lead her to Severin. Instead, all he led her to was spaghetti night at some strange woman's house.

She was too far away to catch the female's scent, but as she watched through her scope, it was clear that there was nothing romantic between them. Their body language was more in line with acquaintances or distant friends than lovers.

Okay, this had led nowhere. She lowered the scope. Maybe she could get something from AKM since this clearly wasn't Sev's house.

Dematerializing from the rooftop, she misted off toward AKM. Maybe she could catch Sev there.

SEVERIN SPED AWAY FROM **AKM,** full of pissed-off and kiss-my-ass. This was the hell he was in for as a mated male, wasn't it? Especially if he was mated to Ari, who wore two faces. One for him and one for the rest of the world. He wanted to be with Ari, and not just in private, but in public, too. To be denied that pleasure, then have to endure Io's jibes and Ari's acceptance of an invite to go out and fuck a pair of whores, was beyond Sev's level of tolerance. It was adding insult to injury.

He had been driving around for an hour, spending the last few minutes zooming north on Lake Shore. He exited on Randolph and within minutes was tromping up the walk to his mom's townhouse. He didn't know where else to turn and his mom had a way of calming him when he got like this. Using his key, he unlocked the door and went inside. All the lights were on, and his mouth watered at the smell of her homemade Italian sauce.

"Mom! Hey, Mom?" He grabbed a plate and loaded it with spaghetti and poured a glass of wine. She was probably up on the terrace. She liked to eat up there even when it was cold outside. He had installed outdoor heaters for her to make it more comfortable.

God, he really needed to talk to her. Hurrying up the stairs, he charged out to the terrace and froze.

"Sev?" His mom jumped up. She had just taken a bite of spaghetti and lifted her napkin to dab the corner of her mouth. "I didn't think you were coming."

Suddenly, Sev remembered that she had told him his dad was stopping by tonight. The plate and glass fell out of his hands and he stared at the tall, broad-shouldered male who slowly stood and gazed at him.

"Son?"

It was scary how alike they looked. His father's lines were harder, though. Sharper and edgier. Sev had softer features, and his eyes weren't as tight.

"What the fuck are you doing here?" he said.

His mom scurried forward and took his hand. She frowned up at him. "I told you he was coming. I thought that was why you were here. That you had changed your mind about wanting to see him."

Sev's night just got better and better. First Ari and now his bastard father.

"I forgot."

Father and son refused to break eye contact. One stared in awe while the other stared in hatred.

"Then why did you come?" His mom knelt and began cleaning up the mess from his dropped plate. The broken wine glass lay in shards.

"It doesn't matter."

"Son, wait. Please." His father walked toward him.

"Don't you come near me." Sev's voice held a warning that his body was prepared to enforce. He had been primed for a fight before coming here. His father gave him an excellent excuse to get into one.

"Severin, please, hear me out. I came here to apologize. I'm different now. I've changed and wanted to tell both you and your mom how sorry I am for what I did to you. I just want to know you, son."

That did it. Sev's fist shot out faster than he could track and connected with his father's chin with a loud thwack as bone met bone. His father flew to the side and his mom screamed.

He pointed an angry finger at Lakota. "Don't you ever call me that again, you bastard. I am *not* your son."

He spun on his heels and raced down the stairs and out the front door to his car, his emotions a hornet's nest of chaos. There was nowhere to go. He wasn't welcome at the compound right now, and he sure as hell wasn't going back inside his mom's house. Only one place remained. Home. And he didn't really want to go there, either.

His phone rang and he glanced at the caller ID Tristan. He had said he was going to call him later and that he *would* speak to him. *Ooo, scary.* Sev waved his fingers at the phone. *Here's what I think of how I will talk to you.* He sent the call to voicemail. *Ha! Talk to that, asshole.* He started the engine, pulled away, and around the park then traveled back down Lake Shore to Buckingham Fountain in Grant Park.

For a while, he simply walked around the park, sitting down occasionally to stare at the boarded up fountain. In the summer it would be a major attraction, but until May it would remain closed and shut off.

The air was colder at the lakefront, but Sev didn't care. The frosty bite actually felt good. Matched his mood. He wandered east and sat down on the great staircase that overlooked Chicago Harbor and Lake Michigan further out.

He didn't know how long he sat there, but when his phone rang again, he jumped.

Fuck Tristan!

Still, he pulled out his phone and looked at the ID.

Ari?

He closed his eyes as his heart weeble-wobbled inside his ribcage. There was no way he couldn't answer a call from his mate. No matter how angry he was at him, he couldn't refuse him.

"What?"

"Sev?"

"Yep. What do you want, Ari?"

Silence.

Sev sighed in frustration. "Why are you calling me?"

"I'm sorry, Sev. I'm so sorry. Please don't be mad at me."

"Too late for that." Sev brushed his hair off his face as the cold, lakefront wind caught it and blew it over his eyes.

More silence.

Sev huffed again. "Is that all you wanted? Will there be anything else?"

"Do you not want me to come over after my shift then?" Ari sounded beyond miserable, which ebbed Sev's anger. As mad as he was for what had happened earlier, the thought that he was causing his mate pain was worse.

"Fuck, Ari." He blew out a heavy, frustrated sigh. "Yes, I still want you to come over. Damn you."

"Are you saying—hold on." Ari held the phone away like he was talking to someone else. "No, no...black coffee. Yeah. Black." There was a rustling sound and he was back. "Sorry about that."

"Who are you with?"

"Malek. Where are you?"

Sev looked up and around. "Grant Park."

"Oh. Okay. We're on the South Side."

Silence again.

"So, will you come over then?" Sev said. Some of the steam had blown out of his sails now that he was hearing Ari's voice, and now the only thing that seemed to matter was seeing him in a few hours. *Welcome to the land of the mated male vampire. Enjoy the emotional roller coaster ride the* calling's *gonna serve up on your ass.*

"If you want me to." Ari's voice sounded hopeful.

"Do you want to?"

A pause. "Yes."

Sev swallowed the lump in his throat. "Good. I need to see you, Ari."

"I need to see you, too." Ari paused.

Sev looked out over Lake Michigan, the tension in his body fading. "I miss you."

"I miss you, too." Ari's voice sounded like he was smiling.

"We'll get through this, babe."

"I know. But it kills me that I hurt you. I'm so sorry."

"Never mind that. Just hurry and get to my place, okay. And don't eat. I'm cooking."

Suddenly, Sev's good mood flowed back into his blood in an instant and he knew just what he wanted to cook for his mate. His mate! Ari. He was still getting used to the idea. But yes, his *mate* was coming over. He was going to see his *mate*. Hot damn!

And while he was at it, he really needed to get used to the violent mood shifts of this mated male thing. This was all new to him and he was feeling tossed around like a rowboat in the high seas during a hurricane. But from what he understood, this was normal during the *calling* phase, but that didn't mean he was enjoying that part of it. He would rather enjoy the other part of it—the part where he got to make love to Ari for hours on end until he collapsed with exhaustion. Yeah, that was the part of the *calling* phase he was looking forward to.

"I can't wait," Ari said.

"Bye, babe."

"See ya in a few."

Sev disconnected and got up. He had to hurry if he was going to make it to the store and get home in time to make a pot of his mom's homemade spaghetti sauce for Ari.

ARI HUNG UP THE PHONE and breathed a sigh of relief. He thought he had majorly fucked up back at AKM, and his heart had been breaking ever since. Obviously, the exchange with Io had hurt Severin, and as soon as he realized what had happened he had been filled with a pain unlike anything he'd ever felt. The pain gripped his chest, knotted his stomach, and pounded inside his head for three hours until just a few minutes ago. Calling Sev and hearing him say he still wanted to see him lifted the ache and pain away like a breeze blowing away ashes from a fire. Suddenly, Ari couldn't stop smiling.

And what the hell was up with his Johnson? He had been hard all night. It had already gotten so bad twice that he'd had to take bathroom breaks to ease himself. Malek was probably beginning to think his bladder had shrunk or some shit, but at least jacking off gave him a bit of a respite.

But fuck, he needed to get his head screwed on straight. Especially where Sev was concerned. What had happened earlier had been inexcusable. He should have known better and been more conscientious.

He would need to find a way to keep his conversations with Io away from Sev's ears, and to also be more careful about what he said to Io. Hell, he had no intention of joining Io or anyone else on some orgy-esque sexcapade with two or more women. The only one he wanted to be with was Sev. He had only agreed with Io because he didn't know what else to say under the circumstances. He hadn't been prepared for convos like that. He would need to start preparing if this was going to work with Sev. And he wanted it to work. It had to. He couldn't live without Sev.

"Here you go." Malek handed him his coffee. "Sorry it took so long. They had to make a fresh pot. Who were you talking to, by the way?"

"Oh, um, uh...my dad." Yeah, he really needed to prepare for how to handle conversations where Sev was involved.

"Did you tell him thanks for inviting us all to his party?"

"Yeah, sure."

After Sev had stormed out of the meeting earlier, Tristan had announced to the rest of the team that Ari's father had invited them all to the St. Patrick's Day party he was hosting at his home this weekend.

Fun, fun. The idea humiliated Ari more than comforted him. He didn't want his teammates to look at him like he was the son of a personal friend of the king, even though that was exactly what he was. Ari worked hard to keep that fact out of the public eye. He swore his dad did this shit just to embarrass him.

"You ready?" Malek said.

Ready to be done with this shift. He was already growing hard again. Ari nodded. "Yeah, let's go so we can get back."

They were on a mass search for cobalt dealers and had already bagged two. Hopefully, they would be able to get something out of the ones they'd caught that would lead them to the primary manufacturer so they could make a dent in production. But drecks had amazing powers of resistance to mind probes, although Trace seemed to have some bionic powers where that was concerned. The guy was a freak of nature. Trace and Micah were working the guys he, Malek, Tristan, and Io took back to the compound. Yep, that's right, even Tristan had slid out from behind the desk to patrol in Sev's place.

Sev. He grinned at the thought of seeing him later.

"What are you smiling about?" Malek said, glancing over.

"Nothing, just something my dad said." The lie came out more easily than the last one. Maybe there was hope, yet.

Malek drove them farther west, and Ari looked out the window. Was his shift over, yet?

CHAPTER 14

GINA HAD STOPPED BY **AKM** for a few minutes, found a lot of nothing, so returned to the hotel. After changing, she went down to the bar until it closed then hung out in the lobby in hopes of bumping into Lakota when he returned from his wineless spaghetti feast.

Her head was buried in a newspaper when she caught his scent. She peeked out from behind the paper as he stopped and looked at the closed bar in frustration before turning around and walking to the desk.

"The bar's closed?" she heard him ask.

"I'm sorry sir. Yes, it closed about an hour ago."

Lakota backed away from the desk, looking dejected. She folded the paper and got up then followed him to the elevator.

"Hey," he said as he turned and saw her step in behind him. "You're the big-breakfast girl. Gina, right?"

"I'm flattered you remembered."

"How could I forget? You eat like I do, but you're three times as small."

"A girl's gotta eat."

The elevator closed and started up.

"I heard you asking about the bar," she said.

"Yeah, well, it's already closed." He sounded frustrated.

"You can come drop by my room if you want a drink." Her voice was suggestive, her eyes provocative.

He laughed. "No, I didn't want to drink. I just wanted to sit in the bar with a glass of club soda and *pretend* I was drinking."

"Why ever would you want to do that?" She made a screwed up face at him.

He chuckled. "I stopped drinking ages ago." He looked at the floor uncomfortably. "But tonight was a rough one and I could use the fake drink—the illusion that I'm drowning myself, as it were."

Ah, so that's why he drank water with his dinner at the female's house.

The elevator stopped on her floor and she stepped out but held her arm over the door to keep it from closing. "Well, I could pour you a glass of water and you can pretend it's a glass of Vodka and I'm the bartender. Then you can tell me all about your troubles and I can give you a bunch of useless advice that sounds wise but is really just a crock of shit."

He laughed and considered her offer. Then he nodded and joined her. "Okay, sure. Why not?"

She led him to her room.

"I bet your advice would be better than some random human's, anyway," he said.

She looked over her shoulder. Until now, neither one of them had acknowledged out loud that they were the same. As in, they were both vampires.

"Oh, why's that?" She batted her eyes innocently.

He grinned and flashed his fangs. "Because you're like me."

She pretended to be scared of his fangs, then laughed as she relaxed her face. "Okay, you got me."

They stopped in front of her door.

"My name's Lakota." He held out his hand and formally introduced himself.

"I remember." She shook his hand. Nice hands. He had nice, strong hands.

He smiled and his face flushed slightly. "Yes, that's right. Guess I'm out of practice."

Gina wasn't exactly sure what he meant by that, but she bumped her arm against his good-naturedly. "You're doing fine."

He glanced at her curiously. "What brings you to Chicago, Gina? Oh wait, you're on vacation, right?"

They entered her room, and he took a seat while she went for the mini bar. "Yep. I needed a break. And you said you're here because of family. Just visiting then?"

He sighed and stretched out those long legs of his. "I'm mending fences. Well, trying to."

She poured him a glass of water over ice and grabbed a Vodka and orange juice for herself. "Mending fences? Is that why you wanted to drown yourself in club soda tonight, Lakota?" She handed him his glass and took a seat beside him.

"Yes, it was a rough night." He rubbed his chin as if it ached. "Some fences are tougher to mend than others."

"Why? What happened?"

He sipped his water. "I saw my son tonight."

"Your son?"

"Yes, his name is Severin. It's been a long time since I've seen him."

This was easier than she thought. Good. Now she just needed to keep him talking. She leaned back as if settling in for the long haul.

"Go on, Lakota. Tell bartender Gina all about it."

He smiled at her and started talking.

SEVERIN SAT AT THE COUNTER IN HIS KITCHEN, tapping the top corner of his cell phone with his finger so it spun on the counter toward his other hand, where he tapped it on the opposite corner so that it spun back. Back and forth, back and forth. *Tap-tap-tap-tap.* He couldn't sit still.

For the third time in fifteen minutes, he hopped off the bar stool and stirred the meat sauce that was simmering on the stove. It was ready to eat, but it was the kind of sauce that the longer it simmered, the better it was.

He took a taste and hovered over the pot as he let the flavor coat his tongue, Then he grabbed a pinch more salt and dashed it into the pan. A check of the clock said it was just after six a.m. Ari's shift had ended an hour ago.

"Come on, come on," he said under his breath. "Get here, damn it."

After their phone conversation, Sev's anger over what had

happened earlier with Io had dissipated, but he knew that sooner or later Ari's need to keep them hush-hush would have to be addressed. He didn't want to live his life with Ari behind closed doors. As mates, secrecy would only hurt them, and more blowups like the one that had just happened would continue to occur.

He had finally talked to Tristan, too, explaining that he was fine and making an excuse that he had some personal shit to deal with. Tristan had offered to give him some time off to sort things out, but he had declined, saying the worst was over—at least, he hoped it was over—and he just wanted to get back to work. He apologized for his behavior and did the necessary sucking up then Tristan had informed him of what else had been discussed during the meeting, including an invite from Ari's father for all of them to attend a St. Patrick's Day party this coming weekend.

That could be interesting. All of them. Together. At Ari's parents' house. What a great time to meet the parents. Somehow, Sev got the idea the party was a bad idea.

Just then the doorbell rang and Sev nearly left his skin behind as he darted out of the kitchen. Taking the time to check the peephole, he caressed one hand over his door when he saw Ari standing on the other side, glancing down nervously. Sev closed his eyes and tilted his forehead against the door as he smiled. Everything would be okay now. Ari was here.

After unlocking the door, he pulled it open and Ari looked up at him, his face a mix of nervousness, hope, and relief. He pulled a rose from behind his back and held it out to Sev.

"When a man shows up with flowers, he knows he fucked up." Sev took the rose and lifted it to his nose and grinned as he stepped back to allow Ari in.

"I'm sorry, Sev. I'm so sorry." Ari stepped inside and shut the door behind him then wrapped his arms around Sev's waist and held him close.

He smelled clean, like soap and Old Spice.

How could Sev be angry at his mate? How could he not hold him, forgive him, and quiet him with kisses? "Sshh, Ari.

You're forgiven. Come here." He nudged Ari's chin with the side of his index finger to turn Ari toward him, and then he kissed those perfect, soft lips until they both moaned quietly at the same time. Ari's body pressed more fully against Sev's, and their hands explored.

"I've been hard for you all night." Ari spoke against his mouth.

"Me, too. And now you're here."

Their lips met once more, tasting and lingering together.

"What are you cooking?" Ari broke their kiss and dipped his head to lick a long line up the side of Sev's throat as if he wasn't interested in food at all. "It smells good."

Sev purred at Ari's oral caress. "So do you." He palmed the back of Ari's head and held his mouth against his neck.

Ari purred back and scratched his fangs over Sev's skin. Up and down, up and down, teasing Sev. "Mmm, so do you." Ever-so-gently, Ari's fangs pierced his skin and sank into his flesh.

"Mmmm." Sev leaned back against the wall and slowly faded into bliss. He thought he would pass out from the euphoria of Ari's venom mixing with his own. The reaction was more powerful in a vampire than a human and Sev felt the room spin in a good way.

Very good.

Ari's bite deepened and Sev teetered drunkenly, unable to remain standing without assistance, too lost in his mate's touch and his total possession of him. The euphoria made him drunk with desire. God, yes. This was what he needed. Arion. His precious Ari at his vein and pressing against him with commanding presence.

Suddenly, Ari pulled away and snapped back as he smacked his lips. He looked as if he had tasted something funny, and he had a frown on his face.

Sev tried to look at him, but he felt like a bobble head doll, unable to control his physical faculties through the euphoric intoxication.

"What's wrong?" His words slurred as he fought through the haze. "Why'd you stop?"

Ari looked up at him and lifted his fingers to his lips. "Oh my God, Sev. What are you?"

"Huh?" Sev was too out of it and didn't understand. The euphoria only lasted a minute or two, but until it cleared, nothing would make sense.

"Your blood. It tastes...I mean..." Ari started to back toward the door, a look of shock on his face. "I know you're a mixed-blood, but I...I just assumed your mix was human." He frowned, looking almost hurt. "But...you're *dreck*." He spat the word out like it was dirty.

Suddenly, Sev sobered, blinking and shaking off the effects of Ari's venom. "Wait, no—"

"You're a goddamn dreck, Sev?" Ari backed further away, headed for the door. "When were you going to tell me? Huh? When? Fuck, Sev!"

"Wait, Ari. No." Sev fought through the last of the haze and reached for his mate.

Ari yanked himself away, practically flinging himself against the door as he fumbled with the handle. "I can't...I need to...fuck!" He glanced back at Sev, looking hurt and confused. "I can't believe you didn't tell me." Ari's glare was accusatory.

Clearly, Sev had fucked up by not telling him sooner, but he hadn't known how. He had been scared of Ari's reaction, and apparently, he had been right to be worried with the way Ari was practically clawing through the door to get away from him. Finally, the door swung open and Ari shot outside.

"Ari, stop. Please!" What had he done? God, he had fucked up monumentally. He should have told Ari last night. Before they had gotten so involved. But, yeah right. When had they really even had an opportunity to discuss it? They had been too busy falling in love with each other, and Sev hadn't been thinking about much else other than holding and feeling Ari against him.

Ari practically flew off the porch, his voice full of pain as he barked over his shoulder, "Don't touch me, Sev. Just don't fucking touch me right now. You should have told me, damn you!"

Sev's heart broke at Ari's vicious tone, and pain broke out

in his chest like a hundred tiny nails had exploded from the center and sprayed out to pierce his flesh. Clutching his chest, his knees gave out from the sudden burst of pain—the *suffering*—and he crumpled to the floor like slack rope. Anguish tormented him. "Please, Ari."

Ari reached his car. As he opened the driver's side door, he turned and looked at Sev. Confusion and pain crossed his features, and he gasped for air, hesitating just long enough that Sev thought he might come back inside. But he frowned and shook his head as if he were arguing with himself then hurried and got behind the wheel.

"NO! Ari! God, don't leave. I love you! I love you, damn it!" The pain in his chest now radiated through his limbs and he fell forward on the floor. "You're my mate!" He yelled out the last right before Ari shut his door and started the engine.

As Ari backed out of the driveway, Sev rolled onto his back and cried out in pain. Then his eyes flew to the clock. It was almost time for sunrise. Ari would never make it home in time.

"NOOO!"

As Ari hit the gas, he finally let his tears fall.

He was shocked more than angry. Well, no, he was angry, too. And hurt. Sev should have told him what he was. Sev should have admitted up front that he was half dreck instead of letting Ari assume he was a human mix. What the hell? How had this happened? How had he gotten involved with someone who was half dreck?

Fuck!

Tears streamed Ari's face as he raced past the stop sign at the end of Sev's street. No other cars were out this early, so it wasn't like anyone was going to crash into him to jolt him back to his senses, even though he was tempting fate to do just that.

He swiped the back of his hand over his eyes and cheeks to wipe the tears away, but he still couldn't see for shit through the blur.

Sev was a dreck? *A goddamn dreck?* How the fuck? When? How? Shit!

But as shocking as that was, what hurt Ari even more was that Sev had lied to him. Well, maybe not lied, because they had never talked about Sev's background. But damn it, Sev should have told him right from the start he was half dreck. If he cared about him even just a little, he should have told him.

The pain he had felt earlier in the evening returned, only this time it was worse. Way worse. As in someone-kill-me worse. The piercing ache gripped his chest so tightly he didn't think he would be able to continue breathing. Immediately, the pain lowered and lanced his stomach then spread upward to squeeze his head as if it were in a giant fist. Then everything in his melon went haywire like his shit was bouncing around inside his skull. He imagined this was what it would feel like to have Shaquille O'Neal use his head as a basketball.

Ari slammed on the brakes and opened his door, gasping for air as he flopped onto the pavement on all fours in the middle of the street to dry heave a whole lot of nothing but net as imaginary Shaq slam-dunked him. Fuck! What the hell was happening to him? It wasn't Sev's blood making him feel this way. Dreck blood couldn't hurt vampires. And, besides, he had felt this pain earlier after what had happened with Io back at AKM. True, this was way worse than how he had felt after hurting Sev, but at the core, the pain was the same.

He rocked back and leaned against the side of his car while he wrapped his arms around his torso to try and dampen the pain.

Sev, Sev, Sev. Sev was a dreck, or at least partially a dreck. Why hadn't Sev told him? It hurt that Sev had kept it a secret from him. Didn't he trust him? Couldn't Sev be honest with him? After he had poured out his own secrets to Sev about his family and about himself, Sev hadn't been able to do the same in return?

Fresh tears streamed his face, and he clamped a hand over his chest and bent his head forward as he sobbed. It felt like his heart was being torn apart. He was in love with the enemy. He was in love with the goddamn enemy.

Suddenly, he stopped rocking himself as he realized what he had just thought. Was he in love with Sev? He searched his heart, seeing the truth that, yes, he was, wasn't he? And then he realized what Sev had yelled to him just before he beat feet. *I love you, damn it! You're my mate!* Sev's words echoed in Ari's ears.

You're my mate!

Ari blinked hard, replaying the memory yet again.

You're my mate!

Sev had looked tortured as he cried out to Ari. Tortured and in agony.

Ari hesitated and frowned, looking down. What was happening here? Realization began to fully dawn on him, his face softening as his gaze searched the shadows in disbelief, as if he could find something in the darkness that would explain the situation.

He and Sev were in the grasp of the *suffering*, weren't they? Shit. The *suffering* was what Micah had gone through after Jackson left him over two months ago. Before Micah had found Sam. The *suffering* was a condition that attacked a mated male when his mate either left him or died. The mating bond didn't like to be severed once it selected a partner, and the *suffering* was its way of lashing out when that occurred. It ensured the mated pair stayed together. But if he and Sev were experiencing the *suffering*, that would mean that they...oh God. They had mated each other.

Ari banged his head back against his car. God, he was stupid. How could he have been so blind? The constant hard-on, the ever-present need to have sex with Sev, the aches, the pains, the way his heart clenched earlier when he had hurt Sev and Sev had been angry with him. Suddenly it all made sense.

You're my mate! Sev had said. Sev already knew. How hadn't Ari seen it when apparently Sev had?

Because you were blinded by your fear of everyone finding out you're gay, you dumbass.

Ari groaned. Fuuuuuuck. He was such an idiot. He had just blown up and jumped to conclusions about Sev and how he should have told him the truth about being dreck, and yet here Ari was, unable to do the same about his homosexuality.

He pulled his knees up and stretched his arms out over them and bowed his head in shame. What a hypocrite he was. Here he was holding Sev to a standard he, himself, couldn't even live up to.

No wonder Sev hadn't told him about his dreck blood. He was probably scared shitless at what kind of reaction he would get. Fear most likely motivated Sev to keep the truth a secret. Fear of how he would be treated. Fear of Ari's reaction. And wasn't that same fear why Ari kept his own secrets about being gay?

Yet Ari had just proven that Sev had reason to be concerned. He had flown off the handle, accusing Sev of lying and withholding the truth. And yet, Ari couldn't even tell his parents or Io the truth about himself.

He had fucked up. Badly.

There weren't many half-drecks who announced what they were, and for good reason. Vampires who were discovered to have dreck blood ended up being forsaken by both drecks and vampires. They were ostracized. Cast-outs from both sides. Stuck in a no man's land where nobody wanted them. Hell, being half dreck was worse than being gay. It was a curse. No wonder Sev kept his mouth shut.

"Idiot. I'm such an idiot!" Ari chastised himself. He of all people should have understood Sev's concerns and fear. Ari, who felt like a reject for his own reasons, should have appreciated the situation. Wouldn't Ari want someone to cut him some slack and understand his reasons for not disclosing his own truth? Wouldn't he want his parents, Io, and everyone else to accept him and let him live his own life without fear of retaliation and retribution? Didn't Sev deserve the same from him?

Yes, he did. And not just because it was becoming clear that Sev was his life mate. Sev deserved it for the simple reason that he was a person like everyone else.

"Stupid, stupid, stupid fuck." Ari chastised himself again and flopped his head back, banging it against the side of the car as he looked up at the sky.

The first light of dawn shone in the east and his skin prickled. He had dallied too long. He would never make it home before sunrise. But his house wasn't where he wanted to be right now, anyway. His home—his real home—was back in the other direction. Going to where he lived would only serve as torture, because he wouldn't be with the male he loved. He wouldn't be with Severin. Yes, there was only one true home for him, now. Just one.

After jumping back into his car, he turned around and sped back to Sev's house. When he pulled into the driveway, he saw that Sev was still lying on the floor in the foyer. The door was still open, and Sev's body was curled on its side. He was tightly gripping himself, shivering so violently Ari could see it from his car.

Was he shaking from the cold early morning air or something more biological? Was Sev locked into the misery of the *suffering* as Ari had been just a few minutes ago, feeling the effects of their separation from one another on a level beyond agony?

Ari stared at Sev, hurting inside for the pain he had caused him. Damn, but that was his mate in there. Half-dreck or not, Sev was his mate, goddamn it. Ari was still too stunned to fully comprehend it.

He looked back at Sev, who didn't seem aware that Ari had returned. Shit, this was bad. Ari knew that all-too-well after what he had just experienced. But once he had made the decision to return, the pain had dissipated and his body had eased. It was just one more sign that he had, indeed, figured out what was happening. He really had mated Severin. He had found the one he had been made for—the one his soul had chosen above all others to fit perfectly with. It was Ari's duty as his mate to make Sev's pain go away and take care of him.

Ari got out of his car and went inside then quietly closed the door before kneeling down behind Sev's shivering body.

Sev was sobbing uncontrollably, not even aware that Ari was there.

Tears formed in Ari's eyes as he lifted his hand to his mouth. God, how could he make this right? What had he done? His other half was in agony because of him. He wasn't supposed to hurt his other half. This was the one person in the entire universe Ari had been made to be with, and hurting him felt like a crime.

Ari had never thought this day would come. All the women he had been with in hopes of finding his mate, and all along, his mate had been a male. A sense of wonder and fascination swept over him, followed instantly by love. Overwhelming, life-changing, I-need-him-in-my-life-or-I'll-die love.

"I love you, too," he finally said on a whisper, placing his palm on Sev's shoulder. He needed Sev to look at him. He needed Sev to see he wasn't mad, anymore, and that he understood.

Sev's head jerked around and he froze, searching Ari's face.

Ari bit back his own emotions. "I love you, too. You're my mate, too, Sev." He bit the inside of his lip to keep from choking up. "I'm so sorry for how I reacted."

Crystal blue eyes that sparkled with tears blinked several times, almost as if Sev wanted to make sure Ari was really there. Then suddenly, Sev lurched upright into a sitting position and reached for Ari and pulled him in hard and held him so tightly it was if they shared the same body.

"You came back. Oh my God, you came back. I thought I'd lost you."

Ari gripped Sev securely, fisting his hands into the back of his shirt so that the fabric bunched within his curled fingers. He wasn't willing to let go of him now that he knew he'd found his one true match. "I'm so sorry. So goddamn sorry, Sev. I didn't mean to hurt you."

"And I never meant to lie to you." Sev buried his face against Ari's neck.

"You didn't lie to me."

"But I never told you, which is the same thing. I should have told you. I should have been honest."

"No." Ari pressed his cheek to the top of Sev's head. "No, Sev. It's not your fault. I understand why you didn't say anything. Me, of all people...I should have known better than to accuse you of keeping secrets."

Sev pulled back, looking confused. "What do you mean?"

Ari leaned forward, not wanting even this tiny distance between them. "Well, look at me, Sev. I can't even admit to my own family and my best friend that I'm gay. Who am I to judge you for not admitting you're half dreck?" He shook his head. "The repercussions of that secret getting out are way worse than if people find out I'm gay."

"You mean..." Sev's brow furrowed as if he wasn't sure what Ari was saying. "You're okay with me being half dreck?"

Ari grinned and pulled Sev close again so that he could rest his forehead against Sev's. He closed his eyes and breathed in Sev's clean, masculine scent. This was all his now. This male in his arms and the way he smelled and felt. Sev was all his. "Yes, Sev. God, yes. You're my mate. My *mate*." He smiled as he repeated it, his whole face lifting as he kept his eyes closed and reveled in the moment. "My mate...God, you're my mate." He sounded almost relieved.

"Yes, Ari." Sev kept his voice soft, almost as if he, too, was savoring the moment. "We're mates." His hands skimmed slowly down and up Ari's back. "I wasn't sure how long it would take before you realized it."

"You could have told me." Ari opened his eyes and looked into Sev's, their foreheads still pressed together.

"I wanted you to figure it out on your own, babe."

Babe. Ari loved Sev's nickname for him.

"Well, it took me a while, but I finally did."

They remained on the floor, holding each other, touching, feeling, and enjoying the closeness.

"I was going to tell you, Ari." Pain edged Sev's eyes. "I promise. I was going to tell you about my dreck bloodline. I just didn't know how. And I was scared."

Ari nodded and took Sev's hand. "Tell me about it. I know scared, Sev. Look at me. I'm scared shitless to come out to my parents. And to Io. I had no right to accuse you of holding out on me. None. It kills me that I hurt you. All I can do is beg forgiveness."

Sev pulled him in again, wrapping him up in the most wondrous feeling of love he had ever felt. "No question, Ari. I forgive you. I love you. You're everything to me."

"I never want to hurt you again."

"Neither do I."

But Ari knew that it was inevitable that as they grew within this new dynamic and learned more about each other, they could and probably would hurt each other's feelings again. It was just the nature of how vampires mated. The biological pull to mate with another didn't always allow for a lot of get-to-know-you up front. So, the newly mated pair oftentimes had to figure shit out as they went. There would be a lot of trial-and-error, but the mating link would never sever and they would always be bound to each other, no matter what happened.

SEV HARDLY DARED TO BREATHE or make a sound. All he could do was stare in awe at Ari. Finally, Ari had acknowledged what Sev had suspected all along. Ari felt it, too. He felt the link growing between them, binding them together. Sure, he had known it would only be a matter of time before Ari realized they were mates, but he hadn't expected it to happen so soon. And certainly not like this.

"Say it again?" A smile spread over Sev's face.

"What? That I never want to hurt you?" Ari grinned quizzically at him.

Sev laughed shortly. "No. That you're my mate."

Ari chuckled at him. "You're so goofy."

"Just say it." Sev leaned closer, smiling from ear to ear. "Please."

The corners of Ari's mouth turned up as he rolled his eyes. "I've mated you, you big oaf." His gaze grew tender. "And I love you." Ari's eyes ranged over his face, down to his chest, his hands, then back up to his eyes. It looked almost as if

Ari still couldn't believe it himself and was seeing Sev with brand new eyes. "You're my mate, and I love you."

"Am I crazy for loving how that sounds coming out of your mouth?"

Ari shook his head. "No. Because I love how it sounds coming out of my mouth, too."

Oh, God. Just the way Ari said it, along with the look on his face as he did, set Sev's insides on fire. Finally, it had happened. He had found his soul mate, and he had been found, as well. Some vampires went their whole lives without finding their mate. But that wouldn't be him.

"I love you so much, Ari." Sev caressed Ari's cheek.

What would their teammates think if they could see them huddled together on the floor of his foyer, declaring their love for one another? Not that he cared, but he sort of liked the idea of showing Ari off. He wanted to walk in to AKM tomorrow, hand-in-hand with Ari. He wanted to kiss him in front of the team before they left for their separate patrols. Then kiss him again as they met back up after their shift.

But until Ari was able to open up and come clean with everyone else, that was a fantasy that would remain just that. A fantasy.

CHAPTER 15

SEV TWIRLED SPAGHETTI ON HIS FORK then held it out for Ari. They were sitting on bar stools at the kitchen counter, facing each other. Sev had his ankles crossed around one of Ari's as if he were loosely restraining him.

"This is excellent sauce." Ari leaned forward and took the forkful of offered food.

Sev was enjoying feeding him. And it was clear Ari enjoyed it, too, as he offered Sev his own forkful of spaghetti. Sev accepted it and pulled the pasta into his mouth.

This was how it had been for the past twenty minutes after they had finally pulled each other up from the floor and made their way to the kitchen. Sev hadn't wanted to continue thinking about Ari's hesitation to open up to the others about his sexuality. He only wanted to enjoy the day with his mate.

Sev dabbed his napkin against his lips. "Do you have questions?"

Ari's topaz eyes sparkled. "A few, but they can wait."

Apparently Ari was enjoying their intimate dinner too much to want to dwell on the issue that had briefly separated them. All in good time, Sev supposed.

Sev lifted his wine glass and held it out for Ari, who leaned forward and sipped as Sev tilted it for him.

"Are you always this romantic?" Ari smiled and licked wine off his upper lip as he sat back.

"Here, let me get that." Sev leaned forward and kissed him, letting his tongue sweep out and run the length of Ari's lips. Then he leaned back with a crooked, self-assured grin on his face. "And, yes, I am." He picked up his fork again and twirled more spaghetti around the tines.

"Well, aren't I the lucky one then?" The smile on Ari's face was filled with warmth and wonder, and it made Sev fall in love with him just a little bit more.

He held out another bite of food for Ari and caressed the back of his fingers down Ari's neck and chest as he took it. "No, I'm the lucky one, babe." He gazed into those marvelous eyes and shook his head affectionately. "You make me want to be this romantic."

Ari set down his fork as Sev did likewise, and they took each other's hands and huddled a little closer together, barely seated on their respective stools.

"When I left earlier," Ari said, "the ache I felt was unlike anything I've ever experienced."

Sev knew what he meant. He had felt it, too. The *suffering* had gripped him fiercely after had Ari rushed out the door and driven off. Sev had never known such horrible pain.

Ari lowered his head and looked at their joined hands. "That's when I realized what was happening between us. The *suffering* was what woke me up and made me realize we were mates." He paused. "How is this going to work, Sev?"

Sev stroked his thumb over the back of Ari's hand. "We'll figure it out."

"But the *calling*...." Ari looked up. "Even now, I want you. I'm hard for you. I've been hard for you for days, and it's only getting worse."

Sev understood his concern. He had been hard since Ari had returned. His body demanded contact and release. It was the way of things with a newly mated male. The *calling* moved in, made itself at home, and forced the male to fuck often and hard for at least a week...usually two. It was why newly mated males had to take time off from work and just about everything else. They couldn't be far from their mates during the *calling* phase, because when the urge hit to plant his seeds, he had to be able to answer. Immediately.

"We'll work it out," Sev said. "We'll find a way."

"It will be harder for us, you know." Ari looked tense and concerned.

"I know."

"The *calling* is stronger when two males mate." It sounded like Ari was talking more to himself than to Sev.

"I know." Sev tried to reassure him. "But we'll make it work."

But it would be tough. Ari was right. Two males who mated each other had extremely powerful *calling* phases, because not only were they answering the call of their own bodies, they were also responding to the call of their mate. The effect was a compounded kind of need that multiplied exponentially.

In a heterosexual *calling* phase, the female reacted to the male, feeling aroused and receptive, but she didn't have to also wrestle with her own body's demands to mate. The male sent the message, she received it, and then she replied.

On the other hand, with two males, they were both sending, receiving, and replying simultaneously. The effect was almost supernatural.

Even now, Sev felt his body responding to the invisible waves of heat pouring off Ari. He imagined the same was happening to Ari. It made for a volatile environment.

Put up the breakables. This could get physical.

"Are you worried?" Sev squeezed Ari's hands.

Ari nodded as he looked up. "Yes."

"Why?"

"What if we aren't together when we need each other?"

Sev shrugged. "You might have to tell Tristan what's going on between us."

Ari visibly trembled. Sev felt the tremor in his hands. The thought of telling someone that he was gay and that he and Sev were mates obviously terrified him. Sev had to feel for the guy.

"Don't get me wrong, Sev. I want to. I want to tell him. But I'm scared as hell."

"I know. Believe me, I know. I want to tell him I'm half dreck, but I'm afraid he'll kick me off the team."

Ari chuffed then broke into outright laughter. "We are so perfect for each other."

Sev loved the sound of Ari laughing, and he adored the way his face shone as he did.

"How do you figure?" He smiled uncontrollably.

"Well, look at us. Both with secrets. Both scared to tell anyone about them."

"Well, you've told me." Sev dipped his head down and lifted Ari's hand to his mouth to kiss the back of it. "And I'm someone."

Ari's face flushed and he sighed. "Well, yeah. That you are. A very important someone, so it seems." He scooted a little closer. "And now I know your secret, too."

"And you're someone very special to me."

"Maybe for now it's enough that we know even though nobody else does."

Sev nodded. "We can figure out how to tell the others later."

"No one else needs to know you're dreck, Sev." Ari's voice grew concerned as he linked his fingers around Sev's. He looked down, appearing guilty.

"But they need to know we're mates. That's what you're thinking, right?"

Ari met his gaze and nodded. "Yes."

"And eventually they will. Because you know we won't be able to hide it forever."

It was hard for a male to keep it a secret once he had mated. Look at Micah, for Chrissake. You couldn't get five feet from Sam without him getting in your grill and puffing up his chest like Sam was his property, and no one could lay a hand on her without his permission. That's how it was. The motto was, touch a male vampire's mate, and it was the same as touching the male vampire. So, best touch carefully or not at all. And the first time a female came on to Ari in public, Sev wouldn't hesitate to go all he's-mine-bitch on her ass. And, oh yeah, that would definitely let the cat out of the bag, wouldn't it?

Ari sighed again. "I know. Just the thought of seeing someone touch you makes me want to bite you and stake my claim."

Fire shot through Sev's loins at the visual image, and he actually growled in approval. Ari sucked in his breath in response, and he looked positively glorious with arousal.

"I was just thinking the same thing," Sev said.

The heat between them suddenly ramped up a thousand notches. The *calling* gripped them full force and in a blink, they were off their bar stools and clamoring to get through each other's clothes to the skin beneath.

The fucking was hard, fast, and furious as Ari bent Sev over the counter and claimed him. And it was perfect. Utterly perfect, even as rough as Ari was with him. And after Ari had spilled his seed, Sev pushed away, spun around, lifted Ari up and slammed him against the wall as he impaled him. In a matter of minutes, it was over, leaving them both breathless and spent as Ari clung to Sev with both his arms and his legs, their bodies covered in perspiration, and their lungs pumping hard as they quivered and panted against one another.

"My God, Sev...."

Sev could only tighten his hold on his mate as he purred against his throat. Making love to Ari was beyond incredible, even when the loving was hasty and frantic.

After recovering, they took turns in the bathroom to clean up, making secret, sexy eyes at each other as they passed in the hall. Then they got dressed and poured two fresh glasses of wine.

"Come on," Sev said, "I owe you some answers. Let's talk." Sexually sated for the time being, it was time to clear the air.

Ari took his hand, and he led him to the living room couch, where they sat down facing each other on either end so their legs wove together and alternated Ari's, his, Ari's, his.

Sev settled back, still in awe that he and Ari had come to this new place in their relationship.

"Remember when you and I met?" he said fondly, not quite ready to face the music about his dreck lineage.

Ari grinned, obviously remembering. "Uh-huh."

It had been the day of his interview with Tristan. He'd

passed Arion just outside the door of Tristan's office as Ari and Io were on their way in for their nightly team meeting.

"I thought you were so sexy." Admitting it made Sev feel the butterflies all over again. "I couldn't take my eyes off you."

"And during our team meetings, I thought you were so quiet. You hardly ever spoke." Ari knocked their knees together playfully.

Sev sipped his wine then chuckled. "And then that night at Four Alarm...when you found out I was gay?"

Ari laughed. "Oh, yeah. I remember that."

"You should have seen the look on your face." Ari had looked deer-in-the-headlights surprised when Sev confirmed he was gay.

An introspective haze came over Ari's face. "That was the first night I really noticed you. As in, *really* noticed." He glanced down into his wine. "I started to suspect that night that I was gay, but I wasn't ready to admit it." He looked back up. "I had this urge to take you in back and..."

Sev perked up. "And what?"

With a blush, Ari huffed as if he couldn't believe where his thoughts had taken him that night. "Wow...I, uh...I wanted to fuck you silly that night, Sev."

"Really?"

"Hell, yeah."

Sev smiled to himself. "And here we are now."

"Yep." Ari lifted his wine glass in a toast. "Here's to all our secrets."

Sev raised his glass. "To all our secrets."

And speaking of which, it was time to spill the deets about the rest of his.

They sat quietly for a couple of minutes, Ari seeming to sense that Sev was getting ready to tell him all the sordid details.

Finally, Sev took a healthy drink, smiling tightly at Ari. Confession time.

"Okay. So, yes, I'm half dreck," he said out of the blue, getting the coming-clean conversation going. "My mom is dreck, my dad is vampire."

"And it scares you that the truth could come out." Ari settled back against a throw pillow as they covered territory already discussed earlier. It got them back into the flow of the conversation.

"Yes. I don't tell anyone. It's why I didn't even tell you."

Ari leaned forward and ran his hand over Sev's shin reassuringly. "I know. And I understand now."

He looked into his wine. "I'm afraid of how I'll be treated." He and Ari really did have more in common than he thought. So similar, and yet not.

"Do you think Tristan would really ask you to resign from your job?"

Sev looked back up and shrugged. "I don't know, but I worry about it, yeah. It's a concern. I mean, I don't show any favoritism to drecks just because I'm half one myself. But someone could easily infer it's a conflict of interest that my job is to maintain the peace."

Ari arched an eyebrow and tilted his head. "I can see that, but how about this: Our job is to maintain the truce. Who better to do that than one who represents both sides?"

"Hell, I never even considered that angle." Sev arched an eyebrow and grinned. "You sure you weren't meant for politics, babe?"

Ari grinned and sat back once more. "Being around my father for so long, I can't help but think like that, but yeah, I'm sure I'm not cut out for politics."

"You're good at seeing the diplomatic side. You know that, right?"

"Well, you don't grow up around the life of a politician without picking up a few things."

Sev chuckled. "True."

"So, tell me about your mom. What's she like?"

"She's sweet. Not at all like what we come up against every night. And I can't remember the last time she shifted into her dreck form."

Ari grinned at him and sipped his wine.

Sev continued. "She's an artist. She owns an art gallery here in Chicago."

"Really? I'd like to see it sometime."

And Sev wanted Ari to see it. He wanted his mom to meet Ari, too. He would be the first person to meet his mom and know who she really was.

"You know, I've never been able to tell anyone she's my mother." Sev looked down again briefly then met Ari's eyes once more. "I've always had to keep her a secret because of who she is. It'll be really nice to introduce her to someone as, 'this is my mom.'"

Ari's warm smile touched his soul. The universe had chosen a pure heart for his mate. Ari was good for him, and in that moment he knew he would never feel thankful enough to express in words his gratitude over Fate's selection for him.

"What about your father? Are he and your mother still together?"

Severin bristled and shook his head curtly. "No. I hate my father for what he did."

"What do you mean?"

Ari sat back and listened as Sev told him about how his father had raped his mother then bailed, leaving his mom to hide her pregnancy from everyone so she could keep him safe.

Sev paused then gave Ari a grave look. "Remember when we went to Jackson's apartment looking for Micah last month? Remember how edgy I was?"

Ari nodded. "Yes, I remember. We talked later and you told me it was because you had lost someone once."

Sev glanced at the glass of wine cradled in his hands. "Yes, that was part of it, but part of my anger over that situation also had to do with what my father did to my mom. She was innocent, and he used her and split, leaving her pregnant with me. What Jackson did to Micah, just walking away and dumping him the way he did, pissed me off. Reminded me of my dad. But, like I said, that's only part of it."

"What's the other part?" Ari sipped his wine and squeezed one of Sev's legs between both of his as if sending him encouragement.

Sev smiled at the gentle gesture. "The part about how I

had lost someone once? Well, I had a boyfriend just over a year ago. We had dated for several months."

Ari stiffened, an automatic reaction of the newly mated link between them.

"Don't worry, babe, we weren't mates. But I did love him. I won't lie about that."

Ari cleared his throat and fidgeted. "Was he a vampire?"

"Yes."

"What happened to him?"

"Gabe was killed in a raid. He was an enforcer in Atlanta while I worked as an agent with VDA."

"You were with Vampire Dreck Affairs?" Ari sounded impressed.

Sev nodded. "Yep, but my commander, Jonas, disavowed me after an AKM raid at a cobalt factory went way wrong. See, I was deep cover and Jonas and Gabe had been lovers before I came along. Gabe had split up with him when he realized Jonas was forming a bond. Gabe didn't feel that way toward him. It wasn't a strong bond, but Gabe didn't want to risk it. Anyway, Jonas sent me into that factory when no agents were supposed to be there. He knew enforcers were going to raid it. He knew Gabe was going to be involved in that raid."

Ari watched him quietly, his fingers playing over his glass.

"At any rate, my thinking is that Jonas wanted to get rid of me. He blamed me for taking Gabe away from him even though I didn't come along until months after they broke up. But his plan backfired. Two kingpins decided to pay the factory a visit for product that night. They were passing through or some shit and took a chance. I don't know. I wasn't involved in that side of it and shit went down before I could find out. Anyway, these guys brought their personal cavalcade of bodyguards with them. If you think what we pull off the streets of Chicago is bad, these guys were like Hell's Angels compared to guys on Schwinn ten-speeds. Top notch firepower. Body armor. The whole nine."

Sev paused to take a deep breath. The memory was still hard to talk about.

"What happened, Sev?" Ari leaned forward and placed his hand over his.

Their eyes met, and Sev bit back his emotion. "Gabe and the other enforcers busted in. They were terribly outnumbered. I hadn't known about the raid, either. Gabe and I never discussed certain aspects of our work with each other. He didn't even know I was a VDA agent. My cover was so deep, I hadn't been allowed to tell him. I mean, listening to him talk about my boss when I had to pretend I didn't know him was brutal. So anyway, the enforcers busted in, the second coming of God let loose, and Gabe was shot. I couldn't get to him in time to save him, and then I had to split with the others so I didn't blow my cover." Sev's face screwed up as he struggled not to break down. "If I could go back, I'd do it all differently. I would blow my cover in an instant if it meant I could save him."

God love Ari. He sat quietly by to let Sev work through the pain before going on.

After he composed himself again, he continued. "I returned to the factory as quickly as I could, and when I got there, Gabe's sister—she was an enforcer, too, named Gina—was cradling Gabe's head on her lap. It was obvious he had just died. I went inside and she turned on me. I don't know what happened or what was said between them, but it wasn't hard to figure out. Gabe thought I had betrayed him, and his sister had dug into his mind to get his memories of what had happened.

"She took one look at me and I could tell she thought I had murdered her brother. She shot at me—and I'll tell you about that in a minute." Sev didn't want to go into his iron skin just yet. He wanted to get this part out first. "But finally I got her to call in to confirm I was VDA, but Jonas denied I was an agent." Sev looked away and shook his head. "Can you believe that shit? He actually lied and told them I had never been an agent." He huffed sarcastically. "Jonas relayed back the message that he had no knowledge of me working for VDA. That's when I knew I'd been thrown under the bus." He paused and huffed again. "Not only had Gabe died thinking I had betrayed him and lied to him the whole time we were together, but then my job was stripped out from under me, too."

"Shit." Ari's expression was a mix of disbelief and compassion.

"Jonas killed himself a few days after Gabe's funeral." Sev paused then said, "And I think Gina is hunting down everyone involved in Gabe's death. I've been keeping tabs. One-by-one, they're all mysteriously dying."

"Do you think she'll come for you?"

"Probably."

"So, how the hell did you escape without her killing you in that factory? Sounds like that would have been the perfect opportunity if she wanted to kill you."

"Are you ready to be freaked out, Ari?"

Ari gave him a look. "I think your dreck blood freaked me out enough for one evening, wouldn't you agree?"

"Oh, you have no idea."

"Shit. Seriously?" Ari groaned. "Okay, well, if you're going to blow my mind, you might as well blow it all the way out. Let's have it."

"Do you still have your knife on you?" He had seen it earlier when they had been eagerly undressing each other.

"Sure, why?"

"Take it out."

It was time to come one hundred percent clean with his mate. Once he shared this with him, Ari would know more about him than anyone other than his mother. He would know more than Gabe had, and there would be no more secrets between them.

Ari sat up and reached behind him, lifted his shirt, and pulled a short, flat knife from the waist of his pants. He extended it to Sev, who took it and made a small cut on his arm and handed it back. "See that?" He held up his arm to show Ari the blood.

Ari looked confused, but nodded. "Sure, I see it. So?"

He licked his arm so his venom could heal the cut. "Okay, now try to stab me."

"Fuck you! I'm not going to stab you!"

"Just do it."

"No!"

"Trust me, Ari. Stab me."

Ari shook his head and looked at Sev as if he were insane.

"For Pete's sake!" Sev grabbed the knife and plunged it toward his belly.

Ari yelled and jumped up. "Fuck, Sev! Are you okay? Shit! Hold on. I'll get a towel. Do you have a first aid kit?" Then he stopped and looked again as Sev held the knife toward him.

The tip of the blade was bent as if it had impacted an iron wall. The point had even snapped off.

"What the…? How did you…?" Ari looked up at him then down at his stomach before bending and inspecting where the blade had sliced through Sev's shirt. There was no blood.

"It seems my mom gave me the gift of iron skin." Sev lifted his shirt so Ari could inspect him more closely.

"No shit." Ari ran his hand over the uninjured ridges of his abdomen and sat down next to him. "But you cut yourself. Your arm. I saw you."

"I can turn it on and off at will, babe." He placed his hand over Ari's on his stomach.

"Wow. So that's how you've been able to fight in so many wars without being killed."

"Like I said before. I was made to fight. I was born with the heart of a warrior then discovered I had the body to match."

Ari turned his hand over under Sev's and wove their fingers together. "I'm almost envious."

"Why?" Sev squeezed Ari's hand.

"Because your life was all figured out right from the start."

"So was yours, babe. You just let other people fuck around with it so much that you forgot what you wanted." He reached up with his free hand and caressed Ari's cheek.

"Well, I'm starting to remember what that is." Ari dipped his face into Sev's palm, closing his eyes.

The simple gesture dissolved something deep inside Sev's soul, liquefying every ounce of hardness he possessed, affecting him in an almost mystical way. In that moment, he realized he literally held his life in the palm of his hand. Ari was his life, his very reason for existing. He gently stroked his thumb over Ari's eyelid, feeling his long lashes brush over his skin. The tip of his thumb outlined Ari's thick, dark eyebrow.

"I love you, Arion."

Ari turned his face into Sev's palm and kissed it. He held his mouth against the concave dip in the center for several seconds then pulled away. "I love you, too. I'm sorry about how I reacted earlier."

"It's okay, babe. I should have told you sooner. I was a big chicken." He made clucking noises and Ari chuckled.

Their eyes met and Ari slid up next to Sev. "It doesn't change how I feel about you. I think you know that. I feel better about it, knowing the truth."

Sev's lips met his for a tender kiss. "Is there anything else you want to know about me, babe? Anything I haven't covered that your inquiring mind needs to know?"

Ari shook his head and their noses rubbed together. "No, but you owe me a new knife."

Sev chuffed and pulled Ari a little closer as the other male's fingers worked at the fastenings on Sev's jeans.

Mmmm, yes. The *calling* was making itself known again, and Sev needed to feel his mate once more.

"Shit, babe, I owe myself a new shirt. How good are you at sewing?" His tone was teasing as he sank back and let Ari undo his fly.

Ari smiled against his mouth, causing Sev to kiss his teeth instead of his lips. "I suck at sewing." Sev's belt jingled as Ari pushed it aside and lowered his zipper so he could wrap his hand around the hardening length inside.

"Mmm." Sev shifted and blinked heavily then rolled his head back. "But you're good at other stuff."

Stroke-stroke-stroke.

"Such as?"

Sev moaned, his body tensing. "Turning me on. You're excellent at turning me on."

Ari's lips trailed over his jaw and down his neck then back

up. "That's just the newly mated male in you. You know how we males get after claiming a mate."

Ari's hand felt so good on him. Perfect.

"Maybe, but no…it's you. God, it's you. You know how to touch me."

"That's because we were made for each other." Ari's mouth brushed over his, then down his chin and across his jaw.

Stroke-stroke.

"Oh God, babe. You're driving me crazy."

Ari's hand increased tempo and Sev thought he would lose it. The night had been an up and down roller coaster ride, but the day looked like it was shaping up to be anything but.

"Is that iron skin of yours turned off, or whatever you call it?" Ari's voice was muffled against Sev's neck.

"Uh-huh. Why?" He thrust his hips into Ari's hand.

"Just didn't want to break a tooth." With that, Ari sank his teeth into his neck and euphoric bliss flooded him again. This time, Ari didn't release his neck until Sev's orgasm pounded through him, the euphoria of Ari's venom prolonging and intensifying his release unlike anything he had ever felt.

He had a feeling the day would be filled with more than one encore. They were newly mated males, after all. It would take a crowbar to pry their hands off each other.

CHAPTER 16

WHEN GINA WOKE UP AN HOUR BEFORE SUNDOWN, she stretched and turned into Lakota's warm, naked body.

Whoa. Wait a second. How had this happened?

Oh yeah, she had slept with him. As in, they hadn't actually slept until after she had ridden him like a rodeo cowgirl and he was the bucking bronco. And buck he could. If all bartenders got this lucky after listening to a guy or girl pour their heart out as Lakota had last night, she imagined bars wouldn't have any trouble filling the position.

She hadn't intended on sleeping with him. It just sort of happened. She had kept his water glass full, and her glass full of Vodka and juice, and had sat for two hours as he spilled his world into her lap. He told her about his deceased wife, his children, the female dreck who was the mother of his son, Severin, but he didn't know much about Severin himself because Sev refused to see him.

He had seen him last night, though, while visiting Sev's mother, Felice. Shit, she knew she should have stayed at that house. But if Lakota turned into a dead end because of Sev's reluctance to see him, at least now she knew where Sev's mother lived. She would have to be careful about going that route, though. The truce between the vampires and drecks wouldn't look favorably on her if she hurt a dreck to get to a vampire, even if he was a mix.

By keeping her mouth closed and her ears open last night, Gina also learned that Lakota wanted desperately to reacquaint himself with Severin. He also knew that Sev worked at AKM as an enforcer and Lakota had told her he had designs on applying for a job there. A hundred different possibilities had rattled through her head about how she could use Lakota if he got hired on at AKM.

At any rate, after all his words had tumbled out, she had gone to him, climbed onto his lap, and pushed his sweater over his head without saying a word. He hadn't stopped her. Even when she removed her blouse and lifted his hands to her lace-covered breasts, he had let her continue, even though it took him a while to relax. He admitted that he hadn't been with a female since Mary had passed away.

She wanted to think she had only seduced him because of her objective to use him to get to Sev. By getting close to Lakota, she could eventually find a way to get close to Sev and kill him. But deep down, she knew that wasn't the reason. His story had touched her. He was hurting and she wanted to help him forget that hurt if just for a little while. Just as she needed to forget her hurt over Gabe's death. In that way, they had been there for each other last night. One pained soul comforting another.

Besides, he was attractive. And when he told her she was the first female he had let touch him intimately since Mary, she couldn't deny she had been excited. It boosted her ego to know he didn't sleep around and had chosen to be intimate with her.

She rubbed her eyes and smeared mascara on her finger. Great. She had gone to bed wearing makeup. After throwing him a cautious glance to make sure he hadn't awakened, she eased out of the bed and wrapped a robe around her naked body and tip-toed to the bathroom where she washed her face and hopped in the shower.

When she came out, he was still asleep, although he had rolled over and now sprawled on his stomach. She smiled and settled on the bed next to him.

Lakota groaned and stretched then scooted toward her.

"Good evening, sunshine," she said.

"Hey, you." He grinned sleepily and wrapped his arm around her waist.

"Would you like me to order room service?"

He moaned and sat up then tossed the sheet off before standing. Her gaze fell to the healthy weight of flesh between his legs, and she bit her lip, remembering just how well he had used that incredible tool with her.

He pulled on his boxers. "No, that's okay. I need to get ready to go to my daughter's house. She's making me dinner."

"Oh, that's right. You told me that."

Lakota slipped into his pants and pulled his sweater over his head. "Thanks for listening to me last night."

"Anytime. It was my pleasure. Really." *Really, it was.*

He seemed to get her meaning and smiled, a hint of darkness stroking his gaze. "Mine, too."

"Would you like to stop by and talk some more tonight when you get back from your daughter's?" The words came out before she could even stop herself, and she instantly wished she could take them back. She didn't need to get emotionally attached to the material. *Any* of the material. And Severin's father definitely counted as material.

"I'm not sure I can tonight. I haven't seen Marie in ages, so I probably won't get back until close to sunrise.

She breathed an inward sigh of relief. "Well, that's okay. I've got things to do, anyway."

"How about tomorrow night? I would like to see you again."

"Sure. Tomorrow night would be great." She reminded herself she just needed to use him long enough to get to Sev, or until she was able to kill Sev some other way. Then she could split and never see him again.

She could do that. Yes, she could. Uh-huh.

CHAPTER 17

ARION AWOKE TO THE SOFT SOUNDS of piano music, lilting and warm, like an embrace for the senses. He was lying on his back with his arm crooked at the elbow and resting on the pillow next to his head. Gentle light washed over him, and he realized he was alone in the bed.

"Sev?" His voice was froggy with sleep. He lifted himself on his elbows and squinted against the light then saw Sev peeking out from behind a canvas on an easel. "What are you doing?"

"Painting you." Sev's gaze scrutinized him then returned to the canvas.

"Can I see?" No one had ever painted his portrait before.

"Not yet. I'm almost done, though."

Ari stretched and turned to look for the source of the piano music and found the sound system in the corner. "What's this music?" He wiped one hand over his eyes, trying to work out the sleep.

Sev peered around the canvas again. "The soundtrack from a movie called *Unfaithful*."

Unfaithful? Ari grinned sardonically. "I hope you're not trying to tell me something."

"What do you mean?"

"The title. *Unfaithful*." He raised an eyebrow and his smile widened at the way Sev looked at him.

"Babe, you don't have to worry about whether or not I'll be faithful to you. I'm there." He winked then returned to his painting. "I just thought you'd like the soundtrack."

Ari settled back and listened. "It's lovely."

"I had a feeling you'd like it." Severin flashed him a smile. "Being my music man and all." Sev worked the brush over the canvas. "What instrument do you play, anyway? You never told me the other night."

Ari lay back down and nestled into the pillow. "Piano. Guitar. Saxophone. Drums. Pretty much anything and everything, really."

"What's your favorite."

Ari thought about it a second. "That's a tough question." He enjoyed every instrument for different reasons, but he always seemed to gravitate back to a couple. "Probably the piano and the guitar."

"Why?" Sev continued to paint as they talked.

Ari watched Sev. He admired his sleek body, long muscles, and broad shoulders. He didn't look like someone who should be painting. His blond hair was hanging down over his face and Sev reached up and tucked it behind his ear, leaving a streak of blue and red across his temple.

"You're damn sexy," he said.

Sev halted in midstroke and darted his eyes to Ari's before a pleased smile popped up on his face. His cheeks colored.

"Look at that. I made you blush." Ari chuckled. "By the way, you've got a little paint on your face."

Sev screwed his mouth up in mock-contempt and flipped Ari off then laughed.

The moment was easy and playful, which was something he wasn't used to feeling after having sex with someone. He loved this intimacy with Sev. He had never had that with anyone, and the atmosphere was calm and lighthearted.

Sev returned to painting. "So?"

"So, what?"

"Why are the piano and guitar your favorite instruments?"

Oh, that's right. Sev had asked him that before he'd become distracted by his sexiness.

"I think I like the feel of the guitar strings against my fingers," he said. "And the piano keys just beg to be touched. Don't you agree? I mean, even if someone can't play, they're drawn to peck on the keys, anyway. You ever notice that?"

Sev considered his words a moment then nodded. "Yeah, actually. I have."

"Can you imagine the allure a piano has over someone like me, then? Someone who actually knows how to play? I don't know, but the piano just draws me to it."

"I can tell I'm going to have to buy a piano, aren't I?" Sev scrutinized the painting then dabbed his brush into a dollop of red and blue paint.

"I can bring my own." Ari glanced down nervously. Were they talking about him moving in? Already? He had to admit, he liked the idea.

"When are you moving in?" Sev turned and looked at him dead on, as if he had been reading Ari's mind.

"We should probably discuss that."

"Yes, I think we'll have to." The hint of a smile touched Sev's lips, and he turned back to his painting. "After you tell your parents about us."

Sev made a valid point. They both knew how scared he was to tell his parents about his homosexuality, and he certainly couldn't move in until he had come out of the closet. Ari nodded to himself then cleared his throat, thinking this would be a good time for a change of topic before things got too serious.

"So, are you coming to my parents' party?"

Ari had mentioned his dad's party to Sev earlier only to find out that Tristan had already told him about it.

"I don't know. It might be hard being there with you when I can't show you off as my guy."

Ari laid back down and fluffed the pillow under his head. "Well, I was thinking…" He paused as he considered his words. "Maybe I should just come out, you know? Maybe I should just tell my parents at the party that you're my mate and be done with it."

Even as he said it, he wondered if he would have the courage to follow through, but damn it, he didn't want to keep Sev a secret forever…and he wanted to be with him. He wanted to live with him the way it should be between mates. The six weeks wasted since that first encounter were bad enough to stomach, but to hide the greatest thing that had ever happened in his life felt completely wrong. And he had hated how it felt to hurt Sev last night. Now that it was clear they were mates, he knew sooner or later he would have to come clean. Might as well make it sooner.

"Are you serious, Ari?"

He glanced up to find Sev had set his brush down and stepped out from behind the canvas. He approached the bed, staring at him. Splashes of paint dotted and streaked his torso and flannel pajama bottoms.

"I think so. I don't want to keep you a secret, Sev, but I'm scared to death, to tell you the truth. I don't know how my father will react."

Sev crawled into the bed and kissed Ari. "I'll be there with you, babe. I'll help you."

But Sev didn't know his father. Gregos could be an intimidating male. "Okay. Good, because I'll need you." The party was in two nights. Was that enough time to build the backbone he would need to stand up to his father?

"Is my painting done, yet?" Ari nodded toward the abandoned canvas.

Sev chuckled and kissed him again then pushed back and returned to the canvas then picked it up and turned it around to show him. His image stared back at him. He sat up and moved closer to look at it.

"Wow. When you told me you painted, I didn't know you meant like this?"

"Like how?" Sev turned the easel around and placed the canvas back on it then joined Ari on the bed and took hold of his hand.

"Like...I don't know, like an artist." He laughed, unable to get over how perfect the painting was. "How long have you been up?"

"A couple of hours."

"You did all that in a couple of hours?"

Sev nodded. "Yep. Not my best work, and it's not quite finished, yet, but that's pretty much how I see you."

Ari could feel the love in the portrait and it filled him with happiness. This was what he had been missing all his life. Love, joy, warmth, compassion, understanding.

"I love you, Sev." He didn't think he could say those words enough. It felt good to finally find someone he could say them to.

"I love you, too, babe."

And to find someone who would say them back.

They sat hand-in-hand for several minutes, listening to the music and gazing at Sev's work. Finally, Sev leaned over and kissed his cheek. "Come on. We're going to be late."

Ari didn't want to go to work tonight, and he didn't want to go tomorrow, or the next night, or the one after that. He wanted to write and play music, maybe even teach it. He didn't want to patrol the streets, anymore, or arrest drecks and break up fights or stop drug deals. Something about being with Sev and learning who he was made him want to embrace the entire package, not just one part of it. Fine, he acknowledged now that he was gay. Now it was time to acknowledge he didn't want to follow in his father's footsteps. He didn't want to be an enforcer and never had. He wanted to be a musician.

"Ari?" Sev squeezed his hand. "You okay, babe?"

"I am when I'm with you." He turned and looked into those pale blue eyes of Sev's. "Come on. Let's go. The sooner we get there, the sooner we can leave and come home."

"Come home?" Sev's eyes twinkled and the corners of his mouth perked up.

"Yeah, come home. I like it here, Sev. This feels like home to me." For the first time in his life, he felt like he was right where he was supposed to be. Now if he could just face his father, he could make it official and actually move in.

CHAPTER 18

THE FOLLOWING NIGHT, Lakota awoke determined to make amends with Severin. He had already made the decision to move to Chicago to be near his daughter, and it was time he returned to work—real work. During his forty-two-year marriage to Mary, he had worked as a night security guard at various places, a job he quit when she died six years ago. Since then he hadn't worked at all, and it was time to get back to what he did best: enforcing. Especially now that he felt he could handle himself better and no longer go off half-cocked in the face of the enemy.

He sat down in front of his laptop and typed in the necessary information to get him to the local AKM site, which fronted as a security detail. But that was just for show for the humans. Vampires knew the real purpose of AKM.

The website was set up like any other, with menu options for About Us, Our Clients, Contact Us, and the one Lakota was looking for, Career Opportunities. He clicked the link and a screen opened with available positions. Of course, everything was coded to appear human-friendly, and like most AKM facilities, they probably did have humans who worked in a separate part of the facility from the vampires. Administrators, daytime security guards, drivers, and the like.

He browsed the open positions. There wasn't much, but there was a listing for security guards. That could mean any number of positions, but most likely it meant enforcers, especially because the job reference number contained the string of characters Lakota knew meant this was a vampire opportunity.

He called the phone number referenced for the position and sat back, waiting for an answer, but got voicemail. Of course. They had to weed out the riff-raff somehow.

Thank you for calling AKM Security. At the tone, please leave your name, contact information, and the reference number for the job you are inquiring about and someone will contact you as soon as possible. No doubt humans thought this was an odd method for gaining information from candidates, but to vampires, especially those who had worked at AKM before, this was perfectly normal.

Beep.

"Lakota Bannon, job reference number V-nine-two-two-six." The V had not been part of the original code, but this was the way a vampire told them he was, in fact, a vampire. He rattled off his phone number then paused before adding, "I have previous experience."

He hung up. All he could do now was wait for them to call him back.

After ordering room service, he was about to hop in the shower when his phone rang. He glanced at the ID *AKM Security.* Shit, that was fast. Not even five minutes had passed.

"Hello?"

"Yes, Mr. Bannon?" The voice on the other end was deep and gruff, a true soldier.

"Yes."

"My name is Stryker. Your message was just forwarded to me. You have previous experience as an enforcer?"

"Yes, sir. I do."

"When and where?"

"Europe and England in the late 1700s and 1800s, just all over. I was part of the King's Guard for about twenty years. Came to the States in 1887 when he relocated, then branched out on my own in 1909 for a few years before helping found the New York division of AKM in 1913. I worked there until 1964."

"Impressive. Why did you quit in 1964?"

"I got married, sir."

"Oh? Was she human?"

"Yes, sir. How did you know?"

"I've seen this before. An enforcer leaves when he gets involved with a human, then returns after she dies."

Lakota winced at Stryker's bluntness, but he understood it. He had been like Stryker once. Worse, actually. He caressed the cross around his neck, remembering Mary. He would never return to the bastard he had been thanks to her, but he had a feeling some of his old ways would return once he got back to work. Not the bad old ways, but the ones that made him a strong enforcer and gave him the edge a soldier needed to make it in the streets.

"Yes, sir, my wife was human."

"Any kids?"

Vampire interviews didn't work like human ones. Questions about family weren't allowed in human interviews, but they weren't as off-limits in those for vampires.

"Yes, sir. One daughter and two sons." He didn't include Sev in this total.

There was a pause. "Okay, how about you come by tonight? Can you be here in two hours?"

"Yes, sir."

"Call me Stryker."

"Okay, Stryker. And you can call me Lakota or just Kota"

"Do you know how to get here, Kota?"

"I've got the address."

"Okay then, I'll see you in two."

"Thank you, Stryker. I'll be there." Lakota hung up and hit the shower. He had hoped to see Gina again tonight, but that would have to wait until later.

After showering and getting cleaned up, his dinner arrived and he quickly ate before heading down to his Suburban in the hotel parking garage. An hour-and-a-half after Stryker's phone call, Lakota was on his way.

AKM's offices were centrally located in the heart of the Loop, and he entered the main lobby to be greeted by a dark-haired, dark-eyed female. "Hello, can I help you?" Her eyes razed him up and down appraisingly.

"I have an appointment with Stryker," he said.

"You must be Lakota?"

"Yes."

She picked up her phone and punched a number. "Yes, Lakota's here to see you." She paused briefly then hung up. "He'll be right up."

Lakota glanced around the windowless lobby at the awards and pictures. All one big for-show to fool any humans wandering in off the streets.

"Kota. Hi, I'm Stryker."

Lakota spun around and clutched the large, outstretched hand coming at him. "That was fast." Not even a minute had passed since the receptionist had called back to him.

"I don't believe in wasting time, Kota."

Stryker was almost as tall as he was, with shoulders just as wide. A black buzz-cut topped his head and he looked and acted more like a Marine than a vampire in his fatigues and skin-tight navy blue T-shirt that showed off what looked like a magnificent pair of pecs.

"Follow me." Stryker spun on his heel and nodded curtly to the receptionist, who grinned slyly and glanced away.

It was clear she had the hots for Stryker, but while she had been easy enough to read, it was hard to tell whether the male returned the attraction.

"Thank you," Lakota said to the female as he rapped his knuckles on the counter.

"Certainly. Good luck." She smiled warmly then dropped her gaze back to a stack of mail she was opening, some embossed with King Bain's royal seal.

"This is the main hall," Stryker said, leading him through a set of double doors. "Dispatch is over there, break room, lockers, prep rooms, conference room, data center, war room." He pointed toward each as his giant strides ate up the hallway. "Over there's the training center – state of the art, by the way." Stryker quickly flexed an arm without looking back at him, and his biceps popped up like a softball—or maybe a small cantaloupe—for a split second before he lowered his arm. "Down that hall is the medical wing, and back that way are the elevators that lead to the dorms. You'll get a room of your own once you come on board. My team takes up the sixth floor. But don't get comfortable. The new facility in the burbs is almost finished. We'll be moving in a month or two."

"Wait? I'm in just like that? No interview?" Lakota was shocked it was that simple.

"With your credentials? Shit, you'll be running your own team before you know it." Stryker shoved open a door and held it for Lakota to enter. "This is my office."

Lakota stepped in and looked around. The space was small but adequate for a guy as big as Stryker, but the sparse walls and desk gave Lakota the impression that Stryker liked to keep things clean and simple. No clutter or personal distractions. He probably lived in a small, one-story house that contained nothing more than a bed, a chair, and a home gym.

"So," Stryker sat down and steepled his fingers in front of him as he plopped his elbows on the desk and leaned forward. "When can you start?"

"As soon as possible."

"Great. How does Monday sound?" Stryker sat back and slid the only file on the desk in front of him and opened it. Then he grabbed the simple, black ballpoint from the pocket of his shirt. The metal clasp snapped and Stryker's thumb click-clicked, and then he made a quick notation on the paperwork.

"Monday sounds good."

"We've got a Bannon on Tristan's team. Is that going to be a problem? I assume there's a reason you didn't volunteer your relationship to Severin?"

This guy was good. "No, sir, that won't be a problem. Not from my end."

"Good. I don't know what you two are to each other, and I don't give a shit, but it's clear you're related. Shit, you could almost pass for twins. But as long as there's no trouble, I don't care. Keep your secrets to yourself and your personal life out of your work, and we'll get along fine."

"Yes, sir."

"I told you on the phone to call me Stryker, goddamn it. I hate being called sir."

Lakota smiled. He could already tell he would like working with Stryker. He had the kind of edge and no-shit attitude that was just what he needed to get back in the game.

"What are you smiling at?" Stryker said.

"Nothing, *sir*." He emphasized sir. "Just that I think I'm going to like working with you."

Stryker started to grin but bit it back. "Yeah, well, I have a feeling I'm going to like working with you, too, shithead. But that won't stop me from busting your fangs if you call me sir again."

Lakota barked out a laugh. He already felt like he had known Stryker for years, what with all the ball-busting going on between them. "Okay, okay. Got it, Stryker."

"That's more like it." Stryker yanked open the top drawer of his desk.

Lakota imagined the inside was just as clean and orderly as the rest of his office.

"Here's your access card and key fob." Stryker wrote down the number on the back of each. "They'll be activated by Sunday night if you feel like coming in and meeting the team, but don't worry. We can do that Monday, too." He pulled out a set of keys. "These are keys to our vehicles. The prep lockers use combinations, but you can bring your own lock for the ones in the training center locker rooms. But I can tell you right now, no one steals shit around here because they know they'll answer to me if they do. And with all the mind-reading that goes on here, no one could hide a theft, anyway."

Lakota imagined that dealing with Stryker alone would be enough to scare anyone away from even stealing a Post-it Note. Stryker didn't seem like one to cross. "Gotcha."

Stryker stood abruptly, and Lakota got the feeling the guy was about to salute, but he simply held his hand out over his desk. Lakota stood then clasped and shook it.

"Welcome to the team, Kota."

"Thank you. You have no idea how excited I am about this." Finally, he would get back to work. He was itching to get his hands dirty again.

His new boss released his hand and strode to the door. "I'll remind you that you said that when you're ass-deep in cobalt dealers."

"Cobalt? Really?"

Stryker opened the door and led him out. "Yeah, we've got a real cobalt problem growing out of control here. It's why all the teams are being asked to add more manpower. It's also why we're outgrowing this place." Stryker swept his gaze around as if encompassing the entire building.

"Outgrowing it, huh?"

"Yep. That's why we're getting the new facility. Well, it's part of the reason why. It's bigger, more sophisticated and modern. State of the art, too. High-tech. Efficient. Partly underground. At least our part of it is. It'll sure be nice to dump this 70s motif and get into a space that will help us do our jobs better."

Yeah, it was clear that the building they were in had seen a few build-outs to make room for additional staff. It looked old, with generic tile floors, partitioned ceilings, and fluorescent lighting.

A few feet ahead, two males stepped out of one of the offices they had passed earlier.

Stryker barked out a greeting. "Tristan, hey, meet Lakota. He just came on." Stryker pulled up and clapped another massive male on the shoulder.

That must be Tristan.

"Lakota?" The other man with Tristan glanced at him and lifted his eyebrows.

"Gregos?" Lakota smiled and took the man's hand. "What a small world. Do you work here, too?"

He and Gregos had known each other as members of the king's personal guard a couple centuries ago.

Stryker and Tristan looked back and forth between them.

"No, I'm retired. My son, Arion, is on Tristan's team," Gregos said.

"Really?" Lakota glanced toward Tristan and shook his hand. "I'm Lakota Bannon."

Tristan's eyes narrowed and he glanced at Stryker curiously, but Stryker held up his hands. "I know. He looks like your boy, Sev, but I'm not prying and he assured me there's no problems."

Tristan didn't look convinced and Lakota got the feeling he wasn't as open as Stryker. Maybe a bit—or a lot—warier, too.

"So," Gregos said, "you're still enforcing?"

"I took some time off, but I'm ready to get back to it. What about you?"

"I still work for the king. I'm a liaison now. No one talks to the king directly, anymore. Everything goes through the liaisons and his consultants."

"Moving up in the world," Lakota said.

"That could have been you if you hadn't left, Kota."

"Eh, I was never the political type. You know that."

Yeah, Lakota had been far from the political type. They didn't usually allow barbaric animals to serve in office.

Stryker cut in to the conversation. "Can you find your way out, Kota? I need to get back to the data center. I'm running intel tonight."

"I can walk him out," Tristan said.

"Okay, I'll see you Monday night, Kota." Stryker nodded to Tristan and Gregos then spun on his heel and marched away, his combat boots thunking heavily on the tiled floor.

"So, what are you doing tomorrow night?" Gregos said as the three turned and began walking toward the exit.

Tomorrow was Saturday, and as far as he knew, the only plans he had would be with Gina if she agreed to see him. "Nothing, yet. Why?"

"It's St. Patrick's Day and I'm having a huge party at my home. We do it every year."

"What? Are you suddenly Irish?" Lakota laughed at him.

Gregos joined him. "Heavens no. I'm still Greek vampire through and through, but I do love a good excuse for a party."

Tristan nodded. "And he throws some of the best."

"I'll bet." Lakota remembered that Gregos always had excellent taste and flourished in social settings. A career in politics suited him so much better than it ever would have suited Lakota.

"How would you like to come?" Gregos said. "I'm sure Christa would love to see you, and you can meet my son, Arion. Christa and I have a surprise for him tomorrow night. It'll be a big evening for everyone."

"Who else will be there?" Lakota asked. He didn't want to be the odd man out in a room full of personal friends, and he hoped Sev might be there. It could give them an opportunity to at least talk.

"Everyone." Gregos arced his arm through the air with a flourish as if to include the entire world.

"My whole team will be there," added Tristan. "If you're worried about not knowing anyone, don't worry. My guys will make you feel at home because they won't know anyone else, either."

That confirmed Sev would be there.

"Can I bring a date?" Lakota wanted to invite Gina. He was really starting to like that female.

"Absolutely," Gregos said. "So, I'll put you down on the guest list with a plus-one then?"

Lakota thought about it for a second then nodded. "Sure. I'll go. Sounds like fun."

This was turning out to be a good night. He had gotten a job, bumped into an old friend, and now had a social engagement on his calendar that he could use to get to know Gina better, as well as his son if all went well, although that kid had a great right hook. He remembered the shot he had taken at Felice's and rubbed his chin.

"Excellent." Gregos pulled out a card. "This is my address. Arrive any time after ten o'clock. Party attire."

"What exactly is party attire?" Lakota said.

"Whatever you want it to be. Christa has provided green masks, hats, and all the typical St. Patrick's Day fare. It will be the event of the season."

They reached the double doors that led into the lobby. The receptionist looked up at them as they stepped through, and he smiled at her and rapped his knuckles on the counter as Gregos and Tristan said a few parting words to each other.

"I'll see you Monday," he said to her.

"Congratulations." She smiled warmly. "You'll like Stryker. He comes off brusque, but he's really a softy."

He winked. "I can tell."

She giggled, and he glanced back at the two males.

"Welcome to the team, Kota," Tristan said.

They shook hands all around then Tristan disappeared into the back as Gregos walked out with him. "It's good to see you again, Kota. Real good. You seem different. Good different."

"I am." He nodded and swept his gaze up and down the street out of habit. "I've only been in Chicago a few days and I already feel like I'm home."

"We'll need to get together for dinner one night next week so we can catch up."

"Absolutely."

"We'll set it up tomorrow at the party." Gregos chucked his shoulder and stepped around to the driver's side of a black and grey Bugatti and waved.

Lakota sized up the magnificent car, trying not to look too impressed, but he was. It was clear Gregos was doing well for himself. When you can plunk down two million dollars for a car, you had to be doing well.

"See you then." Lakota waited for the car's engine to roar to life just so he could hear it purr then he returned to his Suburban and headed back to the Trump.

Severin would be pissed at him for joining AKM, but that was his problem. Lakota had joined AKM for himself, not Sev. The two would have to find a way to work together, but being on different teams, that shouldn't be too hard. Then, maybe over time, Severin would get used to seeing Lakota and the two would eventually be able to proverbially kiss and make up.

Now, to more immediate needs. Before he returned to the hotel, he needed blood then he needed to see Gina. He couldn't get that beautiful female off his mind for some reason, even though his daughter had warned him during dinner last night that she wasn't what she appeared to be.

Marie hadn't elaborated, and Lakota didn't really care. Gina was the first female he had been attracted to since Mary, even though she really wasn't his usual type.

And, really, how dangerous could she be?

CHAPTER 19

GINA STAYED BEHIND LAKOTA, dematerializing and rematerializing at intervals as she followed his Suburban back toward the hotel. She had followed him tonight to see if he would lead her to Sev, but he had gone to AKM instead. Still, Sev worked at AKM. Maybe tomorrow?

He passed the turn-off for the Trump and continued until he came to Michigan and turned north toward the Magnificent Mile. What was he planning to do? Go shopping? His Suburban slowed and he turned west onto a side street, then north on Rush, then east back to Michigan.

He was trolling for blood. Gina could tell. Finally, he parked. Gina ducked into the shadows as he got out, shoved his hands into his coat pockets, and hoofed it up the sidewalk into a crowd. Gina stayed with the Suburban. He wouldn't be gone long.

Fifteen minutes later, he reappeared, walking down the sidewalk, licking his lips and wiping off his mouth as if he were paranoid he still had blood on his face. He got in his Suburban and started back toward the hotel.

She hurried up to her room and deposited her rifle case in the bottom drawer of her dresser and quickly changed into something that looked less military than the black-on-black she had worn to tail him. No doubt he would come pay her a visit. As long as she didn't end up in bed with him, maybe chatting with him would give her some insights into how to reach Sev? But seriously, she couldn't sleep with him tonight. No, no, no.

As she expected, a knock came on her door within minutes.

She opened up. "Lakota. This is a nice surprise. I thought you had decided to stand me up."

"I got a job," he said, stepping inside. He wrapped his arms around her as if he had been eager to see her.

Those strong arms picked her up and she found herself gazing hungrily into his blue eyes before glancing lower at full lips that were still rouged with blood.

"You fed." She pushed the door closed behind him. It closed with a satisfying click of the latch.

"Uh-huh." His body pressed against hers. "I got a job, I fed, I bumped into an old friend, and tomorrow night I'm going to a party." He pulled back slightly. "You want to go with me? Be my plus-one?" His expression read loud and clear that he hoped she would.

"A party?"

"Gregos Savakis's house. He's an old friend." Lakota nuzzled her neck, and her defenses began to crumble. He was sexy and knew just how to touch her to stoke her fire. "My son is supposed to be there."

Severin? Severin was going to be at the party?

"You mean...the one you told me about?"

"Uh-huh." He nibbled her neck and backed her toward the bed.

He really was persuasive.

"So? How about it?" He pulled away and burned her gaze with his. "Go with me?"

Oh, now how could she say no to that? "I'd love to go." She wrapped her arms around his wide shoulders and pulled him closer. "Will you try to talk to him, then? Your son?"

"I'd like to." He leaned down once more and licked her neck as he purred. Well, shit, didn't that just get her juices flowing and turn her all the way on. His hands started to tug up her shirt and she didn't stop him.

Lakota nibbled her nape. "Hopefully, it will be neutral enough ground that he won't punch me again."

"Of course he won't," she said, running her hands over his chest and back up over his shoulders. He was so tall compared to her. Like a lion compared to a house cat. "You feel good." The words came out unbidden.

"So do you."

His mouth found hers and that was all it took. Clothes flew off in record time and his hard, naked body crashed down over hers on the bed, sinking inside her in one smooth stroke. They both gasped and she gripped his shoulders as he bent and took her nipple in his mouth. She was so small compared to him that he had to practically bend like a pretzel to stay inside her and suck her breast at the same time, but it was worth it. Oh, God, it was worth it. His flicking tongue puckered her flesh and sent an erotic pulse straight to her clit.

"Yes, oh God, yes!"

Before she could stop herself she came.

She would kick herself later for falling back into bed with him, but oh, the sacrifices she made for her job.

CHAPTER 20

ARION TIGHTENED THE GREEN TIE around his neck then pulled on the charcoal grey suit jacket.

"Nice threads." Sev stepped out of the bathroom with a towel wrapped around his hips then pulled a pair of boxer briefs out of the top drawer of his dresser.

"It's kind of expected."

"What? That you need to wear a five-thousand-dollar suit to a party?"

Ari sighed. "Something like that."

Sev walked around the bed and slid his arms inside the jacket and around Ari's waist. "After tonight, you won't have to wear that shit unless you want to. I like you just fine in your jeans and T-shirts, babe." He kissed him and shrugged one shoulder indifferently. "Or out of them. I'm not picky."

They smiled at each other.

Ari had officially decided. Tonight was the night. He would come out, tell his father he was gay and that he was quitting his job as an enforcer. Over the past couple of days, he and Sev had talked it over. He would move in, provide music lessons out of their home—*their* home—and play at the local clubs whenever he could book gigs. He had friends at a few of the clubs, so he didn't think that would be too hard.

Hard was what the two of them had undergone the past couple of days. The nights at work were endless and painful for them both. They had both made masturbating an art form just to get through their shifts in one piece, and twice Malek had asked if he was okay. At the end of each night, the two had wasted no time flying out of there to get home and back in bed with one another. Sex had never felt so good, even if it did mean they were running on fumes from lack of sleep.

But all that would end tonight. This was it. Ari couldn't live like this, anymore, keeping secrets when he all he wanted to do was show Sev off to the world.

"I'm scared shitless. Look." He lifted his hand. It trembled. "I'm not even there, yet, and I'm already shaking."

Sev snagged his hand from the air and kissed it before giving it a squeeze. "I'll be there, and you'll be fine, babe. Just think, after tonight you won't have to hide, anymore, and you'll wake up in my arms every night and go to sleep inside them every morning. Won't it feel good to have everything out in the open?"

Sev was right. It would feel good. So why did it feel like he was waiting for the other shoe to drop? "Okay, okay. You've sold me." He checked the clock. "I've got to get. I'm supposed to be there already."

"I'll meet you there." Sev kissed him then pulled away. "I love you."

"I love you." Ari grabbed Sev for one more kiss. "I'll see you later."

He took the stairs two-at-a-time, opened the garage door, and hopped in his BMW. He grinned at how quickly his relationship had progressed with Sev, but that was how it worked between mates. It didn't take long for the bond to develop, and then they became inseparable and the next thing they knew, one was making a space in the garage for the other's car.

Ari thought back to that night in his kitchen last month. That was when the mating had really started. In hindsight, he knew that now, because he could see all the signs from the weeks that had followed before he and Sev had met up in the gym not even a week ago to change the course of their lives together. His body had made it clear he'd mated. The ache in his chest, the confusion and aggression, the moodiness. Those uncomfortable symptoms were side effects and signs of a formed bond that was angry he and Sev hadn't been together. From what Sev told him, he had experienced the same effects, except his moodiness had flown off the charts. Way worse than Ari's.

How had he been so blind? Well, not anymore. His eyes and his heart were wide open now. He was happy. God, he was so happy.

As he drove to his parents' home, he ticked off the plans he needed to make. He would need to sell his house—well, his parents would, since it was in their name—put in his notice at AKM, re-string his guitar, tune the piano, and put together a plan to market himself to the local families for lessons. Sev's house was large enough for him to dedicate an entire portion of the first floor to his piano lessons. He would teach humans in the afternoon while Sev could allow them in, and they would keep the drapes closed and explain that Ari was allergic to the sun. He could teach vampire students at night while Sev worked.

He had his life figured out now. All he needed to do was tell his parents. They were the hard ones. Once he got through telling them, coming out to everyone else would be easy. Well, Io would still be a challenge, but even Io wouldn't be as hard to come out to as his parents.

Ari pulled onto the long winding driveway of his parents' estate and drove up to the house. A few cars were already there. His father wouldn't be happy that he was late. Well, shit, he wouldn't be happy about a lot of things tonight, would he? So, in a way, he was just getting things started off on the right foot.

He parked and proceeded up the wide steps in front of the house. The doorman greeted him inside the foyer and waved him past—no need to check the guest list for his name—and he grabbed a glass of champagne from a tray and looked around.

"It's about time you got here." His mother, dressed in an elegant green gown, appeared from the sitting room and greeted him with a hug. "We were beginning to worry."

"Hi, Mom. Where's Dad."

She linked her arm around his and led him through the

main hall. "He's in the Great Room. Come on, let's go see him" She smiled and her eyes twinkled secretively.

"What is it?" he said.

"What's what?" She tried to sound innocent but failed.

"You're hiding something."

She waved her free hand then laid it over his arm. "You'll see."

Dinner music played through the home's audio system and the entire front hall was decked out in green. Green rugs, green curtains, green bulbs in the chandelier. A variety of green masquerade masks and hats, no two alike, lined a long table covered with a green tablecloth.

His mom picked up a hat and popped it on his head with a tinkling laugh. "Don't you look handsome?"

The way she said it caused the hair on the back of his neck to prickle.

"Um, look, Mom. I was hoping to have a word with you and Dad before the party."

"Certainly, this will just take a moment."

He didn't want to wait a moment. He wanted to get this over with as soon as possible, while he still had the courage to do so. That way, when Sev arrived, he could be by his side without worry. And if his parents kicked him out after he said what he had to say then he and Sev would find a party of their own somewhere else, just as long as they could be together.

Just then his father walked through the door on the far side of the room. He had a stately male with him, along with a tastefully coiffed blonde wearing a shimmering green sheath.

"Ah, there he is," his father said, seeing him.

The female's eyes turned toward him and she blushed.

Somehow this all just felt wrong. What was going on?

The five of them met in the middle of the room and his father shook his hand. "Son."

"Father."

His mom released his arm and stepped to his father's side.

"Arion, this is Ulrich Fenton. Ulrich is another of the king's liaisons. This is his daughter, Persephone. They only just moved back to Chicago a month ago after a year in Atlanta."

"Pleasure to meet you." He greeted them both, playing the dutiful part of a politician's son.

He was just about to remind his mother that he needed to speak to them when his father altered the course of the night.

"Arion, Ulrich and I have discussed it, and we both agree." He glanced toward Ulrich, who nodded and grinned approvingly. "We have arranged for you and Persephone to wed."

Thud. That was Ari's mouth hitting the floor, followed immediately by the abrupt silence as his heart stopped beating. In fact, his lungs had stopped working, too. Everything in Ari's realm of understanding seemed to come to a complete halt.

No one noticed, though, and the bad dream continued to unfold. His father went on as if nothing was wrong, even though it should have been obvious Arion was about to pass out…or maybe keel over and die.

"The ceremony is set to take place one month from today. Your mother has taken care of all the arrangements."

He glanced from his dad to Persephone then to Ulrich and back to his dad. His mom turned around and waved at someone on the second level. Suddenly, a banner—with green lettering, of course—unfolded from the railing. *Congratulations Arion and Persephone on your engagement!* The pertinent details of the ceremony—place, time, etc.—followed. He glanced back at his mom and dad in disbelief.

Suddenly, the soothing piano music playing in the background sounded like a death march. What had looked like festive green decorations now looked like something you would find at a funeral.

"Congratulations, Arion!" His mom hugged him. "This is your engagement party."

Arion was defeated. Trumped by his own parents. He could see the smug victory in their eyes. They had wanted him to take a mate for years, both growing more impatient with each passing week. So they had forced his hand, and at the worst possible time, because he had already taken a mate. But Sev wasn't the gender they wanted for their son, was he?

"Um. Mom? Dad? Can we talk privately?"

"Honey, Arion asked if he could speak to us before the party," his mom said to his dad, sounding as if she only just now remembered Ari's request.

"Yes, of course." His dad acknowledged Ulrich and Persephone then ushered Ari and his mom out of the room and into the library, where he shut the door.

Suddenly, the polite smiles on both their faces disappeared. He had known their performances in the great room had only been for show.

"You will not back out of this marriage," his father said before Ari could say anything.

His mom pursed her lips reprovingly. "Ari, it's time you settled and started a family. Enough of this pandering from woman to woman. Persephone is a worthy female, with strong bloodlines. She will give you political stature and, God willing, your children."

"I didn't realize arranged marriages still took place in the vampire community," Ari said, his voice quiet.

"You'd be surprised, Arion." His dad waved a hand. "It's quite common in the king's inner circle. This is normal."

No wonder few members of the king's council had children. Without mating, there was no *calling*, and without a *calling*, conception became rare. If many of those pairings had been arranged instead of naturally mated, it made sense why few children had been born to them.

Ari didn't have time to think about that now, though, because his own world was crashing down around him. He wanted to shout at them to go fuck themselves, but they had so successfully throttled him out of the blue, he only felt numbness. He couldn't make sense of his thoughts.

His father stepped forward and jutted his chin proudly. "If you have designs on getting out of this marriage, let me forewarn you that if you break this covenant Ulrich and I have formed, I will cut you off from the family fortune. I will repossess your car, take away your house, cut off your credit, and kick you out. It is your family duty to carry on our legacy and the family name. You have been unfit to do this on your own, so we have taken measures to ensure you fulfill your obligation."

And just like that, Ari knew he couldn't tell his parents about Sev. His life had never been his to live, had it? He would forever be held prisoner by the Savakis name, never to live the life he wanted for himself. Happiness wasn't something he would ever be allowed to have. What had he been thinking? Had he really thought he and Sev had a chance? A few days of bliss and that would make everything all right? Apparently, it didn't.

The fact that he and Sev had mated would be inconsequential in the eyes of his parents. He and Sev would have to keep their mating a secret and have an affair for them to remain together. That was the only way this would work. Arion felt his world crumbling around him, but he couldn't lose Sev. He reasoned that an affair would be enough. It would have to be enough.

What had started out to be such a perfect evening had now been reduced to shit.

"Now, what is it you wanted to talk to us about?" his mom said.

"Nothing." Because his life was nothing now. He had no life, only misery.

"Well then, get back out there to your fiancée. She's been dying to meet you." His father gave him a pat on the back.

"Yes, sir." Could his spine have been any more yellow? He felt like a chump. A sniveling, weak-ass chump. He wasn't good enough for Sev. Sev deserved a strong male, not some chicken-shit. And Ari would always be a chicken-shit.

His father opened the door, and once more their façade of happy, doting parents fell into place. "Congratulations, son."

His mother hugged him. "We're so happy for you."

Great. At least someone was happy. Arion just wanted to find a gun and put himself out of his misery.

CHAPTER 21

SEV STOPPED IN FRONT OF THE LONG DRIVEWAY that wound up to a house that was bigger than the entire AKM compound. Shit. He knew Ari's father was someone important, but this was over the top and not what he'd expected. The residence intimidated him, and money and fat cribs normally didn't intimidate Sev. No wonder Ari hadn't been able to get out from under his father's thumb all these years. Someone with that much money exuded a lot of power and influence. He imagined Ari felt he could never measure up.

Well, all that ended tonight. He drove his Challenger up the drive, parked and got out, passed his keys to the valet, and trotted up the steps.

"Last name?" A man behind a podium addressed him. He had a list in front of him.

"Bannon."

"Lakota?"

Sev frowned. What the hell was his father's name doing on the list? "No. Severin." He clipped his response, not caring that the man had called him Lakota by accident.

"Ah, yes, there you are. Enjoy your evening, sir." The man gave him a tight, apologetic smile, obviously aware he had inadvertently offended Sev.

Sev frowned as he walked away from the guy. How the hell had his father earned an invite to the party? Just as long as he didn't see him, there wouldn't be a problem. He wasn't in the mood for his dad right now.

The place was already crowded, but he only wanted to see one person. He needed to find his Ari.

He grabbed a glass of green beer and made his way through the crowds, stepping past groups of people, some of whom wore clothes worth more money than he made in a year. Too-heavy perfume assaulted his senses, making him cough as he wandered from the main hallway into the room where everyone else seemed to be congregating.

Green, green, green everywhere. Someone set a green hat on his head. He didn't know who, though.

"Isn't it wonderful?" someone else said.

"I can't believe he finally did it," said another.

"One of our most eligible bachelors, off the market." A female passed him on her way out, shaking her head at her friend.

"I know. And did you get a look at her dress? I wonder how much that frock cost her?"

What the hell were these people talking about?

He wandered farther into the room then turned, looking for Ari.

That was when he saw it. He almost dropped his beer when he read the sign announcing Ari's engagement to someone named Persephone. The room seemed to spin for a minute then his eyes landed on Ari. He stood behind the balustrade on the upper level that overlooked the room, his arm around the waist of a blonde Sev recognized. Who was she? He had seen her before, but where?

Ari's eyes were dull, his face almost vacant as he listened in on a conversation with the blonde and three other people. Her arm slid around Ari's waist and she nodded and tilted her head toward him affectionately and kissed his cheek. Ari glanced at her and smiled wanly.

Anger coiled up inside him. His mated side reared its head and he suddenly wanted to rip that female apart for touching his mate like that. He was about to roar up the stairs and do just that when someone gripped him hard from behind.

"Out. Now."

"Micah?" Sev was momentarily caught off guard.

Trace grabbed his other arm and the two males pushed him toward the door.

"Let me go," he said, trying to push them off.

"Shut up and fucking chill," Micah said, his voice quiet.

"Excuse us, please." Sam darted in front of them and made sure the path was clear.

"What are you doing? Leave me alone." Sev tried to pull away. He just wanted to go to his mate and pull that bitch off him.

Micah and Trace practically carried him out by his arms and rounded a corner into what looked like a library.

"In here." Sam waved them in and closed the door.

Only then did Micah and Trace let go of his arms.

He shoved off and snarled at them both. "Let me out. Let me go."

"No can do, Sev." Trace joined Sam by the door, arms crossed, making like a roadblock.

Sev needed to get back to his mate. His whole body ached and shivered, the pain growing and spreading. Finally he doubled over and gagged, landing on all fours. The pain—the pain was wretched, worse than the other night, shredding every ounce of dignity he had right there in front of his teammates and Micah's mate.

Sam rushed forward with a trash can and held it in front of Sev just in time to catch his dinner. He retched then retched some more, hugging the can as his stomach heaved and tears of agony streamed down his cheeks.

Micah knelt beside him, and Sev felt something he was sure was a mistake. Micah was stroking his back. His palm smoothed up and down gently, trying to comfort him. Had he entered the Twilight Zone? Hell, this was Micah, for God's sake. Micah didn't do gentle and he sure as hell didn't do comforting.

"It's okay, buddy. I know it hurts. Let it out." Micah wrapped his arms around him, holding him up as another convulsion rocked his body and he vomited again.

He continued heaving for what felt like forever as both Sam and Micah held back his hair. Trace paced uncomfortably to the side, but Sev could feel how hard it was for him to watch what he was going through. He retched again and Micah snapped his fingers and pointed at Trace. "Get his ass in here. Now!" Micah was pissed. "Go get him. He needs to know what he's done."

Him. Ari.

Trace didn't hesitate and barreled out and shut the door behind him.

He felt Sam clasp hands with Micah across his back. This was what Micah had gone through before he had met her, but from what Sev had heard, it had been much worse.

"Yeah, Sev, I went through this. It sucks. It hurts." Micah tucked Sev's hair behind his ear. The gesture was so tender Sev had to look to make sure it was Micah sitting next to him and not someone who only sounded like him.

Yep, it was Micah. And his navy blues were full of compassion and understanding.

"That's right, Sev. I know how you feel. I wish there was more I could do for you to make it better, but I'm here for you. I had hoped it wouldn't end up this way for you. I really hoped Ari would get his head out of his ass and do right by you, buddy."

Buddy? Micah was calling him buddy? Seriously, Sev was beginning to think he had entered another dimension. He had never heard Micah speak so tenderly except to Sam. And he had never in a million imagined that Micah would refer to him as his buddy.

But one thing was clear. He had been right the other night. Micah *did* know about him and Arion.

"How? How did you know about us?" Sev tried to breathe, but all he got was tightness and pain.

Micah let go of Sam's hand and pushed Sev's hair back even more so he could stroke his fingers over the pulse point on Sev's neck. Micah was a fucking magician. The ache soothed, and the spasms in his stomach calmed enough so he could sit back on his heels.

"Is that better?" Micah cupped his palm around Sev's neck and continued massaging.

Sev nodded, watching Micah closely as he panted for breath, still waiting for an answer.

"Sev, I've been around a long time. And I...well...I just know things, okay. I can't turn off my ability to see inside people's minds and into their thoughts. It just happens. Leftovers from my former life, I guess." Micah waved his hand as if dispelling old memories. "So, I've known for a while about Ari, even if he didn't. It's one reason why he and I never got along, because I knew he was living a lie and couldn't see it, but he always wanted to get up in my shit about *my* life. I thought he was a hypocrite, but then you joined us. When you came along, I saw the connection between you two immediately. I knew it was only a matter of time before you mated."

"But..."

"Ari didn't know until recently. Yeah. I know. But I could see what was going on inside his head. I could just tell." Micah paused, his palm still massaging Sev's pulse point. "Sometimes, when you're in the thick of the forest, you can't see the way out even when it's right in front of you. But when you're above the forest and looking down, you can see everything. Ari's too deep in the forest, Sev." Micah gestured and lifted his other arm as if marking a higher level. "I'm above the forest. I could see how lost Ari was, and I could see his way to being found. In you. You are Ari's way out, Sev."

Wow. For real, who was this guy? And where the fuck was Micah?

Sam took Sev's hand and squeezed it. "It's okay, Sev. Somehow this will work out."

Sev turned toward her and knew that Micah had revealed everything to her. Her gentle eyes softened even more as she tried to give him a reassuring smile.

"Ari doesn't want this marriage any more than you do, Severin." Micah stood up and planted his hands on his hips as he huffed. "Fuck, Ari's messed shit up good."

GINA PULLED UP TO THE VALET in front of the Savakis residence and handed over her keys. Lakota came around the back as the valet drove off to a nearby parking space. She made sure she watched where so she could find it later. Her rifle was in the back.

Lakota took her hand. "Thanks again for driving. I don't know what's wrong with my Suburban. It was fine last night."

"That's okay. These things happen."

She knew what was wrong with his Suburban. She had disconnected the battery while out "jogging" before sunrise. While he had remained sleeping in her bed, she had changed into her running clothes, stolen his keys, grabbed her rifle in its compact carrying case, her nine millimeter, extra clips, and then concealed everything under a bulky jacket and jogged down to the parking garage. She loaded her weapons in the back compartment, found his Suburban, unlocked it, popped the hood, and disabled the battery. After her task was done, she hurried back up to her room, snuck in, and deposited his keys back where she found them before he awakened.

After that, they had spent the day *not* getting out the bed. Lakota was insatiable, but she enjoyed herself. Even if there were no long-term plans with him, she had to admit, the sex was good.

"Shall we?" he said.

"Absolutely." She was more than ready. Finally, she would get her shot at Severin and put the past behind her. Then it would be bye-bye, Lakota.

He leaned toward her as they stood at the end of the line of people waiting to have their names checked off the guest list. "You look lovely, by the way." His warm breath whispered over her ear.

"Thank you." She had purposely dressed in black slacks, a black cashmere sweater, and black coat. Black clothing would make her task easier later. At the last second, she had remembered she needed something green and found a simple emerald brooch and fastened it to the turtleneck bunched around her throat.

"You look good, too," she said.

Lakota cleaned up well in slacks and a navy blue sweater.

On such short notice, he couldn't find anything green to wear, but it didn't matter. He was still handsome. And she had already gotten in her pinch.

SEV THOUGHT THE PAIN COULDN'T GET ANY WORSE, but when the door to the library opened and Trace shoved Ari inside, Sev thought his insides were being ripped out. Because he knew the male in front of him wasn't his. Somehow he knew that Ari had backed down. Trace slammed the door as Sev dry heaved again.

"Oh God, Sev. What's wrong with him?" Ari looked at Micah.

"You tell us, genius." Micah ambled over to Trace by the door, looking pissed off and frustrated.

"Did you tell them?" Sev asked when he could speak again. He already knew the answer, but he had to hear it.

"Tell who?" Ari nervously glanced at the others in the room then looked back to him with fear in his eyes.

Sev could tell Ari hadn't told his parents. He was even afraid to admit the truth in front of Micah, Trace, and Sam, when it was obvious they already knew.

"Your parents, Ari! Did you tell your fucking goddamn parents about us?" He could feel the blood rising in his face, the *suffering* claiming him full throttle.

Ari stumbled backward as if Sev had pushed him and his eyes jumped to Sam and the others. "I...what? I don't know... what are you talking—"

"They know, Ari! They fucking know already!"

Micah and Trace looked Ari in the eye and Sam lowered her gaze to the floor.

"What?" Ari's breathing quickened, his hands visibly shaking.

"We know about you and Sev," Micah said. "We know you're mates."

Sev shook his head at Ari. "I'm never going to be good enough for you, am I? I'm always going to be your dirty little secret, the toy you take out to play with when no one's looking but shove under the bed when anyone walks into the room. What are you going to do, Ari? Marry your fucking little princess and see me on the weekends? Huh? Hide me away from the world and leave a few bucks on the nightstand when you leave?"

Ari fell to his knees in front of him. "It's not like that, Sev."

"Then what's it like? Tell me, because I need to know. I need to know where I stand with you."

Ari looked down at the floor and didn't answer him.

GINA AND LAKOTA MADE THEIR WAY INSIDE, and she snuck a peek at the guest list as Lakota gave his name. She found Severin's name and saw the tick mark by it. He was already here. She bit her lip to keep from giggling.

Lakota guided her to the main room. The place was wall to wall with people, but she saw the table of masks and hats. Well, that could come in handy. She grabbed a feather-covered green masquerade mask and slipped it on.

"Mmm, that's sexy," Lakota said.

She laughed and plopped one of the green hats on his head. "So is that."

He rolled his eyes and took off the hat and placed it on her head. "I'm not a hat person."

"Fine, I'll wear it." She tipped it to the side and gave him a flirty look.

He bent down and kissed her. "What do you want to drink?"

She looked over the sign above the bar. She knew he would go for something non-alcoholic, and being that she was working tonight, she thought non-alcoholic would be a good idea for her, too. "I'll take an almond iced-coffee." She had to shout to be heard over the din in the room.

"You don't have to not drink because of me."

"I know, but I want to."

He smiled graciously.

She patted his arm. "I'm going to find the ladies room while you get our drinks."

"Okay, I'll meet you back here."

She nodded then turned and made her way back through the crowd toward the hall. It was time to find Severin.

SEV STARED AT ARI, his anger rising to replace the pain. He was back to feeling betrayed again. Hurt and used. "Are you going to answer me?"

Ari looked up at him. "I'm sorry, Sev. I tried, but they threw all this on me right after I got here. I can't..."

"What? You can't tell them that you and I love each other? That we're mates?"

He hated doing this in front of the others, but right now his mated side was flipping off proper manners and decorum.

Ari looked away. "Shit, Sev, I don't know what to do. I'm dying here."

"You know what. Fuck you, Ari." Sev stood. "Fuck you. You're not the one who just came in here and puked up his breakfast, lunch, and dinner. Don't fucking talk to me about dying." He stormed toward the door, but Trace stopped him, blocking the way and holding his arm out.

Sev glared at him. "Let me out! I want out of here. Now!"

Micah put his hand on Trace's arm. "Let him go."

"Sev, wait," Ari said.

"No."

"Sev!"

But he charged through the door as soon as Trace moved out of the way. He was done. Checked out. But he knew better than that, didn't he? No matter how many times Ari walked away from him and put him through this hell, he would always welcome him back. Even now, if Ari showed up at his house later tonight, Sev would take him in and hold him for as long as they had together, then let Ari break his heart again, only to take him back. There was no other way to exist now that they were mated.

All the more reason to be fucking pissed off at the world and jonesing for a fight.

He broke into a jog through the crowded main hall, pausing just long enough to snag his keys off the valet board before running out and finding his Challenger without waiting on the valet to bring it up. He jumped in, revved the engine to life and squealed the tires. He just needed to get away.

GINA GASPED. The large male who had just jogged past her in the main hall. That was Severin. She took off after him.

"I've got it," she told the valet as she grabbed her keys and darted down the steps outside. Severin's car roared to life and she quickly opened the passenger door on the driver's side of her SUV, pulled out flat rubberized slippers, kicked off her heels, jammed her feet into the slippers, yanked out her guns, and hopped behind the wheel.

Tires squealed as she backed up and hurried to catch up with Sev before she lost him. This was her best chance. She couldn't lose him. Not now when she was so close.

She looked in her rearview mirror to see Lakota rush out of the house with two drinks in his hands.

"Sorry, Kota. I've got places to be right now." She turned onto the road and sped after Sev's disappearing taillights.

ARI DRAGGED HIMSELF UP OFF THE FLOOR and collapsed into a chair.

"What the fuck is your problem?" Micah stormed over and laid into him.

"Not now, Micah. Okay? Not now." His whole world had just rushed out the door and his body felt like it was under a steamroller. His muscles tightened until he couldn't hold himself up, anymore.

"I think now is the perfect time." Micah's voice held a

dangerous edge, and he pointed in the direction Severin had gone. "He's your mate. Your mate, goddamn it! Why the fuck did you let him leave?"

The pain was killing him, diving into his stomach. Ari groaned and clutched his abdomen.

"Sam!" Micah snapped his fingers at her.

She grabbed the waste can and rushed over. Ari grabbed the can and emptied the contents of his stomach then flopped back and looked up at Micah, tears streaming his face. "You were the one who let him leave, asshole! Not me!"

"You'd better check that shit right now." Micah reared back and glared a warning at him.

"Fuck you!"

"Fuck you!" Micah slapped him.

"Micah!" Sam grabbed his hand. "Don't. No."

Micah growled at him. "You idiot. Always in *my* face about *my* life, but look at the fucked-up mess you've made of yours." He paced away then turned and marched back. "I let him go because you had to be the one to stop him, not me. YOU! But you're so goddamned worried about your daddy and what everyone will think when they learn you're gay that you can't even show the man you love how you feel about him. You're pathetic."

"You don't know shit, Micah!"

"Oh, yeah?"

"Yeah, so fuck off!"

"Well, how about you explain it to me, Ari? How about that? Explain to me how you can let your mate walk away without trying to stop him. Explain to me why he means so *little* to you that you can get engaged to some woman you don't even love, because I know you don't love Persephone. It's impossible when you're mated to someone else. So explain it to me, Ari! EXPLAIN IT!" Micah's eyes narrowed and he drew in his breath, as if he suddenly knew the reason. *All* the reasons. And he probably did. He could probably see them blinking like a neon sign on the frontal lobe of his brain.

"I didn't have a choice, okay!" Ari's voice broke as he yelled at Micah. "My father arranged the marriage."

"So? Unarrange it."

"I can't." Ari's voice lowered painfully.

"Why not?"

"Because he'll cut me off!"

The room went dead silent and Ari looked up into Micah's midnight blue eyes.

"My father will cut me off," he said again. "He'll take away everything I have." Ari hesitated and looked away shamefully. "But then something tells me you already knew that, didn't you?"

Micah gave a subtle nod and knelt beside Ari. "Not everything," Micah's voice was uncharacteristically soft. "And your dad can't take everything you have, Ari. Only what you *let* him take."

Ari frowned at him. "What do you mean?"

"He can't take away how you feel about Severin. And he can't take Severin away from you unless you let him, and right now, you're letting him. You're letting your father take away the one thing in your life that's real. Please don't tell me this is about money, because you don't need money to live. But so help me God, I know from experience that you can't live without your mate."

Ari stared at Micah. Who was this soft-spoken, wise male in front of him? Where had he come from? Because just a second ago, he had been yelling and giving Ari the third degree.

Micah reached for Sam, and she took his hand and knelt beside him. "Ari, Sam is my life, and in no way could I survive without her. If anyone told me I had to choose between all my worldly possessions and her, I would choose her in a heartbeat."

Trace shifted his weight and glanced down at the floor by the door.

Ari let out a breath he didn't even know he was holding. "What are you saying, Micah?" But he already knew.

"You need your mate, Ari. You can't live without him. Sev has become the most important part of your life now. More important than anything your father can take from you."

Ari looked down. "I've fucked up too bad this time."

"He'll take you back. He has no choice."

"Why? Why should he? I'm not worthy of him, Micah. I'm not worthy of someone like Sev."

Micah shook his head. "Don't you know anything? Oh, that's right. I'm the resident expert on mating since I'm on my third." He said it almost to himself. "Ari, he'll take you back because *you* are *his* mate. That's why. He can't live without you the same way you can't live without him. You should know that."

Micah was right. And how hard was that to admit to himself? That Micah would be right about something.

Ari clutched his stomach and rocked. He hurt. He needed Sev to ease this awful pain. And he knew if he was feeling like this, Sev was, too. There was only one way for the pain to stop for both of them.

"Go get your mate, Ari," Micah said, as if reading his mind. And who knew? Maybe he was. "I'll help you get on your feet if your dad really does cut you off."

"Why? I thought you hated me."

"I never hated you, Ari. I hated the lie you lived, but I never hated you. Now, come on." Micah helped Ari up then turned to Trace. "Trace, track him, find him. Use that Superman shit of yours if he doesn't come quietly. Sam and I will go with Ari to AKM."

Trace took off without another word.

"No," Ari said, clutching his gut as he winced. "I should look for him."

Micah grabbed his arm before he could run after Trace. "You're in no shape to go after him, Ari. Trace can get to him faster, and then you two can be together at the facility where we can figure out how to get you two through this."

Ari's face screwed up painfully and Micah wrapped his arms around him, pulling him close before reaching up to massage his pulse point in his neck. The ache in his chest eased. Damn, but Micah knew how to take care of a guy whose world was falling apart.

"Is that better?" Micah said.

Ari nodded and pulled back, amazed over how Micah had changed. "I never thought I'd be saying this to you, Micah, but thank you."

"Well, there's a shock." Micah chuffed then led him out and wrangled him through the main hall to the exit as Sam brought up the rear. A tall, broad-shouldered man with blond hair was standing on the steps, staring down the road.

Even from the back, he looked familiar. Shit, the guy reminded him of Sev.

"Excuse me, sir?" Ari said.

When the male turned around, Ari and Sam both gasped. Micah whistled. "Holy shit, no way."

"Do I know you?" the male said, frowning.

Ari remembered what Sev had told him about his dad. "You're Sev's father, aren't you?"

"Yes, why? Who are you?"

He exchanged glances with Micah then looked back at Lakota and sighed. "I'm Sev's mate," he said. "Arion. I'm Arion, and I'm mated to your son."

Well, admitting the truth to Severin's father was a start. Now if he could just admit it to his own parents.

CHAPTER 22

Go! Go! GO!

Sev flew through the streets, reckless, but he didn't care. He wanted to hurt himself. He wanted to destroy something. Suddenly he understood what Micah had gone through in the weeks after Jackson left him and before he'd found Sam. The report about Micah had said he'd actually gone out in search of pain and for someone to kill him, which is how that dreck, Apostle, had gotten involved. Sev definitely saw how such abhorrent behavior would be possible, because right now, either would work just fine for him. Pain, death. It was all good.

With just the barest pressure on the brakes, his car jumped the curb as he turned into the parking lot at AKM. With a whip of the wheel, he barely missed crashing into one of the company vehicles as he gunned the engine and flew into the underground parking garage.

Once parked, he stormed inside, using the stairs because the thought of riding in the elevator made him feel like a caged animal. He shoved open the doors to the main hall, not caring if anyone was on the other side. If anyone else got hurt during his rampage, so much the better, as long as they hurt him back.

He made a quick stop at his prep locker, where he at least had a change of clothes to get out of the monkey suit he had worn to the party. After strapping on his weapons, he shoved the suit into the trash can on his way out then practically ran to dispatch.

"What's available?" he said as he threw open the door.

Adam spun around in his chair. All the dispatchers were taking calls. "Sev? I thought you were off tonight."

"Change of plans. So, what's hot? Send me out on something."

Adam eyed him suspiciously, obviously noting his new and improved kiss my ass and fuck off attitude. "Um, I just got a call about a potential cobalt dealer on the South Side. I was about to assign it to—"

"I'll take it." Sev turned for the key rack by the door.

"Are you sure? You don't look good, Sev."

"I'm sure, and keep your opinions to yourself."

"Suit yourself. I'll forward the details to your phone."

Sev snagged a set of keys and showed them to Adam so he could note the tag number.

"You're set," Adam said. "I'll radio any developments if and when I get them."

Sev flipped the keys back into his palm and closed his fist around them then marched out of the room, down the hall, and out the door. After he got into the Suburban whose bumper number matched the one on his keys, he felt his phone vibrate and pulled it out. He had three missed calls from Ari, but fuck if he was going to call him back right now. He was too intent on laying a trail of mass destruction to bother with talking to his mate who was too ashamed of him and their relationship to tell anyone about it. The text from Adam flashed on the screen with the details of the call.

Pulling the Suburban out of the parking space, he tore out of the lot and hit the streets. He would probably lose his job for disobeying and going out on his own like this, but he didn't care. At least if he lost his job he wouldn't have to see Ari every day. That would make his shit all better. Not!

GINA TAILED SEV TO **AKM** and parked across the street. While he was inside, she put together her rifle, loaded the bullets, checked her Glock and loaded it, then tucked the extra clip inside the pocket of her black, leather jacket. Snatching a skull cap from the glove box, she tucked her short hair inside then got out and slung the rifle's strap over her body and dematerialized to the roof of a nearby building.

As soon as Sev barged out of the compound a minute later, she dematerialized to another building, and then another as she followed his Suburban south.

FIFTEEN MINUTES LATER, Sev entered the general vicinity where the suspected cobalt dealer was doing business.

The computerized com system in the Suburban buzzed to life. "Unit Victor one four seven, be advised, a second party is on the scene."

Sev pressed his transmitter. "Copy. Do you have more information?"

"Two females are with the subject and were seen entering an alley behind Bosco Electric."

"Witnesses?" Sev said.

"Negative. The one who called it in split. Said he wasn't sticking around."

Which meant the report had probably come from a vampire who didn't want to be anywhere near the shit that was about to go down, because he knew the players and knew peripheral damage could occur to bystanders.

"Copy. I'm on the scene." Sev parked the Suburban at the entrance to the alley and shut off the engine.

"Sev, you should wait for backup to arrive."

He didn't answer.

"Sev?"

What he needed was in that alley and he wasn't going to stand by like an invalid waiting for backup. Ignoring Adam's repeated transmissions, Sev hopped out and wasted no time chewing up the pavement as he charged into the darkness.

GINA PULLED THE NIGHT VISION GLASSES out of her jacket and put them on. Her vampire vision was good enough on its own, but this shot was too important to not use the extra visual acuity the night vision glasses gave her. Maneuvering over the rooftops of the surrounding buildings, she followed Sev as she pulled the rifle into her grasp. This was it. She was finally going to avenge her brother. A moment would come, and she would get her shot.

SEV TURNED THE CORNER AND SAW THEM. One dreck stood to the side while the other knelt down next to — it was the female from a week ago. The one who had called herself Candy who had been driving that swank Jag.

Suddenly, Sev realized how he knew Ari's new fiancée. Persephone had been the passenger in that car. *Sue.* Yeah, right. Sue his ass. He knew the names had been fake. What's more, Ari was engaged to an addict. The irony almost made Sev laugh. Ari couldn't tell his father he was in love with a clean, honest, safe guy like Sev, but his father could hook him up to a junkie in the making. Ah, but she possessed the right parts in her trunk to please good old dad, didn't she? What a fucked up world this was.

Sev turned his attention back to what was doing ten yards in front of him. *Candy* sat on the ground, her black hair falling over her shoulders and the dreck injecting her with what Sev imagined was cobalt. Her head rolled back, and her friend, another brunette this time since Persephone was busy taking his mate away from him this very minute, eagerly stood waiting her turn.

Without waiting for an invitation, Sev charged down the alley and tackled the dreck who stood to the side.

Then it was on.

Candy's friend screamed and took off, leaving *Candy* to slump in convulsions as the drug entered her system and did its damage. It's why you took the drug sitting or lying down, so you didn't hurt yourself by falling.

The dreck who had injected her jumped up and attacked Sev.

Soon fists where flying, legs were kicking, and the satisfying sound of flesh hitting flesh echoed off the walls.

"Hit me!" Sev yelled at one of the drecks, shoving him hard.

The second dreck flew at him, jumping on his back. He laughed as the guy's blue-black hair swung around his face and his fist smashed into his jaw.

"That's the spirit!" The pain felt good radiating through his neck and shoulders.

He hardly ever fought with his iron skin down, but that was precisely what he needed tonight. Keeping his biological shield hidden allowed their punches to do the damage he needed—to give him the pain he longed for. But the drecks were no match for his superior strength and before the fight had really even begun, it was over and he was looking down at their unconscious forms lying at his feet.

"Lightweights." Sev growled with disappointment, not even close to the threshold of pain he needed to reach to feel content.

He turned and stalked toward *Candy*. She had another needle in her arm and was passed out cold. His gaze swept to the ground beside her. The dreck had left his stash, and apparently *Candy* had helped herself to more.

Fuck! Overdose!

Suddenly, his mind cleared. He was hurting, but he had a victim who could die if he didn't help. He had to do something—help her—get her back to AKM where the medics could do whatever it was they did to drain the shit out of a person who had overdosed.

With his own problems suddenly pushed aside, he scooped her up, rushed her to the Suburban, and tossed her in as carefully as possible even though he needed to hurry. But there was no way he was leaving those assholes and their stash behind. If *Candy* died, they would pay. He ran back into the alley.

GINA DIDN'T CARE THAT SEV had just beaten the shit out of two drecks. She was of a single-minded purpose that had ruled her every minute for the past year: kill Severin. Nothing else at this point registered. She was locked into bloodlust, ready to take the opportunity and end the hunt. She had found him, and now she would kill him. Her mind was completely obsessed with the task at hand.

When Sev rushed back into the alley, she had her chance. It was now or never. She only hoped his iron skin wasn't engaged.

Pht! She fired off a round, and the rifle's silencer whispered the shot.

Sev flew back against the wall as the bullet pierced his shoulder.

Pht! Pht! Two more rapid shots. The first tore into his chest and the other bounced off his skin. Shit! She knew she shouldn't have fired a test shot. Still, the two that had hit could do the job. She would have to wait and see.

She was about to swoop down to the alley and wait for him to lose consciousness so she could finish the job if the bullet wounds didn't when a tingling sensation prickled her skin. She looked over her shoulder then froze in place. Literally froze. She couldn't move.

A dark-skinned, bald vampire loomed over her, his hand outstretched and fingers splayed.

"I'd love to kill you right here, bitch, but I need to know why you just tried to kill my buddy. So, get ready to take a little ride. You're coming with me." He picked her up and flung her over his shoulder. "I'll kill you later, and trust me, it will be very unpleasant."

CHAPTER 23

TRACE FELT HIS POWER STRETCHING and trying to consume him, and he knew he would need to pay his Domme a visit later to help bring him back down, but right now he had more important matters to attend to. Such as Severin and that new hole Queen Sniper had blasted into his chest.

With the bitch tossed over his shoulder, he jumped off the top of the building, glided down eight stories, and landed in a crouch on the pavement.

Severin groaned and gasped a few feet away.

"Hang on, Sev. Don't you die on me."

Shit, the injury looked bad. Trace needed to hurry.

He half-released the female from compulsion so he could gruffly bind her wrists and ankles. Her squeak of pain made him grin. He hauled her to the SUV and shoved her in then rushed back for Sev. Fuck the drecks. These two just got a free pass. Sev needed medical attention STAT.

"I've got you, buddy. Come on." Trace picked Sev up. Damn, but he was losing a lot of blood. "Don't you die, Sev. Ari is waiting for you."

Sev groaned and dropped his head back as he passed out.

"Fuck!"

Trace got Sev in the passenger seat then rushed around to the driver's side and jumped behind the wheel.

Keys! Keys! Where were the keys?

Fuck it.

He started the damn thing with a touch of his finger. *Presto-start-o!* Without hesitation, he stomped on the gas and rocket launched out of the alley before hitting the transmitter. "Dispatch, this is Trace!" He didn't wait for them to acknowledge and started rattling off the details. "Get medical ready. Now! Sev's been hit. I repeat, Severin is down."

"What happened?" Adam's voice shot back.

"Took two bullets to the chest."

"Shit. Condition?"

Trace glanced at Sev. "Bad. Losing a lot of blood and unconscious."

"Hurry him home. Medical's been alerted."

"Get security to meet me at the back door. I've got his would-be assassin, too." Trace shot a glance at the female in his rearview mirror.

She glared back.

"Copy."

Trace remembered his third passenger. "And I've got an overdose, too. Female."

"Fuck, Trace. What *don't* you have?" Adam said.

"The kitchen sink."

Trace ended the transmission and looked in the rearview mirror at the dark-haired female as he flew through an intersection. "You'd better hope Sev doesn't die, bitch." He shot the words at the female like bullets of his own.

"Fuck you."

"No, you'll be the one who's *fucked*." He barely slowed down at a red light then gunned it.

"He's a sympathizer!" She sneered at Sev. "He's half dreck. He's one of them. I've done you all a favor. You should be thanking me instead of hauling me in like a criminal."

"Bullshit! Just shut the fuck up." Trace scowled at her, but he quickly darted a questioning glance toward Severin. Was she saying Severin was half a goddamn dreck? No way.

She chuffed. "You'll see soon enough." She looked and sounded so self-assured, which made Trace want to slug her. "He helped killed my brother and ten other enforcers in Atlanta."

The Suburban practically went airborne as he shot through another intersection.

Trace glanced quickly at Sev again. Sev had come to them from Atlanta, but Trace couldn't see him being capable of the shit this bitch was accusing him of.

"I'm not buying it, sweetheart." Trace lurched the Suburban around a corner and gunned it again.

"Don't believe me? Look inside his mind. Go ahead. See for yourself."

Damn, but Trace wanted to wipe that smug look off her face. With his fist.

Undaunted by his scowls in the mirror, she continued. "He claimed to work for the VDA, but they said they never heard of him. He was working with a band of cobalt dealers the night my brother raided the factory. Sev was there. He helped kill—"

Trace held up his hand and growled at her. "Just shut up. I'm done with your goddamn Mickey Mouse voice."

She sat back and glowered at him.

Trace didn't buy her line of shit for a second, but he poked inside Sev's unconscious mind, anyway. If he died, Sev's memories would be lost forever and Trace would be the only one to provide witness to the truth so they could convict this female and sentence her to death by beheading. Which he would happily see to personally.

As he dug through Sev's thoughts, he pushed past a lot of things he didn't need to see - personal things about Ari and a male named Gabriel—Gabe as Sev called him. A quick shuffle through the memories of Gabe showed he was this bitch's brother. Her name was Gina.

Okay, so Trace got that.

Next he saw Sev's mother. Well, fuck him sideways. Bitch Gina was right. Sev's mother *was* a dreck. That didn't mean he was a sympathizer, though.

Trace kept sorting and sifting then found the memory he was looking for. Sev in the middle of a firefight in a factory. Drecks and enforcers were unloading a lot of hard ammo on each other, bullets bouncing off Sev's skin—iron skin, huh? Nice mixed-blood power there—as he raced for Gabe. Sev's panic in the memory took Trace's breath away as he watched bullets tear through Gabe's body armor and his blood splatter the air.

Fast-forward. Sev returned to the factory. Gina was there. Gabe had just died and Trace could feel Sev's pain even through the mind link.

Damn. Shit. That brought back memories of his own that he didn't want to think about.

He refocused on Sev's memories. Sev used to be a deep cover op. No one knew of his assignment, not even Gabe. Then Trace saw confusion and anger. Sev's boss at VDA had disavowed him. *Why?* Oooohhh, jealousy. Sev's boss had been jealous. Trace raced through all the memories. He saw Jonas, how Gabe and Jonas used to be lovers, and how Jonas blamed Sev for their breakup even though Sev had nothing to do with it. Shit, Sev had been royally fucked over, and this bitch in the back seat had leaped before she'd looked.

Tears bloomed in Trace's eyes. Sev had endured so much pain and suffering over Gabe's death. The agony was overwhelming and Trace forced himself to disconnect from Sev's mind before the sorrow overtook him and tilted his power balance, especially when Sev's pain reminded him of his own past.

"Are all Atlanta enforcers as careless as you are?" Trace glared at Gina in the rearview mirror.

"Fuck you. I'm not careless." She lanced him with an icy glare.

"Like fuck. You've got it all wrong about Sev. *Gina*." He emphasized her name to ensure she got the clue that he had taken a trip through Sev's mind.

"Like hell I do." She frowned as doubt crept over her face.

"You didn't bother looking at the whole memory, did you? You only saw a piece of what really happened."

"Gabe died before I saw it all, but I saw enough. Sev killed him." She didn't sound as confident as she had a few minutes ago, though.

"Look again. This time, look inside *Sev's* memories." Trace felt his impatience and anger coiling like a deadly python.

"I don't need to. I know what I know." But her voice wavered.

"LOOK AGAIN!" Trace's power nearly broke free to crush her skull, but he deflected it in time to crack the windshield. He was unbelievably angry. He needed to be careful.

Gina cowered and trembled, obviously feeling the waves of darkness emanating from his body, but her eyes darted to Sev.

"That's right," he said. "Look. Again. Take a good long look, sweetheart. You just shot an innocent male who's already endured enough pain over Gabe's death. And so help me God, if he dies, I will enjoy hurting you."

He would break every bone in her body, crushing them one-by-one, starting with her fingers, then her toes. Then her hands and feet. He would work his way from her extremities and save her skull for last so she felt every painful blow. The thought made his hand twitch eagerly.

Oh yeah, he really needed to be careful. His power was eating its way into his body. If he unleashed himself now, he could very well find himself tipping the scale into full-blown transformation to the land of the mutants.

Chill, Trace. Just a bit longer and you can have your release.

He glanced into the rearview mirror and saw Gina staring at Sev. She was looking inside his mind. He knew she would. Curiosity had a way of pushing people to do things even when they wanted to resist. Horror stretched over her face and tears welled in her eyes as she clapped her bound hands over her mouth. And then she broke down.

Trace felt nothing of compassion for her. "Now you see. And now you have to live with what you've done." Fucking reckless bitch. "What kind of an assassin are you that you go into a job without all the facts. Do us all a favor and find a new line of work if Sev makes it through this."

And that was a very big if at the moment. Sev's breathing had grown shallow and his face had lost all color. Vampires may be immortal, but they could die just as easily as humans under the right circumstances. And these were the right ones.

He reached AKM and sped around to the back entrance. The medics rushed out and unloaded Sev onto a gurney then grabbed the overdose victim from the back. A sextet of enforcers yanked out Gina, whose face was locked in numb shock. She didn't even attempt to resist as they shoved her through the doors.

Yeah, you fucked up, bitch. Trace glared after her as he followed everyone in, his stride long, purposeful, and measured.

The mass of bodies pushed hurriedly down the hall toward the medical wing then disappeared through a set of swinging doors. The overdosed girl was swept into another room, and personnel ran back and forth in what looked like chaos. But Trace knew they were like bees in a hive. To his eye, the buzz of activity looked haphazard, but to the doctors and nurses rushing around, they knew exactly what needed to be done and where to go.

A herd of footsteps charged up behind him and Trace turned in time to catch Ari before he ran into the fray of doctors attempting to save Severin's life.

"No, Ari! Stop!"

"Let me go. I need to see him."

The entire team was there, including some tall fucker Trace didn't know but who looked a lot like Sev. The guy looked as anxious as Ari to push his way through, and Micah and Tristan were trying to wrangle him back.

"What happened? What happened to him?" Ari twisted and tried to get out of Trace's grip.

"He was shot."

CHAPTER 24

FOR A SPLIT SECOND, Ari thought he had heard wrong. No! Not Sev! No! He had iron skin. He couldn't be shot. Not unless he...Oh God! He hadn't had his iron skin engaged.

"How?" Ari continued to struggle to get free.

Trace's pale eyes narrowed as he frowned. "An assassin. Some dark-haired bitch named Gina."

Severin's father perked up behind him. "Gina? Are you sure? Dark hair? Petite?"

Trace turned and nodded. "That's right. Who the fuck are you? And how do you know her?"

"Lakota. I'm Sev's father. And she was my date at the party tonight."

Trace had been out of the loop, so all this was news to him. "No shit?" Trace said.

"Yeah, no shit. Where is she?" Lakota sounded primed to kill.

"In a holding room," Tristan said. "We detain prisoners in the holding rooms."

"Where are those?" Lakota sounded even more menacing.

Obviously Tristan caught on to the bloodlust Lakota was rocking because he said, "You stay away from her until we've had a chance to get to the bottom of this."

"She's mine," Trace said, his voice deep and filled with lethal warning.

Ari got the impression Trace had plans for Gina if shit went badly. But if that happened, it would mean Sev.... No, Ari couldn't think like that. He couldn't think Sev wouldn't pull through this.

"Like hell she is. That's my son in there!" Lakota pointed toward the emergency room. "And that bitch used me to get to him."

Tensions were high. Testosterone was flowing. The aggression levels were off the charts, and all Ari wanted was to get to his mate.

My mate's been shot!

The crowd pushed forward and Trace let go of Ari to push Lakota back. Lakota retaliated. Fists flew. Bodies hit the walls and Ari turned to see Micah and Io holding Trace back while Tristan and Malek restrained Lakota. Sam huddled to the side to avoid being hit.

This was his chance. He darted down the hall and ran through the double doors just as Sev's heart monitor flatlined.

"No!" he rushed forward and pushed past the doctors and nurses who tried to hold him back.

"He's crashing!" someone yelled.

"He needs blood, STAT!" another shouted.

Ari jumped on Sev's body and thumped his chest hard below the gaping wound. "Don't you die on me, Sev! Don't you fucking die!"

He hit his chest again as a nurse rushed in with a bag of blood. They didn't have time for that. Without a thought, Ari grabbed a scalpel and sliced his wrist open and shoved it over Sev's mouth as he thumped his fist against Sev's chest again.

"Drink! Fucking drink, Sev!"

The doctors knew better than to try and pull him off, so they worked around him, hooking up bags of blood and injecting syringes of blood directly into his veins.

Ari collapsed over Sev's lifeless body and started crying. His tears fell over Sev's face as he kissed his closed eyes. "Don't you leave me, Sev. I love you. I love you, goddamn it! You're my mate. You can't leave me!" He felt hope slipping away. "Please drink. Please don't die. I love you."

His chest ached, and the pain only worsened with each passing second. Sev was slipping away.

The blood flowed from his wrist into Sev's mouth, but Sev didn't move. His throat didn't work to swallow the life-giving blood Ari offered.

"We're losing him!" someone yelled.

Ari wrapped his free arm under Sev's body and held onto him, sobbing. "No, don't go. Don't give up. I'm ready to fight for you, Sev. I'm ready to fight for *us*. Please." He pressed his lips to Sev's ear, his voice a whisper now. "I love you. I need you. I can't live without you."

The continuous monotone shrill of the heart monitor filled Ari's ears. Sev was dead. His mate was dead.

"No." He whispered the single word before sucking in a wretched sob of air. "Nooo!"

Suddenly, Sev's body shuddered and tensed then arched up violently as his fangs sank into Ari's wrist. The monitor buzzed to life again, beeping wildly as Sev's heart re-engaged inside the land of the living.

The pain of Sev's bite was nothing compared to the joy that leaped into Ari's heart as he pulled back and looked down.

Oh my God! Oh my God! He's alive.

Hope burst from his soul. "That's it. Drink my blood."

Vampire blood trumps human blood.

Sev's arms jerked and wrapped around him and pulled him close. His strength was off the charts and Ari could tell he was struggling to control his movements, causing tubes and monitors to whip around, shift, and fall over. But Ari didn't care. The only thing that mattered was that Sev's eyes blasted open and his beautiful, perfect blue irises flashed to his, full of life and panic.

Ari smiled down at him, his tears turning to tears of joy as they fell on his face.

"I love you. I love you."

Sev nodded as if he wanted to tell him he knew and loved him, too.

A doctor tugged at Ari's suit jacket, now covered in Sev's blood. "We need to prep him for surgery. Please. Let us do our job, Arion."

They were right. There was still a long road to make sure Sev was safe, but as he moved to get down, Sev's arms locked around him and he shook his head as fear filled his eyes. Sev's fangs released his wrist.

"Don't leave me," Sev said. His pleading voice was raw and weak.

Ari bit back another sob. "I won't. I'll be right here. But the doctors need to work on you. They need to save you and they can't do that with me in the way."

"Stay...with me." Sev shivered, and his teeth chattered.

Ari licked over his own wrist since Sev obviously hadn't released any venom to heal his bite, which explained the lack of euphoria. "I'll stay. I'll be right here. I won't let go of your hand the whole time, okay." He moved to get off the gurney and Sev nodded as he let him go.

"I love you." Sev's voice was deathly quiet, but at least he was alive.

"I love you, too, now sshh." He wrapped both his hands around one of Sev's. Damn, he was cold, but Ari held tight as the doctors went back to work.

CHAPTER 25

ARI LOST TRACK OF TIME, but after what felt like several hours and two more close calls, the doctors sewed Sev up and transferred him to a recovery room. They assured him Sev was stable, but Ari just wanted him to open his eyes again and look at him. Only then would Ari believe he was out of the woods.

The rest of the team shuffled in except for Trace, and Io glanced down at Ari's hands wrapped tightly around Sev's. He could imagine the questions going through Io's head.

"How is he?" Micah said.

For the first time, Ari saw Micah in a new light. Something had clicked between them earlier at his parents' home. Ari let go of Sev's hand, stood up, and hugged Micah. "Thank you."

Micah seemed to take the hug in stride, but a couple of others in the room gasped. Seeing the two of them hugging like old friends was something he doubted anyone would have laid bets on. He and Micah weren't known to be the best of buddies. Punches were more likely to be thrown between them than kind words.

"Thank me for what?" Micah held him close and patted him on the back of the shoulder, all big brotherly and shit.

Ari pulled back and nodded at Micah. What Micah had made him see through his eyes changed him. He knew what needed to happen now.

"For helping me see what's really important."

"And? What is that?" Micah looked him in the eye, arching a brow in a way that almost looked like he was daring Ari.

Perhaps he was daring him to reveal the truth in front of

his team, including Io. Something Ari was finally ready to do.

Ari couldn't believe the changes in Micah since he had taken Sam as his mate, and this wise, compassionate side was just one more surprise Ari had never expected to see. Ari placed his hand on Sev's leg. "Him. Severin. He's what's important."

"And why is that?" Micah looked him dead in the eye.

Ari kept his eyes locked with Micah's and took a deep breath. "Because I love him. Because..." He glanced around the room and met the eyes of everyone there. "Because Sev is my mate."

Io's mouth fell open, and Ari watched him look away uncomfortably.

"That's right, Io, it was me Devon heard in the shower with Severin, not Bauer. It was me."

Io's gaze lifted. He looked betrayed and angry. "You're... oh my God, you're a faggot?"

Micah shot away from Ari and had Io by the throat and against the wall and suspended off the floor so fast he hadn't been able to track him. "You check that shit right now, Io. You got me. You're half to blame for Sev over there with his chest sewn up like a Raggedy Ann doll, so you need to put a lid on that shit like yesterday."

"Okay, Micah, calm down," Tristan said.

Ari felt something brush against his hand, and he glanced down to see Sev's fingers reaching for his. He turned toward the bed and looked up to see Sev's eyes opened and a weak smile on his face.

"Sev!" He gripped Sev's hand and moved toward the bed. "How long have you been awake?"

Sev blinked heavily. "Long...enough." His voice sounded like someone had rubbed sandpaper over his vocal chords.

The commotion coming from the others fell away as Ari knelt beside Sev. "You heard me, didn't you?"

Sev's gaze followed him as he lowered himself to Sev's eye level. He nodded. "Yes."

It felt like they were the only two in the room, despite the arguing and bickering carrying on in the corner among

Micah, Io, and Tristan.

"Well, it's time I lived my own life, don't you think?" He traced his fingers across Sev's brow. "How do you feel?"

Sev grinned. "Like I've been shot." He still sounded so damn weak, but the fact he was smiling was good news. "When can we go home?"

Ari smiled. Sev must have been doing better to be thinking about going home already.

"Let me buzz the nurse and we'll find out."

Within seconds the nurse came in and took his vitals.

"How long does Sev need to stay here?" Ari said.

"I've called the doctor. He should be here in just a minute. I'll let him discuss that with you."

"Who shot me?" Sev said, sounding a little stronger.

"Gina." Ari looked down.

Sev had been afraid she was after him. He had been right.

"Gina? Gabe's sister?"

Ari nodded.

"She found me."

Lakota stepped to Sev's bedside. "I think it was revenge or something. That's what Trace said."

Sev's eyes flashed with anger and his heart monitor spiked. "What's he doing here?"

Ari squeezed his hand. "He was at the party with Gina. He—"

"You led her to me?" Sev's voice sounded stronger than he looked. "Get out of here."

"Sev, no, I didn't lead her to you. She used me to get to you. I didn't know. I never would have—"

"Get out!" Sev's shout quieted everyone in the room just as the doctor pushed his way in.

"What's going on in here? Everyone out, now." The doctor hit everyone with the hairy eyeball then approached the bed. "That means you, too, Ari."

"No." Sev clutched his hand, making it clear he wasn't going anywhere. "Ari stays." Sev was clearly struggling to speak again, his voice scratchy and labored after yelling at his father. "Anything you have to say to me can be said in front of him."

The doctor shrugged. "Okay, fine, but the rest of you have to wait outside."

Ari got the impression he just wanted to quiet the place down and keep Sev calm.

"When can I go home?" Sev said as soon as everyone had left.

"We should keep you at least a couple of days. You're already healing very nicely thanks to Ari's blood. There's no permanent damage." The doctor turned toward him. "Ari, if you'll agree, we'll transfuse you so Sev can drink from you again in six hours. It will help speed up his healing. But we need to make sure you keep your own strength up, too."

"Of course." He just wanted Sev back home, where he could take care of him, dote on him, and feed him chicken soup or whatever the hell else Sev needed. Right now, he would give his left arm for Sev.

"Okay, I'll send in the nurse in a few minutes to begin the transfusion." The doctor patted Sev on the shoulder. "You're a lucky vampire, Sev. Ari saved your life." He smiled then turned and left them alone.

"Sev, I'm so sorry about earlier, at my parents' house. You deserved better than that."

"That doesn't matter, anymore, babe." Sev cleared his throat. "What matters is that you're here now." He still struggled to speak.

"But if I hadn't behaved the way I did, you wouldn't have left and you wouldn't have been shot."

"Sshh." Sev raised his free hand limply to shush him. "Gina would have found another opportunity to try and kill me. Maybe one with better odds of success. So, stop worrying. If anything, it's my own fault for letting my guard down."

"Still, I'm sorry. I hurt you and I don't ever want to do that again." He kissed Sev's hand and lowered his forehead over Sev's chest. Right over the bandage covering his heart. The heart he never wanted to hurt again and would cherish forever.

Sev placed his hand on the back of Ari's head. "Hey, the doc was right."

"About what?" Ari turned his head and looked up into eyes that made him feel like he was home.

"I am lucky," Sev said. "Because I have you."

CHAPTER 26

TRACE HAD SLIPPED AWAY from the group earlier. His skin crawled. His muscles twitched. His power was seeping through every cell of his body. Once he got himself relatively composed, he knew it was time to go.

As he hurried out back to his custom chopper, he quickly pulled out his phone and dashed out a text to his Mistress.

9-1-1 On my way.

He didn't wait for a response and slipped on his sunglasses, climbed on to the seat, and started the engine. He revved it once then put the bike in gear and hauled ass, his leather duster flapping like a cape in the wind.

That's right. *Super Sub* was on the move. And he had a bad itch that needed scratching by *Wonder Domme*.

It took him no time to reach the elegant home in the suburbs. No one would ever imagine the depraved actions that went on inside the pristine home set back from the road with manicured lawns and a Hallmark card effect.

But inside those walls was what Trace needed. Pain and humiliation awaited him, and he couldn't get off his bike fast enough before stripping out of his coat and flinging it over the seat.

His power clawed at him. He needed fixes more frequently these days. He was getting worse. It terrified him that one day soon he would lose total control of the power he was cursed with. His mother had intended the power as a gift to save him, but that showed how little she had known about mixed-bloods at the time. And now the burdensome spell couldn't be undone.

The front door swung open as he reached the porch. Immediately, he put his head down. He wasn't allowed to look her in the eye until she gave him permission.

"Mistress."

"My servant." She stood aside. She knew he had little time. "Undress and get on your knees."

Trace stripped and fell to his knees after she closed the door. Already, he could feel his power ebbing. Thank God he had made it in time.

"What would you have of me, my Mistress?" He kept his gaze on the immaculate marble floor. With the heels clicking on the hard surface, her leather boots came into view in front of him.

She strapped a collar around his neck and hooked a length of leather to it. "I have work for you to do, my pet. But first, downstairs." She tugged on the leash and he fell to all fours and crawled after her as she led him through the house.

He could hear the subtle tap-tap-tap of a riding crop, as if she was gently tapping it against her own thigh as she walked.

Trace didn't love her, and she didn't love him. They trusted one another, but that was as far as their relationship went. Sexual congress wasn't the objective during these scenes, control was. He needed the pain and to be controlled to bring his power down. Even so, they rarely wasted the erections he obtained during these sessions and had sex. Trace wasn't able to get an erection without feeling humiliated, dominated, or otherwise tortured in some way, so it seemed a shame not to enjoy a carnal relation when he got the chance.

He crawled behind her, the marble and hardwood floors biting against his knees until he reached the door to the basement. He began to stand, but she smacked him with the crop.

"Crawl down backward, servant."

He bowed his head to the floor. "Yes, Mistress."

Trace turned around and slid his knee back until he found the edge of the first stair then lowered it to the next. Then he lowered his other knee until he found the next step. And so forth. It was slow going, and the mistress tapped her booted foot impatiently as she tugged on the leash.

"Hurry up. You move like molasses, my pet."

Trace tried to move more quickly, but he could only go so fast.

She whipped the riding crop down over one ass cheek then the other. "So slow you move."

Then Trace shuddered as the tip of the crop slid down the crack of his ass and rested against his scrotum.

Yes, yes, yes!

With rapid, gentle swats she spanked the tender sac of flesh. *Tap-tap-tap.* The sting was delicious, and Trace groaned as he went still halfway down the stairs. For him, pain was pleasure. *Aaaahhh.*

She tugged on the leash again. "Stop wasting time, servant."

The riding crop was pulled away from his balls and switched down over his ass again, spurring him to get moving.

"My apologies, Mistress."

He crawled backward the rest of the way down the stairs, following the scent of leather and disinfectant. He wasn't her only submissive, and she kept her equipment expertly cleaned. Not that he really cared. It wasn't like anything the others left behind would hurt him.

As he turned around at the base of the stairs, he looked up at her as she walked over to a shelf of accoutrements. Her long, blond hair was pulled up in a high ponytail, and he imagined that her lips were painted blood red.

Other than the knee-high boots, she wore a leather bustier and cuffs, as well as a leather choker around her neck.

She turned around and he quickly ducked his face to the floor. She tsked and slinked back to him before kneeling down in front of him. "Are you looking at me, pet?"

He kept his gaze on her boots and nodded. Guilty.

"Awe, now. That's a bad pet. Bad bad pet." She brushed her hand over his bowed head, scratching his bald scalp with her fingernails.

Trace had looked at her on purpose, because he needed the punishment. "Yes, Mistress. I've been bad. I need to be punished."

She swatted him across the back with the riding crop. "And you shall be. Follow me, bad little doggy."

Trace began to stand, purposely looking to disobey her, and he was rewarded with a strike of the riding crop across the back of the thigh.

Fuck! That shit was beginning to sting like hell. And didn't that just get him all fucking excited.

"Stay down, servant. I didn't tell you to stand."

He bowed and knelt once more, crawling behind her to the area of the basement she used for suspension.

The air was cool, but that would change soon enough. Before long, he would be covered in sweat as she pushed him to his limits of pain tolerance.

She stopped and stepped her boot up onto a raised block of wood. "My boot needs shined servant." She switched him lightly on the back of the shoulder.

Not wasting time, Trace leaned forward and licked the shiny, patent leather, eager for the debasement.

"Mmm, you are in need tonight, aren't you?" Her voice crooned as he continued swiping his tongue higher, licking up the seam of the zipper on the inside of the boot until he reached her knee.

After a few minutes had passed, she shoved him away with a wicked laugh, as if she were amused by some debauched thought of what she planned to do to him. "Now you may stand," she said, turning away indifferently.

Trace rose to his full six-foot-five, naked, his dark skin gleaming in the faint light, his cock already stiff. He knew what lay ahead and it excited him. He didn't arouse easily, but during these scenes, he always did. It was as if his power subsided enough while being worked over that he could feel the rest of his body and experience other sensations than tension. Because tension was all his power allowed him to feel outside these walls. He had to exercise constant control over his power to keep from losing himself and his mind.

And didn't powerful, control-freak types often make the best subs? Trace had often heard at the scene parties he attended that the more powerful or controlling someone was in the real world, the better they responded to submission. That was certainly true of him.

"What's on your mind, my pet?" Mistress Diamond prowled around him, inspecting him, trailing the tip of the riding crop over the curve of his ass before giving him a gentle swat. It would get worse. It always did.

"Answer me, servant!" She smacked his thigh.

Trace winced. "You, Mistress. You're on my mind. You're always on my mind." A lie, but his training required such an answer.

"Is that so?"

"Yes, Mistress. I can't stop thinking about you."

"And what do you think about?"

His deep voice lowered even more as he replied. "The gift of pain you give me."

"And you like that?" She struck his ass with the riding crop.

Trace bit back a grunt. "Yes, Mistress."

"Give me your wrists, servant."

Jesus! Yes! Trace's knees trembled at the thought of what was coming and he lifted his arms.

With expert fingers, she secured thick, wide, leather cuffs around both wrists then attached a heavy clip connected to a chain to the hook between the cuffs. In a matter of seconds, he was hoisted into the air, his arms pulled tight above him as she cranked the handle of a pulley until he was suspended at least a foot off the floor.

His muscles pulled and stretched, and his cock sprang nearly straight up. Shit, she hadn't even had to use a cock binding on him tonight. Probably would have helped keep his already-looming orgasm under better restraint if she had, though.

"Mmm, you *are* ready for me, I see." She knelt behind him and he felt her secure the spreader between his feet, cuffing his ankles to each end after prying his legs open.

Fuck! He was about to come.

She seemed to sense this. "Do *not* come, yet, my pet. I will be very displeased if you come before I am ready for you to."

Rainbows and unicorns. Rainbows and unicorns. And rotten

meat. Yes, rotten, spoiled meat. That works. It was the only thing he could think about to bring his erection under control, but it worked and his pending orgasm took a breather and chilled out.

"You may look at me now, my pet." She stepped in front of him.

As he suspected, her lips were blood red and her hazel eyes appraised him scornfully. She was a beautiful woman, and an excellent Mistress as far as humans went, but he felt nothing for her besides his trust that she could give him what he needed.

She held a horse-hair flogger in her hand and brushed it down his chest. Trace shivered. With soft strokes, she brushed it side-to-side over his torso. The coarse texture of the hair scratched his skin. Lower still the flogger crept, stopping just before brushing over the head of his cock. She knew that would send him over, didn't she? Then she pulled back and lashed him with it. In two diagonal strokes, she whipped it down over his chest.

Trace winced and jerked in his restraints. She circled him and repeated the whipping action on his back until he cried out.

Mistress Diamond stopped and gave him a rest from the flogger, but not from a verbal berating. "Quiet down! You're weak, servant. Weak!" She waited another couple of seconds then lashed him again before rubbing the horse hair over his ass then down and against his exposed scrotum. The rough texture hurt against his sensitive skin, but that only made it better. He liked the pain. He needed it. And she knew that.

Trace's orgasm pushed forward again, unable to withstand the pain.

The flogger skimmed back up to his shoulder as he felt a cold, metal cylinder press between his ass cheeks. It was thick and heavy and breached him as she pushed.

He saw stars from the tight fullness and the way it stretched him. She pushed the cylinder in slowly, then drew it back out, back in, and out, taking turns whipping him with the flogger. She hadn't used lubricant on the cylinder and he winced at the dry, slow strokes. He knew the intent of the cylinder wasn't to hurt him. Just to make him uncomfortable. And it worked. Very well, in fact. In combination with another whip of the flogger, the stroke of the cylinder had Trace on the verge. He wasn't going to be able to wait.

"May I come, please, Mistress?" He was barely holding it in as it was.

His jaw clenched and his teeth bit together. His more urgent sessions usually progressed this way, with a relatively rapid release followed by hours of intense submission that usually included at least two more orgasms. On good nights, he could come as many as a half-dozen times. Trace had a feeling tonight would be a good night.

She stepped in front of him and scowled, but Trace could just sense the pleasure in her eyes that she could drive him toward the brink so quickly. She stood there, not speaking, not moving, just watching him.

"Please, Mistress." The muscles in Trace's neck and shoulders strained and his abdomen quivered. He couldn't hold back much longer. "Please, may I come, Mistress?"

She clamped her hand over his balls and squeezed. "Yes, you may."

His entire body convulsed as she gripped and twisted, and almost immediately he released a violent shower of semen that sprayed into the air then fell over her arm and rained down on the concrete floor. The chains and equipment holding him rattled and shook, his whole body wracked with endless spasms as she continued to squeeze his scrotum. The pain—the beautiful pain—blew him apart until nothing was left, and he slumped over, spent, feeling like a lamb left for sacrifice.

A minute later, he felt himself being lowered to the floor, and his widespread feet touched the cold surface within seconds. Then the chain and cuffs were removed from his wrists and the spreader removed from between his legs. The cylinder in his ass had already been removed. Hell, maybe it had fallen out on its own during his orgasm, and he had simply failed to realize it while in the throes of ecstasy.

After being unbound, he moved his arms and legs, loosening them up, his body coming back alive as he prepared for more.

"Over there." She pointed to the St. Andrew's Cross against the wall. It was a large, X-like rack he was very familiar with.

His cock was already growing hard again, and he trudged to the rack and lifted his arms to the manacles on each side of the upper half of the X. She strapped him on then shackled his ankles to the bottom.

Aaaahhhh, now the real beating would begin.

Trace closed his eyes and smiled blissfully. His power was completely shut down. He couldn't even feel it, anymore. Sweet Jesus, praise God. He was free. For just a little while, anyway, he was free.

CHAPTER 27

Io LEANED WITH HIS BACK AGAINST THE WALL outside Sev's room, his face the visual definition of the phrase *stunned stupid*. He wasn't sure how to feel. His best friend was gay. When had this happened? How the fuck had Ari become a faggot? The two of them had fucked plenty of women, sometimes together. How did you go from fucking women to being gay and mated to a dude?

He cringed. What if Ari had been hoping to score with Io during those group scenes? Had Ari wanted to tap his ass instead of the female tail he had been getting?

The thought made him shudder.

He closed his eyes and thunked the back of his skull against the wall. Io had seen Ari with plenty of females, but the fact he had mated Sev was unavoidable. His bestie had taken Sev as a mate.

How did he feel about that? His stomach knotted like he was about to get sick, that's how he felt.

"I know what you're thinking, Io," Micah said.

"Oh, you do, huh?" He opened his eyes and scowled across the expanse of the hall to level Micah with a lot of silent eat-my-shit. Micah had taken a male lover before he had met Sam. Did that make Micah gay, bisexual, or just a freak?

"Fuck off, Io. I don't work with labels. And, no, Ari never thought of you like that. He never wanted to 'tap' you, so shut that thought process down right now."

"Get out of my head, Micah."

"Funny. Sam says that to me all the time. And yet...." He cocked his head to one side, leaving the thought unfinished.

Yeah, the message was clear. Micah wouldn't be stopping his thought intrusion any time soon. As if he could. And Io had learned long ago that he couldn't.

Sam wrapped her arm around Micah's waist. "Stop it, honey. Come on, aren't you tired? I am. Let's go up to your dorm and get some sleep."

The sun was already up, so Io was trapped here until nightfall. Fuck! Trapped with a couple of faggots and a freak.

Trace strode around the corner. "Is he okay?"

"Where have you been?" Tristan said.

"Out." Trace shrugged out of his coat, and it was obvious he didn't have plans to go into detail about his whereabouts for the past several hours. Wherever it was, the guy looked way more chilled than he had six hours ago.

Micah pulled Trace into a one-armed man-hug, and the two exchanged solemn glances before Trace looked down to the floor. Micah glanced around for Sam and wound his other arm around her waist.

"How's Sev?" Trace asked, looking back up.

Micah gently clapped his shoulder. "He's okay. Ari's in with him." He ran his palm over Trace's bald melon. "Sam and I were just going to get some sleep. You wanna crash with us?"

Trace nodded. "Yeah, sure. I'm beat." The corner of Trace's mouth ticked as if he'd just made a joke.

Micah grinned and looked away as if he got the punch line no one else in the room was privy to. Then the three turned and headed out without another look in Io's direction.

Tristan stretched. "Me, too. I need to get back to Josie." He looked at Lakota, who stood away from the rest, his head bowed. "Lakota, come on. I'll find you a room for the day."

"I want to stay here. I want to be near my son."

Tristan shook his head. "I don't think that's a good idea right now. Come on, let him rest and then you can try to talk to him tomorrow."

Lakota relented with a sigh and followed Tristan out.

Malek glanced up at Io. "I'm going to go check on the prisoner. You need anything?"

Io shook his head, still too numb to think. "No."

"Interesting night, wasn't it?"

"You could say that."

"Okay, well give me a shout if you need anything." Malek exited the medical wing, leaving Io all alone in the hall.

Arion. Gay. Homo. Fag. Io felt like punching something. Yeah, like Arion's face. His best friend was—he cringed—gay.

A feminine moan caught his ear from the room across the hall and he looked up. The cobalt overdose.

Io shivered and ran his hand through his thick crop of brown hair before scratching his fingertips back and forth over his scalp like it itched. But that's what remembering his own cobalt addiction did to him, made him itch all over. He pushed away from the wall and worked his blunt nails up and down his tattooed right arm then over his collarbone as he walked to the door and pushed it open.

The female was sitting up in bed, her head bent forward so that all he could see was long, black hair hanging down over her face.

"Hey," he said quietly.

She lifted her head and brushed aside her hair with one elegant, long-fingered hand. When her crystal blue eyes met his, Io nearly gasped as his blood instantly heated. She was the most beautiful creature he had ever seen. Even with brown circles under her eyes and her hair a mess of tangles, she was stunning.

"I feel sick," she said.

He entered her room and found a tray then hurried to her side. "Are you going to be sick?"

"I-I'm not—oh, God..." She grabbed the tray and retched, but nothing came up.

Io knew what she was going through. His own addiction had become so bad before he got off the shit that a night hadn't gone by when he didn't throw up at least once.

When she finished dry heaving, he set the tray down and went to the small bathroom in the corner of her room and filled a cup with water. He returned to her bedside.

"I'm Io." He helped adjust her bed so she could sit up then handed her the water. "Thirsty?"

"Miriam, and yes." She took the water and sipped then collapsed back against the pillow after Io fluffed it for her.

"So, Miriam, you like cobalt, huh?"

She rolled her head to look at him but didn't say anything.

Io shrugged. "It's okay. You don't have to talk. Do you mind if I stay with you a while, though?" He knew from his own experience that addicts didn't willingly talk about their addiction, but maybe if he just stayed with her she would eventually open up. Not like he had anywhere else to go except his dorm, and he didn't feel like going there right now. And he liked the idea of staying with this beautiful creature and learning more about her.

Her eyes ranged him up and down then she shook her head. "No."

"Good." Io pulled up a chair. Suddenly, Ari's homosexuality didn't seem like such a big deal. He suddenly had something more interesting occupying his thoughts.

MALEK NODDED AT THE BEEFY GUARDS outside the holding room where they were keeping Gina, the assassin who had gone after Sev. Pushing open the door, he cleared his throat.

"May I come in?" She may have been a prisoner, but it didn't mean he had to treat her like one.

He was of the mind that you got more bees with honey, anyway. And from the sound of it, Trace had already verbally worked her over.

She snapped her face to his. "Hey, this is your place, not mine. You can do whatever you want."

"No need to be rude, Miss. We can do this the polite way or we can rough you up. I'd rather be nice, but the choice is yours."

She glowered and looked away, a real tough guy in a female's body. Her anger seemed to be self-directed, though, and she looked like she had been crying.

Malek closed the door, which locked behind him with a clank. "Not the kind of accommodations you're used to, are they?"

"Not exactly." She huffed and looked away.

He sat down backward in the room's only chair. "So, tell me what happened."

"I already told the other guy." She refused to meet his eyes.

"Well, tell me now."

"What if I don't want to?"

"Do we have to have this discussion again? Polite or roughed up." Malek lifted his hands as if they were scales, rocking them up and down. "It's your decision." Malek hated the idea of getting physical with a female, but this chick didn't seem like just some ordinary femme fatale. And after what she had done to Severin, he had a feeling Gina could damage a guy pretty good if she caught him off-guard.

"Look, I'm done talking to you people. If you're going to kill me, then kill me and get it the fuck over with."

"You're not helping yourself, Gina. Now, drop the attitude and talk."

She jumped up and lunged for him. "I don't want to talk!"

With lightning speed, Malek burst from the chair and blocked her as the chair went flying. Gina went after him again, swinging haphazardly as if trying to provoke him. He deftly slapped her errant fists away, backing up. He may not have had Sev's hand-to-hand skills, but he wasn't a schlep when it came to self-defense. He was a black belt in several disciplines of martial arts, after all.

Suddenly, the door flew open as the guards realized what was happening.

Gina's head snapped around and Malek knew what was about to happen.

"No! Close the door!"

Too late. Gina rushed toward the massive guard then dropped at the last split-second to slide underneath his outstretched arms and legs. She snagged his gun from the holster then hopped up and took off down the hall.

Fuck!

Malek hurdled the guard as he fell down in the commotion then sprinted after her.

"Don't kill her!" He didn't fully understand why, but he needed to keep Gina alive.

Lakota paced in the small dorm room Tristan had let him use. He couldn't sleep. All he could think about was the image of his son with his chest blown open and how he had almost lost his chance to earn the right to call himself Sev's father.

That bitch had used him. Gina had used him to get close to his son. Anger prickled the hair on his arms to stand at attention and he suddenly needed to get out of this tiny room that felt more like a cell. After rushing out the door, he took the elevator down to the main floor, pacing inside the cramped space until the doors opened and he could walk again. Movement. He needed to keep moving to escape his thoughts. He passed the break room then stopped and backed up. Maybe if he ate something he would feel better. Better yet, maybe they had some alcohol stashed in there. No better time than the present to fall off the wagon.

The sudden commotion and shouting coming from down the hall drew his attention and he spun around in time to see Gina fly around the corner with Malek close on her heels. His anger directed his thoughts. He would take that bitch down. Now.

"Here's your iced coffee," he said right before tackling her. The gun she had been carrying slid right into his hand. He smiled. Time for this bitch to die. He cocked the gun and sat up before pointing it at her head.

"This is for my son."

She didn't fight back, and only stared up at him as if waiting for him to get it over with and pull the trigger.

Gina wanted to die. Malek could smell it on her like stale bread as he chased her.

No, no, she can't die. You have to make sure she lives.

"STOP!" Malek knocked Lakota off her just as the gun went off. The bullet caught Malek in the arm, but it was only a flesh wound. "No! She has to live!" Why he felt so certain of this he didn't understand, he just knew that killing Gina would be a mistake.

She scurried to her feet to chase after the gun that skittered across the floor again, but Malek jumped back up and grabbed her.

"No!" She screamed at him as she flung her body around to backhand his wounded arm.

Malek winced and she briefly hesitated, her eyes panicked. Then she tried to kick him to get away, but he was too quick and dodged aside.

"Kill me! Just kill me!" She wrestled with him as he fought to get a hold of her wrists.

"You're not dying today, Gina!" He growled in frustration as she bucked and shoved against his shoulders.

"Please, just kill me!"

Finally, he got hold of her and slammed her back against the wall so hard his own teeth rattled.

"No." In a flash, he had his knife in his hand and up to her throat. She instantly stilled. "See, you don't really want to die after all, do you?"

Her face contorted in mental agony and tears flowed down her cheeks before she inhaled harshly through a violent sob.

"Please." The fight oozed out of her, and she relaxed under his forearm pressed to her throat.

Her plaintive plea choked his heart.

"What?" he said, loosening his grip.

"Please kill me." She broke down, her body convulsing through heavy, anguished sobs.

Malek lowered the knife and pulled her against him with his free arm. Her face pressed into his shoulder, and her arms wrapped tightly around him. Malek got the impression she hadn't cried in a long, long time. Not like this. Her sobs were too deep, too ragged, feeling as if they spilled unbidden from a part of her she had kept tightly locked and closely guarded. Her sorrow came from a place so deep that it nearly decimated Malek as it crashed over him in a wave of escaped anguish, as if her grief was relieved to be free from the restraints Gina had shackled it with for too long.

"No one is killing you today, Gina. Now, come on, let's go. I'll help you figure this out."

He didn't even look at Lakota or the others as he turned her back in the direction of the holding cells. Malek kept his attention on Gina. Even when he bound her wrists, he did so with tender care then guided her gently by the arm back to her room. Once inside, he cut off the plastic cuff then massaged her wrists as she lowered her gaze to the floor. Why wouldn't she look at him? All he wanted was for her to look at him. What was it about Gina that touched him? Why did he feel so close to her when he had only just met her?

CHAPTER 28

Io slipped back into Miriam's room and sat down next to her again after taking off his jacket.

"What was that?" she said.

"Nothing, just a prisoner trying to escape." He placed his hand over hers and she smiled.

"You're nice," she said.

"Thank you." He hadn't been called nice in a long time. At least not by anyone he didn't have in the throes of seduction.

She reached across her body and traced her index finger over one of the swirls of ink on his right arm. "Wow, that's some tattoo."

He pulled back and pushed the sleeve of his T-shirt up to show off his ink. "Yeah, me and my best—" Io paused, not sure what Ari was to him, anymore. "Um, me and one of the other guys here got our arms tattooed at the same time. He did the left arm and I did the right."

"You two must be pretty good friends then."

He lowered his shirt sleeve and shrugged. "Eh, maybe. I don't know."

Miriam—he loved her name—inspected the tattoo some more. "I want to get a tattoo," she said.

"You should. They're sexy."

She shook her head. "I don't know. My dad won't let me."

"Why not?"

"He says that tattoos aren't proper or ladylike." She rolled her eyes.

"Do you do everything your dad tells you to do?"

She looked away uncomfortably. "Usually, yes. You have

to know him to understand."

"Well, maybe I can meet him someday." Io had no idea where those words came from, because he never wanted to meet the parents of any girl he dated, but somehow they sounded right with Miriam. And he hadn't even tried to hold her hand, let alone take her on a date.

"Um, I don't know." She fidgeted.

He held up his hands and smiled. "Hey, I'm just making small talk here." *Uh-huh. Nice save, stupid.*

She grinned almost shyly at him then looked toward the bathroom. "Could you help me to the bathroom, please."

"Of course." He helped her out of bed. She was tall. Almost as tall as he was, which was saying something since he stood at six-foot-six. Where the hell had she gotten her genetic makeup? Damn!

She closed the door while she did her business. Then he heard running water as she washed her hands.

"Oh my God!" she said from behind the closed door.

Io turned, startled. "Are you okay? Is everything all right?"

Miriam opened the door, her face deep red and her gaze averted. "I look awful. My hair." She tried to hide herself behind her hands.

Io stopped her, taking her hands in his and turning her toward him. "You're beautiful."

Her eyelids fluttered and those crystal blue irises turned up to his. "Really?"

He nodded. "Breathtaking."

She blushed and looked away. "But my hair, it feels awful." She pulled one hand from his and ran her fingers through her black mane.

"Would you feel better if I found you a brush?" He gave her a look that made her laugh. The sound was husky, airy, and perfect, just like she was.

"Yes, please. If you don't mind."

He helped her back to bed then rummaged through the cabinets. Nothing. "Hold on." He left and found a nurse, who scrounged a brush out of the supply room. When he returned to Miriam, she was wiping a tissue over her face.

"Ah, a brush!" Her smile lit up the room. Io loved a girl who got excited over the simple things.

"Here, let me." Io scooted onto the bed behind her as she made room for him.

He started at the ends of her hair and brushed out the tangles before working his way up, gently pulling the brush through her long hair. She dropped her head back so he could brush even higher.

Before he knew it, he found his mind drifting toward fantasies of reaching around to stroke the graceful arch of her neck before easing lower to cup one of her ample breasts. He had to force himself not to act on the impulse, instead combing his large hand in the wake of the brush as it smoothed over her silky soft hair.

"That feels so good," she said.

Yes, it does. "I'm glad. You had a rough night."

Suddenly, the door to her room pushed open and Tristan walked in, looking like hell had just frozen over with him in it. He gave Io an abrupt frown as if to ask what the fuck he was doing in there, brushing Miriam's hair no less, then he turned toward Miriam.

"Well, I just got a very interesting phone call." His voice boomed harshly.

Miriam tensed and Io swore he felt anxiety roll out of her.

"What the fuck, Tristan. How about some bedside manner. She's been through enough already."

Tristan ignored him. "Why didn't you tell us you were King Bain's daughter?"

Io nearly shit himself. "You're King Bain's daughter?"

Tristan scowled at him. "Get away from her, Io. You're not allowed to touch her."

Miriam looked away as Io practically fell off the bed in his haste to get away from her. He sure could pick 'em. Fuck. If the king himself had come through the door and seen him touching Miriam like that, he wouldn't have seen his death coming. It just would have happened.

Tristan took a deep, exasperated breath. "He's sending someone to pick you up at sundown."

Miriam huffed. "He's not coming himself?"

"No."

"Surprise, surprise." She huffed again and looked away.

"You know your father doesn't go out in public," Tristan said.

She flipped her hair, her chin jutting out proudly. "Guess not. Not even for his own daughter."

Tristan pursed his lips and propped his hands on his hips. "Well, someone will pick you up in about eight hours. I'm supposed to watch over you personally until he's here."

Io frowned at that idea. "I can watch her."

Miriam's hopeful eyes shot to him and he forced himself not to smile at her.

"No." Tristan shut him down in a heartbeat. "Direct orders from the king himself. And after what I just saw, I think it would be better that you get the hell out of here right now, Io."

Yeah, Tristan knew Io's reputation. This was one time he wished he didn't have such a track record with the ladies. He wanted to stay with Miriam. The thought she would leave and he'd never see her again was disconcerting.

Miriam's face fell and his chest ached for her. "I'm sorry." He handed her the brush.

"It's okay, Io. I'm used to it."

He wondered what she meant by that as she took the brush from him and held it to her chest like a treasure.

"Thank you for brushing my hair." Her doe-like eyes blinked to his and he nearly came undone with desire.

"You're welcome." He couldn't take that first step for the door. He could only stare at her.

"Now, Io." Tristan pointed to the door.

Io scowled at him. "Fuck, Tris. I'm going, okay? Cool off."

He turned and gave Miriam a final glance, smiling wistfully at her. Then he waved to her and she waved back as he left the room. In one way he hoped he never saw Miriam again, because that would mean she'd gotten off the cobalt, but in another way, he hoped her addiction only got worse, because that would mean she would be back here again someday. And then he could see her again.

Hmm, he usually avoided cobalt calls while on patrol because of his past addiction. After this, he might have to change that. One never knew where Miriam would turn up again, and if she was using, it was a sure bet she would. And Io wanted to be the one to take that call.

CHAPTER 29

THREE NIGHTS LATER, Sev woke up with his arms around Ari in the bed of his room in the medical wing as the nurse came in to open the curtains and blinds. The medical wing was the only place in the compound with windows because being exposed to the outside world was supposed to have a positive psychological effect on the sick and recovering. Or at least, that's what he'd been told. And he had to admit, seeing the lights of the city did make him feel better.

"Good evening," the nurse said when she turned to see him awake. Then she lowered her voice and smiled at Ari, who was still sleeping. "He just refuses to leave you, doesn't he?"

Sev looked at Ari's face and slid his hand over his tattooed left arm, which rested across his stomach. He turned back to the nurse. "What can I say? He loves me."

"That he does, that he does." The nurse proceeded quietly to the door then whispered, "Your dinner will be in shortly. One last meal before you go home."

He nodded and mouthed *okay*.

Sev felt so much better. Ari's blood had helped heal him quickly, and the doctor had removed the stitches in his chest this morning. Right where Ari's head now lay with his ear pressed against him as if he wanted to make sure he could hear his heartbeat while he slept.

He bent his head and kissed the top of Ari's. "Hey, sleepyhead. Time to wake up."

Ari stirred and pressed closer.

"Come on, babe. Wakey-wakey."

Ari turned his face into Sev's chest and kissed him through

his hospital gown, then looked through sleep-filled eyes into Sev's. "I love you."

Since the accident, *I love you* was the first thing Ari said to him every night upon waking and the last thing he said every morning before going to sleep. And Sev always said in reply...

"I love you, too."

Ari pressed his mouth to Sev's.

The door to the room flew open and Micah barged in, followed by Trace. "Get a fucking room, you two."

Sev jerked back, breaking the tender lip-lock as he scowled at the intrusion. "We have a room, asshole."

Micah chuckled.

Ari pulled back and turned around. "Don't you knock?"

"Fuck no. I own the place." Micah pulled up a chair and plopped down on it backward while Trace stood at his side.

"Is that so? You own the place, huh?" Sev actually chuckled at Micah. Who would have thought he would ever find the fuckhead amusing?

"Nah, but speaking of owning the place." Micah leaned his forearms on the back of the chair. "That girl Trace brought in? The overdose? She was King Bain's daughter."

"What?" Sev thought back to that first night when he paid her and Ari's fleeting fiancée a visit in that Jag. Now he understood all the bling and rich kid vibes. The fucking king's daughter, for Chrissake. And she was a junkie, or at least she would be if she didn't slow down.

"Yep. We just heard. And she made quite an impression on Io."

"Oh?" Ari glanced down.

Io hadn't been to visit them once. Everyone else had, even his father, who had hovered in the background wordlessly while Tristan checked on him. But Io? Ari's best friend had all but abandoned him.

Micah gave them a facetious look. "Yep. Io has had fucking hearts in his eyes ever since. As if he has a chance at tapping that shit. The king would chop off his balls and cook them for breakfast if he even caught Io looking at his daughter."

The nurse came back with a cart of food.

"Mmm. Speaking of food, what's for dinner?" Micah lifted the lid off one tray and snagged a French fry.

"Back off, asshole. That's my dinner." Sev laughed as the nurse slapped Micah's hand. "Thanks, Isabel. You show him who's boss around here."

Isabel smiled at him. "I can handle Micah. Sometimes I think I'm the only one."

"It's because I like you, Izzy." Micah tossed the fry into his mouth.

Sev and Ari sat up in bed, side-by-side, and the nurse set their trays on the make-shift table then situated it in front of them.

He and Ari had become quite the attraction in the medical wing. The nurses practically doted on them, loving that they had a newly mated couple to take care of. Something about the females around here made them love that he and Ari were two males who had gotten together. Maybe it was because they saw it as a novelty. Sev couldn't say. But it made him laugh how they all just gushed around the two of them.

He opened his carton of milk and took a drink as Ari started on his own fries.

"So, what about the female who capped me? Where is she?"

"Holding cell." Trace's deep voice rumbled to life. "Malek has been with her. Won't leave her, actually. It's kind of freaky how he won't leave her."

Sev had already been told that Gina knew the truth about what had actually gone down in Atlanta. Apparently, she hadn't taken it well and had tried to get herself killed by faking an attempt to escape.

"I want to see her."

Ari tensed beside him.

"Not a good idea." Micah stole another fry. "And not just because Malek will finish the job she started if you touch her, either."

Okay, that did sound freaky. What was up with Malek? He glanced between Micah and Trace then looked at Ari.

"I don't care. I want to talk to her." Sev spoke to Micah, but kept his eyes on Ari.

"After what she did to you? You sure you don't just want to go in there and kill her?" Micah shook his head. "Like I said, not a good idea. Malek would blow out."

"What's up with that?" Ari said, shaking his head in confusion.

Micah made a you-don't-want-to-know face and huffed. "He's gotten a bit protective of your would-be assassin."

"I'm not going to hurt her," Sev said. "I just need to see her."

Gina was Gabriel's sister and she deserved to hear the truth from him. Besides, he had something Gabe would have wanted her to have.

Trace snuck a fry and eyed him. "I know about you, you know."

"What do you mean?" Sev stopped with his burger halfway to his mouth and glanced quizzically at Ari then back to Trace.

Ari half-shrugged and gave him a sheepish grin. "I think he's saying that he knows about your mom."

Trace chewed and swallowed then glanced at Micah. "I haven't told anyone else. Micah knew already, though."

Yeah, Micah would know because he had been poking around in his mind. But damn if it didn't impress Sev all to hell and back that Micah had known and hadn't said anything. That guy was better than Master Lock when it came to keeping his mouth shut.

Micah grinned at him and held his gaze. Sev arched an eyebrow at him and Micah chuckled before looking away.

"You got that, didn't you?" Sev said.

"Loud and clear." Micah grinned. "And yeah, I am better than Master Lock."

Ari looked back and forth between them. "What are you two talking about?"

"Oh, nothing. Just Micah's five-finger action on my thoughts."

Micah leaned back and threw his arms up like he was innocent. "Hey, I'm not stealing them. I'm just window shopping."

Everyone laughed.

Sev turned back toward Trace. "So, Tristan doesn't know?

Or the others?"

Trace shook his head. "Nope. And they won't. Not unless you tell them. Not my place to."

Man, Trace was good people. Sev was starting to feel a camaraderie growing among the four of them he never would have imagined just a couple of weeks ago.

"What about Gina? She knows." Sev took a bite of burger. "Has she told anyone?"

Trace shook his head. "No. And I doubt she will. She already feels guilty about what she did. And I bet if you ask her not to say anything, she won't. She feels she owes you."

"Well, that's something, I guess." Sev exchanged glances with Ari.

He was grateful for Trace's and Micah's understanding about the sensitive nature of his lineage, and he hoped Trace was right about Gina. He wasn't ready for the entire compound to know what he was. At this point, with all that had happened, most would probably look past it, but he was sure some would shun him and demonstrate prejudice against him for being half dreck. And there was still a chance he would be asked to resign.

Micah pushed out of the chair and gestured toward Trace that it was time to go. "We'll let you two get back to it." Micah stopped at the door, turned around, and made kissing noises at them then laughed.

Sev grabbed a handful of fries and threw them at him. "Get out of here, Micah!"

Micah and Trace ducked, chuckling.

"Get well, Sev. Let us know if you need anything." Micah hesitated and nodded toward Arion. "But I think you've got all you need right there."

Meaningful glances were exchanged and Sev felt the kinship strengthen between him and Micah. He had a feeling he would lay down his life for that male right now if it ever came to that.

Micah grinned. "That won't be necessary." With that, he led Trace out.

"What did he mean by that?" Ari's brown furrowed.

Sev shook his head and smiled. "Nothing. Just that I think Micah and I have an understanding now."

The two gazed at each other for a moment then looked back toward the door as it hissed shut.

"I never thought I'd say this," said Ari, "but I'm really starting to like that black-haired freak."

Sev took a bite of his burger. "Me, too."

They exchanged glances again and grinned at each other.

"And I don't care if you are half dreck. You're *my* half-dreck, and I love you."

Damn, Ari knew just what to say to make his heart beat a little harder. He kissed Ari's cheek then brushed his lips over his ear. "I love you, too."

AFTER FILLING THEIR BELLIES, the doctor came in and gave Sev one final examination then cleared him to go home with orders to rest for the next week.

"Do you want to see Gina before we leave," Ari said.

Sev slipped a shirt Tristan had loaned him over his head. He was still stiff as hell, but at least he was upright and alive.

"No, I need to get something from home first and get cleaned up." He hadn't had a proper shower in over three days. "And I need you."

They were still in the midst of the *calling* but it had taken a brief hiatus while Sev recovered. But it was reawakening and they had already had to lock the door once for some privacy.

Ari licked his lips and his gaze smoldered. "I see."

Uh-huh. They really needed to get home and get back to being newly mated.

Sev was still weak, though, and as a precaution they rolled him out to Ari's BMW in a wheelchair and helped him into the passenger seat. Ari tossed their things in the back and got behind the wheel and drove him home, holding his hand the whole way.

Once home, Ari helped him inside and downstairs to the bedroom, where he sat down on the bed.

"What do you want to do first?" Ari said, grinning.

"Shower. Definitely a shower." No question about that. Sev felt disgusting. As much as he wanted to get inside his male, like yesterday, he wanted to be clean first.

Ari went to the bathroom and Sev heard the water turn on. In a moment, Ari was back, kneeling in front of him. "Doc says I'll have to help you bathe."

"Oh, is that right?" He grinned at the way sly twinkle in Ari's eyes.

So, maybe he could have his cake and eat it, too.

Ari nodded and palmed his knees, smiling affectionately. "Yes, we can't have you falling down or hurting yourself, you know."

Sev arched an eyebrow. "Well, you'll definitely have to join me in the shower then. Save me from myself." He winked.

"Absolutely."

"What else are you supposed to help me with?"

Ari's fingers rubbed up his thighs to the waist of the nylon sweats he had borrowed from Trace. "The doc said I might have to help you undress if your muscles are still stiff." His fingers grazed over the erection that had popped up the instant Ari had mentioned the shower.

"I'm definitely stiff." Sev stared into Ari's sexy, topaz eyes.

"Yeah, I should probably lend you a hand, huh?"

"Or two."

Ari pushed his hands up Sev's shirt and lifted it over his head, then kissed the angry scar that was still healing over his chest. In another day, it would only be a pale pink mark, especially if he drank from Ari one more time.

"What did the doc say about physical activity?" Sev rested his arms over Ari's shoulders.

"Mmm, I think he said physical activity was good as long as it wasn't too strenuous." Ari hooked his fingers in the waist of the sweatpants and pushed them down. He pulled them off along with his shoes and looked back into Sev's eyes before pulling his own shirt off.

"So, I guess you'll have to be gentle with me." Sev took the shirt out of Ari's hands and tossed it aside as Ari took off his own pants.

"I'll be anything I have to be as long as I can spend the rest of my life with you." Ari took his hand and pulled him off the edge of the bed and led him to the bathroom.

Ari stood behind him and raked his blunt nails up and down his back while he brushed his teeth. The head of Ari's cock bumped against his ass then slid between his cheeks. Sev quickly finished brushing and wiped the extra toothpaste off his mouth with his hand then spun around and pulled Ari to him with a possessive growl.

In an instant, their mouths came together and Ari's tongue darted into his mouth to taste him.

"Mmm." The deep moan vibrated from Ari's chest into his own and their cocks slid together.

Without breaking the greedy lip-lock, Ari maneuvered him into the luxurious, open shower and slapped his hands around on the shelf until he found the soap. Sev grabbed the shampoo and poured a generous portion into Ari's hair, then his.

Within seconds, between Ari's soapy hands and Severin washing both his and Ari's hair, they were covered in thick dollops of suds that fell down their bodies to slap onto the tile floor. All the while their lips never parted, and their tongues never stopped dancing.

When one of Ari's slippery, soap-covered hands dove down the crack of his ass and the other wrapped around his shaft, Sev grunted and staggered forward. Ari caught him, letting go of his cock long enough to steady him before getting back to work on his hard-on.

Just when things were getting interesting, a thick stream of shampoo bubbles dribbled down Sev's face and into one eye. He jerked back with a laugh.

Ari joined in and directed them both under the water spray to rinse off. "Problems, babe?"

"Fucking soap." Sev splashed water over his face then worked the suds out of Ari's hair.

"It has its advantages," Ari said, working the bar between his hands before setting it aside and going to work on Sev's cock again.

"Mmm, yes it does."

The hand job made Sev's legs shake. This was only the second time Ari had touched him like this since the accident, and it was as if they both had been eager to get home and back to the business of loving each other. Ari stopped stroking him and rinsed him off then eased him back until he sat down on the shower bench. Then he knelt in front of him.

"What are you doing?" Sev said.

Ari pushed his legs apart and slid between them. Keeping his gaze locked to Sev's, Ari leaned forward and took his cock between his lips.

Sev's hands gripped the edge of the bench. Oh, fuck! This was the one thing Ari hadn't yet done to him, and he could only stare down at his shaft as it disappeared into Ari's mouth. His tongue swirled around and around the head, causing Sev to shudder. Then Ari's fist started pumping the shaft as he sucked lightly on his glans.

"Oh my God, Ari. Fuck, yeah."

Sev's fists gripped the bench so tightly it was a wonder he didn't break it. Ari knew just how to touch him. He knew when to apply pressure, when to back off, when to pick up the tempo and when to slow down. It was almost as if he was inside Sev's head, but that's why nature had made them mates. They were designed for each other. Perfect complements. Mating was nature's way of saying they had been made for each other.

"You're going to make me come." Sev tapped Ari's head to tell him if he didn't want a mouthful he had better pull back, but Ari only doubled his efforts. "Fuck, Ari. Are you sure you want this."

Ari didn't stop. He only looked up through his long, water-beaded lashes and nodded once when he found Sev's gaze. His lips sealed around his shaft, sucking and pulling, his tongue teasing the head. His topaz eyes practically sparkled as he watched Sev.

"Then don't stop. Keeping do—unh—yes, that. Keep doing that. Oh God. Don't stop-don't stop-don't stop." He clamped his hands on Ari's head like he was holding a bowl in place to catch his release. "Close, so close!" his chest and shoulders pumped hard with each ragged breath. "Fuck! Uuuuungh!"

Ari moaned as Sev's offering spurted down his throat. He swallowed reflexively as he reached down to pound his own erection. Within seconds, he jumped up off the floor and climbed onto the bench to stand in front of Sev, his feet on either side of Sev's hips.

"Take me in your mouth. Hurry!" Ari commanded.

Ari bent his knees slightly and pumped his cock as he slid the head inside Sev's open, greedy mouth. Sev closed his lips around it, flicking the tip with his tongue, making Ari shudder. He could tell Ari was close and knew just how to send him over. He rubbed his palm between Ari's legs and over his scrotum. Then he slid his thumb inside Ari's ass as he gripped his cheek.

"Aauugghh!" Ari cried out and orgasmed instantly, his ass clenching and releasing around his thumb as cum sprayed over his tongue.

He had blown Ari a couple of times already and eagerly swallowed what Ari gave. He loved the way Ari tasted, and he licked and licked until he had taken every last drop then pulled Ari down to sit on his lap.

"Thank you." Ari was still gasping for air.

Sev stroked his fingers over Ari's back and smiled at the way Ari wrapped his arms around him and held him like he would never let him go. "For what, babe?"

"For being alive. For loving me. For everything."

"My pleasure," he said.

Ari barked out a breathless laugh. "Mine, too, apparently."

"Apparently." Sev closed his eyes and smiled against the side of Ari's face then kissed his cheek.

They held each other a minute longer, then reluctantly got up.

"Do you think we followed doctor's orders then?" Sev rinsed one last time before shutting off the water.

"Absolutely. Do you want to follow doctor's orders again later?" Ari snagged their towels and tossed one to Sev.

"Do I look like I need that much medical attention?" He

rubbed the towel over his hair and brushed it down his arms, chest, and stomach then secured it around his waist.

Ari stepped closer and licked his shoulder. "I think you need at least two more days of bed rest. At least."

"And I think you're looking a bit under the weather yourself, babe. Maybe you should stay in bed with me." He wrapped an arm around Ari's waist.

They embraced and Ari nibbled his bottom lip. "I hope I'm not contagious."

"I don't know if you're contagious, but you're definitely my antidote, and I think I need another dose before we go back to AKM."

Ari kissed him, licking his lips. "I think I can handle that."

"I hope so." Sev crowded him out of the shower and back to the bedroom, where they fell onto the bed already wrapped in each other's arms.

ARI WAS STILL HARD FROM THE SHOWER and only wanted more of his mate. His *mate*. Nothing would tear them apart. Not Io, not his parents, no one. This was where he belonged and he would never doubt that again. He rolled Sev to his back and slid inside him, ready to give Sev everything he wanted and needed for the rest of their lives together.

Sev's legs locked around him and he pulled him down until they were chest-to-chest and mouth-to-mouth once more.

"I'm never letting you go," he said, thrusting into Sev, their lips brushing together.

"I'll never let you." Sev grunted as Ari thrust again, harder this time.

"Am I hurting you?" Ari knew he needed to be careful with Sev for a few days.

"No. Feels good. Harder, babe."

Ari rammed into him, and again, faster, their flesh slapping as their bodies came together.

Sev moaned. "Yes, I like that." His eyes closed briefly as his face contorted in ecstasy.

"Must be my mate. He's really sexy and I can't stop myself."

Sev smiled at him. "Your mate's a lucky guy."

Ari licked Sev's lips and just ever-so-softly kissed him as he pressed both palms against Sev's hips, driving into him harder.

"Oh, God!" Sev groaned hard. "Check that. He's a *very* lucky guy."

"I'll be sure and tell him." Ari grunted as he pushed forward inside Sev again.

He fell more in love with Sev every second he was with him. Almost losing him made him appreciate that much more what they had together.

Ari fucked Sev harder, another orgasm tickling his spine, growing on a crescendo until it exploded and shot fireworks through his balls. He grunted and clamped his mouth over Sev's then shuddered as he pulled out and came on Sev's stomach.

After the last spasm rippled through him and he lay spent on Sev's torso, Sev grinned against his mouth. "Doctor's orders."

Ari chuckled. "Who would've thought, right?"

Sev laughed then Ari joined him.

Ari was happy. He was finally happy.

CHAPTER 30

Sᴇᴠ ᴘʀᴏᴜᴅʟʏ ʜᴇʟᴅ Aʀɪ'ꜱ ʜᴀɴᴅ as they walked through the main hall toward the holding rooms. The stares only made him stand taller as he squeezed Ari's hand reassuringly. He knew it would still be a while before Ari was completely comfortable with public affection, but he hadn't pulled away when Sev linked their fingers around one another. Ari seemed determined to show Sev how important he was to him, and just as determined to overcome the fear still inside him that they would be the subject of ridicule now that they were *out*.

But they had a couple of big guns in their corner, which made it easier. Micah and Traceon had been busting anyone's chops who dissed them. Sev was still surprised about that, but sometimes allies came from unusual places, and Trace and Micah were two vampires Sev and Ari both wanted in their corner. Nobody fucked with Micah, and Traceon was proving to be just as intimidating. The two of them together? Well, it seemed everyone was smart enough not to push their buttons.

He and Ari turned down the prisoner hall and stopped in front of Gina's door. Apparently, she was no longer a flight risk, because the posted guard was gone. He had heard she'd tried to escape that first night—well, one story said escape, another said she was trying to kill herself. At any rate, the posted guards had been removed from in front of her door, so she must have calmed down enough that they were no longer needed.

"Do you want me to go in with you?" Ari said.

"I want you to do everything with me, Ari." Sev gave him an earnest look.

Ari smiled and nodded then followed as he pushed open the door.

Malek was inside the room with Gina and stood up and moved in front of her like a guard dog.

Sev frowned at him. "I'm not going to hurt her, Malek."

"What do you want?" Malek sounded defensive.

Gina sat up behind him. She had apparently been napping.

"I knew her brother. I brought her something I think he would have wanted her to have." Sev paused. "And I want to talk to her. Just her and Ari, not you."

"Forget it. No one sees her without me present."

What the fuck was up with Malek? Did he think he was Gina's bodyguard or something?

"No, Malek. It's okay." Gina brushed back her hair. "I'll see him. I owe him that."

Malek softened at the sound of her voice then nodded. "I'll be right outside if you need me."

Malek stepped out and he and Ari exchanged perplexed glances before he turned back to Gina.

Gina's tears began immediately. "I am so sorry. I didn't know—I thought—Gabriel's death—and I saw you—Oh God, I almost killed you." She dropped her face in her hands and cried.

"Gina, calm down. I'm not angry at you. I'm as much to blame as anyone." He looked at Ari. He and Ari had already talked about how he should never have let his iron skin down in the first place. He had been careless, so it wasn't just her fault. He had known better.

"No, it's my fault. All my fault."

Severin pulled her into a hug, and she latched onto him, her fingers gripping his shirt. She suddenly broke into harsh sobs, and he knew part of her sorrow came from having lost her brother and never having properly dealt with her grief. Now she finally could. Her guilt over trying to kill Sev gave her the perfect excuse to do so.

"Gina, I've been told what happened. At least the bits and

pieces that you've shared, but I wanted to make sure you knew the truth about what happened between Gabe and me."

"I already know. I saw in your mind."

Sev frowned. Nobody had told him this. "When?"

"When you were unconscious. I know now. You tried to save my brother. And I mistakenly thought you were part of the group that killed him."

Sev wiped a tear off her cheek. "I couldn't tell Gabe what I was. I couldn't tell him because I worked undercover. When he showed up at that raid, my heart nearly fell. He and I weren't mates, Gina, but I cared about him. He was the closest thing to a boyfriend I've ever had until I met Ari."

Gina looked up as he gestured toward Ari, who nodded politely to her.

"Hi," she said.

"Hi." Ari smiled.

Gina looked back at Sev. "I know that now. I know that when you returned to the factory, you wanted to help him. I saw the truth. I know your boss lied and that you did work for VDA. I just wish..." She sobbed. "God, I wish for so much." She covered her face with her hand and cried. "I wish I'd known. I wish I hadn't been so careless. I wish I'd listened. And I wish Gabe had known the truth, too. He died thinking—"

"That I betrayed him. I know." Sev squeezed her free hand. "But I'm sure he knows the truth now. Wherever he is, I'm sure he sees the truth."

She nodded curtly, wiping her face. "I hope so."

He reached into his pocket and pulled out a locket and an envelope then handed them to her.

She gasped and put her hand over her mouth when she saw the locket. "I gave that to him when I was just a little girl." She popped it open and choked back tears. "He was my hero. My big brother. I wanted to be just like him. It's why I became an enforcer." She gazed at the locket.

Gabe had put a picture of her and him inside. Sev had looked at the pictures often in the months that followed

Gabe's death just over a year ago.

"We both know the truth, now, don't we?" Sev took the envelope that remained unopened and pulled out a picture. The edges were worn and the picture was creased in one corner as if it had been folded down. "Gabe kept this picture in his wallet and took it everywhere with him, Gina. Before he died, he had taken it out and put it in a small picture frame in his apartment. I went back and got it. I wanted something to remember him by, but now..." He paused and looked at Ari. "I don't need it, anymore." He turned back to Gina. "You should have it." He held the picture out to her. "He bragged about you all the time. He loved you so much."

Fresh tears flowed as she took the picture and stared at it. It was a picture of her and Gabe that had been taken at Christmas. They both had Santa hats on and huge smiles on their faces, arms around each other on the floor in front of the Christmas tree.

Gina looked up at him. "Thank you for this."

Out of the corner of his eye, Sev caught Ari wiping a tear off his cheek.

"You're welcome, Gina. He was a good male. A worthy male."

She nodded. "He was. And so are you. I wish I had seen that sooner." She hung her head. "I really fucked up."

He exchanged glances with Ari. "We all do, Gina. We all do." And didn't he and Ari know that all too well? "Some of us just do it better than others." He looked back at her, smiling.

She frowned at him, then her face twisted. She rolled her eyes and smiled wanly. "I guess I'm an overachiever." She sighed and looked down. "So, what happens to me now?"

"Well, I'm here to bust you out." Sev clapped his palms down on his thighs.

"Excuse me?" Gina frowned at him as if she didn't believe him.

"You heard me. Let's go." Sev stood and took Ari's hand.

"You've got to be kidding."

"Nope. Come on." He reached for her hand.

She took it and stood up hesitantly then followed him to

the door. Ari knocked and Malek opened it from the outside.

"Where do you think you're taking her?" Malek said.

"She's free to go." Sev pulled on Gina's hand to leave the room, and Malek practically burned holes in him with his gaze.

"I wasn't told," Malek said.

"I'm telling you now," Sev said warily.

They all stood in the hall at a stalemate, Gina appearing afraid to move, and Malek refusing to let her go.

"It's okay, Malek," Tristan said, coming down the hall. "Severin isn't pressing charges and asked us to let her go. We've decided under the circumstances to agree. You're free to leave, Gina." Tristan stopped in front of her.

Malek looked from Tristan to Gina in disbelief. Sev didn't know what to make of his strange behavior.

"No, she can't go." Malek frowned as if confused then shook his head.

"Yes, she can, Malek. We've concluded that the circumstances surrounding this incident were out of the ordinary, and since Sev is so passionate about wanting her released, being that he was the one who was shot, we've decided to honor his request."

"But...." Malek looked positively stymied.

"It's okay, Malek. You did a fine job keeping an eye on her, but it's time to let her go. Come on, Gina. I'll walk you out." Tristan held out his arm and she took his hand, which sent Malek into a fit of growls.

Ari let go of Sev's hand as everyone exchanged wary glances and prepared for what sounded like a shit storm about to blow up. But then Malek simply quieted, looked down then back up, and smiled.

"Forgive me," he said. "I'll walk out with you." Malek joined Tristan, and after an uneasy moment, the three strolled down the hall. Gina turned and gave him one last look and mouthed the words *thank you* just before they disappeared around a corner.

"You ready to go home for good now?" Sev took Ari's hand once more and pulled him to his side as they started down the hall.

"Not quite." Ari flashed him a mysterious smile. "One more stop, and then I'm all yours."

The way he said it made Sev wonder exactly what he meant by that.

"Okay, where are we going?"

Ari pulled up in front of Tristan's office. "It's a surprise. Hold up a sec. I need to put something on Tristan's desk." Ari ducked inside and was back out in a flash.

A few minutes later, they were cruising to the North Side.

"Come on, Ari, where are we going?"

"You'll see soon enough."

Fifteen minutes later, Ari turned into his parents' neighborhood.

"Ari?" He looked over as Ari offered a tight smile.

"I owe you this, Sev. I'm finishing what I started."

"You don't owe me, anything. You don't have to do this."

"Yes, I do. Not just for you, but," Ari glanced at him, "I need to do this for me, Sev. I need to stand up to my parents. It's time for me to live my own life and not the life they expect me to live."

"But Micah said they'll cut you off."

"They'll cut me off, anyway. I'm not marrying Persephone. I'm not. The only person I want to marry is you."

Sev had known this was coming. He had known when Ari refused to leave him while he recovered. But they hadn't talked about it. Hearing Ari say out loud that he wasn't marrying Persephone and that he wanted to be with him and only him filled his heart with joy.

Ari pulled into the drive, drove up to the house, parked behind a black Suburban, and shut off the engine.

"I'm proud of you, Ari. And I'm damn proud you're my mate. I just want you to know that before we go in there."

"Thank you." Ari took a deep breath. "You ready?"

Sev chuckled. "Me? More like, are *you* ready?"

THAT WAS THE QUESTION, WASN'T IT? On the surface, the answer was no, but Ari knew deep down he was going to do this now. To hell with everything else. Sev deserved to have Ari proclaim to his parents that he belonged to Sev and that he didn't care what they did to him. He would spend the rest of his life living the truth, not hiding behind lies.

"Yes, I'm ready." Ari got out of the car and walked around to the passenger side and took Sev's hand, gripping it hard as his knees wobbled like they were filled with gelatin. "I'm not letting go of you in there. If I do, I might fall over. I'm so nervous."

Sev nodded at him. "I'll hold you up if that's what it takes, babe. Now, deep breath. I love you. You can do this."

"Okay, let's go."

Ari walked side-by-side with Sev into his parents' home, not bothering to ring the doorbell. This was as much his home—at least until his father disowned him in the next ten minutes—as it was theirs, so he had every right to barge in unannounced.

The smell of roasted meat and herbs drifted on the air, and Ari followed the aroma into the dining room.

Unexpectedly, his parents were having dinner with Sev's father, Lakota, and all five of them stopped and looked at each other. Sev tensed and Ari reached over with his other hand and steadied him. His father's and mother's gazes dropped to his hand clasping Sev's, and the color drained from their faces.

"Arion?" His mother said.

"Son?" Lakota stood.

"This is your son?" Ari's mom stood with a gasp.

Lakota's gaze never wavered from Sev's. "Yes. That's my son." Lakota's voice sounded strong and proud, and Ari thought he felt Severin bend emotionally just a little bit, but in a good way.

"What's going on here?" Ari's father rose from his own chair and took a step forward, his scowl fixed on their clasped hands.

Ari cleared his throat and tightened his grip on Sev. He felt so small in the gigantic room big enough to comfortably fit more than twenty dinner guests. The massive table shined, freshly polished after every meal. The chandelier sparkled, the windows gleamed, everything in the room was spotless and perfect, and suddenly Ari realized how wrong this entire house and everything in it was for him.

He lifted his head proudly, almost regally, and pulled Sev farther into the room. "Mom. Dad. This is Severin Bannon, and I love him. I love him with my heart and soul, and," he turned and looked into Sev's amazing blue eyes, "he's my mate."

"This can't be happening. Oh my God, what will our friends think?" His mom sounded positively panicked.

Ari rolled his eyes dramatically and looked at Sev, who grinned back at him.

"Oh, and I quit my job," he said, keeping his eyes on Sev's. Then he said, "That's what I put on Tristan's desk. It was my notice."

Sev nodded approvingly.

His parents fussed and stammered, blabbering about their friends, the king, Persephone – everyone and everything but Ari.

"I love you," Sev said.

"I love you, too." Ari leaned forward and kissed him.

His mom gasped. His dad growled. But Ari didn't care. He had what he wanted right here in his arms.

"You're marrying Persephone, Ari, and that's final!" His dad slammed his fist against the table and stomped his foot like a petulant child.

"No, I'm not." Ari refused to look away from Sev.

"He's marrying me." Sev's eyes twinkled. "He'll be *my* husband or no one's."

His parents fell into uproar, but their protests and pleas fell on deaf ears.

"Come on, babe, let's go home." Sev kissed his forehead.

Ari nodded. "You *are* my home."

SEV GLANCED BACK AT HIS DAD as he and Ari turned for the door.

His father had a grin on his face the size of Montana, and while Gregos and Christa argued and consoled each other, his dad tossed his napkin on the table and stepped away from his chair.

Once he and Ari reached the front porch, Ari stopped and looked up at the night sky.

"God, this feels good," he said.

"*You* feel good." Sev pulled Ari back into his arms, and they looked up at the stars together.

The door opened behind them and his father stepped outside. He hardly slowed down as he passed them, but he did meet Sev's eyes for the briefest moment. "I'm proud of you, son," he said. "Ari." He nodded a greeting at Ari then descended the steps in three long strides.

Sev just watched him go.

"Do you think you and your dad will ever kiss and make up?" Ari leaned back against him and placed his hand over Sev's around his waist.

"I don't know." But Sev had a funny feeling they would. Not tonight and not tomorrow, and maybe not even next month, but maybe someday. Hell, if he could forgive the person who had tried to kill him, anything was possible. He watched his father's Suburban pull around and head down the driveway.

"Come on, I've got more doctor's orders for you when we get home." Ari turned and kissed him.

"Mmm, doctor's orders, huh?" Sev grinned. "Do they include digging into the drawer of your nightstand?"

Ari blushed and bit his lip. "Maybe. If you can handle it."

"Oh, I think I can handle it." Sev's left eyebrow shot up confidently.

Ari grinned and placed his palm on Sev's chest. "I'll take good care of your warrior heart, Sev." He caressed his hand up and down tenderly over Sev's sternum.

Sev shook his head. "Huh-uh, babe." What Ari had just done in his parents' dining room had taken more courage than anything Sev had ever faced. "You're the one with the true heart of a warrior, Ari, not me."

"Seriously? You really think so?"

Sev shook his head again. "I *know* so." He brushed their mouths together. "Come on, babe. Let's go home."

Ari's fingers linked with Sev's and he took a deep, satisfied breath as they started down the steps. It felt good to be openly mated.

CHAPTER 31

ARI CHECKED HIS REFLECTION IN THE MIRROR for the fifth time. "Are you sure I look okay."

Sev stepped up behind him and wrapped his arms around his waist. "This is what I love about you. You're going to meet my mother, who's a dreck, and who most vampires wouldn't give a rat's ass about making an impression for, but *you* want to make an impression." Sev grinned and kissed his cheek.

He leaned back against Sev. "Dreck or not, she's your mother. She's important to you. So, yeah, I want to make a good impression. I want her to like me."

Sev's arms tightened around him. "You look perfect, babe. My mom'll love you. Stop worrying."

Okay, so maybe Ari was being a little neurotic, but he really wanted Sev's mom to like him. They were going to spend the rest of their lives loving her son, and that would go over much better if they got along.

Sev kissed his cheek again then pulled away to finish getting ready. Ari sighed and brushed his palms down his black cashmere sweater then wandered past the bed they had spent the last three days soiling. They were making up for the time they'd lost while Sev had been in the hospital. Even now, the urge to take Sev again was already building inside him, and they just made love an hour ago. And an hour before that. And just a few hours before that, when Sev had awakened him in a fit of need.

He knew the pull was stronger between them since they were both males, but he had a greater respect for females of the newly mated now. Man, what the *calling* phase put a body through. It was both bliss and agony.

"We'll need to hurry home," he said.

"I know. I feel it, too." Sev darted a smoldering glance at him.

God, Sev really shouldn't look at him like that. Especially when they needed to be walking out the door.

"She won't be upset that we can't stay longer?" Ari grabbed his jacket.

Sev shook his head and joined him. "No. She understands."

"Just don't touch me a lot and I'll be okay." Ari started up the stairs.

Sev's hand caressed his ass and he nearly fell over from the strike of hormonal heat that surged through him.

"Damn it, Sev!" Ari turned around on the stairs and slapped Sev's hand away.

Sev chuckled at him. "I'm sorry. I couldn't help it."

Ari shook his head in frustration, but ended up laughing, anyway. "I'll make you pay for that later."

"Promises, promises."

Ari turned and continued up the stairs. "Oh, I mean it. Count on that."

SEV GRINNED AT THE BACK OF ARI'S HEAD as he followed him up the stairs then out to the garage, where they got in his Challenger.

After backing out of the garage and pulling onto the street, Sev reached for Ari's hand at the same time he reached for Sev's. He loved how they always seemed to be in sync with one another.

The last few days had been exhausting bliss with Arion. All the shit that had been interfering with their relationship finally found a place in the past, leaving only the two of them with no obstacles to overcome. No secrets. No meddling parents. No one trying to kill him. Just Sev and Ari. And they had taken advantage of the *calling* as it re-engaged at full strength. They shut off their phones and holed up in his basement bedroom except to eat and drink. And wash the sheets, of course. Sev had changed the sheets more times in the last three days than he had in a year.

"Do you want to have kids someday?" Ari said out of the blue.

Sev glanced over. "I don't think either of us has the right equipment for that, babe."

Ari grinned and rolled his eyes. "No shit."

Sev laughed.

"I mean, we can adopt. Or even try in vitro with a willing female."

Where was this coming from? Was Arion feeling the instinct to nest with him? Build a family. Sev liked the idea of having a family with Arion.

"Well, if we do anything, we'll have to decide whether we want a human young or a vampire."

"Or a dreck." Arion looked at him and gave a slight shrug, as if to say, *Why not?*

"Okay, yeah. That's a possibility, too." Sev squeezed Ari's hand. "I didn't know you wanted kids, babe."

"I didn't either, but for the past few days I've been thinking a lot about it."

Not unusual for a male caught in the throes of his newly mated hormones, which demanded he sow his seeds often to ensure fertilization. Sev had to admit, he had been considering a child, too.

"Let's wait until the *calling* wears off and then talk about it again. That way we can see if it's just the *calling* or if we really want a family."

"Good idea."

A child of their own. What an idea. Sev had never thought he would have a family because of his sexual orientation. Can't have many kids of your own when you like to dip your wick into people of the male persuasion. You didn't see a lot of pregnant males, after all. Try never. Sev hadn't even considered adoption, though. But then, he had never been mated. Taking a mate had a way of changing your plans for the future, including the idea of creating progeny.

His mom would love having a grandchild, but, like him, she had never thought it would happen. Now, with Arion, Sev thought it just might.

It took them twenty minutes to get to his mom's house.

"You ready?" He looked at Ari as he shut off the engine.

Ari took a deep breath and nodded. "Yep."

Ari really didn't have anything to worry about. His mom was going to love him. But apparently that was something Ari would have to find out on his own.

Hand-in-hand, they headed up the walkway to her townhome and he rang the bell. Within seconds, his mom pulled open the door and beamed at Ari.

"It's about time you boys got here." She stepped aside and the smell of homemade lasagna assaulted his nose.

"That smells delicious," Ari said.

"My mom cooks the best Italian." Sev hugged his mom and kissed her cheek. "Mom, this is Arion. My mate. Arion, this is Feelee. My mom." He had never introduced her to anyone as his mom before. This was such a relief. The two most important people in his life, and he didn't have to hide from either of them who they were or what they meant to him.

He stepped back after making the introductions. His mom's gaze danced over Ari's face, her artistic eyes taking in his features and coloring, no doubt comparing the real thing with all the portraits Sev had given her of him.

"Such a handsome one." His mom's eyes jumped to him. "He looks just as you painted him."

Ari glanced at him. "Painted me? You mean, there's more than just the painting of me in your basement?"

Sev nodded. "Yes. I've painted you a lot, Ari." He looked at his mom. "Did you bring them?"

Her smile lit up as she took Ari's hand and led him through the front room and up the stairs. Sev followed behind and grinned when Ari turned and flashed him an inquisitive look over his shoulder.

"In here." His mom opened the door to a spare room Sev knew she used as a makeshift studio.

White sheets covered the floor, and an easel was set up in

the corner. Her painting supplies were laid out neatly on a table against the near wall.

"Oh my God," Ari stepped into the room, his eyes skimming the portraits hanging on the wall as he stood in place and turned.

Every painting was one that Sev had painted of Arion after their interlude nearly two months ago.

"You painted all these?" Ari turned to Sev, awe and disbelief coating his features.

"Yes."

"When? When did you do this?"

"After I took you home when Micah tried to give you a facelift with his fists." He didn't want to disclose in front of his mother the sordid details of what had happened that night, so he only said enough to let Ari know when his painting frenzy had started.

Ari understood and smiled as he looked down almost bashfully. Then his gaze drew back up to the paintings. "They're incredible."

"This one's my favorite," his mom said, lifting a canvas that had been propped on the floor, facing the wall. She turned it around as she set it on the easel then stepped back. It was the oil he had painted of the two of them, holding each other, their foreheads tilted together.

Ari stepped forward and stared at the painting, speechless.

His mom continued. "The first time I saw it, I felt the pain within the color. But now..." she stepped beside Ari and put her arm around him. "Now, I just see the love."

Ari's shoulders jerked then Sev smelled his tears.

"My son loves you, Arion. And that's enough for me to love you, too. Welcome to the family."

Ari turned toward his mom and wrapped her in a tight embrace as she hugged him back. Sev wiped a tear from his own eye. Ari had lost his own family to be his mate. And he knew that had to hurt Ari on some level even if he pretended outwardly to be strong and not care that his father and mother had disowned him. But that didn't matter anymore, because now Ari was a part of his family. *Their* family.

"Thank you," Ari said into his mom's shoulder. "I'm honored to be part of your family."

So, drecks and vampires could get along. Sev smiled at the two people he loved the most but who came from two sides of the same war. He never would have imagined introducing a mate to his mother would be this easy or emotional.

"You honor me, Arion," his mom said. "I've always wanted my son to be this happy. And I can tell he is with you."

They hugged again then his mom stepped away. "I'll go downstairs and finish getting dinner ready." She gave Sev's cheek a little pat. "Don't be too long or it'll get cold."

"We'll be right down." Sev hugged her and let her go.

"Well?" He said to Ari.

Ari rushed forward and locked Sev in an embrace worthy of the Incredible Hulk. "I love you."

Sev pulled him in even closer, holding him. "I love *you*. And I told you my mom would love you, too, didn't I?"

"Yes, you did." Ari nuzzled his neck, kissing him and sending fire through his limbs.

"No, no. You have to stop that, babe."

Ari pulled away and sniffled as he wiped tears off his cheeks. "Sorry...I just..."

"Ssshh. I know." Sev grinned. "Let's go downstairs. Otherwise, I might not be able to hold back, and your portraits will have to watch me make love to you."

Ari composed himself and took a deep breath. "Yeah, okay." He looked around at the portraits again. "I'm, uh..." He swung his awestruck gaze back to Sev. "I'm a bit overwhelmed emotionally right now."

Sev followed Ari to the door before stopping with his hand on the light switch. He turned and looked around at all the paintings of Ari. So much pain, emotion, and love had gone into each one. It seemed like a lifetime ago, and in a way, it was. He no longer needed to paint Arion's portrait to feel him. All he needed to do was reach out and Ari was there.

"Hey, you okay?" Ari touched his arm.

Sev smiled and sighed. "Yeah. I'm perfect."

He switched off the light and took Ari's hand.

"You *are* perfect," Ari stepped forward and dipped his forehead against Sev's.

"We're perfect together, babe." He closed his eyes and let his forehead rest against Ari's as they gently held each other. It was the oil painting come to life, the two of them still and holding each other, foreheads resting one against the other as they savored the love between them.

Hmm. His mom was right about her favorite portrait. He could feel the love in it, too.

DID YOU ENJOY READING THIS BOOK?

If you did, please help others enjoy it, too:

Recommend it.

Review it at Amazon, iBooks, or Goodreads

If you leave a review, please send me an email at donya@donyalynne.com or message me on Facebook so that I can thank you with a personal e-mail.

ABOUT THE AUTHOR

DONYA LYNNE is the bestselling author of the award winning All the King's Men Series and a member of Romance Writers of America. Making her home in a wooded suburb north of Indianapolis with her husband, Donya has lived in Indiana most of her life and knew at a young age that she was destined to be a writer. She started writing poetry in grade school and won her first short story contest in fourth grade. In junior high, she began writing romantic stories for her friends, and by her sophomore year, she'd been dubbed *Most Likely to Become a Romance Novelist*. In 2012, she made that dream come true by publishing her first two novels and a novella. Her work has earned her two IPPYs (one gold, one silver) and two eLit Awards (one gold, one silver) as well as numerous accolades. When she's not writing, she can be found cheering on the Indianapolis Colts or doing her cats' bidding.

For more information on Donya's books or just to say hello, visit her on Facebook or swing by her website.

www.facebook.com/DonyaLynne

www.donyalynne.com